FICTION

Hateful Pitches
Unfortunates
The Grimhaven Disaster
Jesus of Scumburg
Bonespin Slipspace

FILM

Cancelled Plans
Cherophobe
Mr. Sleepy
Students
Searching for Veslemøy
Face Boy
Burnt Portraits
The TrutherNet Apocalypse

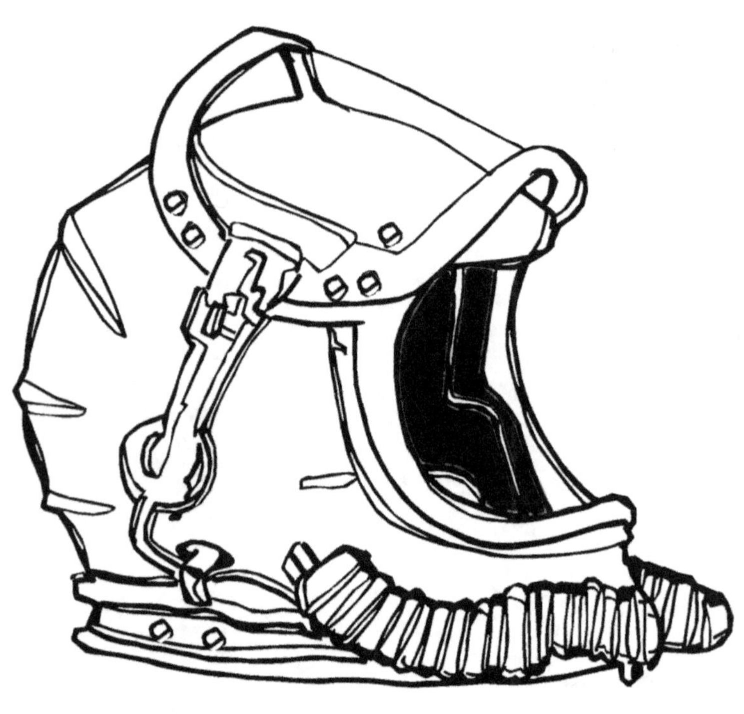

BARHOPPING FOR ASTRONAUTS

COSMIC HORROR, LATE-STAGE CAPITALISM, AND OTHER LIGHT READING

LEO X ROBERTSON

Library and Archives Canada Cataloguing in Publication
ISBN: 978-1-988865-77-5 (paperback)
ISBN: 978-1-988865-78-2 (ebook)

Material in this collection was originally published: 'SnapShots', *Pulp Literature* Issue 22, Spring 2019, reprinted in *Best of British Science Fiction 2019*, NewCon Press; 'Killing Time', *Pulp Literature* Issue 47, Summer 2025; 'The Hundred-Year Storm', *Fiction on the Web*, 2016; 'WE TOUCHED A REAL DINOSAUR! (NOT CLICKBAIT)', *Horror Sleaze Trash*, 2019; 'Bar Hopping for Astronauts', *Pulp Literature* Issue 30, Spring 2021; reprinted in *Best of British Science Fiction 2021*, NewCon Press; 'Levels for Sustainable Living', *Helios Quarterly* Volume 2, Issue 2: Redux & Progression, 2017; 'The Headphones of Damocles', *Antipodean*, 2020; 'Love You to Death', *Close to the Bone*, 2019; *The Glow*, Aurelia Leo, 2022.

Cover art and design: Kate Landels
Interior design: Amanda Bidnall
Frontispiece art: Mel Anastasiou
Printed and bound in Canada by Fraser Printers
International version printed by Ingram / Lightning Source and KDP

Published in Canada by Pulp Literature Press
www.pulpliterature.com

ADVANCE PRAISE FOR BARHOPPING FOR ASTRONAUTS

"Leo Robertson's stories are vivid, playful, and charming. *Barhopping for Astronauts* is a delight!"

"With the stories in *Barhopping for Astronauts*, Leo X Robertson shows us that a better future isn't always the best future for everyone. This is heartbreak sci-fi, pushing the aches and pains of modern existence forward just enough to stimulate imagination, while refusing to sacrifice those universal truths strong enough to cross timelines and interplanetary distances and technological advancements."

"Like the implanted hidden thoughts of HAL-9000, Leo X Robertson's stories walk an intoxicating line between the soulfully humane and indefinably sinister. His skill is to draw you in to these shimmering new worlds and show you visions that are at once mind-bendingly fresh and intimately relatable … Robertson weaves his futuristic landscapes in ways that not only incite genuine wonder, but also tap into the very nucleus of what makes us who we are."

PRAISE FOR LEO X ROBERTSON

"As carefully crafted as it is imaginatively conceived, Leo X Robertson's aptly titled fiction collection *Unfortunates* is engaging, nicely written, and often as thought-provoking and challenging as it is entertaining. One of the better up-and-coming talents I've had the pleasure of discovering in recent years, Robertson's work is not to be missed."

GREG F GIFUNE, AUTHOR OF *THE BLEEDING SEASON*

"Much like seeing the aftermath of a car accident, Leo X Robertson writes the kind of horrifying, all-too-human stories that keep your eyes clearly affixed to the beautifully written prose no matter how grotesque or emotionally scarring they are. And I always want more."

SAM RICHARD, AUTHOR OF *SABBATH OF THE FOX-DEVILS* AND *TO WALLOW IN ASH & OTHER SORROWS*

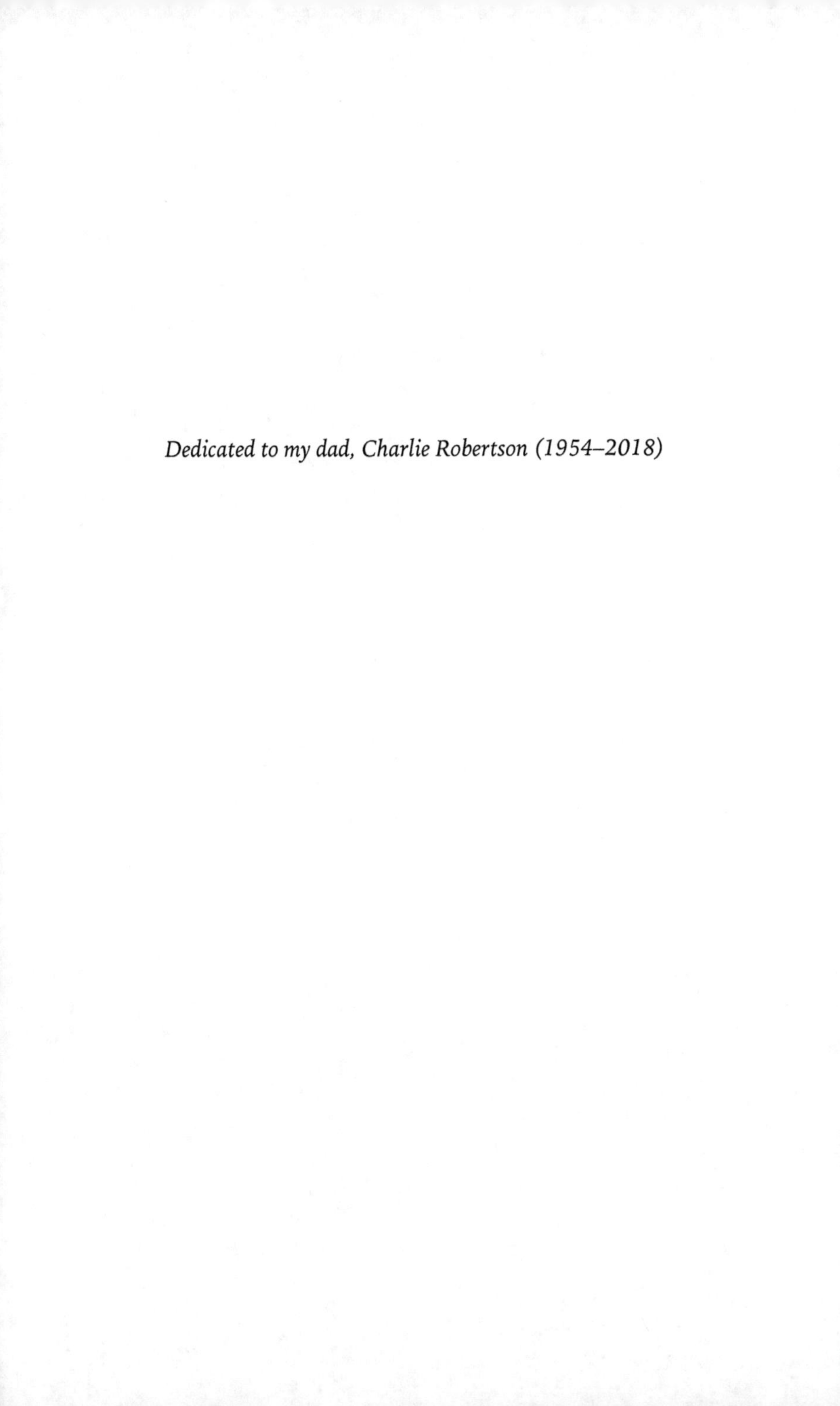

Dedicated to my dad, Charlie Robertson (1954–2018)

CONTENTS

POVCAST

TEARS FILL MARIA'S EYES AS SHE STARES IN THE window. Within the dino diorama stands the MechaDinoRanger, in blue, surrounded by his biomechanical dino buddies, all cast in brightly coloured plastic. Bob's choice—the treat that she will buy to cheer him up but cannot afford.

Jaunts with Bob are her happiest memories. His excitement would ramp up as they neared the water park, arcade, or art gallery, his little hand heating hers. Later they'd find a park bench, sit and enjoy some roasted chestnuts, cinnamon churros, or freshly baked pretzels.

The joy of the jaunt, that was the thing. The toy is near pointless to own now that he can't accompany her on the trip to buy it.

She observes her reflection in the glass. Modest beige coat, shoulder-length brown hair, no makeup. As nondescript as she could be. As if that is any protection.

Don't go into debt if you can help it, they all told her. She was managing, until an autobus ran over Dad in order to save a dozen schoolkids from plunging into a ravine. It wasn't the bastard's fault he became the casualty of a real-life trolley problem and passed on all his debt to her. She knew this for a fact, having insisted on watching dashcam footage of the bus ploughing into him to check that he hadn't jumped in front of it.

She couldn't pay for a funeral, but there was no escaping it. And even if she'd dragged his corpse into a cardboard box and kicked it into a hand-dug grave, the land rights alone would have set her back tens of thousands.

This was weeks ago. Add on interest, and the net total she owes is ten times what it was. Probably. She's too afraid to check.

She opens Povcast on her phone. The empty notification bar gives her palpitations.

If they don't give you a target, you're the target.

Not necessarily, she tells herself. She doesn't currently have a target, but that doesn't mean she is one.

The system doesn't tell her. Benefactors probably enjoy plaguing her with fear, paranoia, and a constant state of unknowing.

There's a tap on her shoulder. A pain in her gut. It happens so quickly that she only sees the knife when it slides back out of her. A hand-span long, a monstrosity of metal glistening in crimson.

The killer is a woman about her age. Hair tied back in a ponytail, sorrowful green eyes. Sleek leather coat, tight pants, dirty black plimsolls. She places a hand on Maria's shoulder and lowers her to the ground, whispering, "Shh, it's done."

Indulgent shoppers and impatient businessfolk widen their berth to give the pair space. Some tut in disapproval or groan in disgust, but most are silent.

"How much?" Maria says, her vision closing in. "Please, at least tell me that."

The killer holds up her phone's camera as Maria's eyes deaden.

"It's okay," Maria says, coughing. "I would do the same."

"I know you would do the same, Maria. That's how the system works."

Sarah clenches her jaw and looks at her phone. A green tick appears over the footage of Maria, and she reads a familiar message: *Kill confirmed! Calculating relief: $10,000.*

Is that what Maria asked—how much her death was worth?

Povcast doesn't tell you while the target is still alive. Perhaps this Maria didn't watch the tutorial vids. She had noob all over her, the way she just stood there, gawping at a window and feeling sorry for herself.

Best not to learn your bounty—nor why your killer wants it.

This season's ruby-heeled Louboutins, have mercy!

She was on such a tight killing schedule she couldn't even wear them; she just kept them in the purse she ran around with. It was enough to feel a trace of their power.

Beside the point. Maria signed up for the system. That's enough solace for me.

Targets nominate themselves voluntarily by signing up for Povcast. There are no rewards for random killings. You do unto others only what they would do unto you if given the chance.

It wasn't like Povcast created this city-wide barbarism. The system simply puts it out in the open, and maybe for the better. Now, everyone can see what they are doing to one another, and each new murder is a reminder that no one has yet devised a better debt relief solution. And deaths will rack up until they do, like some massive opt-in terrorist network that holds a fraction of society hostage until everyone bows to its demands for a fairer economy.

Sarah gets up and walks briskly ahead, checking her banking balance: -$990,038.57.

Joy!

Once, she was horrified to read an initial debt of 50K, and now she celebrates that it's beneath a million—for at least the next hour, interest rates and new kills allowing.

Sarah does seem to get a lot of targets. Do the benefactors like her? They keep paying her, sure enough, but never that much. Maybe they want her in the game longer. If she ever got close to being debt-free, would they make her the target of the Povcasters in her area? That's what she would do if she was privileged enough to entertain such sadistic notions.

Thank God they can't read my thoughts. Yet.

Then again, what choice does she have? If she kills any slower, the growing interest will erase her progress—an insult to her and the ones she leaves neutralized in her wake.

Her phone pings. A new target, two kilometres northwest.

She slips her knife back in its holster and sprints towards the pin on her map, between the city's faceless skyscrapers and spires, tackling anyone who gets in her way.

She's running to the next target.

No—she's only outrunning whoever chases her.

SNAPSHOTS

When Dad arrives, he twiddles a dial in the panel, and SnapRoom gets brighter.

He's wearing the same slacks and mustard-coloured cardigan that I expect Mum to have thrown out by now. His face is hollow, eyes empty. Strings of white hair fall from the ring of still-functioning follicles on his head. The white whiskers on his face give his skin a greyish hue.

I've never seen him look so old. Best not to mention it.

The SnapShots adjust to the new light. The bluish glow of Five, Fifteen, Nineteen, and Twenty-One makes each a petal in a ghostly peony at the room's centre.

"Cheers," I say. "I was too scared to touch anything."

There are basic options on the panel, like *lighting, EQ, mute, reverse, record,* and so on—but also more serious-sounding options: *delete, modify, enhance.* I almost pressed *reset memory,* thinking it was the light switch—which would've erased everything the SnapShots had learned since their creation.

Five runs to Dad for a hug. "Daddy!" He giggles as his hands run through Dad's legs with a buzz. Holes, like dead pixels, pock-mark his blocky hologram all over, from the bowl cut down to the dungarees.

"What took you so long?" I say.

Dad pretends to pat Five's head, his hand going straight through, fingertips lit up in blue. There's a resting tremor in his hands. I've had those before, from antidepressants and hangovers. Neither are topics I broach easily. I hope Dad's shakes are something else.

"Some new customers wanted to book golfing lessons," he says. "It takes a while to register them in the system." He walks to the TV monitors embedded in the wall and turns them on. They display CCTV footage of his golf course up above us. Golden light spreads over the greens. There's a white cart by the ninth hole, where I parked not minutes ago. "What were you guys talking about before I showed up?"

"Tell him what was on your mind, Twenty-Five," Fifteen says to me, rolling up the sleeves of his school shirt.

I let them call me Twenty-Five so they don't feel excluded.

"I need your advice, Dad," I say. "I've been seeing Flossy for a few years. She's itching for me to propose."

I'd never known a 'Flossy' before I met her in the bank one evening. She squeezed rain from her ebullient mop of pink hair and screamed at a camera that she wasn't leaving before speaking to a human. In a cringeworthy but effective move, I said that if she was looking for human connection, we should go for a drink instead of waiting longer in that forgotten, sterile cubicle. In my office daydreams of her, a shimmering ream of gossamer floss surrounds her. She's my Flossy by name and nature.

"That's how it usually goes, Twenty-Five," Dad says. "Your mother and I got married at your age." He giggles. "The most wonderful decision I ever made! Until we had you, Son." He points at me, finger wobbling. "Grandkids! They'll follow soon enough."

"One thing at a time!" I say.

"A dad can dream. You'll bring Flossy next time, won't you?"

He used to complain that I wasn't visiting enough. Now I'm

here so often it feels like I never leave, so he guilts me about not bringing Flossy. It's always something.

"You're right," he says, reading my face. "I shouldn't say things like that."

"I-I didn't mean—"

"Hooray!" Five says, star-jumping with excitement. "What's the wedding gonna be like? How many cakes? You guys need to get a big house for all our kids!"

Dad sits cross-legged beside Five but meets my gaze. "Remember visiting me in the garage when you were five? I'd be tinkering away with my tech, and you'd pad across the backyard to see me, getting grass all over your grippy socks."

Mum would entrust me with a steaming espresso to take on my journey. I'd hold it up to Dad, careful not to spill any. Back then, he looked several orders of magnitude larger than he does now.

Dad looks to Five. "I knew from this age that you'd make something of yourself. Remind me how high you can count, Son!"

Five's face screws up in thought as he taps numbers across his digits. "One, two, three, four ..."

These days, now that anyone can make a SnapShot and all of them are immaculate, Dad seems to love Five the most. Over our lunches at the restaurant that overlooks the golf course, Dad has told me countless times that Five is "a special early fragment of a tech with boundless applications."

Nineteen interrupts Five. "Ugh! Marriage." He slumps on the brushed aluminium wall. "Are we that conventional?" He scratches his bald head.

I had long hair for most of that year but shaved it off just before I turned twenty. Dad so enjoyed that act of bravery that he kept it for the SnapShot.

Nineteen has a point. Flossy's friends are all getting married, and it does seem like it's our turn—but is that all any life event is? Our turn?

That's the weird thing about SnapRoom. I come here sometimes just to see how far I've progressed, but my former selves can be insightful. In the end, I'm the same as these kids in front of me once were: I improvise some approximation of a life in the face of epic choices I feel too small to make.

"Thought we'd have spent a few more years single," Nineteen continues, "riding suicide over the magnorails between the cities. Living off the land."

What an insufferably idealistic dream. It's so painful to look at my own smug face from that age: its insincere smile, the whole snake-like, hooded-eye, brooding thing I always did. I thought I knew so much more than everyone, rambling on about how I should've been born in the 1960s. I extolled the potential joy of living out of a Volkswagen van when I wouldn't even join Dad on his weekly hikes.

"Can you even play the guitar any better than I can?" Nineteen adds.

I shake my head with feigned dismay. Nineteen can tell. The last person he needs treating his pursuits as a silly phase is himself.

It's cruel of me to hang out with these guys, really. They derive so much hope from the it-gets-better potential of the different futures they envisage. Here I am, the finite reality, robbing them of that hope simply by existing.

I frown at Nineteen and say, "We have a happy life?"

"Fantastic," he says, pushing himself up the wall with his feet, grazing its panelling, his arms firmly folded. "I'm sure that makes us all so memorable. People will flock here to meet us one day. 'Come hang out with this guy's SnapShots, for here lies a man who was once *happy*.'"

They used to visit SnapRoom, Dad's golfers and B&B guests. Later, SnapShot Soft LLC's patented holoproject technology became reasonably priced. Now everyone has their own

SnapShots. It's hard to see even these first iterations as meaningful, what with proliferation like that.

What's that sound? Oh. I cringe as Dad sings some made-up tune to himself while playing an air guitar. "Hey, Nineteen, remember letting your dad take you to see The Mechabots in concert? When their drummer closed with that ten-minute solo, and his platform rose up into the air? Then all those fireworks launched out of the base. You'd never seen anything like it." He smiles. "I watched you watch them. The light of the sparklers in your eyes."

Nineteen sighs. "No one else wanted to go with me."

"Your guitar's here at the club, up in the attic! Will you teach me how to play if I bring it down?"

"Oh, come on, Dad," I say. "Why would you wanna do that?"

Nineteen ignores us both. "How do you think Twenty-Five is doing, Fifteen?"

Fifteen is Nineteen's favourite, even though they make each other bluer, their neuroses feeding off one another.

"Honestly?" Fifteen says, loosening his tie. "I can't believe we even have a girlfriend."

An eternity in school uniform! Why not? That's what Fifteen's existence felt like. His is an age I wouldn't repeat. On my mental to-do list for most of it was *find ANY bearable direction for life, hide misery from others, try not to kill self (will to live pending)*. 'Pending' lasted months until I witnessed the purple balloon of my own pee bursting across Terry Coraghan's sour face at high school graduation. It was a petty humiliation to cap the many he put me through. Whatever keeps you going, I say.

Dad tries to pinch Fifteen's cheeks. "True, you didn't have anyone to go out gallivanting with—but it worked out great for me. We spent weekends playing backgammon together." He clicks his tongue in thought. "And you had so much to be proud of. A handsome young gent with your whole life ahead of you? I wish you could've seen that."

It wasn't so simple. I kept all my suffering internal at that age. I guess that's one reason why Dad holds on to Fifteen: he has happier memories with me than I have with myself. I'm glad, in a way—but shouldn't I have enjoyed my own company at least as much as anyone else?

Dad gasps. "Fancy beating your old man at backgammon again? I'll bring a set. Just tell me where to move your pieces!"

Twenty-One slicks his brown hair out of his face then snaps his fingers. "Oh, yeah!" He laughs. "How quaint to think of the age before girlfriends! Don't worry, Fifteen. Let's just say you make up for lost time."

Nineteen takes Five's little hand and pulls him closer, blue sparks flying from their fingertips. The wireframe shape of their holograms bursts through as the room's computer struggles to interpret their crashing together. Nineteen glowers at Twenty-One, who says, "What's the big deal?"

Twenty-One: the edgy, all-black-wearing, experience-collecting party boy. Never missed a club night out, memorized album reviews on obscure websites and spouted them at friends to impress. When I look at him, I feel the elbows of all those partygoers in my ribs. The tinnitus of blaring techno rings in my ears. The sugary film of vodka mixers coats my teeth. The frozen fear, of waking up in a field in muddy clothes, jags through my chest.

At least he kept me alive, but should I attribute that to him or luck?

Dad cocks his head at me. "You've something to learn from Twenty-One. All that creative energy! Remember the thirtieth anniversary party for your mother and me? The caterers with those fancy canapé-laden slates. You rented a champagne fountain." He presses a hand to his heart. "The speech you gave —it brought me to tears."

I must've used the fountain more than Dad, because I don't remember that at all.

"Sometimes it's more about indulging in the day's fun than working for the future. So slow down! You won't be Twenty-Five for long."

"That's the opposite of your usual advice," I say. "What's going on?"

"Since no one likes my suggestions, Twenty-One, maybe you can choose the activity for all of us today? I know you guys don't agree on much, but there must be something. Anything to distract Twenty-Five from his troubles."

"Why are you so against helping me?"

He hangs his head but doesn't speak.

"You didn't do much living-in-the-moment at my age. You already had your own company." I hold my arms up and gesture around the room. "I've gotta get cracking if I want silly playrooms like this in my manse."

"Hey!" Twenty-One says.

"Y-You know what I mean," I say.

"We sure do," says Fifteen, looking to Nineteen, who nods.

"I wish you could just enjoy yourself," Dad says. "We never get enough time together, and your mind's always elsewhere." He's almost in tears. I have no idea why.

I shrug at the SnapShots, who've spread around the room and appear like the blue fingers of a giant's hand.

I clench my fists. "I didn't mean to upset you, Dad. Let's just drop it. Wanna go for lunch?"

Dad goes to the door, opens it, and bends down. He slides in a silver tray and picks it up. On it are a single BLT, a glass of milk, a carton of orange juice, a box of raisins, and a red plastic tea set. "Why don't we have lunch here today? I brought the teacups for Five, to serve with his favourite—orange juice with raisins in it!"

"Yay!" Five runs to Dad and jumps up, trying to grab the tray. His hand passes through it, to his bemusement.

I know it's fun for Dad to be here with the SnapShots too, but as the eldest version of myself—and the only *alive* one, in every sense—I don't want to share. He puts me in the awkward position of inventing some excuse for why we can't stay, without insulting the rest. Oh, well. If I mess up, maybe I can press *reset memory* when Dad's not looking.

"Twenty-Five thinks we don't know what he wants," Fifteen says, looking at Dad but jerking his head in my direction.

Five is on the floor, crying. He's realized his flesh isn't solid.

Dad puts the tray down and kneels beside Five.

Did I sound like that at five? I figured it was endearing, evoking only sympathy. This is one occasion when I prefer my memory's partial view of the past to these digital replicas.

I look between Five and Dad to indicate my discomfort, but Dad's back up and chatting to Nineteen now.

"Dad!" I say.

"… don't know why we humour him," Nineteen says, tailing off to look at me and say "Hm?" to show that I've interrupted.

He knows I resent him. I'm disgusted to have been someone so sneery, though I do admit that it's easier to judge him from the outside.

"Okay, this is ridiculous," I say.

I reach for the door handle. My hand goes straight through it, buzzing with blue sparks.

Five keeps wailing. I can only hear a few words of Dad's conversation with the others, who form a bright blue wall around him.

Their voices blur together. I struggle to hear my thoughts over the sound of them.

I shout, "How did it happen?"

The shock of it shuts up Five, who sniffles.

Dad looks in dismay at his sandwich. His plan of a pleasant lunch has shattered. How many times I've done this to him, I've no idea.

"You and Flossy were celebrating your engagement," he says.

"Took an unlicensed autocab back home. It went haywire. E-Exploded. Neither of you, you know …"

I think back to my first spontaneous date with Flossy. The knock of her knee against mine. Her manic laughter. How she characterized her office's staff room with such loving detail that I saw everyone with her: mad Karen, kind Sophie, Bob the slob. I think of her now in a haze of grapefruit perfume, with an aura of colourful ticker tape all around.

The guilt of leaving the world Flossy-less presides over every other pain now flooding me.

"But I don't get it," I say. "I parked a cart outside about half an hour ago." I gesture to the TV, to my cart by the ninth hole.

Dad looks where I'm pointing. He walks to the panel and taps some setting into it. Across the TV screens, a granite sky appears. Beneath it is black, ash-like rain. The grass and dunes now fester with eerie black weeds. Why? He'd made it to retirement, to the simple pleasure of running this place.

His rheumy eyes roll at me. "What was the point? Let nature take it all." He looks around the room. "This is about all that matters." He addresses each of the SnapShots in turn. "Five, my first and favourite assistant. Fifteen, my little rebel. Nineteen, who emerged from his funereal adolescence with the ambition to live forever. Twenty-One, who first discovered how to enjoy life." He turns to me. "Twenty-Five."

I shudder to hear the name.

"Your final reluctant birthday present to me. As close as I can get to the day I lost you."

I'm jealous of the tears streaming down his face.

To think I'd shown these other SnapShots such disdain. I'm the most deluded and pitiful of them all. I hope my future self is kinder to me than I've been to my younger versions. Oh, right, there won't be one. How many waves of awful revelation can my heart take? Oh, right, I don't have a heart. There goes another wave.

"I want to see Mum," I say.

Dad waves a dismissive hand at me. "Your mother came here once. It's—not for her." He rolls his shoulders as if to rid himself of the idea. "But I just want to forget what happened."

"That's not fair."

"Isn't it?"

I think of the alternatives, for both of us. I don't know the answer.

Dad turns away, too saddened to look at me any longer, at any of us. He makes to leave, but I shout after him, "Take me with you."

The others meet this plea with laughter, murmurs, saddened exhalations.

Dad stops by the door, still with his back turned. "Why did I save any of you? Your mother was right. This isn't helping."

I growl with frustration. "I've just learned I'm … nothing more to you than, than a height mark on a kitchen wall and … and now you're gonna delete us? Go on, then!"

"Let him," Fifteen and Nineteen say to me in unison.

"No!" Five wails.

"Chill!" Twenty-One says.

Dad inhales, turns around, and says, "The eldest SnapShot is the most likely to think it's still alive." He smiles bleakly. "I advised customers to keep SnapShots of the same person in different rooms. I was mostly thinking of the profit I'd gain from the extra projectors required." He walks between us, reaching out to ruffle Five's holographic hair, stroke Nineteen's sunken little face. "Split you guys up? That was like asking whether I wanted to see only your hand today, your leg tomorrow." He looks between us all. "Not height marks on a kitchen wall. More like, I don't know, cross-sections from a full-body MRI scan." He holds out his palm and chops up and down upon it with his other hand. "Instead of the 3D image of a body, together you're the 4D reality of my entire son." He lowers his head. "You're each a person I wish I could've kept. And just a part of someone I loved dearly."

None of us know what to say.

"I-I'll try again later," he says, turning back to the door. "One more time. Just once more."

"Well done," Nineteen says to me.

"You ruined it," Fifteen says.

I feel Twenty-One's touch like a fuzz of static on my shoulder. "It's okay," he says, bringing me in for a comforting embrace.

Five wraps his arms through my legs.

"All of you stand before me now," Dad says, "proof that my son has gone forever. But each time I come here, I think it'll go differently."

Before I can say anything, he's out the door.

His hand reaches back in. I run to it as he presses *reset memory*.

KILLING TIME

When Tabby closed the door on the world, she created a darkness in which something worse manifested itself. One day, it turned its key in the lock.

She was on the couch at the time, wrapped up in fusty blankets, picking at her self-cut fringe while binge-watching *DreadTech,* a show about miserable dystopian futures that brought her pleasure for reasons she didn't understand. For maximum immersion, she'd hung black blankets from the curtain poles, near-eliminating the sunlight, but square streams of it shot around the edges in white, dusty streaks.

She heard the key turning, gasped, and paused her show.

Who would dare invade her tiny sanctuary, the place she left as little as possible, where she bothered no one? Couldn't everyone do her the same courtesy and leave her alone?

The door opened to reveal a double of Tabby herself. Perhaps a better Tabby. Sleek hair, immaculate eyeliner, beige mac with matching designer handbag.

The double placed the bag on a nearby armchair with a smooth and effortless gesture.

Tabby picked up a large knife from the coffee table in front of her. It had dried cheese and tomato sauce on the blade.

The double paced towards Tabby. "I'm sure you have questions."

"Wh-who are you?" Tabby croaked back.

The double clasped her hands. "You hate guessing games, but indulge me, please. Who do you think I am?"

"My twin sister?"

The double shook her head.

Tabby looked to *DreadTech,* paused on the TV. "A-Are you me from the future?"

"Closer, maybe." The double grinned.

Tabby let the blankets fall off her, feeling ashamed. "Why 'closer'?"

"I can be you if you want me to." She hung up her coat and bag by the door and joined Tabby on the couch. "Think of me as your slave."

Tabby shuffled away from her.

"You haven't gone to work for two months, three days, five hours, six minutes, eleven seconds." The double smoothed her hair back. "But that's okay. I'll go in for you. You mostly hated it, and you don't have to return. Filing can be therapeutic, but you didn't find it so. It brought you pleasure only thirty-three point four eight nine per cent of the time. You deserve more than that."

Tabby was speechless.

The double shuffled to the couch's other end, mirroring Tabby with a crossed knee and folded arms. "With your permission, I'll take over all your duties. I know them inside out. I've been watching you since your creation." She looked to the screen and smiled. "While you watched TV, I watched *you.*" Then back to Tabby: "I'll do a better job than you and give you all the credit and benefits."

Tabby let her arms fall to her sides. "What would *I* do?"

The double grinned and held up a finger, returning to the door to retrieve something from her bag. She took out a screen and two wireless earbuds. The screen was a curved triangle shape, like it would rest perfectly on a sphere. The earbuds were angry-looking and insect-like.

"Stay here," the double said. "Entertain yourself."

"You're going to live my life while I stay here and watch Netflix."

The double's laugh was smooth and practised. "It's better than Netflix." She clicked on the screen, and it hovered before her, projecting misty white holograms.

Tabby watched, mesmerized, as images from vague dreams of hers emerged from the clouds. Elaborate castles, chisel-jawed men, the perfect outfit, Shakespearean vengeance enacted on high-school bullies. These images washed elaborate emotions over her: the sensation of having arrived, of life happening now with nowhere else to be, nothing to fix, and everyone pleased.

When the double spoke again, the images collapsed. "A stream of perfectly entertaining shows, tailored to your unique needs and desires."

Tabby half listened, irritated by the distraction.

The double walked back over to her. "These shows have a target audience of one. And they never end. There's always another episode, another series. It just goes on and on."

"Why?"

The double's face snapped to sympathy. "Haven't you been through enough? Overeducated, unappreciated, tossed aside by a world that only acknowledges you when it wants something, and barely even then." She mirrored Tabby's body language, leaning in closer after each sentence.

An obvious, manipulative ploy. But Tabby felt the words needle their way in, poking at the inextinguishable parts of her that wanted them to be true. "So you've been watching me."

"Your whole life." The double held up her front door key. "Printed this myself from the footage."

"So you saw when—"

"You were in the shower. I can provide you with that comfort myself. It would be my honour. You needn't feel alone ever again, in any capacity."

Tabby looked away and shook her head. "N-No, I—y-you saw what *happened.*"

The double cocked her head.

"Two months, three days, five hours ago," Tabby said. "You're not the only one keeping track."

The double sighed. "I so badly wanted to help. You were my assignment, after all. But I was nowhere near here at the time." Her face remained flat, but tears leaked from her eyes. "It hurt me more than it did you. My species is sensitive far beyond the spectrum of human emotion." She reached for Tabby's hand.

Tabby flinched. When doubles had touched in *DreadTech,* they erupted in a matter–antimatter explosion. But when Tabby's double took her hand, all Tabby noticed was the softness of her skin.

An oxytocin rush ran through Tabby's system. Pure safety.

"The police did nothing." The double's look was hypnotic, like her eyes were expanding.

Tabby bit her lip. "It wasn't like that. I didn't describe him properly. Because of the shock. That's why they couldn't find him."

The double pointed vaguely towards the street, but kept her eyes trained on Tabby. "He lives just a few streets away. It could happen again at any time."

They stared at one another.

"It's a lot to take in." The double held the screen and earbuds out to Tabby. "Why not watch something while you think about it?"

Time lost meaning for Tabby as she lay there on the couch, bathed in the endless dopamine bliss of her self-designed shows.

When she'd first put those earbuds in—whenever that was—the screen had floated up and expanded into a sphere that enveloped her head, spritzing pleasant smells and filling her field of view with constant gloss.

She spent most of her time in her favourite role, as the cool, sophisticated teen protagonist in a high-school drama set in some unnamed, affluent region of California.

All the parents had money and lived in enormous houses, so they made sure to complain as a courtesy. They never committed the transgression of enjoying a lifestyle few could afford.

All the girls at school were hot. They swarmed around Tabby and proclaimed her the hottest, which was the ultimate compliment.

All the boys had abs and infallible hair. They created endlessly epic and intricate love polygons around Tabby. Tabby with the good figure and best grades. Tabby who threw the best parties that they'd all remember forever. Tabby with the interesting and tragic back story, which she'd learned about through tenderly treated and dreamily rendered flashbacks. The guy who did all the show's music sang with a voice ethereally beautiful, imbuing her character's longings with such striking poignancy that he simply had to be an alien. That or a masterfully designed algorithm. But Tabby tried not to think about that. Or about anything, really. She just let the sights and sounds soothe all her woes away.

Slam.

Tabby jumped up and took her earbuds out. The screen collapsed and fell into her lap, revealing her ruinous surroundings.

Dust motes clouded the air. Black fungus rotted through the walls, fluffs of white extruding from their spots. A freezer sat open by the front door, its contents thawed, water pooling on the floor, packets of vegetables wilting in the room's stale heat. Thick grime, like some weird discharge, coated the coffee table.

She couldn't say when last she'd looked around, but she'd trusted it wouldn't look like this. Why hadn't the alien cleaned?

Tabby could ask it herself: it stood there in the foyer.

"I shouldn't hear you come in!" Tabby yelled. "I don't even want to look at you."

This was her usual spiel. The alien would normally cower and mouth *I'm sorry* so as not to further offend Tabby with the sound of its speech.

This time, it scoffed at her.

"How dare you respond to me like that!" Tabby got up on her atrophied legs and walked to the door.

Something tugged on her arm. Plastic tubing ran from her vein to a drip bag that hung from a stand beside her. She gripped the stand and wheeled it with her.

"It's been weeks since you last secured a promotion for us." Her legs shook, unaccustomed to supporting her body's weight. "What have you even been doing?!"

"I just came to say goodbye."

"I don't think so. You're my slave. Or you're supposed to be." Tabby's lip curled with distaste at all this empty exertion. "You need to up the dose of sedatives in my drip. You're not changing my catheter fast enough. And we haven't made love in God knows how long."

"'Made love'. Hah!" The alien recoiled. "It nauseated me more than you could ever understand." Its laugh had a timbre like a shaken sheet of metal. "The latest reports are in. Our entertainment protocols have weakened your species to below the critical takeover threshold."

"What?" Tabby was almost in tears, desperate to defend herself—but she found her reasoning skills vastly weakened.

The alien dissolved its human hand, letting its dark feelers escape for the first time. At the sight of this, Tabby scurried to the comfort of the couch.

"We isolated you from each other." It examined its feelers

with pride. "Depressed you all." It stretched the feelers behind its back, its many unseen joints popping like bubble wrap. "This was the humane option, believe it or not." It paced around the living room on newly released forelegs, which clicked on the lacquered wood. "Most declined our offer, so we ground them up for fuel. Sometimes the devices malfunctioned, which led to a suicide here and there. The rest of you we simply subdued." It turned to look at Tabby, its real eyes emerging. No cornea, iris or pupil, just two balls of pale jade. "Thank God it's over. I could hardly stand to look at you. That expression on your face as you watched your stories."

More facial features poked through the Tabby mask: dark green chitinous protuberances at bizarre angles. They were seemingly superfluous, but surely possessed functions in the alien's home environment.

"That slack-jawed face of yours," it continued, "with its dead, cow-like eyes and bitter mouth." Black feelers took over its lips, intertwining like fingers. "The more pleasure you received, the more misery it caused you." Furry antennae sprouted from its temples. "Pitiful!"

The alien tossed her coat to the floor and dropped her Tabby illusion entirely, the skin melting away to nothing. It was a slick, human-sized mantis with a wedge-shaped head. Blade-like ridges ran along its armoured shell.

Tabby howled and bunched blankets around herself. All this time, if the alien had wanted, it could have pared her out of her skin in a second.

The alien opened the front door. "It's been a blast. But I'm off to scour this stupid planet of its resources, darling." It held up a feeler. "I do have one final gift."

It tossed something that skidded across the floor.

Tabby recoiled, then gingerly peered over the edge of the couch. A round pocket mirror wobbled around. As it came to a stop, Tabby examined her bloated face, greasy hair, flaking nails.

Her greying and waxy skin. 'Etiolated' was the word for it: pallid from lack of sunlight.

When had she learned that? When had she last learned *anything?*

Only the alien would know—but it had already left.

***

Before she could emerge from her cocoon-like dwelling, Tabby had to overcome her pre-alien agoraphobia *and* the killer withdrawal symptoms that raged through her after she pulled out the drip. Uncharacteristic waves of fury. The alien had fed her heavy opiates mixed with just enough nourishment for survival—but not a drop more.

She writhed on the floor, clawing at the wood, splinters digging beneath her nails. It was painful, but more lucid than anything she'd experienced in so long.

It was a full week before she stumbled out of the flat in her pyjamas, hungry and confused, a vice-like headache gripping her by the temples.

The air was thick and poisonous, brown smog insulating the world in an unbearable heat. It seemed to obscure the buildings and streets—but when she approached where once there had been a lamppost, a newsagent's, a bar, she discovered levelled plains grazed by amorphous black vehicles that hoovered the dust.

She backed away. A humming in the distance got louder. She turned in its direction and took slow paces ahead.

Pipes emerged from the dim. They were big shimmering metal tubes, flared at their bases where they connected seamlessly to the ground. From there, they launched high into the sky, their tributaries connecting to massive terminals that branched off higher still, through the atmosphere itself, enormous cylinders tapering out of sight. The whole network vibrated fiercely.

She steadied herself as she shuffled forward, wondering if the pipes sucked out the planet's very core. The ground nearby buckled into depressions as big as buses, which were almost filled to the brim with corpses in tattered clothing.

"Hey."

Tabby jumped, shook, cowered.

A man, who himself looked sucked out, stood before her. Skin peeled from his face. Stringy hair fell to his shoulders. His jeans and hoodie hung from his slumped skeleton.

"D-Do I know you?" Her voice was hoarse. She hadn't spoken to anyone since the alien's departure—and not to another human in who knew how long. She could barely form sentences.

"Yeah, I'm … uh." He took her arm gently and moved them both away from the pipes' humming. "I'm the guy who mugged you."

She'd thought, if she ever saw him again, she'd recognize him immediately—but this wasn't the face that had appeared in all those nightmares. Though it did share some of the same features. The unwashed hair, the craggy wrinkles around the eyes. The scars, two ragged slices at either corner of the mouth that tore up to his ears. The divots all around them where someone—another gang member, probably—had failed to sew them up.

He wasn't afraid to share his identity for the same reason she wasn't afraid to learn it: even if they had managed to maintain scraps of their former selves, this new world obliterated their meaning.

"This is like something out of *DreadTech*," he said. "Or maybe *DreadTech*'s like something out of *this*."

She frowned. "*DreadTech*?"

"It was a TV show."

"Oh. Yeah." She rubbed her eyes. "It barely counts as one compared to what I've been watching lately."

A large metal bowl dug itself into a corpse-laden concavity, filling itself with bodies.

"Did they get you too?" she asked.

He nodded. "He looked like me. He told me he knew why I was like this. Mentioned stuff about my childhood even I'd managed to forget. He knew I wanted to change. But he said I didn't have the self-control to do it. All I'd ever known was all I'd ever know, he said. I could be no other way."

A black impenetrable monolith in morphing, non-Euclidean shapes floated along the street. Magnets selectively filtered favourite particles from the ground below. The particles rose in a fine mist, the monoliths leaving silt and dust in their wake.

The mugger continued, "My alien knew I wanted to help society. The kindest thing someone like me could do, he said, was stay indoors. He would live my life for me, better than I ever could."

More humans emerged from the remaining buildings. Most cowered in the shadows, holding their arms over their heads as if to block the sun. Some padded around in horror. All must have watched shows of their mind's design. Not only had they nothing to say to one another—unique entertainments having destroyed their once-common cultural ground—but reality clearly terrified them.

The mugger was in tears now. "We wasted so much time." He grabbed Tabby by the shoulders. "Is it like the aliens said? Is it too late to do anything?"

She went limp in his grasp, knowing he couldn't hurt her even if he wanted to. She looked back at the dust and dirty sunlight, at the indifferently humming pipes and meandering alien equipment. "I know they *want* us to think it's too late."

"But what should we do?"

She saw, in the weariness of his face, his desire to abdicate any authority, to outsource all of his thinking to her, simply because she was the nearest 'anyone else' around.

She stretched her neck, fighting off outrage. She would

pretend he thought of her as important. "We can start by bearing witness." She shrugged. "It's better than what we've *been* doing."

This thought seemed to pass like a wave over others in the toxic murk. They gathered in the streets, straightened their backs, dropped their arms to their sides and stood tall.

"It's the start of something," Tabby said.

Survivors murmured to one another in loose clusters.

"It hurts to see, but at least it's real."

The mugger smiled. "We'll learn what we can. Maybe there are still actions we can take."

But as they squared their shoulders and looked once again to the street, their grins dropped.

A roaming alien vehicle passed by, using big chitinous claws to cart up bodies, both alive and dead, and toss them into an industrial shredder on its back. It crunched them with deafening volume, spraying the buildings' nub-like remains with a confetti of bloody viscera.

A ripple of survivors fell to the ground in horror as it passed by, the sight of it excruciating.

Some gripped their heads. Some screamed for the pain to end. But some got back up again.

"I LIKE THE MISCALCULATIONS."

We were several kilometres underwater in the viewing deck, right above the colony. Dr Schwarz and I were on the platform, in the centre of the crystal globe. Before me was a triplet of screens with readings on high-contrast backgrounds: warnings beeping in warm colours, graphs running with real-time numbers, and a 3D diagram of the globe that registered external disruptions.

"I can't get used to it," Dr Schwarz replied.

Shoom, shoom, shoom. A stream of corridor lights died off behind him.

I looked at him. Dimples tightened and broke across his scarred cheeks. His scalp shifted as he smiled, but his hair didn't. He'd gelled it into a rigid bowl.

I folded my arms and looked at the globe itself. Silky purple liquid rushed across its outer surface. "If there's no chance of evacuating, maybe a chain will crash through and drown us all."

"Yeah, yeah." He watched it with me.

The globe sat on a crater-shaped plinth atop the Smart Dynamics facility's black metal shell, the only of its kind here on Hypnos. Long chains attached to the globe's surface and waved around to gather the force of the eddies that thrust against them.

A chain crashed down upon the globe, and purple lightning fired off it in all directions, crackling as its energy dissipated. The chains were poorly tuned.

"Follow me," Schwarz said. "The subject is speaking again."

———

The subject's room had walls like a copper burial chamber, slanting upward and covered in weird etchings. Soot coated each panel above the flickering yellow torches.

It smelled of heavy incense.

Schwarz addressed the subject: "Hi, son. How've you been?"

The subject, a pale-faced kid swamped by an ill-fitting hospital robe, looked haunted. Had the experiments changed the colour of his eyes? They were a foggy blue, but I couldn't remember if they'd ever looked different. Being down here messed with my memory.

I walked over to the zinc slab slicing out of the wall and opened the journal that lay atop it, reading from the last test transcript.

The corresponding case report read:

Case #0000289: "JR"
Absolute: 1578.83
Harnessed: 899.93
Efficiency: 57%

"When was the last experiment conducted?" I asked Schwarz.

"Three days ago."

"Without my consent."

"There were complications with your globe. You were busy all day."

I tied my hair into a low bun. "It's fine this once. But that's it."

"It was a good one, though. Right, kid?" Dr Schwarz said.

"I used to go by Junior," the subject said. "Call me that."

"How do you feel, Junior?" I asked.

He pressed two fingers to his temples. "Splitting headaches three times a day. The white light flares up and I have a five-minute window to stop it with painkillers or the day's gone."

"And the fits?"

"Only one since last time."

Schwarz turned to me. "Progress."

Junior stuck up his middle fingers behind Schwarz's back.

"Ready to go again?" I said to him.

"As ever," he replied.

Dr Schwarz turned to a clean page in the journal, hopped onto the table, and poised his pen. In the wall's embedded autoclave was the exchanger, a large sleek metal spike with a circular base. I took it and slipped it into the aperture drilled into the base of Junior's skull, poking it up through each of the brain's structures of interest and triggering a release of the device's electrolytic adhesive. The screen on the base lit up, and readings—images of the many voices of Junior's mind—flowered out from a central point on its little screen.

I walked around to stand in front of Junior and nodded to Dr Schwarz, who clenched his jaw with determination. I sat down on the table beside him.

"When you're ready," I said.

"I'm embarrassed about this one," Junior said.

"Hey," I said, "it's not like you're in control of the visions. Let's just get it all written down and you can stop thinking about it."

Junior chewed on a knuckle and looked away, but subsided and met my eyes again. "I'm a little boy. I just have that sense."

"How old?" Schwarz said.

"Doctor!" I said.

He looked at me like I'd lost it.

"We agreed that you wouldn't guide the visions," I warned him.

"I'm walking through a house," Junior continued. "It looks like my old family home, but all the walls have aged and turned grey. There's a snail on the ceiling and a smell of mould. Something is wrong."

Dr Schwarz continued scribbling, noting in the margins: *Snail description? Obtain later.*

The exchanger beeped its heightened pace.

"I'm walking to the upstairs bedroom door," Junior said, closing his eyes tightly. "It's grey and peeling. The wood beneath the dead paint is weathered. I feel the wet floorboards beneath my feet and look down at them. The floor is rotting, the fibres splitting from each other like hay. I open the door and trace my eye along the boards. I see the bare legs of what I know are my nan and grandpa. If I keep looking, I'm gonna see them naked, you know? I'm scared to be in this house alone."

Faster beeping.

"Continue, please," Schwarz said, looking at me. I frowned back.

"I hide a little," Junior said. "I breathe deeply. I open the door fully and see an ebony cross on the wall in front of my grandparents. It's upside down."

!!! Schwarz wrote. *Is he sure ebony? Or painted black?*

"They're kneeling by the bed," Junior said, and I can see his child's horror in his eyes, his creeping posture, his wavering voice. "Their hands are together in prayer and … their underwear is pulled down to their knees. They turn to face me, and I try to scream but I can't. And I see their faces and they're—"

The beeps got so close together that they merged into a single stream of high-pitched noise, which held for a second then broke apart again.

Schwarz got up and marched towards him. "They have snakes' faces, don't they? Tell me what you see!"

I gripped Schwarz's elbow to hold him back, but he tugged it free and marched forward.

"They're not—" Junior began, but a stream of milky vomit erupted from his mouth and splattered on the floor. He sounded like a demon resisting exorcism. He fell face forward and seized, flopping around, his mouth still full.

"Shit!" Schwarz's trousers and smock emitted a vapour of sick.

I lay Junior on his side and twisted the exchanger to disengage it.

"You're not supposed to do that!" Schwarz said.

"And you agreed not to guide him," I said.

Schwarz pushed the emergency button by the door. He took the exchanger from me and held me back from the door with one arm.

Two medics in yellowy-green nylon uniforms ran in: generically handsome men with strong jaws.

"Hey!" the shorter one said. "Can you hear me?"

Once Junior stopped seizing, they carried him back to his bed.

"Whatever is making this happen is getting worse," the other medic said. "You can't keep doing this to the poor kid."

"He's the reason you're not down below," Schwarz said.

"Can't you at least get a new subject?"

Schwarz sighed. "He's the only one who scored high enough in clairvoyance. No one else was proficient enough. You knew this going in."

The medics shot Schwarz dirty looks.

Schwarz ignored them and handed me the exchanger. "Tell me it's good."

I wiped away the synthetic mucus and turned the probe to read the dial. "Three ninety-one over two seventy."

"Is that all?"

"We didn't go on for very long this time."

"The efficiency, at least?"

"About seventy per cent."

He grabbed the device from my hands and looked at it, holding his breath. "That's the biggest leap since—"

"Ever, but I've never seen him get ill so fast."

"I've examined the data. His reactions are flukes. Nothing to do with our experiments."

The medics walked out.

Schwarz grunted and left.

The room's light grew dimmer. I walked to the dumbwaiter and requested a standard pack of toiletries. Once it arrived, I used wet wipes to clean Junior's face, toilet paper to mop up the floor, and sanitizer to clean my hands. "Incinerator," I requested, and dropped the used supplies back in the dumbwaiter. Watching Junior made me feel weak, so I returned to the table to lie down for a while, on my side, a parallel of Junior.

Fields of artificial grass had grown all over Hypnos.

They were made of smart fibres that predicted the motion of the wind down to the molecule and bent to catch the greatest fraction of its energy, much like real grass bent towards the sun.

But the flood destroyed most of them.

By then, I'd already been working in the Smart Dynamics facility. Ours was the planet's first and only subsea smart fibre plant. The 'fibres' were more like heavy chains than grass, and the building's walls had to be thick enough to withstand the sea's hydrostatic pressure—heightened by Hypnos's gravity, which was double that of home.

The facility was about a tenth the size of a standard industry plant. As a postgrad, I'd been working with bench-scale models of the plant in my lab, so Smart Dynamics employed me to get the facility up and running.

The flood happened when we were still in the testing phase. Nevertheless, other citizens soon arrived and dug out a city-sized bunker beneath us. They told us we were getting the first colony, with a population as large as could be sustained by the energy of our one inefficient subsea globe. The government halted my smart fibre testing and forced me to maximize energy efficiency as far as was safely practicable.

They had no choice. The only ones who'd survived the flood were subsea at the time. There was neither enough space nor enough resources for all of us. Other colonies had to make do with less developed means to harness wave or geothermal energy, lest they return to more primitive energy sources. The luckiest colonies had the resources to develop long-term, sustainable subsea cities, or cities that could float and weather the storm. The floating cities-in-progress were anchored to the seabed and constructed by divers until they were ready to be launched to the surface, taking their colonies with them. Some rested on precarious floating platforms tethered to the colonies by long, tense wires. How depressing it must have been to build a new city in the same raging storm that had sunk the old one, in that purple darkness, on a black sea, in thick rain from a sky of black clouds, lit harshly by white floodlights.

Every colony had to prove that at least some of its constituents could contribute something new and useful to the surviving civilization. There were colony-wide projects related to clean water, waste recycling, food production, the military, and even the arts: theatre pieces with thousands of actors, enormous murals, and full-colony symphonies that took days to perform. Most colonies elected to develop technology to harness energy from new sources, working on everything from compact thorium reactors to volcanic probes and cold fusion. There were even attempts to harvest radiation from black holes. If a project made it, the whole colony associated with it would be saved.

It always seemed to go that way.

Dr Schwarz had come with the colony. He was an esteemed scientist and pioneer in the field of oneiric engineering. When he presented the colony with his exchanger, the colony leaders ordered me to stop optimizing the Smart Dynamics facility. Our mission was no longer to scale up our wave energy–harnessing technology. Instead, the leaders expediently sanctioned Schwarz's dangerous patent-pending exchangers that dug directly into the brain.

I convinced him he needed my expertise in nanofluidics to perfect the exchanger's electrolytic membrane. That meant I could carry on performing some sort of research; spend as much time as possible in my globe, away from the bunker below; and minimize the number of new people I had to meet. I'd always liked being alone and underwater, even as a kid. I was one of the few who was subsea by choice.

Our colony was set to join a floating city if we could create an affordable and suitably efficient exchanger before the globe crashed. The globe was designed to weather a hundred-year storm—a theoretical overdesign at the time, a way of making the facility inherently safe by protecting it from conditions we never expected to experience. But now, after the flood, with the waters eternally roiling, a hundred years was a very real measure of the facility's eventual destruction.

A slap woke me up. My right shoulder ached, and my head slumped on the metal table.

"Hey!"

I was looking right up Junior's nose. "Sorry, I didn't mean to —I was just making sure—"

"Did you stick that thing in my head while I was asleep?"

"Don't you think Schwarz would have done that already if it worked?"

It just slipped out. He looked at me, horrified.

"I made sure the device only works if it registers consciousness," I added.

"Hah! That's reassuring. You need to leave."

"Wait!" I held out my hand. He had no authority to make me go, though I did want to respect his decision. "That house, your grandparents … Did that really happen to you?"

He sat in the revolving black chair we used for the experiments, spinning around. "They're just visions. They don't mean anything." He shot me a sardonic smile. "What do you dream of, Dr Xiphias?"

"When we don't have to do more of these experiments. Anything you can offer to help us get there?"

His smile faded. "What would you have me tell you?"

I didn't know.

The light in Dr Schwarz's office revealed every last pore on his face.

"Do you have coffee?" I said. "You'll never believe that I—"

"Slept in the subject's room?"

Did he have cameras in there? "I was worried."

"And I was trying to earn his trust," Dr Schwarz replied.

I grabbed at the clipboard on the table to examine Schwarz's scrawling. He snatched it back from me and said, "Coffee's over there," flicking me a sharp nod.

I poured a cup from his personal canteen. Our conditions were monumentally better than those in the bunker—but Schwarz's coffee still tasted better than mine.

I sat in front of him. On his desk were several sheets of paper, all set at skewed angles and linked by obscure drawings.

"I've been trying to map his world," Schwarz said. "I'm convinced all the visions take place in the same space. The kid was raised by his grandparents. Did you know that?"

"How did you find that out?"

"Bribes. But he wasn't much of a talker back in the bunker either." He flipped up pages of a clipboard, skimming through his notes. "In earlier dreams, someone kept visiting the city of his mind. Some weird version of Junior's father, cobbled together from early memories and distorted through an impressionistic lens. Why?"

"Asking why makes a wild assumption," I said. "Dreams don't have rules. They're never obliged to mean anything. You can't make deterministic sense out of chaos."

Schwarz leaned forward and clasped his hands together. He stood up, and his aluminium chair skidded behind him. "Didn't they say the same of turbulent fluids, Dr Xiphias? Did you ever think you would see a globe like ours?"

"Like mine," I said. "I enjoyed the mystery. Before we had a theory for turbulence, technology could only approach its true movement, minimize errors, improve predictions—never gain a clear picture. I trusted that idea. I felt the same when I tried to make sense out of anything in life." I swirled a spoon in my coffee and watched the resulting vortex as it lost energy. "I hate dreams. They sound like stories, but they aren't. They don't have any rules. They don't proceed with any transference of consequence or meaning. They're totally pointless. And the only thing duller than keeping a dream journal is journaling the dreams of someone else."

"But what do you suppose is the purpose of clairvoyance? These aren't just dreams. They mean something."

"How can we translate them into something useful?"

"I have my theories. But surely you wouldn't want me to know the outcome before I investigate?"

"You should know intuitively which investigative paths won't lead anywhere."

He shook his head. "You're trying to tell me that the fate of our colony—"

"As if you care."

"—rests on the work of an uncurious scientist."

"An efficient scientist," I said. "I don't waste my time examining outliers."

"I have a strategy."

"Your interference is altering the trajectory of his accounts."

He walked around his desk, approaching me. "Then how do you explain the jumps in efficiency? Each night I take the exchanger from the autoclave. I speak to it, telling it my predictions about the world it sees. Together, Junior and I are getting closer to this world's description. Improving the prediction, minimizing the errors."

"This is insane."

"You disappoint me. I wanted to brainstorm with you."

"'Thought shower' is the appropriate term. Especially when our patient is an epileptic."

He cocked his head at me. "We're giving Junior the fits."

I took a step back. "But you said to the medics—"

"Lies. He would be perfectly healthy otherwise. But think of the—Where are you going?"

I was at the door. Schwarz went over to a screen he used for presentations and tugged on its string so that it curled up and away. Beneath it hung a large touchscreen with mind maps, drawings, and notes scrawled across it. I read around the spiral of his schematic:

DREAM 1
Case #0000289: 'JR'
Description: Available in case file.
Symbols: Improbable return of the father. MOTHER MISSING.

Tattoos of eyes and cross. VISIONS OF OUR SAVIOUR.
Smoking. ASHES/REBIRTH.
Comments: First dream deemed of sufficient symbolic merit for
record. Some symbols were not captured by the subject (additional
tattoos). Likely a serpent or ♀

<u>DREAM 2</u>
Case #0000290: 'JR'
Symbols: The upside-down cross. ANTI/COUNTER/CONTRARY
Grandparents. OLD REGIME.
Comments: Promising but as yet inconclusive. Predictions for
Dream 3 based on personal experience:
FEMALE ∩ TRANSPORT ∩ STRENGTH
The world is building!!

"More wild assumptions!" I said. "What are you looking for? And what do you mean by 'personal experience'?"

"The scars." He stroked his face. "My father's bulbous head. A flying serpent with a metal tongue. An inverted cross branding my stomach black. Every symbol Junior ever mentioned—I've seen them all before."

I scoffed.

"I'm a clairvoyant, Dr Xiphias."

"What? Then—why aren't we experimenting on *you*? You know how valuable every subject is to us. Why didn't you tell me?"

He held one hand over the other and rested them in his lap as he sat on the edge of the desk. "Soon, I will be able to dream while awake. Using Junior's visions, I have noted the common symbols between us. I'll command my dreams at will."

"Is that the real purpose of our experiments?"

"Through my dreams, I will call her. She will evaporate the roiling seas into a gentle cleansing rain." He rubbed his hands up and down his arms and shoulders.

"Who is she?"

"The Serpent of Antimatter." He touched upon the screen.

A sketch of a long black snake faded into view on the touchscreen, drawn over Schwarz's notes.

"To call her," he continued, "we must describe the world she wants to save. The world of Junior's mind."

"Antimatter? You think that will get us out of this? If there's any truth to what you're saying, it will destroy us all!"

"She will restore the suns." Schwarz's eyes glazed over as he stared at the ceiling and heralded the imaginary serpent. I backed out of the room and slammed the door behind me, but Schwarz continued talking to himself, his voice bellowing through the door. "Through her arrival, our world will be reborn."

I returned to the globe to see if I could catch a crashing chain. No luck. But the motion of the fluid on the glass was enough to calm my nerves somewhat. Purple streams flowed this way and that, a dark communiqué.

When Schwarz had first arrived, I'd briefly engaged in a fantasy of a clean future with an exchanger in the brain of every clairvoyant. It would be an attractive, luxury object, safe enough to wear at all times. Kids would point at them with excitement. On sunny days, you'd see the base's blinding sheen, like the head of a brass split pin, and look on in awe. "What good people to wear something like that to look after our energy needs," people would think, their energy pooled wirelessly from every viable subject in our new floating city.

The dream had slipped away.

The exchanger was not an energy-harnessing tool but a divining rod, gauging the accuracy of Junior's visions against the city that Schwarz was trying to describe. Our experiments were riddled with more bias than I could have imagined.

It wasn't my mind that I listened to; it was the sea. She wanted me to find the answer, to develop the right technology. If we didn't, she would kill us.

But I had a plan. First, I had to convince Junior to return to the colony beneath the lab and use the emergency transport channels to the Delphi Colony. There he could strike a deal to provide us with backup energy. We could form an alliance with them to ensure our combined success. Why not? I had my globe —developed technology—at my disposal. I just had to get back to calibrating it. With Junior gone, Schwarz would have no test subject and our colony would have no better option than the globe. Through their mutual allegiance, Delphi and our colony, Asclepius, could be the first non-city colonies to secure their survival.

I returned to my room and stayed up late, plotting Junior's route to Delphi Colony, trying to obtain permission from the relevant layers of authority. On the off chance there was any truth in Schwarz's ramblings, I didn't have much time. He sounded too close to obtaining what he wanted from Junior, and, given his treatment of the boy so far, what then for either of us?

I met Schwarz back in Junior's room. Junior pleaded at me with his eyes, but I proceeded as usual.

"I want the medics present this time," Junior said.

Fury contorted Schwarz's face.

"We can do that," I said. "Doctor, if you would?"

Schwarz hopped down off the table and left.

I paced over to Junior and lowered my voice. "I have a plan. I need your help."

He could see in my face that I was serious.

"Tonight," I said, "we're returning to the colony. But if you stay there, Schwarz will come looking for you. We need to get you to a neighbouring colony, and from there you'll—"

The doors opened, and Schwarz returned with the medics.

"Let's not have any more delays," Schwarz said. "If you would, kid, proceed."

"Fine," Junior said. "This isn't over."

Schwarz sat on the table. Junior bowed his head to look at me past lowered brows. I ignored them both and inserted the exchanger rather too briskly. Junior grabbed his head in pain.

"I'm in an underground station this time," he said. "The walls, floor, and benches—they're all covered in ashes. Ashes and broken spider-webs. They look like carrier bags of dust hanging from threads that line the ceiling."

"What does decay mean to you, Junior?" Schwarz said.

"You don't have to answer that," I said.

Beep beep beep.

"There's no exit or entrance to the station," Junior continued. "I figure I must be waiting for a train. The tracks are the colour of coal. The stones beneath are damp and grey. The ashes shake and fall and—"

"Look at the tracks, Junior!" Schwarz said. "There's someone there. Tell me who it is!"

"A girl."

"Doctor!" I shouted.

Beep beep beep beep—

"She's running on the tracks." Junior forced his eyes shut and punched fists into his cheeks. His jaw locked.

"Resist it!" Schwarz said.

"Stop it. You're forcing him to make this up!" I walked to Junior.

Schwarz shoved me. I hit my shoulder hard on the table behind me.

The shorter medic came over to me to offer his hand, but I shuffled beneath the table. He crouched in front of me to keep a barrier between me and Schwarz, who towered over Junior's meek frame.

"Behind her are large, rusty freight train carriages," Junior said. "But they aren't carrying anything. The girl doesn't have any arms, and—" He fell to his knees and vomited. There were spots of blood in it this time.

"Get out of the way!" the other medic said. "We need to deal with this."

"I need the exchanger," I said to the medic crouched over me. "The thing in his head!"

"I can't touch that."

"Pull it out. It's doing more damage in there!"

The medic held Junior's head to keep his tongue from flopping back over his airway. The other medic placed his fingers carefully around the exchanger's hilt, pulling it out and examining it with horror before handing it back to me.

"Give it here!" Schwarz snatched the exchanger from me. I stayed on the floor. I looked to the medics, but I couldn't help them.

Schwarz walked briskly out the room.

Junior lay in the recovery position. I knelt beside him and stroked his hair. The experiments were becoming shorter, the damage more severe, as if Junior's trauma and Schwarz's mission were converging.

"Rest, son," I said. "I'm coming back this evening. He can't do this to you anymore."

Junior's eyes shot open. He stood up with a start, pushed me out of the way, and bolted out the door.

I ran into the hallway after him, but found only Schwarz there, empty-handed.

"He took the exchanger," Schwarz said.

"Shh!" I could hear something. Like glass smashing. "We need to get to the globe."

We ran along the corridor tiles, propelled by the rubber grip of our boots. The clatter of metal on crystal grew louder, until out of the darkness ahead emerged Junior, standing on my desk, chipping away at the globe. It looked like he was punching it. But then I saw the spike of the exchanger in his hand.

"You're destroying it!" I shouted.

He turned to look at me, balancing on the desk's edge to get as close to the globe as possible, his atrophied legs clouded in the billow of his hospital robe.

"What am I destroying?" he said. "The exchanger or the globe?"

"My plan!" I said. "I was gonna get you out of here."

Schwarz clapped his hands together. "Now, Serpent! I offer you the world you desire. Take it from this boy. Give us back our land."

"What is he talking about?" Junior said.

"Come with me," I said. "I'll fix this."

"Clear his world of decay. Accept its offering of rebirth!" Schwarz continued.

Junior grabbed at his head, and we crept forward. If he snapped and stabbed himself with the exchanger, or broke the globe, we were done for.

"No!" Junior opened his eyes again. "Stay where you are!"

We froze. Schwarz's eyes were alive with mania.

"The globe," Junior said. "I heard you talking about it. It's designed for a hundred-year storm." He tapped his temple with the exchanger's sticky probe, now coated with shattered crystal. "But what about the storm—in my head?"

"Now, Serpent!" Schwarz said.

We felt a soundless shockwave from outside that blew us backwards along the corridor. I cracked my head. I tried to raise myself back up on a handrail, but it vibrated too much and hurt to touch. The lights glowed brighter than I'd ever seen. In the globe was light, and outside was air. No water, just sky. Clear, bright sky. Kilometres of ocean depths cleared in one explosion.

A shadow took over again. The water rushed back in like a big dark blanket. All the chains smashed against the crystal globe at once. Purple lightning spread out and burst into a beautiful spiral of fractals. As one branch made contact with the chipped-out fissure, a crack spread across the surface of the globe, like we were in a water balloon bursting in slow motion.

The purple glow blasted us, and black waves rushed in.

WE TOUCHED A REAL DINOSAUR! (NOT CLICKBAIT)

WHAT UP, DINOFAM? IT'S YA BOY THE SALTOPUS, SAFE and sound here at DinoManse, ready to launch our most anticipated video of all time. You found me here in the merch room, lying on our latest batch of hundred per cent ring-spun cotton T-shirts! Mm, so comfy!

Enjoying this exclusive look at our newest designs? Hope so, because if you're just wondering why it's me in the vlog intro and not my big bro, Lil' T-Rex—where the hell have you been? Have you not watched the news or anything?

Sorry. P-Please don't cut the stream. There's some boss content coming up.

For you youngsters out there, it is graphic, and viewer discretion is advised. Guys, this is no joke.

That being said, what you're about to see is a guaranteed vlogging exclusive, so bring in your parents, grab on to your DinoPlushies—link to purchase in the video description below—or do whatever necessary to witness this amazing footage.

Here we go.

What up, DinoFam? Lil' T-Rex here, back at it again with my little bro the Saltopus.

Can any of you bros out there recognize where we are?

Yeah. That's right. Legit insane, no?

We kept quiet about it because we didn't want to be, like, intercepted or anything? But we've travelled down here from China—saw some wicked temples and shit, so humbling, uploading the vid as we speak—thanks to some help from our newest DinoFam recruits, these two Chinese piratebros!

That's right, we legit bribed two pirates to take us here! You think anyone else on the stream would do that just to bring you fresh content?

They don't speak English, and our translator gets a patchy signal out here in the open water, so we didn't catch their names. Instead we nicknamed them Callisto and Titan, after our albino Pomeranians back at DinoManse in LA, duh!

No, they don't get the reference. They don't even appreciate all this excellent DinoMerch that we brought them—the latest hoodies, and these killer gold backpacks! Can you believe they don't care that we hooked them up? These piratebros are hashtag…

"Merchasaurus *Wrecked!*"

That's this week's discount code! How fun, how cute, how spectacularly unique and fantastic is this new DinoPlushie? If you squeeze him, he says "Merchasaurus Wrecked" along with a whole bunch of other DinoBros catchphrases. Well, *yours* will— this is just a prototype—so if you wanna hear the rest, preorder using the link that's flashing up on your screen right now.

Anyway, the DinoPlushie is coming with us as we arrive at the biggest and therefore best of the five Dino Islands! You knew the DinoBros *had* to make it out here, right? I mean, it's in our name. We didn't have a choice!

Okay, it's not just that. Not to put any negativity out there, but the DinoFam hasn't grown as much since the incident last month. Check out my apology video about it, went up last week—y'all know I demonetized that shit. We're from Ohio, all about that sincerity.

If you didn't hear, our biggest competitor, Teddybear Kid, the streamer with the second biggest family out there? He died attempting the world record for highest handstand ever on the edge of the Floating Freedom City.

I admit to the showing-up-at-his-funeral-wasted thing. And, sure, I did some burpees on the casket—but there's no *way* I opened it and dressed his corpse in DinoMerch! Like, he landed in Times Square after free-falling for twenty thousand feet. You think there was anything intact left to dress? Use your head, bros.

Enough outta me for now. We're about to arrive.

Okay, we're off the boat and making our way to the first destination. Look how high the grass is, bros. I don't think anyone's been here for years.

Wow. You see that, Salty? The facility's exactly where they said it would be.

Let me get the drone out and we'll just scan the full area. Switching to aerial shot, so to those of you watching with VR, get ready for a trip!

Whoa, you see those footprints in the mud? Salty tells me they're from a stegosaurus. See how they emerge from that forest? Must be conifers, bros. Legit majestic!

Check out these buildings. Kinda beautiful, don't you think? The crumbling concrete, smashed windows. The moss, the vines in the crevices? So, *so* Lil T-Rex's aesthetic.

Okay, we'll switch our view back to Salty's headcam.

This is the Alpha facility. It's the first stop on our journey across the five islands. They say this is where MuskCorp grew the dinos! Cool, right?

Know why I wanted to take you here first, Salty?

I know you love dinos, buddy. We all do. But, why come to this facility?

I don't know if they had saltopuses. Or is it saltopi? Anyway, good guess—but that's not why.

Hm? Speak up for the cam, lil' bro.

You got it! These dinos never knew their parents either.

Salty and I are always about the upside. Since we don't know anything about our family, we choose who gets to be in it, without limits. That goes for you, watching this. You're DinoFam4Life! You're the reason Saltopus and I got out of Ohio. The reason we could pay for DinoManse in LA. And, as you saw in our video earlier this year, the reason we have a place for Janet, StepDinoMomSupreme. You got her miles away from our stepdad Chris, and with your donations, you pay for the guards that keep him and his cronies off the manse perimeter. Plus, you keep Salty out of school so he can just hustle like me, all day every day.

I declare every dino on this island an honorary member of DinoFam!

I'm super stoked to see what the facility looks like inside. But before we go in, let me remind y'all out there that safety is a must. I don't want any of my fans—or fellow streamers—copying the content you're about to see.

So I found this box by the entrance? It's got this cool explosive warning label on the side. I tossed out whatever was in there and put in these shotgun shells, test tubes, and torn-up bits of danger tape! And—Salty, are those bones on the floor? Look like ribs or something. Can you scan them for me? They're human? Bro, that's insane. And there's still space in the box!

If we turn the box like this, it should fit in the backpack. There.

Oh my God, check out these lab coats! Looks like no one ever wore them. And they've got MuskCorp insignia embroidered on the pocket! Let me just fold some of these up and we'll take them too.

Bros, see how much space there is in these authentic DinoBros backpacks? They're really quite something. Just saying!

I think that switch is connected to the emergency generator. Salty, can you press it?

There. Much easier to see where we're going with the lights on! Bros, look how long this corridor is. It's trippy as. But you don't need to see us wandering past all these locked rooms. Jump cut!

Okay, so we followed the maps on the wall to the birthing chambers. You see this? Don't you think it's like a dry-cleaner rack with empty plastic bags hanging off it? Well, these bags are way bigger and more complicated—got wires running through them and shit.

Those of you HD subscribers can smell what it's like in this room. I know it's weird, but, guys! That's the super-exclusive scent of rotting dinosaur remains. Try and find that anywhere else!

Salty, come over here! Dude, this stego could have been an ultimate beast. Ew, his skin's still moist! It's so damn humid in here.

What you got there, Salty? A tail spike? Neat, hand it over. I can carry it. Because you were gonna put it in the backpack! We need to keep the lab coats clean. We can always leave some stuff with the piratebros and come back. I paid them to wait as long as it takes for us to return.

Whoa. Is that what I think it is? Salty, you see that? In that bag at the back. It's still full! That looks like a control panel over there, too. See if you can bring it over to us.

Here it comes. What's in there? Is that a raptor?

Guys! You seeing this shit? It's wild. Is there a button on that panel to get it out of there? Must be.

Why you so scared, Salty? Would Lil' T-Rex ever let anything happen to you? Damn right I wouldn't. You're safe. So press the button.

Press the button, Salty. I didn't take us here so we could pussy out from going all the way! I *just told you* nothing's gonna happen!

Good.

Whoa, he's a capital-B Beast! Like, four stepdads in size!

Oh, shit, he's breathing. Salty, keep your voice down.

I'm gonna touch him.

This stuff is super sticky. Some kinda nutrient paste.

Uh-oh. He's moving. Salty, get back. He won't hurt us, no. We rescued him, so why would he?

Shut up! I don't like the way he's looking at us either. It'll be fine, I swear. Even if he gets up, it's not like he'll have the energy to—

Shit, he's up. Go, go, go!

Yeah!

Salty—you missed it—I totally nailed him in the face with that tail spike. I hope it was enough to let us get away.

I ... I know you're tired, but don't toss the backpack. I'm gonna scoop you up.

God, you're heavy. Can you look back? He's still there, right? I can hear him.

Oh, God. Oh, Jesus, Salty, I'm so sorry. We're almost outside. It's okay. If we get outside we can hide somewhere. We'll be okay, Salty. We're gonna be okay.

Okay, guys, we're back outside. We made it as far as these ferns for cover. You can't see him, but he's still too close for us to get away. Still, thinking positive, he hasn't found us yet. We're waiting until he gets far enough away from us that we can make a run for the boat.

Crap, there he is. See? Just there, that's the outline of his head.

No, he's turning. He's coming over here.

Phew, he's looking away again.

Don't be scared, Salty. I'm here for you. Not gonna let anything happen. I've just gotta sit down for a moment. My legs are so tired.

"Merchasaurus Wrecked!"

Hey, DinoBros, you're back in the merch room with me, the Saltopus. No, I'm not gonna show you what happened next.

There are a ton of write-ups about it, and I've done interviews for all the big news channels, so I'm sure you've already heard: Lil' T-Rex bravely sacrificed himself so that I could escape the island.

If you wanna pay your respects, head on over to our site, link in bio, where you can buy the lab coats and all the other stuff my bro collected from the island. Oh—apart from the bones. Mainland Chinese police wouldn't let me keep them.

All proceeds go towards Lil' T-Rex's funeral. I sent you VIP subscribers out there your invites to the wake at DinoManse this Friday. For those of you lower-tier bros, we're livestreaming the funeral right here on DinoBrosChannel, three o'clock Pacific.

You'll wanna tune in, guys. It'll be the bossest funeral of all time.

BARHOPPING FOR ASTRONAUTS

DODGY BARS, LIKE THIS ONE, SPORT FAKE WOMEN AND real bartenders. The opposite of what a mostly male clientele wants. But the astronaut isn't picky anymore. Besides, he doesn't much mind the prospect of spending an evening in the company of robostrippers, their skins torn and peeling, the ragged mechanics of their limbs peering through. Decay into obsolescence merely adds to their humanity.

He finds a stool at the bar's far end and sits, leaning his rubber-sheathed elbows on the counter's stinking wood. Govcams on the walls turn to him, but amber rings of light around their lenses signify inactivity. 'Manually disabled', no doubt, by local glowlife gangs.

Flies buzz lazily between beer puddles. A woman shoots him a sneering glance as she walks back to her posse of friends, all of them with glossy hair and clear heels. They gossip in tight circles, their thin voices needling in his ears. Through the chip in his head, he mentally pings a noise reduction to his helmet, reducing their sound by fifty per cent.

The middle-aged bartender approaches, his metallic pupils glowing, bloodshot streaks firing out across his corneas. Black market implants—for what purpose, the astronaut doesn't know.

The bartender doesn't react to the astronaut's suit or to the darkened smartglass visor covering his face. If people asked about that stuff here, the clientele would vanish. He says something, muffled words with a rising inflection.

The astronaut de-mutes.

"Drink," the bartender says, miming a glass.

"Do you do Lunar Juleps?" he asks.

"We might've lost it a few barware updates ago, but I'll check." He eventually returns with a dirty highball of slime-green fluid.

The astronaut dips his finger into the glass and his glove sucks it all up. Nanites metabolize the alcohol for him before the drink even reaches his bloodstream. Nanites are many things, but fun isn't one of them.

As the astronaut tries to place the highball back on the bar without causing a fuss, he feels people looking at him funny. The gecko pad of his palm sticks to the glass like Velcro. He carefully unpeels it.

The bartender sighs. "What the hell are you doing here?"

"Huh?"

"By the looks of your suit, you must be, what, late sixties? Try the Caloris District. You know Tycho Singles? That's more your speed."

The astronaut shakes his head. "They don't let me in with the helmet on."

"Then take it off."

"I can't!"

"I'm not babysitting some dementia-ridden old coot, okay? I'll do you this one last courtesy. Then be on your way." The bartender eyes up the suit. "I can see the flap for the emergency cord from here. The red one, right? Here, I'll get it—"

The astronaut bats the hand away. He turns and pushes through the throng, heading back outside.

He catches his breath in the street. Snow stills the air, quelling the city noise. Teens pass him by, shooing pesky ad drones that quiz them about alcohol consumption and sexual appetites. Strumpbots stand at regular intervals, maximally optimizing the sidewalk's revenue without intruding upon one another's territory.

White clouds of vape juice bloom before him, and the nanites, alerted to this anomaly, replicate the smell for him in his helmet. Cotton candy, mingling with poor-quality weed.

Red light shimmers off the astronaut's visor. It settles on his chest as a flickering laser dot. He traces its source to the thick black bangle of a glowlife with a blue quiff, who leans on a nearby defunct autocab.

"Pew pew!" the glowlife says, making finger guns.

The astronaut flinches.

A woman in the glowlife crew laughs. She has studs of metal pierced seemingly at random across her face. Braids of light in her hair stream rainbow colours. Dog holos caper around her poodle skirt. "He actually thought you were firing at him! Old man, you think that's possible?"

"What's his suit all about?" says the third guy in the posse. A green animated graffiti tag shimmers on his muscle tee, and red biotats of demons smirk on his deltoids.

Quiff cocks his head. "Is that the Vitus New Moon model?"

"What's Vitus?" Poodle Skirt says. "Oh, wait." She sings the Vitus jingle: *"Overcoming limits of biology / Colonizing space with technology!"*

"Weren't those ads from, like, the seventies?" Biotats says.

"Dude, how old are you?" Quiff says.

The astronaut can't help himself. The words bubble up inside him. "I-I was on the moon."

"Hah!" Quiff says. "Who wasn't? I was there last week."

"I got back yesterday," Biotats says.

Poodle Skirt spits. "You can take the suit off now."

The astronaut walks away, but Quiff grabs his shoulder, takes out a blade and slices the suit open.

In a reflex, the astronaut slaps his hand over the opening.

"Sorry," Quiff says, "did I breach your suit?"

The friends rush over and tug at the rip, tearing the suit all over. The astronaut wrestles them off and runs away, their mocking laughter trailing behind him.

Sleek-looking autocabs roll up beside him and open their doors. "Sir," they say, "you look tired. May I assist?"

He doesn't live far away enough to risk falling victim to a hacked cab's kidnapping protocol or worse, so he walks all the way home in the snow.

He arrives home with the suit almost completely peeled off, revealing the T-shirt and long underwear he has on beneath. The suit doesn't know what to do, and self-repair only causes further damage. After all, if this were space, the astronaut would be dead by now. Its warning sirens blare inside the helmet, ringing madly in his ears.

He screams, clawing at the suit. Nanites in the material melt its torn edges, reaching out at each other in silvery threads, trying to knit the seams back together. But the tears are too big, the nanites too far from one another. As programmed, they try to stick the suit to his skin. In ultra-critical conditions, better to create any kind of seal and let a patch of skin get frostbite or sunburn than to do nothing and risk a fatality. That's the theory in space. Here on Earth, melted polymer scalds his chest. He tugs the suit off and leaves it in scraps on the floor.

He walks through to his living room, tearing away the T-shirt and picking strips of burnt rubber off his naked torso.

"Sir! Were you assaulted?" Jenny's voice comes from the ceiling's speaker. "We ought to file a report—"

The astronaut waves his hand. "Don't fuss."

"It's no fuss, sir," she says. "I'm not real."

"I know, Jenny. You don't have to remind me."

He sits on the edge of his couch, balancing the helmet so it doesn't fall. Empty foodule packets litter the table in front of him, and dirty boot prints coat the carpet.

As his adrenaline subsides, the apartment's chill rushes over him. He hadn't noticed how comfy the suit was, how like a second skin. Its sensations had become sensory background noise. Now, he's palpably bare.

Out the window, a haze of neon blends the buildings together, a dim redness on the horizon revealing the outline of so many concrete blocks all seemingly fused into one.

One last scrap of the suit flops off his shoulder. He examines it with a sorry glance. Nanite threads glint silver. In space, they bridged together throughout the suit to keep it firm during pressurization. They agglomerated where needed across the suit's many membranes. Made repairs. Relayed biomedical data. Vaporized micrometeoroids. Expelled carbon dioxide and water vapour. They strung together into synthetic veins, sending cooling water coursing across his skin. They eradicated dead cells and other detritus from his surface, and other excreta from elsewhere.

He goes to the window and opens the delivery box. Shiny foodule packets spill to the floor. Out of habit, he picks one up and squeezes it. That was usually all it took for nanites to suck out the juices and inject nutrients into him like reverse mosquitoes. Not anymore.

He closes the box and orders some pyjamas on its touchscreen.

"Connect me to Vitus support team, please?" he asks his visor.

Ellipses flash inside the visor as it makes the call for him.

A smiling cartoon face appears. "Hi!" says a female voice. "Did you mean to reach me? I heard something about Vitus."

"Yeah, I need repair for a New Moon."

"Sorry, sir, we no longer offer support for that model. May I order you a replacement?"

"I can't afford that. I couldn't even afford my Vitus. They gave it to me after I—"

"Would you like to hear more about our latest, the Tharsis? It's a flexible and durable polymer suit with—"

"I want to go back inside! Now!"

"Sir, yelling isn't good for your health. Just saying. I don't mind it, of course. I'm not real."

He pulls the helmet off and throws it to the floor. Instead of smashing, it dents the wooden boards with a *dunk*.

"Sir?" the AI says.

He leans on the wall, sliding down, hugging his knees. The suit kept his skin young, supple, hairless.

"Intruder! Intruder!" Jenny says.

He looks to the ceiling. "Settle down, Jenny. It's still me."

"Voice recognition confirmed, sir. Glad to see you again. You look different! New haircut?"

He feels the perfectly trimmed bald pate. It seems to itch only now the nanites have gone. "Good different?" he says.

"Why not see for yourself?"

He grits his teeth, then gets up and heads to the bathroom.

"By the way," Jenny says from her speaker in the tiled wall, "you forgot your pills again, silly billy."

The mirror spits a handful of green liquid capsules onto a ceramic dish.

"Thanks, Jenny." He picks one up and squeezes it with thumb and forefinger, again to no avail. He sighs, winces, and looks at his face.

He'd seen warped glimpses on the visor's inner surface, or

reflected dimly in puddles and shop windows sometimes, but always softened by the smartglass's resting darkness setting. The unmasked thing is something else. Sunken eyes. Thin lips. Incipient jowls. Wrinkles like deep gouges sliced across his forehead.

"Handsome as ever, sir," Jenny says.

"Well, Jenny," he says, "that's the visor off. All my settings are disabled. You might as well tell me the year now. I can't block it out."

"You sure?"

"Yep."

She tells him.

His mouth gapes, revealing pale, receding gums. "I've been in that suit for twenty-two years?"

"Yup."

He shrugs. "Time flies when you barely leave the house."

"Would you like to know anything else? How about the latest water shortage on Mars? Want to know what happened with that organ cloning scandal? There's talk of a new viral epidemic in a biohab—"

"That's enough crisis for one day, thanks. I'm going to bed."

Light wakes him up. It's Jenny, warming him with an artificial sun from the screen in his bedroom ceiling.

He groans. "Disengage protocol, Jenny!"

"I may only have seen your new face for fourteen hours and twenty-six minutes," Jenny says, "but to my vast knowledge base, most humans don't display an expression *that* consistently sad. Especially not in their sleep. So come on, get up."

He slams a pillow over his face.

"Sir?" Jenny says. "I was thinking. I'm not real, but I do think."

The pillow muffles his words. "Again, Jenny, I know how this works."

"Great! Look, you know I would never wish you any harm. I'm literally incapable of doing so. But maybe what happened to you wasn't the worst."

"I don't want to hear this right now."

"But it might do you some good, and that's what I'm here for!"

He stays quiet.

"I thought of something that might cheer you up. Go look in your delivery box!"

He lies there, immobile. Jenny ramps up the light intensity until it makes an unhealthy whining sound.

"Fine!" He gets up, tosses the pillow aside, and heads to the living room.

In the box are the clothes he ordered yesterday and a clear vacuum bag with a pre-sliced pizza inside, squished until its orange oils run into the plastic's creases.

He reaches for the T-shirt and joggers but withdraws his hand like he just touched an iron. The screen on the box reads *60°C*.

"To keep the pizza toasty!" Jenny says. "And I had it ordered in that bag so your clothes wouldn't smell."

"Very considerate of you, Jenny."

He unzips the bag, its plastic relaxing, and slides the pizza onto the table. Its smell is familiar and distant.

He tugs at the crust, dislodges a slice and—

"Ow!"

"Sir?"

"I forgot how to use my tongue."

"Well—take care."

"Okay, okay!"

He tries again. Mozzarella melts over his taste buds, accompanied by a tang of tomato sauce. He bites down on a crunchy piece of pepperoni, burnt a little on the edges, but it hardly matters. "Mm!"

"What do you think?"

"This is amazing," he says between chews.

"I'm glad!"

A piece falls out of his mouth. He smiles up at the ceiling. "I need more eating practice, though. What will we try next?"

"Oh, I'm so happy this worked, sir! We'll try whatever you want!"

He frowns. "Wait, wait."

"What is it?"

He grimaces. "Can you show me a video of someone putting on clothes? Project it onto one of the walls once you've got it."

"Uh, sir, did you mean 'taking off clothes'? I know this is the first time you've requested such a thing, but as always, I'm not a real person. Couldn't judge you if I wanted to."

"Ugh." He looks up at the ceiling as he goes back to the box, lifting the clothes out and brandishing them accusingly at Jenny. He shuffles out the long underwear, puts the T-shirt on backwards, and nearly falls over when slipping on the joggers. He crosses his legs on the floor and catches his breath.

"Sir, was that necessary? Please be strong enough to clarify your requests for help in future."

"Yes, Jenny."

"Back to it, then?"

"Yeah. Hey, get me a coffee!"

It's not long before a drone buzzes by, dropping an insulated pouch into the box.

He opens the door from the inside and takes the pouch to the kitchen, where he pours its contents into the one clean glass he uses to top up his hydration. Out of habit, he dips his finger into the brown liquid.

"Ouch!"

His skin is tender, like it's missing a few layers. More than a few.

He takes a sip. "Delicious."

"Cool! What now?"

"Surprise me."

Over the next few hours, Jenny delivers an assortment of test objects.

He thumbs books and savours the crisp feel of their freshly printed paper. He spritzes himself in the face with a cologne bottle, catching himself in the eyes, but the scent of citrus and sandalwood seems worth it. He even sticks his finger in a little plastic prank toy that gives him an electric shock.

"Play me some music," he asks Jenny.

"What kind?"

"Anything, anything!"

Noise blares into the room. It sounds like static from an old radio that's clattering around in a washing machine.

"What the hell, Jenny? I said 'music'."

"It's from a local stream," she says like a partner taking offence on behalf of her choice.

"No, no, give me—jazz. Play me some jazz."

The reedy sound of a saxophone fills his ears, and notes from a double bass reverberate around the living room. The soft hiss of drum brushes makes his skin shiver. He grips his head, closes his eyes, and grins. His eyes flicker open, and he bolts to the window, unlocking the latch and pushing back the glass.

"Sir, no!"

"Relax." He sticks his head out.

Drones buzz by like big cicadas. A nearby advert simulates the sound of a rushing waterfall. Several storeys below, autocabs shout robotic warnings at pedestrians.

The breeze rushes over his face. It's thick as a blanket and pungent with smog, but he doesn't care.

"What is it, sir?" Jenny asks.

He's crying now. "It's wonderful."

Sensory exploration soon begets the difficult work of relearning old habits. The nanites have gone, so they can't baby him anymore. He has to shower, brush his teeth, clip his nails, and shave without nicking himself.

Days and weeks pass in frustration. Soon, he's back in bed again, refusing to get up.

Jenny beams her light over him. "Sir, it's time to wash the sheets. It's been over a month since suitgate. You're entraining dirt everywhere."

He's silent.

"I had another idea, if you wanna hear it."

"You're just gonna tell me anyway."

"Remember Tycho Singles?"

He pushes the sheets back like an insolent teen. "What about it?"

"Why not go back there? It still has a consistent four-point-two rating, above average for the area. You used to love it back when—"

"I was young, happy, famous, successful, and rich. Cheers, Jenny."

"Oh, please."

He shuts his eyes in thought and pinches the bridge of his nose. "I've passed by there before. It used to be young and happening. Looks like the same crowd has hung around there for decades. So now it's—"

"Still an age-appropriate place for a gent like yourself?"

He kicks the covers off and looks at the ceiling. "You getting cheeky with me?"

"Did I violate a boundary? Are you dissatisfied with your service? Because I can always—"

"It's fine. I like it."

"Good. Because I took just *one* more additional liberty."

"Did you, now?"

"Go take a look in the box!" Her autotuned squeal grates in his ears.

"Fine!" He gets up and heads to the living room.

In the box is a full tuxedo and black bowtie.

"Jenny, can you tell me your budget settings again?"

"Of course, but why?"

"You think I can afford fancy clothes and expensive cocktails?"

"Not all the time." Jenny adopts the tone of a benevolently scheming wife trying to sound nonchalant. "But you deserve to celebrate your progress."

Tuxed up, he hesitates as he approaches the facial recognition scanner at Tycho Singles—but it gives him the green light and invites him in. He reaches up to feel the helmet, but it's long gone now.

Tycho is much nicer than the last bar he chose for himself. Ornate cornices, white pillars, bronze light fixtures.

As he walks in, his new dress shoes clacking pleasantly on the lacquered hardwood floor, he notices how much lower-tech the bar is than the average locale. There's a champagne fountain holo here, an android waiter there, but not much. Surely because of the clientele. All around, sophisticated elders on dates sit around tables of expensive marble.

Why would he want to hang out with all these old people?

Oh. Right. He's one of them.

He approaches the bar and sits down. A woman nearby catches his eye. She has delicate wrinkles under her eyes and her hair is in a high, silvery do. Placid waves roll over the fabscreen of her dress.

He stares at the marble counter, too nervous to make an introduction.

"What'll it be, sir?" A bot-tender in a white tux wheels himself over. Its head is a gunmetal cylinder, and a screen on the front shows its few emotions in Technicolor pixels. "A quiet type, eh? I can offer you a recommendation."

He nods.

A green circle loads to completion on its face. "For an esteemed gent like yourself? A Lunar Julep." A door opens on its chest and a silver cup appears. A small tap deposits the julep inside, and the bot-tender places it on the table.

The cup gathers frost. He reaches out to touch it, startled by how cold it feels. He peers at the green liquid within and brings his index finger to its surface before remembering. He stops and, as practised, raises the drink to his lips with both hands, taking a sip.

He coughs.

"Sir? You don't like it?"

"It's fine. It's just—got a kick." Alcohol rushes straight to his brain. "Whew!"

"I recognize that voice, sir," the bot-tender says. "Have you been here before?"

He lowers his head. "A long time ago."

"I thought so. I'm examining some photos of us from the seventies." Its blocky eyebrows pinch in a frown. "Huh. You sure looked different. You're wearing something weird. Do you remember? There are all these women crowded around you. You were sitting about where you are now. But you had much more company back then."

"I don't really wanna talk about it."

The bot-tender leans in. "Well, I can't just leave you here."

"Yes, you can."

"It makes the other patrons awkward. If you want to sit here, we have to talk about *something*."

They're both silent.

"Hey," the bot-tender says, "you were in pay grade XZ back then. Impressive!"

"I can take it from here." The wave-dressed woman has a sultry, gravelly voice. "What brings you to Tycho?"

He dares to meet her eyes briefly, then looks back at the counter. "I'm, uh, supposed to be celebrating."

"Cheers to you, then." She raises her martini. "May I ask the occasion, Mr … ?"

The words form in his throat. The stream of all he's ever been before. He stifles it, his face contorting with worry.

"Sir!"

He turns.

It's the scanner on the door, addressing someone outside. "I can't let you in if you insist on covering your face."

On the street is a man in a grass-green Vitus New Moon. The helmet's visor is dark, his shoulders slumped.

"Friend of yours?" the woman says.

He smiles at her. "Just might be. Excuse me for a moment?"

She nods and he walks back to the door.

"I used to come here all the time!" says the astronaut in the green suit.

"We both did," he says.

The visor swivels, fishbowling all it reflects.

Who's that old guy in the tux? Oh, it's me.

"I don't know you," the astronaut says.

"Yes, you do. You just don't recognize me." As he approaches, the chip in his head illuminates the surname *Zhang* on the suit.

Zhang looks down at his chest. His shoulders square and relax. "I haven't seen it do that in a long time. Who are you?"

"Bob Jones?" Bob says. It sounds painfully ordinary out loud, but it's his name nonetheless.

The astronaut takes some tint out the smartglass visor. The

tired face of an elderly Asian gent appears, his hair thinning and silvery with nanites. "It *is* you! What were you, an engineer?"

Bob nods.

The astronaut taps his chest. "Mike Zhang. I was an architect, see? Green suit!"

"I remember."

"Am I glad I ran into you! No one else gets it anymore. The importance of what we did, that is." He bumps Bob on the arm with a fist. "These days there are colonies all over, but *we* made the moon habitable, man. We were pioneers!" Mike looks at the bar. "They used to let me in here dressed like this when we came back. You remember?"

Bob nods.

Mike pats his chest. "People went to bed with me while I was in this suit." He smiles. "Felt like it would be that way forever."

Bob puts his hand on Mike's shoulder. "Now it's almost like it never happened." The suit warms his hand as nanites cross its external membrane to assess the threat.

"But w-we're trailblazers," Mike says. "We got to do more than most ever could."

"At the time." Bob smiles sympathetically.

Mike mirrors the smile. "Yeah." A thought makes him shudder with excitement. "What are you doing now? Let's go talk about the mission! Hey, remember that time we thought we'd lost two whole oxygen bottle racks? Or when Montero welded himself to an airlock and we thought he'd die if we tried to remove him?" He made fists of his hands. "What do you say? Wanna go grab a drink somewhere else?"

Bob bites his lip. He looks at Mike, then back to the bar, where the wave-dressed woman raises her glass to him.

"If it's okay with you," Bob says, "I think I'll go back inside."

LEVELS FOR SUSTAINABLE LIVING

Hundreds of glass bubbles, like floating, building-sized marbles, clouded over the Thames. They filled the air with their nacreous sheen, shining in London's champagne sky. In the biggest of them stood a man in a dandruff-free tux and a woman in a vintage skirt and cable-knit sweater. In the effervescence of their champagne glasses, bots danced like grains of steel in an updraft.

The woman squealed as their glass bubble clinked off another; the man caught her, dipped her Hollywood style. With the jolt, she'd spilled a hundred thousand pounds' worth of tech on the bubble's floor.

"Sorry," she said.

The bots that landed on the smooth glass swelled up like ticks as they sucked up the spill.

The man brushed her copper hair behind her ear. It reminded him of the wire nests that addicts kept stealing from the company basement.

"There's still enough bots in your glass," he said. "They'll proliferate all the same."

"Then we'll be the same?"

"You'll still be you," he said, chucking her under the chin, his hand tingling as the cells shed from her face onto his knuckles were destroyed. He looked at his shiny, ridge-free nails. "You, 4.0. No risk of heart attacks, strokes, diabetes. No infiltration of viruses, bacteria, parasites, you name it."

His skin heated into overdrive as she cupped his perfectly moisturized face—free of blackheads, moles, skin tags, dents, scars, zits—and their combined sweat evaporated. He had no shaving scrapes or bumps to speak of, given that bots laser-annihilated every bristle of beard seconds after its formation—he was looking to speed up that process.

She shrugged so the chicken pox scars on her chest disappeared beneath her sweater. She hand-washed all her clothes with love, but they still faded with time.

They took a deep breath together.

His lungbots selectively absorbed the free radicals looking to cross the membranes of his alveoli, and they chopped up every particulate at the molecular-bond level. These bots were body-optimized versions of his first product, the NanoAngels, billions of which skated across the ozone layer, repairing its rich fabric and keeping oxides at acceptable levels for sustainable living.

Her brow furrowed—he didn't smell of anything.

"What's wrong?" he said.

"I was just wondering if they'll take the kink out of my nose."

He grinned, revealing self-mineralizing teeth. An invisible photovoltaic mesh kept them sun-bleached. "They don't do that."

"But your face is symmetrical," she said. "Maybe it's just because I think you're perfect."

He frowned. It was Friday, and outside of business hours, so confusion and boredom were unproductive, undesirable. Knowing this, bots flooded the synapses of his brain's nucleus accumbens with dopamine, making him happy. They filled the creases of his brow and injected acetylcholine inhibitors into the muscles of his forehead, keeping them relaxed.

He reached for her waist, but she flinched at his touch. "I'm chubby," she said.

"Not for long," he said. "Soon, we'll spend guilt-free hours together on the couch, watching series after series, eating all sorts of junk and selectively digesting it for required energy content down to .0001 calories. That's right; with 4.0 we added an order of magnitude. Bots will deliver a personalized recipe of vitamins and minerals to your small intestine every day, oxygenate all your tissues with maximal efficiency, and maintain the complex architecture of your bones' internals." He ended his speech—taken directly from the new manual—before he reached the paragraph stating that yes, users occasionally passed gas, but no, it never stank.

"Just what every girl wants to hear," she said, blushing.

Muscarinic agonists encouraged vasoconstriction in the capillaries of his cheeks and prevented him from responding alike; this was to conceal weakness and avoid unnecessary heat loss. But Viagra released from subdermal bots around his crotch prepared him for the spoils of flirtation.

"If we develop the product enough," he said, "you, me, and everyone who can afford it will live like this forever."

She ran her hands through his hair, which was kept in the Stasis 4.0 style so everyone knew just how important he was. But when she looked at the reflection of her designer glasses in the constant film of fluid that coated his eyes (which no longer needed to blink), her expression dropped and she began to cry.

"What is it?" he said.

In the silence that followed, cancer cells developed in his liver, their membranes promptly ruptured by nanobot knives.

She placed a hand over his heart, feeling it beat with expert regularity. At rest, it never faltered from its marathon-runner pace. Bots couldn't comprehend any biological anomaly for which a racing heart was necessary.

She threw her champagne flute to the floor. Rivulets of bots dispersed like living mercury.

"Take me down!" She turned her back to him and looked out at the city below, at the reflection of the glass bubbles in the river's pure water. A cloud passed, and the sunlight shone too brightly for her to see herself.

He looked at the glinting fragments of glass on the floor. An unwanted thought made it past the bots. He reached out for a shard to run across his wrist. Bots caught wind of this desire and dosed him, paralyzing the hand. Now the impulse seemed absurd. Even if he harmed himself, the wound would heal just as soon as it opened. He was impenetrable.

"I'll do better next time," he said. "These bubbles won't clink together. The next girl will toast my achievement with a self-mending flute and swallow whatever I gift her."

The woman ran a finger along her nose's dent. "For as long as I live, I hope there are kinks you can't remove."

1

"We saw Deakin out food shopping the other day."

Late morning, brunch with the boys. Bathed in blue neon from the buzzing signs above us, we sit around a high table at Gangnam Taqueria, our favourite Korean-American fusion shack. Jalapeño fairy lights, scuttling cleaner bots, hissing griddles. Cricket tacos for me, bibimbap for Eric, and blue noodles for Jon. He's probably on some new fad diet as content for his vlog.

A standard Saturday, then, or so it seems until Jon announces, as if casually, though how could it be, that Deakin is leaving his apartment again.

Jon adjusts his metal choker, which he's paired with a black vest and shorts. He's trying to incite something, can never resist insidiousness, especially not against his friends.

"So Deakin's feeling better, then?" I scoop guacamole, salsa, and sour cream in various proportions onto a new soft-shell taco.

"It would seem so." Eric, likely coordinating with Jon this morning, wears a grey linen romper. He pulls the peak of his trucker cap over his eyes, squinting. The neon above us is so bright, even against the day's blinding sunshine. "We thought you'd want to know." He speaks loudly, above the AI-generated café music that fails to string together a memorable few bars, probably by design.

I stuff the taco in my mouth in one go, crunching on lettuce and crickets.

"Deakin wasn't alone." Jon dexterously pincers a chunk of chicken from his noodle bowl and eats it up. Chicken and fried eggs have emerged from beneath the noodle density! It actually looks pretty good. I eye the menu and try to figure out what it is so I don't stroke Jon's ego by asking him.

"Seems like he made some new friends," Eric says. "Four, to be precise." He gestures to the modded and silicone-packed gays who pass us by on the stony plaza, in day-glo short shorts and sandals. All with the same wave of shiny blond hair. Models, all of them. The 2070 model gay, to be exact!

"Muscled-up gym rats like these," Jon says. "I saw Deakin's friends at SF Fitness before, on the east side? But Deakin was here, in Forest Hill, right in our neighbourhood. The dudes surrounded him like bodyguards. One at each corner, Deakin in the centre of a queer quincunx. How often do you get to use that word?"

"You think he hired them?" Eric asks. "The gym rats?"

"Probably," I say.

Jon interrupts me to add, more crudely than I would have, the reason why we suspect this. "I don't think he'd fuck one guy who looks like that, let alone four."

Eric places a hand on mine. "We always thought you and Deakin would end up together."

"I did once too," I say. "Before I learned I wasn't his type."

Deakin and I bonded over our shared attraction to guys who looked like him. While I am slim, blond, vaguely muscled, and nicely dressed, Deakin is chubby, bearded, tattooed, and dresses in black metal T-shirts, cargo shorts, and high-tops. You just wanna lie in bed with a guy like that all day, eating pizza and watching Netflix.

Eric plays with an earlobe. "Neither you nor Deakin would let appearances stand in the way of a relationship if you thought it was right."

"Yeah." I take a napkin from my red plastic taco basket and clean my fingers. "I guess I love him so much as a friend that I didn't want to ruin it. Or I wasn't ready to risk the friendship."

Jon strokes his beard, his black nail polish glinting. "I find it interesting that no one would ever accuse Deakin of being one of those gays who just wants to fuck himself, even though he and the guys he goes for look pretty much the same. No, it's always the gym rats who get accused of narcissism."

I smirk. "Always standing up for the little guy, Jon."

He flicks me with ice from his tumbler of biodegradable plastic. The establishment doesn't trust him with glass. Quite rightly. I can no longer fathom how much of it he's smashed.

"But look at Jeremy," Eric says, the name adding a chill to our conversation. "He was the biggest narcissist of all."

"Are you hurt?" Jon asks me.

"That Deakin hasn't gotten in touch? A little. I guess I was trying to pretend he doesn't exist."

Jon scoffs. "So, not much change from your friendship over the last few years."

"Unfair. I didn't want to ignore him. He wouldn't let me contact him anyway." I roll my shoulders as if to shrug off the chat's discomfort. "The whole thing is just so painful. Look, whatever's going on with him, he'll tell us when he's ready. Give him time. He'll come around."

"Will he?" Jon is always prone to little digs like that.

I put the conversation back on track. "So he hired some men for protection."

Eric shrugs. "Most likely. They might even be androids. But all white gays look similar to me. I can't even tell if they're copies of one another."

I smile. "Sometimes you see a rubbery seam here or there. What do you think?" I ask Eric. "Can you tell?"

"I'm no expert," Eric says. "I only make objects, not people."

Eric, an artist, prints 3D dioramas from photos and scans he takes around the city. He hand paints them and assembles them in new formulations, asking the audience how much his art is found or created, and how much ownership we have over the world we walk through each day. I always say I would love his work even if he wasn't my friend. I hope he believes me one day.

"Eric," Jon says, "why not just ask people if they'll let you make models of them? The critique you got at your last showing was that your dioramas looked sparse without any humans."

Eric clenches his jaw. "That's what I was after. It was about the loneliness of landscapes."

Jon places a hand on Eric's shoulder. "This could be the progression of your work! You could go around the city, snapping randoms all day and printing models of them. They'd be flattered, I promise you. Don't you think that would be cool, Ioan? Little robots wandering around the dioramas?"

I shake my head. "I'm not an artist."

Eric crosses his arms. "Well, I would only do it to friends who offer consent."

Jon shoots him a look, like he's no fun. "That reminds me of this story I reported on. There was a killer who went around copying bodies of folks then murdering the copies! He was doing it so he wouldn't have to kill real people. They take care of him in some institute now."

Eric looks at me. "It's a crime, right?" He expects me to know, since I guess it is somewhat related to my job.

"It's illegal to create more than a twenty-five per cent likeness of someone, without permission. But you can't precisely quantify a person's image with that metric. It's down to reasonable doubt." I shrug. "A killer could easily circumvent that by making androids copy-pasted from five different people, for example. If so, that makes him clever *and* considerate."

"How do you figure that?" Jon asks.

"Well, when it comes to guys like that, maybe we should ensure they have an adequate supply of android bodies they can defile or dispose of."

"What, like, through taxes?" Eric asks.

"I mean, yeah," I say. "We pay for these people one way or another. Maybe that's the cheapest, most ethical answer."

As always, I watch Jon drain of joy as my compassion sucks the stinger out of his sensationalist chatter.

"Settle down, guys." A human server collects our empty tumblers and plates. Geometric tattoos across his arms, black denim shorts, white cut-off shirt. "The whole restaurant doesn't need to hear your opinions."

"Oh, I'm sorry," Jon says, touching his arm.

"It's okay."

"No, I mean are you a new friend in our entourage, or are you just a server?" Jon's wasted already. "I get it, honey. You're not the last surviving human drone who doesn't care about his job." He takes out his pebble and clicks on it. "I'm sure there's much more to you, but that's not for us to learn."

The server pauses, considering what to do, before walking away.

I fold my arms. "Guess you didn't plan on letting him know that you're a server too."

I'm so used to referring to Jon and Eric as vlogger and artist respectively that I sometimes forget they're also scraping by, doing jobs that androids are taking over.

"Oh, please." Jon shoots me a wry smile. "There's much more to us than that." He looks back at his pebble. "We should go anyway."

"Where?" Eric asks.

"Olympo!" I say.

"Nah," Jon says. "Don't want to spend the afternoon indoors on such a lovely day. That place is no longer that safe. You don't even know if you're going home with a real person or a killer robot anymore."

"Where, then?" I ask.

Eric gasps. "The fair!"

2

As my friends and I pace our way to the magnotram stop, I think of the Ship of Theseus, that thought experiment where parts of a ship are gradually replaced over time until you can make an entirely 'new' ship from all the parts that got replaced. So in what sense is the ship of replaced parts the original ship? Isn't the new ship, made of old parts, in fact the original ship?

It surely applies to our chat about Deakin and his makeshift gym-rat militia. But I don't want Jon to pollute my pontification with dick metaphors. Every other time I love it, but this time not so much. Not sure why.

We get on the tram, the boys sitting on either side of me. It's nice and cool, like sitting in a fridge, and there's a warmth in my stomach. The affection of hanging out with my silly friends on a sunny day when I'm filled by great food—nothing else like it.

We're quiet at first. There's a harried-looking mother in a denim dress with two dungaree-clad kids beside her. A real SF rarity.

I grip a love handle.

Jon pokes me in the side. "What are you up to, Ioan?"

"Guess my metabolism has changed in the last decade, even if nothing else has."

Now Eric has a feel. It tickles. "Getting doughy because you're having too much fun is something to be proud of."

"Yeah." I jiggle my chest with a palm. "This is the body I

covet in others, so why do I have such mixed feelings about living in it myself? You know, when Deakin and I were teenagers" —back in South Bend, Indiana—"I used to get hammered and force older men to spend their evenings looking after me. I treated them with contempt. It was funny how much they'd put up with just because they liked my young body. They deserved it, I thought."

Eric touches my arm. "You did that *too?*"

"I thought it was just me!" Jon says. "My god, you bitches are cruel."

I laugh as if surprised. Truth is, Jon and Eric are still at that game. They use their jobs in fancy restaurants as ways to climb socially, targeting rich older men to fund their projects and wild lifestyles.

"I got my karma, though, when I moved here." I look around at the others on the tram. A fleet of chiselled Spartans, SF being a veritable gay enclave. Thank god I do not consider these men competition, else I'd be a lifelong loser.

"With each passing year, my mainstream appeal fades," I say. "I see how little I can get away with. Glad I had my fun, I guess."

"Speaking of sexual pasts, I have dildos of everyone I've ever dated," Jon blurts, barely holding it in.

The mother glowers at us. I try to mouth *sorry* when Jon isn't looking.

"Proud of your collection?" I ask Jon, humouring him with pretend offence.

"He sure is." Eric rubs his eyes.

"Are you okay with it?" I ask.

Eric shrugs. "I mean, what choice do I have?"

"I earned them!" Jon says. "And it's not like they're real dicks."

Eric taps me on the knee. "You should see them, Ioan. They're getting so realistic these days. They look … freshly severed."

"It's my version of a trophy cabinet," Jon says, giggling.

The mother ushers her kids towards the door. They complain that they haven't yet reached their stop.

Jon ignores her. "Ioan, I hope Nerve develops a full-body service one day. Would you like a boyfriend who looks just like this person, except you don't have to hear him talk about conspiracy theories, diet and exercise, or his latest breakthroughs in therapy?"

I narrow my eyes at him. "So basically you want to date a blow-up doll."

"Yeah. Arm candy you can take to functions, except it doesn't embarrass you by getting drunk or opening its mouth."

"Sounds like a great business opportunity," I say. "I should make a proposal for Gabe."

"Ooh!" Eric says. "You call him Gabe now?"

"He'd rather call him Daddy," Jon says.

I hold my face in my hands. "You guys."

Jon turns to Eric. "Have you seen his boss? He's so fucking hot." He takes out his pebble. "Show me Gabriel Flores, Nerve employee."

From his palm spring holos of my husky boss: smiling atop Twin Peaks; lying on the grass on a sunny day; at a bar having cocktails with Ben, his grim-faced, angular, and weathered husband.

Eric examines the holos. "This is obviously Ioan's dream guy."

"I can't go after my own boss." I gesture towards Ben. "They've been in a relationship for twenty years."

Jon slips the pebble back in his pocket. "But isn't he uncomfortably vocal about how it's going down the toilet?"

"Hah!" Eric says. "We all know how attractive that is."

"Don't you see?" Jon says. "That's exactly why you can go after him! Gabe's all vulnerable and wondering, 'Have the good times passed? Will I ever find true love again? Where is my youth?' Then in you come, like, 'Bam! You wanna know what the future looks like? Me, bitch. I'm the same age as your relationship!'"

"What the fuck?" I say. "I'm thirty, not twenty."

Jon waves a hand at me. "It's the same thing when you're fifty."

It would be great if things worked out with Gabe one day. I know it would please my parents too. They worry about the disposable aspects of queer culture, which are admittedly in hyperdrive here.

The mother has had enough. She tuts loudly at Jon as she ushers her kids off the tram.

"Oh, fuck you, prissy fish!" Jon yells at her. "If you don't like it, you're in the wrong city."

"Sorry," Eric and I say in unison.

"Don't apologize on my behalf," Jon says as she leaves.

I rarely see hetties anymore. Just gays and their fancy little bioengineered kids, who will likely grow up and engineer more gays of their own. It's all they know, after all. We live in a bubble, sure, but after a mere sketchy century of 'tolerance', don't we deserve a homo homeland?

I place one hand on Eric's knee, the other on Jon's. "Guys, I think I'm gonna stop at my office first."

"What?" Eric says.

"No!" Jon objects. "You have to stay with us."

I grit my teeth. "I think I left something out on my desk. I need to go in and check or I'll think about it all weekend."

I get up and head to the door.

"But can't you just check the CCTV from here?" Eric calls after me.

"Catch up later!" I say, jumping off.

Eric and Jon have gone from being the friends of mine that simply everyone has to meet to the ones I invite last, if at all. I think they've noticed. When they tell their party stories of debauchery, they look at me with these pleading eyes, like they want me to jump in and run their lives for them. I'd be amazing at that, but it would detract from Task Number One: running my own damn life.

My point being, I'm two stops away from the office, but Eric and Jon don't know that. I just need a break from them.

Sometimes I'd rather be around normal, calm, non-judgemental, stable, chill people.

Then again, who can resist friends who don't want you to better yourself?

3

I don my Wayfarers and head towards the Nerve office, located in a converted warehouse. The facial scanner recognizes me even— *especially*—with my sunglasses on, given how often I stagger into work with a hangover, gripping a coffee. Gotta love those flexible hours.

Inside, light streams big dusty beams through the old warped panes. Historical windows, Nerve building the future, something something—there's some interesting metaphor there, I'm sure. Hope Gabe discovers it in time for his next TEDx Talk!

I do love this office. The original wooden flooring, the scent of its recent coat of varnish. The standing desks with little metal cube projectors for screen, keyboard, and mouse. We mostly work through voice activation anyway, telling AIs what to do for us. Soon they'll read our minds, and we'll be able to just stay in bed all day, thinking creative thoughts. Can't wait.

I duck into Gabe's office and steal a beer and lime from his fridge. It's not a big deal, but I'll replace them so he doesn't know. Charles runs the CCTV here. He'll keep quiet too.

In my department, robot bits on desks glint in the sunlight: slivers of carbon fibre, the dull sheen of titanium and stainless steel, the soft texture of brushed aluminum. If you put glass display cases over them, you could easily mistake this place for an art gallery. A meek little android caretaker would wheel around the corner, whispering something like, "Beautiful pieces, aren't they? Just let me know if you want any more information on the artist."

I head to my desk, on which sits a throat, all pink silicone and metal pistons, linked up by wires to my CPU.

This job wasn't my original plan. I once worked in a vintage shop with comic books, vinyl, iPods, Blu-rays. But when the economy last tanked, Deakin got me a position here, where he also worked. Still works. I assume.

Mechatronics gets me thinking: if you could start again, design a person from scratch, what would you keep? What would you throw away? Except, they're making me spend months trying to give a gag reflex to an artificial throat. And given how much effort I've put into losing my own gag reflex—hey, if I die as a result, it's a pretty good way to go—I'm not even sure, if the decision were mine, that it would be something I'd necessarily teach.

I flip open the penknife on my keychain and cut a lime wedge on the desk. It'll get sticky, but the cleaning routines will catch it over the weekend.

When I slam open the beer on the slate desk's edge, chipping it a little, the noise wakes up Charles.

"Ioan! Good to see you again."

The shadow of his printed proxy looms behind me. I turn and there he is, in a navy Nerve polo and dark jeans. Wavy black hair, chiselled yet rubbery face, airbrushed freckles, and cool grey eyes. This is my other work crush, an android whose appearance and personality were generated by neural networks. What that says about me, I don't want to know.

He scratches his head. "What are you doing here? It's Saturday. Brunch with the boys?"

"Yeah, I know." I lean on the desk and sip my beer. "I sent

them off to the fair. I just came by because I forgot to lock away the throatotype."

He looks at it, puzzled. "I could've done that for you."

"I was thinking of coding for a bit now that I'm here. I always find it easier when I'm a little buzzed."

In our company, there are so many automated and human processes for catching errors. With a few drinks, my mind clears of its more scolding impulses, the ones that slow me down or stop me completely.

"Plus," I add, "you can deduct the hours from Monday morning so I can lie in."

He eyes up my beer. "Giving you more time to nurse your inevitable hangover."

I frown at him. "Uh, you'd have one too if you had some way of metabolizing alcohol."

He takes a cloth out of his pocket and wipes the lime residue from my desk. "I can see why Nerve has not provided me with that capability. By the way," he adds, with an auto-tuned singsong lilt, "Gabe doesn't come here at the weekend."

I gasp and clutch my chest. "What are you implying?"

He raises his eyebrows at me. "I've seen you two together since literally day one, and I have an immaculate memory of your every interaction."

I shake my head. "Of all the candidates I had for office gossip, Charles, you weren't even under consideration."

He walks over to the back of a leather couch and sits on the headrest. "Ugh, I wish. I'm forbidden from sowing discord in the office environment."

A wave of tiredness hits me. I rub my eyes.

"You okay, Ioan?"

"I think I caught too much sun on the way here or something. Gonna take a quick nap on the couch."

"Want me to monitor your REMs so you feel rested enough to meet the boys later?"

"Yes, please. And let them know what I'm up to."

"I doubt they'll be surprised."

I shrug my backpack to the floor, take out my vape pen, and throw it at the charging pad on the wall. Just before I close my eyes, I see it stick there in the gel.

"Ioan?"

I blink my eyes open. When the blur clears, I'm looking at an upside-down face. Dark skin, salt-and-pepper beard, moustache waxed into curls, shaved head. Fresh smell of aftershave.

I sit up straight. "Gabe? What are you doing here?"

He wears pink pastel shorts and a black Hawaiian shirt with red parrots printed across it. A pair of aviators hangs from the neck. A plus-size squishy Styrofoam peanut of a man!

He licks a vanilla cone. "I got a message from Charles about an intruder? He sent me blurry footage of someone. You, I guess."

Charles is standing by the wall, staring forward, holding his arms gently behind him and his legs slightly apart. Standby mode.

"There must be condensation on his lenses or something." Gabe looks around. "Hope there isn't a problem with the air conditioning. It might damage some components."

"Yeah." I glower at Charles. "Those components better watch out."

Gabe gestures towards me with his cone. "I'm glad to see you, actually."

"I, uh …" I look down and see flip-flopped feet with big flowery black mandalas tattooed on them. "If it's about that new medical contract, I don't think I can help you out today. I had a bit too much to drink at brunch."

He grins, revealing the adorable gap between his front teeth. "That's not what I meant."

I look in his eyes. They're bloodshot. Did I wake him up? Is he tired? He, being more mature, can hold eye contact longer than I can. I look at the wall.

"Is that your pen charging?" he says. "Didn't know you vaped."

I hold my hand out for it. "It's just for weed." The gel spits it into my hand. "I shouldn't have said that."

"No worries." He sits on the armrest. "I have a port."

He tilts his head. There's a clear rubber stopper behind his left ear, like a beach ball. He flips it open so I can see inside.

I sit up to examine it, arching my back. I'm pretty sure he looks down my vest!

"It was an impulse installation when Ben and I separated." He motions to sit on the couch.

I shuffle over for him. "Sorry to hear it." I can barely even pretend.

"Well, as you can imagine," Gabe says, "I've been using the port a lot."

I peer at his eyes again. "You're high right now!"

"A little." He smirks. "What? It's the weekend." He kicks off his flip-flops, places his cone on the floor, and brings his legs up onto the couch. "So, if you didn't know, Ben and I separated. Is that why you haven't been returning my advances?"

Is this really happening? Is this some tipsy dream?

"Your *advances*?" I grin. "Maybe your style of flirting is too old-school for me to have noticed."

He laughs, belly jiggling as he does. "So mean to tease me when I'm putting myself out there, dude."

"It is, dude. It is."

Silence. We've reached a tipping point. We could go either way. And it feels like my job to send us in the right direction.

I play around with my vape pen as I consider what to say next. "Can I touch it?"

"The port, you mean?"

"Uh, yeah?"

He smiles and leans his head towards me.

It's a lovely excuse to touch his skin. So soft! I circle the port with a finger. "If I blow vapour in there, will you get high?"

"Not if you blow it in *there.*"

I get it.

I take a hit from the vape and hold it in my mouth as I crawl on top of him, gripping the pen in my fingers as I place my hands on either side of his head. His mouth opens into a loose pout as he takes in my face. I press my lips against his, open my mouth, and blow. As he exhales through his nose, his tongue enters my mouth. And mine plays with his.

You ever feel like you're so very much getting what you want that you've entered some other impossible reality, some what-if scenario from which you must unfortunately return, since entertaining it will do nothing but hurt you, make you yearn further for something you can't have? That's the exquisite weirdness I feel as I brace for Gabe to disappear into smoke. But as he wraps his arms around me, and I taste the vanilla of his kiss, the moment just becomes more real. Satisfaction, it seems, is not an insatiable collection of dildos or an army of identical gaybots. It's just a pair of lips away. Right now, Gabe's are the only ones I want to kiss, probably ever. But I'm grateful for the feeling that it matters right now, that this is exactly where I'm meant to be, rolling around on a couch with my boss.

"Weed makes me horny," I say.

"Me too," he says. "But you're drunk."

"So? I've wanted this for the longest time anyway." I shift away a little to disguise my growing erection. Why did I have to wear these flimsy-ass shorts today?

I see the time on the wall. "I'm late for the fair!"

"The fair! Can I come?"

"You want to meet my friends?"

"I ... thought we were being spontaneous and fun?" He holds his head in his hands. "Oh, god, what am I doing?"

"Starting your second wind!"

"Is that it?"

I take his hand. "Well, I do know I want to spend the day with you."

"Then—let's do it!" He grips my hand in his and we run together, giggling.

I wink at Charles on the way out.

When Gabe isn't looking, Charles winks back.

4

I cannot stop beaming. Every now and then I look up at Gabe sitting beside me on the tram. When we meet eyes, it fills us both with excitement, and I need to look down again.

The tram is packed now, but still nice and cool. All the rest must be going to the fair too. Their hair is dyed and shaved in different formations. Their fabscreen tops and skirts display GIFs of fireworks exploding or psychedelic repeating patterns. Some wear light-reactive clothing, which conserves the sun's heat during the day to use during the evening's chill.

When others catch my eye, they share in the thrill that I am holding my Number-One Crush's hand! I've always thought shit like that is super cute when I see it. Gabe and I are now a travelling two-man troupe of joy.

"I really wanna kiss you right now," Gabe whispers.

"A real gentleman," I say. "Won't do it here because it's déclassé."

"But I don't know if I can help myself."

I feel the back of his thick hand stroke my cheek. He sends electric currents through my skin with his touch.

"They have a big wheel at the fair, right?" he asks.

"Duh. It's a fair."

"You could just say yes! Well, we'll go on it, and then I'm gonna kiss you so much."

We—reasonably intelligent grown-ass men—sound like schoolboys. A portal to youth was in front of us the whole time, unlocked with a hold of the hand.

When we reach our stop, we get out and order separate UberAirs.

Our drones fly down towards us at about the same time and release their harnesses. We strap ourselves in, and their white propellers cart us into the air.

The UberAir is the gayest method of transport there is, so here we break our hand-holding lest, before reaching the park, we explode into a beautiful rainbow in the sky. I'm not opposed to doing that—what an interesting legacy!—but I can always do it later, and I want to see how things turn out with Gabe.

Did I just hope? Do I have a reason to live? Does that mean I'll have to, like, take care of myself now? Getting older is the worst!

We buzz through the sky, which is ablaze with warm colours. A summer wind cools our backs. Around us, more one-person helicopters gently weave through one another's predicted geodesic paths. We're all carted around like Amazon packages through the sky, over silvery cars and solar-panelled rooftops that gleam in orange sunlight.

I make a mental note that reads, *Business idea: Droneboys.com?*

I know we're close when I see the decaying remains of the Golden Gate Bridge. Nothing but two rusting masts. It fell into disarray during the Singularity Wars. Before my time. I know embarrassingly little about them beyond the laws they incepted, such as the one that integrates a string of specially devised do-no-harm code so deeply into every system, Nerve's included, that we can't even access it. Its success rate is debatable, but its inclusion non-negotiable.

The UberAirs deposit Gabe and me beside one another, as requested, at the entrance to Golden Gate Park. We smile and link hands once again.

Glowing lights streak across the encroaching evening sky. Spotlights reveal the faces airbrushed on the backdrops of rides. 1990s dance music fills the air—Black Box, Corona, Haddaway— as does the nostalgic scent of muddy grass.

Futuristic dragdroids grind on podia around the park. There are ostentatious pastel-coloured wigs and metal faceplates like Japanese Noh masks, with sparks flying out of them in rainbows, serving me neo-Tokyo realness!

I do hear myself. I'm just having too much fun to care.

But I'm also nervous. I wanted to be spontaneous with Gabe, but will the boys mind? They're a couple already, but they've been together long enough that they exist in a fairly stable 'friend mode' when they're around me. Gabe might change the energy.

Oh, whatever. What do they care about making *me* uncomfortable? It's Jon's constant mission. And they're probably hammered on another round of frozen margaritas by now. At least.

They confirm my suspicions when I see that sensible Eric now has his arm around a staggering Jon, who has the characteristic dinner-plate pupils of a guy who's triggered his pleasure centres with a dodgy app and a black-market wireless probe. I look forward to pretending to read his future article about it.

"Well, hello there!" Eric gleefully stretches a hand towards Gabe. "Seems like you picked somebody up on your way here? I wholeheartedly approve."

"Gabe." He accepts Eric's hand.

"We know aaall about you."

Jon's eyelids flare. "Exactly his type!" he attempts to whisper to Eric, but we can all hear him. He turns to Gabe. "Ioan does *not* shut up about you."

Gabe squeezes my hand. "Really now?"

"I knew this was a bad idea." I'm blushing.

Gabe cannot stop grinning. It feels wonderful to flatter a beautiful middle-aged man following a separation. I haven't seen such a glimmer of joy on his face since I started working for him.

Jon holds out his hand, in which are two paper tabs. "Party favours?" he says.

Gabe takes one and examines it. "Is this a good idea?"

"Oh, no," I say. "None of this is."

We take a tab each, and the four of us walk into the park together.

5

I'm explaining to Gabe how I first met Jon and Eric—Jon on Grindr (nothing happened, bad match) and Eric at 3DCon when I went there representing Nerve and perused his art stand—when the tab kicks in. It streaks the fair into a blur of coloured lights. I think it's a mild dose of ecstasy and acid, or maybe psilocybin. Jon must have gotten it here, what with how well it enhances the experience. People flicker past us with big blue coifs, stiff rings of skirts glowing fluorescent, fabscreens pulsing in time with the music. Holo ghosts bloom out the walls of haunted houses in primary colours, their misty nature feeling solid and cozy to my drug-induced synesthesia.

Our bumper car interactions provide us with any number of stupid innuendoes. When we strap ourselves into the antigravity harnesses that blast us at high Gs into the air, it's like the hard plastic seats melt and envelop us. Same with the railless coasters that fire each pair of chairs across a randomized course through the air and even briefly underwater, blasting a sphere of air around us. No worries, though. They can't expose us to dangerous acceleration forces or crash into anything—and they have to come back to earth after a few minutes.

We head through the stalls, stopping to knock coconuts off their stands and throw hoops over milk bottles. I have my eye on a purple teddy bear with a mohawk, but it isn't my lucky day. Timeless entertainment, though!

Then it's time for popcorn, pretzels, and churros. None of this is terribly expensive, but Gabe always insists on beeping his chip for both of us. It's like an impromptu first date and yet beyond that. It's been a long time coming.

The four of us pace our way past the bowling pin and raffle stalls, catching our breath. More dragdroids walk by on big metal stilts. They hand us bead necklaces and more tabs, which Jon sprinkles into the beers we clutch in plastic cups. As he does, we pass a guy vomiting while his boyfriend rubs his back. I really hope he has worse tolerance than I do, or that I'd started earlier in the day. I don't want my own evening to end up like that!

Jon waves an arm around, his new glow bracelets leaving a bright blur in their wake. "Why are there so many kids here?"

"Huh?"

He's spotted a petting zoo, where kids play with genetically engineered abominations: miniaturized giraffes, extra fluffy penguins, and defanged tigers with enormous cartoon eyes. All born without the ability to reproduce and kept around for nothing beyond entertainment value. As an early twenty-first-century non-SF-born gay, I can relate.

Eric smacks Jon on the back of the head. "It's a fair, for Chrissake."

"For adults!" Jon grabs Eric's hand and plays with his fingers. "Not these homegrown imitations, these creepy clones with their tiny teeth and dirty hands."

Here he goes again.

Gabe just laughs—and not in that manner of, 'I tell you your friends are fun but what I really mean is they make me uncomfortable and I don't want to see them again'. It's the kind of laughter I heard throughout my twenties from stuffy types I soon stopped dating. I guess by the time you're Gabe's age, there are no new types of people, that everything is familiar. That must have its ups and downs.

"Okay." Jon turns back to us. His pupils have constricted somewhat. He's coming down. "I know what you're gonna say. If my parents hadn't made me, I wouldn't be here. But if I'd made others, I would've squandered the life my parents were kind enough to grant me."

I tap Jon on the shoulder. "Who's asking you to have kids?"

"No one!" He vaguely gestures in the direction of what I assume is a local wombshop. "But I could print myself six of the little fuckers by this afternoon. Except I wouldn't, because I'm not an idiot."

With talk like that, there has to be a bullied child inside him—unless I'm projecting.

Gabe takes me under his arm. "To be fair, this place isn't that safe for kids. So easy for predators to take surreptitious photos with their eye implants and later print some dolls for themselves."

I clap my hands over my ears and sing, "La la la, don't want to hear more!"

Jon bats my hands away. "Such an awful phenomenon. Especially since the government will provide anyone with their own child bot, no questions asked. They have neural network-generated appearances that make them unlike any child in existence."

"When you say no questions asked," Eric says, "you mean—"

"Maybe you want to raise a child but you're not ready for a real one." Jon raises a finger. "Or some other reason."

"I'm so sorry for this," I say to Gabe.

"I started it!" Gabe scoffs.

Why do I have this weird impulse to parent all the people around me? They're adults just like I am.

"How much more compassionate can the state be with these people?" Gabe walks between Eric and Jon and slings an arm around both of them. I swell with pride at how quickly he has integrated. "And still it's not enough to stop them stealing the appearance of real kids?"

"Couldn't agree more," Jon says. "But asking for a free kid might put them on some sort of register, even if the government claims otherwise."

Gabe lets go of my friends and comes back to me, taking my hand. Eric and Jon walk on ahead.

"Hey," Gabe asks me, "where's that Deakin guy? Did you both break up?"

I shoot him a confused look. "You thought we were together and you're only asking me that now?"

"I don't know! I'm just seeing where today goes."

"Hah. Well, Deakin was my best friend. He can be again if he wants. But we don't know where he is."

Eric doesn't even try to hide that he was listening. "He was supposed to come meet us."

"Let's call him again!" Jon takes out his pebble. A green phone holo pulses gently above it.

I don't know about this.

A holo of Deakin appears. He's in knee-length camo shorts, a black Cradle of Filth T-shirt, and a dirty lab coat. He's shaved his head recently, but the beard is long and unkempt, with more grey in it than before. We can't see any of his environment. He's blocked it from display.

"Deakin!" Eric says. "You're looking well."

"Thanks," Deakin says. "I've been sleeping better."

"Better—or less?" Jon says. "You've met someone!"

"Maybe." He smiles bashfully.

A vague sadness hits me. It's mostly, *How did he meet someone and when? Why didn't he tell me? Why haven't I seen him? What the hell is going on?* I may well be envious that I am not Deakin's new partner, even if, logically, I don't want that. Even in the midst of living out a fantasy date with the literal man of my dreams. The human heart, I swear to god.

Jon pinches the holo's cheek.

Deakin recoils. Receptors have conveyed the sensory message to him, wherever he is.

"We're so happy for you," Eric says.

"We are," I add in quickly, piggybacking off the sentiment without having to express it myself.

"You deserve it," Eric continues, "and bravo. It can't have been easy, after … I know it's been tough."

"Hey!" Jon says. "Isn't that them now?"

Deakin's face takes on a panicked look.

"Don't worry," Eric says to Deakin. "Jon has white gay blindness."

"Ah, yes," Gabe murmurs to me, "I know it well."

I grin at him.

Jon points ahead. "I swear I see Deakin's buddies."

There are two couples in front of us. Blond, topless, bright shorts and trainers. Gym bags and water canteens strung over their shoulders. They notice Jon pointing and squint, looking with confusion at one another.

Before responding, Deakin signs off, his holo collapsing back into the pebble.

The gym rats keep walking, looking with confusion towards our hapless gang.

Jon shrugs. "Well, that was weird. What now?"

Gabe pats my back. "Big wheel!"

6

Jon and Eric take a separate Ferris wheel cart without even asking, even though there's space for four in each. Kinda cringe, but also not.

It's not like the wheel of my youth. It's freaky. There are no spokes, and the 'carts' are simply long white plastic benches that float beside a big metal circle, the 'wheel' itself. Maglev, I think.

I must have the type of brain that suits my job, because I cannot switch it off.

Gabe and I take a bench together. He pulls the bar down over us both. Up we go, watching our legs dangle, swinging them about in the warm evening air. I take Gabe's soft hand in mine, looking at the fireworks shimmering in his dark eyes. I stroke his cheek and lean in to kiss him.

As our cart ascends, there's a little over-the-shorts action too. We're simply capitalizing on what is maybe a year's worth of built-up sexual tension. Nothing but an appetizer for … later, whenever that will be. As I suspected, he has one of those adorable short but chubby dicks. I picture him naked, me holding it in my hand, burying my face in his armpits or sucking his nipples, pressing my body against his. All this is surely destined to happen eventually.

For now, we're high in the sky, making out beneath purple clouds lit up by spotlights that sway across them. Gabe wraps his arms around me, holds me close. I am aglow.

And then—of course—I hear bickering.

I lean back to see Eric and Jon, their cart now descending, arguing fiercely with one another.

"What the hell, guys?" I say.

Gabe strokes my leg to get my attention back on him. "Just talk to them when we're back on the ground."

"Sure," I say.

We start kissing. But I frown. My friends are shouting now.

"Should we just tell him?" Eric says.

"Oh, just say it already!" Jon says.

"I caught Jon in bed with you this morning," Eric yells up at me.

"What?"

Gabe rolls his eyes. That's right, Gabe: younger means more energy *and* drama. I like it as much as you do. That's why I want to date *you!*

I lean back again. The bar restricts my motion. I turn too quickly, and my neck punishes me for it.

Jon folds his arms. "You're breaking the news to him like that? It's inflammatory!"

Eric has shifted as far away from Jon as he can. "Well, sorry, darling, I know that's usually your thing." He looks back at me. "I thought it *was* you. Turns out it was an android of you."

"That I purchased for research purposes!" Jon slaps a hand across Eric's mouth.

I'm bent over the back of the bench, shaking a finger at them. "That is such a violation, Jon."

"That's what I said!" Eric says.

"After joining me in a three-way with it," Jon retorts.

Beneath us, fireworks eject from exhaust ports in the shoulders of dragdroids. We shout over them.

"Oh, thanks, Eric," I say. "That makes me feel *much* better."

Gabe groans. "Ioan—"

I get one leg free from the bar. "Look, whatever you did with this thing, it's all terrible."

Jon pushes Eric. "You can fuck your high horse."

"Not unless you fuck it first!" Eric shouts back.

The operator down below, a skinny teen in an ill-fitting polyester uniform, shouts up at me. "Buddy, sit properly in your seat!"

I'm leaning way over the back of the bench.

Gabe grips my thigh. "Let's have a talk with them when we get off the wheel."

Why does he have to be a part of this? I ask myself.

So I'm thankful to discover, as we descend, that Jon and Eric have already run off to god knows where.

When Gabe and I get free, he turns to me. "Time to go?"

I take a deep breath. "Yes."

7

Gabe and I walk together silently. We're not holding hands anymore. It's getting darker. I don't know where we are, but it isn't a nice area. Fabscreens turn blue for the safety of their wearers, lighting up at night in the universal colour of the police. The muddy grass beneath our feed gives way to a dirty pavement. The purple sky dims, and ragged clouds blow slowly through the sky. There are needles in the gutters beside our flip-flops and puddles of puke lining the alleyways.

"What's on your mind?" Gabe asks.

I look at him, weighing up what I should say. I'm getting cold in my vest. I hug myself. "I'm sorry."

"What are you sorry for?" He takes me under his warm arm. "What your friends told you? That was fucked. I wouldn't know what to think. And, look, we had a lovely day together—"

"Up until now." I put an arm around his waist. "I always say you should leave an event at peak fun, when you'd love it to continue. That's when to go. Not now, when the fun has run out."

"I know this was a pseudo–first date, but we've known each other for ages. There aren't the same expectations." His smile brightens as he spots something. "Hey! Let's stop for a slice of pizza, and you can talk to me about it."

Red neon lines the pizza place's window and a big slice reads *PIZZA PIZZA PIZZA* in green, flashing in case we don't get the point. Precisely designed, I am sure, for people of our chemically induced intellect.

We amble in and find a booth by the door, sitting in the cool plastic chairs that jut out of the wall. Our legs intertwine beneath the touch-screen table. We tap our order into the screen, and a metal waiter bot fires towards us on rails, sliding menacingly over to our table, his head flailing on a broken axis. He fires two slices from the slots in his oven-chest.

The pizza is flavourless but warm, comforting.

Gabe strokes my arm. I squirm. A reflex. It seems to scare him.

"Sorry," I say. "It's like I've been assaulted by proxy or something. It's not like they made my body do something it didn't want. But ... it doesn't feel far beneath that."

"Yeah, I get that."

I take another bite of pizza. "I'll start by giving them an evening to have a massive falling out and doubt the future of our friendship."

"They deserve worse."

I nod. "I just realized. They were alluding to this earlier. Eric said that for his art, he would only make models of friends who offer consent."

There had been a glimmer of resentment in Jon's eye when Eric said that. Like Eric had used one of those coded personal attacks that couples sometimes deploy in mixed company. You know communication has broken down when they resort to this enigmatic talk at the expense of their confused friends. But I've been in that situation before. As uncomfortable as it is for those around you, sometimes it's impossible to resist.

Gabe lowers his head.

"You're a great listener," I say. "You always have been. It's one of the reasons I like you so damn much."

He smiles to himself. "You're not just doing this because you want my organs?"

"When I could print newer, fresher ones for cheap?" I grin. "Okay, there are a few of your organs I would like my hands on, but I don't plan to treat them in a way that will cause you discomfort."

He laughs dirtily, resting his chin in his hands. "Maybe we should head home?"

Does he mean to our separate homes? I really don't know. My mood has changed, and, after Jon and Eric's announcement, I can't offer the same range of options. I feel like I can't trust myself.

"Can we have another beer?" I ask.

"You think that's a good idea?"

"Not really." I tap an order of two beers into the screen. "Oh my god! You can order cards here? Let's play!"

I'm just trying to get our evening back on track, but I end up completely derailing it. Because it's somewhere into this last beer that I black out.

8

I wake up with a headache. Still drunk, definitely still high.

I'm in my apartment. It smells like cozy new man and aftershave. Gabe's arm presses down on my chest.

I'm on the floor, on my air mattress. Gabe is asleep on the couch beside me, beneath a blanket. His other arm is above his head. He's in a black vest and boxers only. The blanket drapes vaguely across his figure.

He appears to have been respectful last night. I do not return the favour. I take it all in. The outline of his dad bod through the sheets. Ropey black tribal tattoos. Nipple rings slipping out of the vest. The bulge in his boxers.

Jesus Christ, man.

I have to pace myself. I've wanted him so badly for so long, and this could really be something above and beyond the superficial pettiness of the meat and rubber market. Someone truly special.

Unless I already fucked it up.

I stroke his head. He wakes up quickly, like he wanted me to spy him like that. Maybe.

"You slept on the couch," I say. "What a gentleman. I feel like we're in Victorian times."

He yawns and stretches. "What does that make you? The scrappy chimney sweep disowned by his parents?"

"Put a pin in that for later. Um, why are we at mine? I didn't plan on you seeing my place this quickly."

"I don't mind. Like I said, it's not like we don't know each other."

I press the heels of my hands to my temples, as if trying to crush my skull into remembering. "Nothing happened last night, right? Oh, god, I knew it."

He sits up and folds the sheets. "What?"

"You don't want to hang out with me again."

"If I didn't, would I be here now?"

I get up slowly and head to the kitchen to make coffee. "Uh, yeah. If you felt guilty, and obligated to look after me by sleeping on the couch."

He paces to the window, looking out, stretching his back. "We had innocent fun, that's all. Played some of your retro game collection."

I clatter cups around, toss coffee pods into my machine. "Oh, really?"

"Yeah. Mostly *Smash Bros.* We stripped an item of clothing each time we lost. You called *us* the Smash Bros."

I cringe.

"I thought it was cute." He shields his eyes from the morning sun filtering through my thin curtains. "And there was a lot of kissing. But definitely nothing more."

I bring us back a coffee each.

Gabe holds his cup and breathes it in. "Smells great."

"*You* smell great," I say, and sniff his chest.

"That tickles!"

"I can't help myself. Your scent is intoxicating."

I'm hungover for sure. My god. Getting wasted is like an emotional sneeze. It leaves behind this open, floaty feeling, cracking open new conversational possibilities.

"The right people have a pheromonal attraction," Gabe says. "Huge problem for our products, don't you think?"

"Only if you consider them in competition with human relationships."

"Not with ours," Gabe says. "Not that I'm implying we're in a relationship."

I wave a hand at him. "Relax, old man. I know what you mean. But I feel like this requires more research." I put my cup back down on the coffee table and inhale from his chest again. "We'll partner with pharmaceutical companies and artificially manufacture pheromones! Study the nasal mucosa of prospective clients and design chemicals that fit the receptors on their membranes even better than human pheromones can. Make people addicted to our androids!"

He takes my hand and pulls me onto the couch with him. "You really want to go there?"

I pull my leg over his. "No. I just want you. Bottled."

"Sometimes the real thing is irreplaceable." He buries his nose in my pit and takes a deep sniff.

Holy fuck, am I in love?

"You, uh ... you want breakfast?" I ask him. "Eggs and bacon?"

He licks at the crease between my arm and pec, sending shivers throughout my body. "Sounds great."

I scurry back to the kitchen, happy to hide my lower half behind the central counter. I press the breakfast preset on my printer, twice.

Gabe cocks his head. "Is that …? Shit." He stands up warily and ambles towards me. "I guess I'm gonna do a lot of that."

"Of what?"

"Showing my age."

I brandish a spatula at him. "You actually cook it, don't you? Your own breakfast."

"I'd love to do it for you sometime."

He walks up and pushes me against the cool counter, biting my lip. I feel the growing erection in his boxers pressing against me. Cute and chubby.

He coughs and shifts away. When he isn't looking, I tuck my dick away, beneath the elastic waistband of my boxers, under my vest. We both seem to be in agreement about taking it slow. It just turns me on more.

Gabe returns to the couch and leans over it, getting something out of his bag. His vest rides up and boxers fall down, revealing a sliver of hairy crack. I love it. He doesn't even seem to notice.

He gets back up with a box of green tablets and pops one with coffee. "They say the way to navigate the 'emotional journey' of a divorce is to feel everything that comes to you." He smiles softly. "Feel everything, ride the emotions—that's like saying you should let someone hit you with a sledgehammer because they'll eventually tire themselves out." He shrugs. "Maybe. Maybe you'll die first."

I don't know what to say.

He shakes off the thought. "So. What are your plans today?"

Our plates are ready. I take our eggs and bacon over to him. "Well, after I drink so much, I usually go to the gym because I feel guilty."

Gabe toasts this with a forkful of bacon. "Enjoy!"

"You don't wanna tag along?" I bump him on the knee with my fist. "It can be more effective than medication."

"I'd sooner kill myself than go for a jog this morning. How's that for effective?" He grins. "I have my own errands to run today."

"Ah, okay. When will we see each other again?"

"Monday morning, probably."

"Well, duh." I punch him in the ribs. I'm trying to be playful, but it's a little too hard. "But don't you want to meet sooner? Like this evening?"

"Of course!" he says. "I was just waiting for you to suggest it. Let's meet at my place. I'll make you dinner."

"Deal."

When we finish breakfast, we get dressed and head out together, UberAirs carting us off in separate directions.

9

Why on Earth am I—the guy who subconsciously chooses partners based on the unlikelihood that they will invite him to the gym—going to the gym?

Well, it's not any gym. It's the SF Fitness where Jon and Eric say they spotted Deakin's new friends.

There's a low morning smog, so I don my face mask. When I land at the entrance, a thick wall of glass, the filter deposits a compacted pellet of dirt into my palm. I toss it in the trash as I enter.

I beep my chip on the turnstile, turn on my music, then head to the treadmills. There are ten or so gym rats over by the weights and mirrors, including two pairs of blond boyfriend twins in yellow, pink, green, and blue tank tops.

When guys who are basically dating themselves come here and make each other work out, they should call that 'polishing the mirror'.

They admire one another and post selfies. Surely the joy of a relationship is that only one other person needs to find you attractive? I once posted a selfie that got nine hundred likes. It filled me with dread. What did it mean, that nine hundred people liked the look of me? Nothing could happen between us all—there's only one of me! Never say never, I guess. Still, I opted out of the selfie game entirely.

The blond in yellow catches my eye in the mirror. Oh, shit. I look straight ahead, but I see him approach in my periphery.

"Hi." He leans his muscular arms on my treadmill. Up close, his green eyes shimmer in the daylight. He's beautiful.

I take out my earbuds. "I wasn't staring."

"Uh, okay."

"We saw you at the fair yesterday." Another of them, in pink gear, with blue eyes.

"Okay."

"You were talking to the holo of that guy who's been creeping on us." The other two come over, four of them addressing me now.

I frown. "Deakin was—?"

"Deakin."

"So that's his name."

Shit.

"Do you know him?"

I slow my pace. "He's my best friend."

"He cloned us, didn't he?"

"Is that what he did? I honestly don't know." I lean on my thighs, catching my breath.

"Bullshit!"

One reaches a hand and turns off my treadmill.

"Hey!" A roomba yells at us to behave.

But the men carry on. "If we see him back here again—"

"We're gonna kick his ass."

"As for you, get the fuck out."

"You know why."

I bite my tongue. These four guys could easily take me before any robot could intervene. "Fine. I'll just take a shower and go."

"I don't think so, perv."

"We know what you get up to in the showers."

Unnecessary! "You know what?" I say. But then I take another look at them. "Fine. Fine."

I throw up my hands, collect my stuff, and bugger off.

———

Back outside, I put my mask back on and walk off with my head lowered. I haven't earned their hostility, yet I still feel ashamed. How does that work?

So. Deakin cloned them. Allegedly.

So what? They don't know what he's been through. If they did, and they had hearts, maybe they'd donate their own time to him. If we lived in a world like that, Deakin wouldn't have to do what he did. If that's indeed what he did. And why he did it.

I'm sure men like that would love to donate their image to such a service. They can't get looked at enough to satisfy themselves, and then a company comes along that will pay to replicate them? Easiest sell imaginable.

I take out my pebble. "Find escorts in my area," I request aloud.

At first, no one on the street turns their heads at this commonplace request, but then someone shouts, "Right here, baby!"

I turn to see two gents in floaty kaftans, short shorts, and roller skates. They have thick black dreadlocks, big smiles. They turn gracefully and skate backwards, eyeing me up and down.

"Thanks," I say. "But I'm just researching."

They get mad, shoot me the evil eye, give me the finger, and skate onwards again.

The pebble returns a holographic map with escort profiles that I can touch for more info.

There the four of them are: the gym rats. Darryl, Brent, Hunter, and Cody. Which cannot be their real names. (I wonder where white adult actor aliases came from. Who knows, but they're instantly recognizable as such. What a curious feature of language!)

They boast many five-star reviews, mostly from lonely-seeming older men who felt cared for during their massages. How nice. Seriously!

I guess it explains the gym rats' indignation. They implied offence at being copied, but perhaps they disapprove of piracy that encroaches upon their revenue.

I swipe through their profiles. They've posted their gym selfies as bait to get people to subscribe to their OnlyFans. If these sites have any sense, they'll soon let users add 3D scans and body specs so users can print their own sexbots. Of course, data will get leaked and pirated, as always. Maybe one day that won't be inevitable, but I don't see how.

Such a dark age it was in our history when sites like OnlyFans cropped up. Not because of the services they provided—I don't care about that—but because of how quickly folks went from condemning sex workers to becoming them. Their puritanism caused I don't know how many deaths, but it was okay when they did it?

We're all whores to some degree—or did nobody learn anything from Paul Verhoeven's 1995 classic *Showgirls*?

10

I tried respecting Deakin's space. I tried tracking down his new companions. But I'm stumped. I just don't think I can wait any longer for him to contact me. I hope he understands that I interfere as his friend. But I'm willing to accept the risk that he doesn't.

I take out my pebble and dictate a message to Gabe: "Hi,

mister. Unfortunately I have to postpone our dinner this evening."

He calls me straight away, and I see a projection of his upper torso and head, buzzing in a range of blues. "Well, this is disappointing."

"Yeah, you're a caller," I say. "I thought people stopped that even before your time."

"Isn't it cool again? Your friends did it at the fair."

"No, it's still weird. Not that it isn't lovely to see your face again."

He presses the bridge of his nose. "Listen, Ioan—cut it out, would you?"

I cock my head at him. "What?"

He holds out a palm and points an index finger into it. "Look. You had nothing better to do, so you thought you'd kiss your boss. It's the light of a new day now, and you don't know how to get out of it. I thought we could be adults about this, but apparently not."

The midday sun fires off the skyscrapers around me, so I don my sunglasses. "It's mostly sad that you don't see your worth. Though it is also a little adorable."

"Stop it. Yesterday was what it was. I was feeling tender about my separation, and you were just there."

I stop walking. "Oh, is that what happened?"

"Yeah. And maybe I reminded you of Deakin, the guy you really want to date. I saw the way you looked at his holo at the fair. And I see where you're heading now."

"Are you tracking my pebble?"

"It's your work pebble. I have a right to—"

"At the weekend, for personal reasons?"

This is exactly the type of bullshit I was trying to avoid by going for an older man, but here it is once again, in full force.

Gabe takes a deep breath and closes his eyes, like he will rise above my drama. "I'm used to this. Just … See you Monday, no harm done, okay?"

"I don't know about that."

He frowns. "About which part—the harm, or Monday? Because we have some major deadlines to—"

"Yeah, good luck with those."

I toss his holo down the drain. It leaves me without my pebble, but I can't have him tracking me. And it was symbolically worth it.

I consider it a bonus of my proclivity for middle-aged dudes that I get to breathe new life into men who often need it. But the risk, I've learned, is that once they're reinvigorated, they bugger off. Sail round the world, take up golf, or return to their partners when they learn I can't hold my own in discussions on sustainability or international politics. I've felt used, sure, though I'm ultimately relieved that if men have other desires, they're honest about them.

Because who the fuck wants to go sailing?

So whatever. I'll shake it off. Despite the wider world's best efforts, Deakin needs my full attention.

———

The door to Deakin's building slides back for me, as does the elevator at the back of the lobby. I take it up to his floor. He doesn't bother to collect me. Perhaps it's still an effort for him to leave.

Inside his top-floor apartment, there are robot arms everywhere on a wide U-shaped desk in the room with splintered floorboards. Outside, neon signs too close to read make the outside world look like a big glowing pattern of cross-hatches, whorls, and exploding circles.

His desk is also cluttered with grease, gears, and circuit boards wired up to laptops—for tests and programming, I assume. Components hang from stands around the room, ready for manual assembly, for painting on rubber skin and airbrushing details and blemishes. All the personalized handiwork that Deakin puts into our products.

I look through to the bedroom. There are heaps of clothing and junk food detritus. Since Deakin spends most of his time in his head, most of what I take in now is probably invisible to him. Even so, this is undeniably the home of a depressed person.

"You must be Ioan!"

I turn and flinch when I see one of the SF Fitness dudes. Same blond hair and blue eyes, same megawatt smile. This time he wears a black cotton shirt, black trousers, and leather chisel toes. He takes my hand in both of his, shaking once, firmly and just beneath the threshold for pain, then letting go.

Here come the other three from the gym, similarly overdressed.

"Ioan!" they say, smiling.

"Good to finally meet you."

"Thanks for checking in on your friend."

"Here he is now!"

They part to reveal Deakin in his black T-shirt and cargo shorts, in his dirty lab coat. He looks deflated, gaunt, quite different from the holo we saw yesterday. He must have sent a false projection so as not to worry us. The real Deakin has lost too much weight too quickly. Compulsively exercising after Jeremy got in his head? That would explain how he met the gym rats. The real ones, not these copies. Maybe the men were kind to him, showed him how to use the equipment.

I will not ask unless he feels like telling me.

I gently wave at him. "Hi."

"I see you've met my new friends," he croaks.

I look between them. "A very polite crew." They stand at attention in a row, looking at me.

"They've been taking good care of me," he says. "Around the

house, I mean. And helping me get out sometimes, when I need food and stuff."

I smile. "That's great. Jon mentioned that he'd seen you with them. I was pleased to hear you were getting back out."

"Sorry I haven't been in touch."

I shake my head, my eyes getting watery. "You've nothing to apologize for."

"Gents," the green-eyed guy says to us, "might I suggest you sit in the living room and I bring you a selection of teas?"

I nod at him politely. "Sounds ideal."

Long Island iced tea is one of the available teas, apparently. I don't know why that counts, but I can't resist. So Deakin blows on his mug of chamomile while I sip a ridiculously alcoholic thing through a pink silly straw. The very image makes us giggle.

"So," I say eventually, "you made a wall of muscle to separate yourself from the world."

"I guess you could put it like that. And it made the real guys mad."

"Yeah, well." I don't know how to finish that thought.

He places his cup down and rests his hands in his lap. "You think I should've asked you for help."

"I did at first, but—"

"You didn't notice. You didn't stop it."

I crash my drink down too forcefully. The sound of it clattering on the table scares both of us. "What could I have done, honestly? Tell you Jeremy was no good for you? Confront you about your bruises? Express my concern about your weight loss? Well, I did all those things, and it only pushed you further away." I don't want to cry or make this about myself. "Isn't this what you wanted to hear, what I really felt?"

We're silent as two gym rats shuffle in with bowls of chips and peanuts.

Deakin watches as they leave. "Are you gonna make me get rid of them?"

I reach over and touch his arm. "No. I didn't come here to judge you or tell you what to do. But if you're gonna take them out again, maybe slap a fake moustache on them or something so you don't get in trouble."

He chuckles darkly.

I place my hand on his, interlacing our fingers. "Do whatever you need to while you're healing. I bet when you're ready you'll let them go. And you'll come see us again. We can't wait."

Deakin shuts his eyes forcefully. Tears stream out. He stops breathing for a while, then finally lets out a big sigh. He raises his shoulders and looks at the ceiling.

I can tell it's a pressure release for him. And thank god. He's been through enough.

I stand up, move behind his armchair, and kneel down, hugging him.

He leans his head against mine. "I know you knew. And tried to stop it. You, all of you, kept telling me Jeremy was hurting me. I wouldn't listen. So finally I managed to get him out of my life, and—now I can't look any of you in the face because you think I should've done it sooner."

"Not at all," I say. "We felt like we failed *you*. Even Jon and Eric."

"Did they say that?"

"You can tell. It's there, beneath the callous jokes. How much they wanted to help."

"But what could they do?"

"You know what they're like," I say. "They're not about to open up or let you cry on their shoulder. But they would get super drunk and watch *Golden Girls* with you on repeat."

"That only goes so far."

"Farther than nothing."

We're silent again.

"I've missed your hugs," he says finally.

I kiss his bald spot. "Little brother."

"Not really."

"But as good as."

We rest like this a while longer, gripping onto one another with love.

Deakin jerks forward and turns to look at me. "Did I see Gabe with y'all at the fair?"

I stand up. "Yeah!"

"He's so cute."

"Isn't he, though?"

He gets on his knees on the chair and grips me by the shoulders. "How did the evening end?"

"It didn't."

He claps his hands. "When are you going to see him again?"

I scratch at my neck. "Probably just at work."

"What happened?"

"I … You know what? I'll tell you everything at brunch."

"Unfair." He's just teasing.

The gym rats have assembled by the front door, having fussed over us so much they've run out of ideas.

I bow politely at them as I pick up my bag. "Gentlemen," I say. And I turn to wink at Deakin, who presses his hands over his heart.

I leave so much lighter. I can see the glowing embers of our friendship's once-full flame.

I know we can get back there again.

11

After the Long Island iced tea hits me, I collect a six-pack of beers on the way home so I can keep the buzz going. It's not the best idea, but this weekend is draining me like no other.

When I open my apartment door, who do I see sitting in a pair of boxers on the stack of folded sheets that Gabe left on my couch, but me

"Aaah!" I drop the beers.

The cans crack open and fizz, spritzing the air. I just know my foyer is going to smell like old beer for the next month.

Jon and Eric peek from behind the living room doorway.

"Sorry," Eric says.

"We didn't mean to scare you," Jon says.

I walk forward and peer at my synthetic self. He's in standby, but his eyes are still eerily open, staring upwards.

I peer at the threads of fake veins in my android's corneas. "Do I really look like this?"

"You sure do," Jon says. "You ever send any nudes?"

"So, what? I was asking for this?"

"His appearance," Eric says. "It comes from cloud-owned images. They sold the data to us to make this android, uh, anatomically correct. Totally legal, all in the fine print."

I pull back the elastic of his pants and look at his crotch. "Jesus Christ."

It slaps my hand away and says, "What do you think you're doing?" in my voice.

I recoil. "It even acts like me! That's so much worse."

Jon reaches out to me. "How?"

"Because it's not just my likeness. It's … *me*, as best you could make."

Eric flicks Jon on the forehead. "See, that's what I said!" He looks at me. "Jon had me convinced it was less offensive because it was less of an abstraction."

Jon holds up a finger like he's about to protest. "I—Oh, it's all bad."

I scowl at Jon. "What were you thinking?"

"That it would make good content for a vlog about introducing new partners into your relationships." He ruffles the android's hair. "But Eric and I slept with a fair share of people before we met."

"Yeah," Eric says, "and we don't feel like we've had to give that up for the sake of monogamy."

Jon hooks an arm around Eric. "Our relationship outcompetes the notion of casual sex with others."

"How sweet," I say, on the way to mop up my beer spillage with paper towel. "You're trads. Who knew?"

"Real conservative, it turns out," Jon adds.

I return to the living room.

"And we learned that from you," Eric says. He gestures to the android. "Well, from *this*."

I sigh. "You're welcome."

"You don't seem that mad," Eric says.

I run my hands through the android's synthetic hair. Again it bats my hand away. "Well," I say, "it reminds me of the gym rats."

I tell them what happened at SF Fitness and that I looked up the men on escort services. That I'd wondered if they didn't have a right to act offended about being copied since they were the ones putting themselves out there—only to come home and get confronted by the very same principle, this time with a version of *me*.

"But since this is a case-by-case thing," I conclude, "and it *is* me after all, I can choose how to react. So just between us? I'm a little flattered."

Jon gasps. "You are?"

I shut my eyes tightly. "Just don't quote me on that at a pride parade or something, okay?"

Jon's pebble rings. "Sorry, I have to take this."

I throw my hands up in disbelief and look at Eric. "Is he really taking a call in the middle of his own reconciliation attempt?"

"You know Jon," Eric says.

"All too well, I think. He's gotta tone it down. I'm getting tired." It feels terrible to talk about him when he's not in the room. Don't know why. I'm sure he does it all the time.

Eric sighs. "I agree. By the way, he didn't choose you for sexual reasons."

"Whatever you need to tell yourself, buddy," I say.

"No, I mean—it's because you were safe to experiment with. But also so trusted that he didn't want to put your friendship at risk." He gestures to the doll. "This is about as close to you as he wanted to get, for fear of fucking things up between us all. Except he ended up making it … weirder."

"Wow," I say. "That's much more careful than you'd imagine him to be."

"He runs deeper than he pretends. Just don't tell him I said that."

Eric pulls me close and kisses me on the cheek. It's so affectionate, and he smells so good, that for a moment I'm sad that they didn't ask me, the *real* me, to join them in bed. But the moment will pass, and our friendship will persevere. And that's the point. Probably.

Jon comes back. He's off the pebble. "So what do we do with Cloan?"

"I think you'd better get it away from me," I say.

"Are you that disgusted by it?" Eric asks. "By us?"

I shake my head. "The opposite."

"Hah!" Jon kisses Cloan on the cheek and turns him off. "Then we'll take it to get dismantled. Lest you never leave the house again."

"Let me see if I didn't smash all those beers," I say.

"Fuck that," Eric says. "We brought whiskey and coke on the off chance this went well."

"Well here's to that, guys. Jon, get us takeaway from

wherever. Eric, turn on the TV and get some blankets. I need to turn this Sunday around."

12

Late Saturday. Gangnam Taqueria. Brunch with the boys.

Eric and Jon have coordinated in dark string vests, which must be in this season. Deakin is in a Hawaiian shirt, denim shorts, and flip-flops. He's trimmed himself a carefully waxed moustache. Trying out something new.

Jon has his pebble out, and he's swiping through potential matches for Deakin.

"Leave the poor guy alone," I say.

"Oh, let me have my fun," Jon says.

"Yeah," Eric says. "Now that we're off the market for good, we need vicarious excitement."

Does this mean marriage? Deakin and I, best men in matching pastel tuxes with little bow-ties? Fingers crossed.

"There are so many gorgeous daddies in this city," Deakin says.

Jon keeps swiping. "Totally. You could eat a new middle-aged dick for breakfast, lunch, and dinner in this city for the rest of your—"

Eric almost spits out a mouthful of rice. "That's one way of putting it."

A shadow falls over our table. I flinch as two hands slap down on my shoulders.

Jon nods at the figure behind me. "Gabe."

Deakin's eyes flare. "Mr Flores. We're just having brunch."

I shake a finger at Deakin. "Don't explain yourself to him."

"He's right," Gabe says. "You don't have to."

I turn to look up at his shadowy face beneath a floppy straw hat. "I got a new pebble," I say.

"I'll reimburse you," he says.

"No, I—I'm just wondering how you tracked me here this time."

"Margarita?" Eric holds up an empty tumbler.

I reach over and rest his hand back on the table. "Gabe was just leaving."

"No, he wasn't," Jon says. "He's our guest."

He scrapes a chair up beside me. "I'll leave if I'm not wanted, but I'd like to say my piece first."

"Guys," Deakin says to the boys, "let's go order another round at the bar."

Jon watches us and shakes his head. "They upgraded their systems since you were last here. You can just dictate your order into the … "

Eric puts a hand on his arm. Jon gets it. They head up to the bar together and talk to the serverbot.

"Didn't see you at work this week," Gabe murmurs in my direction.

"I, uh, decided to work from home."

"Charles told me. I stayed home too."

"And Charles told me *that*." I can't help but grin. "We're as immature as each other."

"You have a better excuse." He takes my hand in his. "Do you ever feel like something is going suspiciously well?"

"Whenever anything good happens."

"Well, that's what my date with you was like. It got me thinking about how I used to behave when I was younger. Before I came here or met Ben, even. I ensnared older men for my own entertainment. I thought it was funny how they went gaga over someone like me. A pretty shell."

"I'm familiar," I say.

"I thought to myself, 'That simply must be what Ioan is doing to you.' Nothing else made logical sense. It couldn't possibly be that you really liked me."

"Wow. Something must have bashed your confidence."

"For one," he says, "Ben cited my appearance as a reason for our relationship falling apart."

I lean back in shock. "After you were together twenty years?"

"There was more to it than that. There always is."

"I should hope so." I stroke my chin and look at the neon glow above us. "I wonder if I would even be attracted to a younger, skinnier version of you."

He smiles to himself. "Are you saying I'll totally lose my chance to date you if I lose weight?"

I look at him. "If I say I like your body the way it is, would you hold it against me?"

He laughs.

"I take it back only if you answer in the negative."

He squeezes my hand. His skin is just as soft as I remembered. Could I forgive him for freaking out over how pretty he thought I was, how lovely a time he was having with me? For thinking me capable of something I used to do *a lot?*

Hm, let me think. Yes.

The boys return to the table with a new margarita pitcher.

"The server from last time is gone!" Eric exclaims.

"Oh, yeah?" I say.

"He made it as an artist, apparently," Jon says.

"I should try and get his number," Eric says. "For networking."

Jon's shoulders slump. "I hope I didn't fuck that up for you."

Deakin pats Eric on the shoulder. "As long as we're alive, no opportunity is our last."

Eric stands tall again. "Cheers, Deakin. Ever the optimist."

They sit down and dispense fresh tumblers to each of us.

"That's a big pitcher," Gabe says. "Are we celebrating something?"

"My date this afternoon," Deakin says.

"Who did you pick in the end?" I ask.

He shows a holo of a chunky dude. Tanned, blue eyes, blond hair, big ginger beard. Boiler suit, hard hat, and boots.

Jon clutches his chest. "Love a scruffy factory worker."

I laugh. "How do you make everything sound like a porn description?"

Deakin spins the holo. "I took this on the assembly floor."

"At Nerve?" I ask.

"Yeah," he says. "We met IRL."

Once we all have a margarita before us, I raise my tumbler. "A toast to your date!"

"Not just that," Gabe says. "My divorce is finalized."

"Awesome!" Jon says.

"You must feel amazing," Eric says.

"How long were you trying to get divorced?" Deakin asks.

"Like, a year." Gabe holds up his hands. "My fault. I couldn't let go. But I actually signed everything last Sunday."

When he said he had an errand to run.

"And what convinced you to make the final push?" Jon asks.

Gabe looks at me. I blush.

Jon wipes chicken grease from his fingers. "So your marriage, like Ioan's gag reflex, is yesterday's news."

I press my palms together and take a deep breath, like, *Guys, can we not, just once?*

I feel Gabe looking at me. "Is that so?"

Deakin looks at Gabe with feigned confusion. "I thought you knew." He winks at me. It's not like him at all!

Eric eyes Jon up. "How do you know that?"

Jon sticks a stack of used napkins on his plate. "I'm tempted to make something up, but honestly, Ioan, you just told me when you were drunk one time for no reason."

"Sorry," I say to Gabe.

He winks. "You should be proud." He addresses the boys. "So, where to after this?"

Jon clasps his hands together. "Eric's working on some new pieces and wants to show me."

"Oh, yeah?" I say to Eric.

He tries to answer me, but Jon interrupts: "'The most intimately human art of the year.' 'Most promising emerging artist.' 'Mesmerizing, resonating, powerful!'"

Eric rubs his temples. "No one's even seen them yet."

"Wait," Deakin says. "Are these—"

"Yeah," Eric says. "The ones with the little versions of you guys walking around in them. My Microcosms of Joy series."

"We'll go too, then?" Gabe says to me.

I was kinda hoping we could hang out alone this afternoon, but I don't know how to refuse.

"You're not invited," Jon says. "You two should go hang out alone this afternoon."

Gabe salutes him. "Yes, sir."

"Sometimes it's good to have a friend who tells it like it is," I say.

Eric points at me. "*Always*."

"But we still have to get through these margaritas first," Jon says. "So, Deakin?"

"Hm?" Deakin says.

"Pictures, pictures!"

We look at more holos together, commenting on how good a fit this date looks for Deakin.

Our taste in men can be so different. Maybe it means there *is* someone for everyone.

And, hey, if you don't find him, you can always print the next best thing.

But that doesn't mean you should!

THE HEADPHONES OF DAMOCLES

IT'S FRIDAY EVENING AT THE AIRPORT'S BUSINESS lounge, where the executives luxuriate.

He has arrived far too early for his flight, to avoid catching a taxi with the manager. Had he cab-shared, he might never have made it to the airport, might have barrelled out of the taxi on the motorway to escape the manager's chat about, say, company regulations on printer paper usage.

The dining area fills with bald men in blue shirts who sit with terrible posture. Their laughter is cold and calculated. "What project are you on?" they ask one another. "Where do you live? How big is the company-provided apartment at your commuting location? How big is your house? Are you renting out any of its floors? For how much? What do you drive?"

After these questions, the chatter ceases. Why talk more? What else would they even say? They know how to treat one another now. They have all the information they need. This isn't conversation but data exchange. A status download as purely distilled as the beer in the chalices they clatter—though nowhere near as effervescent.

His wireless headphones mercifully muffle the sound of all this. Removing them is forbidden, but why would he ever take them off? How else would he listen to endless Muzak while answering emails, or hear co-workers when he calls to ask if they received his emails?

He didn't buy them until they became mandatory for all executives. He has that as an excuse, at least. Were he to change professions, he wouldn't have to wear the headphones, blue shirt, jeans, boots, or the backpack that came free with his laptop. Though he'd likely buy all this business paraphernalia anyway. So no one thought he was poor.

But he *is* different from them.

Like them, he gorges on the buttery croissants and sugary yogurts of the free continental breakfasts at the hotels and airport lounges of his various business trips. To stay trim, he goes on gruelling hikes with his superiors. On the morning walk to work, he bitches with other business folk about his co-workers' poor performance. At lunch, he compares his university degree to theirs again, having forgotten his ranking since last time. At the pub, he shares their frustrations about IT's poor handling of the latest Microsoft Outlook update. He smiles until he can't remember if he means it. And, whenever a spare moment arises, he initiates conversations about the chance of rainfall or restrictions on the use of PowerPoint colour schemes that aren't associated with the company's brand.

Can't he think of anything to talk about other than weather or shop? He doesn't even laugh and excuse it anymore. Better that he resists dissenting thought entirely.

He takes a beer from one of the fridges and sits down at a free spot.

It's one hour before his flight. Oh, what an imaginative person could do with that hour ...

He takes out his laptop and checks his email.

One new message from the manager: *Thanks for reminding me to approve the technical query regarding purchasing orders—but you forgot to formally sign off on it in the system. It's after five now. I can't issue a response to our vendors until the weekend is over. We could've fixed this together if you'd grabbed a taxi with me.*

Oh, no.

He slams the laptop shut, gets up, and retreats to the toilet.

Maybe they don't know yet. Maybe he can—

He tries to wrench off the headphones, to no avail.

The familiar alert plays through everyone's headphones: "Attention. Attention. One amongst your ranks has performed poorly this quarter."

The headphones drag him up off the toilet and out towards the middle of the business lounge.

"Let this be a lesson to you all!"

The headphones tighten like a vice. It feels like a mild headache at first, but soon his skull buckles excruciatingly under the pressure and breaks through the skin.

He lets out a final scream as the headphones turn his head to pulp, one earcup meeting the other through a mush of his skin, bone, brain, and blood.

Some glance over. But mostly they sip their beers and check the weather for the weekend's hike.

WHAT WOULD MARINA ABRAMOVIĆ DO?

I want to get old, really old so that nothing matters anymore. I want to understand and see clearly what is behind all this. I want to not want anymore. —Marina Abramović, *The Onion* (1995)

THE GALLERY DOORS OPEN, AND ABOUT FIFTY OF US rush in. It's a white room, about sixty square metres in size, at the Archivio D'Arte Contemporanea in New Naples. The year is 2075. *Rhythm 0.5* will soon begin.

A woman stands upstage. Short black hair, strong Slavic features, haunting eyes. Silent, unwavering, in a long black dress. Identical to Marina Abramović in her late twenties. We can tell because photos of Abramović's famous *Rhythm* performances, from the 1970s, decorate the walls. *Rhythm 5:* she lies unconscious in the middle of a burning wooden star, the Yugoslavian star of communism and the Satanic pentagram in one. *Rhythm 2:* she ingests two drugs, one for catatonic patients, another for schizophrenics. She sits in a chair with a glazed look in her eyes and a painful rictus on her face. *Rhythm 0:* naked, crying, holding up a mirror with *IO SONO LIBERO*—'I am free'—written on it in lipstick.

Prints are available in the gift shop.

As for us, we're mostly young hips in recyclable fashion. Dresses and suits of paper, cork, seaweed, compressed mushroom. Minimal jewellery, mostly coral. Half of us are reals, half proxies: robot avatars controlled from home with VR sets by people who couldn't attend on account of their schedule, disability, illness, or perhaps a desire to remain anonymous. Our apparent ages range from teens to forties, but of course the appearances of proxies rarely correlate with those of their operators.

Beside the woman standing upstage, there's a table with seventy-two objects on it, just as in *Rhythm 0*. There are objects for pleasure, like a feather, honey, olive oil, a rose, perfume. Others are for pain: needles, a knife, a razorblade, a pistol and bullet.

"This is where *Rhythm 0* took place, right?" asks a dreadlocked guy to his friend in a vegan leather waistcoat.

"No, that was Studio Morra," the friend says. In 1974 or '75, according to different sources. "But the gallery got obliterated, along with the rest of Old Naples, during the Third World War." He approaches the Marina clone. "Is that *her?*"

"How could it be?" asks his date, a fem-presenting individual in a white cotton tunic. They read from a placard on the wall. "It explains here."

Marina Abramović lived lucidly to the age of 103.

"Like her grandmother," Waistcoat Guy says. "I'm not surprised."

We read on.

Prior to her death, she had her consciousness preserved.

"*That* surprises me," Cotton Tunic says.

The consciousness usually resides in this robot host—though it is not present today.

Another of us, a woman with multiple coral eyebrow piercings, admires the robot. "I take it Abramović's e-ghost commissioned this piece?"

E-ghost is the non-PC but most common term for the agglomeration of diaries, memoirs, video clips, audio recordings, and fMRI data into a 'living' record of, in this case, Marina Abramović.

More murmurs pass through our group.

"Would she really choose this?" we ask. "Why?"

"It's not the first gallery curation by an e-ghost," someone replies.

Others run with the idea. "Damien Hirst put himself in a plastic pill inside a rotting cow's head. It created this really interesting semiotic discourse between the decaying flesh and the infinite capsule of consciousness within it. He gave some really cool interviews about it."

"You know that big pink mechanical balloon dog outside the San Francisco MOMA? That's Jeff Koons. He rears up on his hind legs and wags his tail to show love for passersby."

"You *have* to check out Tehching Hsieh's consciousness in the Guggenheim. It's locked in this black box and a sign in front of it reads, 'Planning art. Will never make it'."

"I took in some of Matthew Barney's latest VR experiences. He's enjoying the additional mass and power of artificial muscles. He has a set of e-ghosts inhabiting various modified Barney-esque robots, from the androgynous to the downright alien. Quite the trip!"

"And you *must* have heard about Ai Weiwei. He had his e-ghost and ashes stored in a satellite that's locked in geostationary orbit. It's in the shape of a big metal hand giving the middle finger, forever pointed at China."

"They're all wonderful pieces."

"Hardly. I feel cheated. It completely invalidates the work they did in life, which always had an implied context of their ultimate passing."

"Oh, no, I'm in full support of it. It's giving birth to whole new genres and movements!"

"It's a travesty and an embarrassment. What happened to their principles?"

"Yeah. Look at Abramović. She used to enlist other artists to perform her work. Why not just keep doing that?"

A woman with a necklace of cardboard beads kneels and examines the Abramović robot's hands. "Inauthentic. There are none of the scars and wrinkles accrued through her life and performances."

"On her hands," we continue, "where she stabbed them during *Rhythm 10*."

"From smashing glass during *Warm/Cold*."

"From whipping her back during *Lips of Thomas*."

"Pentagrams carved into her stomach for various pieces."

"The marks left by rose thorns and razor blades from *Rhythm 0*."

"What the hell is she up to?"

As if Abramović herself is listening, a projection appears on the wall. It reads as follows:

Performance.
Robot is the object.
Use anything from the table on it.
Duration: 6 hours.

We murmur once again. The instructions are similar to those of *Rhythm 0*—except in that performance, Abramović herself was the object.

We gingerly approach the robot, starting off gentle at first. A woman with an Abramović-esque braid of black hair marvels at an antique Polaroid camera at the end of the table. She points it at the audience and clicks just to see if it works. We delight in the developing photo that extrudes from this ancient device.

A woman in a wide-brimmed hat tickles the robot's face with the feather. When the robot twitches in reaction, the woman flinches. She leans in again, feeling the heat off the robot's skin. It is, if not alive, made to appear as real as possible.

A slim woman takes the robot's hand in her chainmail gloves, squeezing it and feeling the springiness of its fake muscles. She pulls a finger towards her and kisses it, giggling. The robot neither assists nor resists. When she lets go, the hand remains with the index finger outstretched, the other fingers gently curling.

We prod at her. We take the rose by its flower and poke the robot's side with the stem. We take the mirror and show the robot to itself. We put the book, Dostoyevsky's *The Idiot*, in its hands. We open it at a random page to see if the robot will read. We receive nothing but a blank stare in return.

Some hours in, a plain-looking man in an expensive black suit struggles to pick up the knife. It must be a proxy handled by an inexperienced user.

We call to him. "Why not try picking up something safer, just to practise? How about that pen over there?"

"No." He's determined. He uneasily grips the knife in two hands and staggers towards the robot.

We grab at his forearms. More of us join in and clutch at him. But his proxy's mechanics are too strong. He drags us towards the robot.

When we make a last attempt to tackle him, he slips, falls, and slices down the robot's front.

We gasp.

The robot winces, sighs and opens its eyes again. An oval rip runs between its breasts, the revealed skin flushing pink, blood dripping from a shallow cut across its sternum.

We disperse and stare at the robot.

"So real," says a bald man with wooden gauges in his ears. He assertively snatches the razor blade, cuts across the robot's index finger, and wipes it across his tongue. "Warm. Metallic. Like blood."

A pulse of disgust travels through us. We take a step back.

The robot winces again, gritting its teeth. Tears water its eyes.

A linen-dressed woman grabs the robot's head and licks its tears. "Salty."

"As human as possible," says a woman wearing a tie-dyed hair scarf. "As passive and prepared to 'die' for art as Marina once was."

"Prove it," says a man in a black boiler suit.

"No!" some of us shout back.

The audience's barbarism towards Abramović, during her twentieth-century performance of *Rhythm 0,* was legendary. They tore her clothes, stuck her with thorns, cut her neck, drank her blood, and forced her to point a loaded gun to her head: an apparent inevitability when everything is permissible and nothing is forbidden. Proof that civilization is a thin veneer, a farce. But less well-known is that there were warring factions that day: a team that wanted to hurt her and another that protected her.

The same is true now, a century later. Some take the mirror and book from the robot. Some tug at its torn clothes to preserve its dignity. A man bats the mirror out of the protectors' hands, shattering it. He and others grab the shards and hold them around the robot's neck to see if it will react. A short, snub-nosed man pours olive oil through its hair. A nervous, hunched-over woman takes a dishtowel off the table and wrings the oil back out. In homage to Abramović's original performance, a tall man pulls thorns off the rose stem and sticks them into the robot's bare chest. A woman in a beige muumuu takes ice from a glass and numbs the thorn wounds.

The proxies go further than the reals: a new outcome, but hardly surprising. Certainly not to the elderly, though presumably they are not in attendance. What could they learn from such a performance? Now we have absolute surveillance—everything is seen and recorded all the time—but the elderly remember a time before this. Back then, you didn't need to attend a gallery to experience maximal anonymity and minimal accountability. You lived your life in it. You saw GamerGate, iCloud leaks, Twitter dogpiling. Who, with any sense, would want to go back?

The performance is nearly over. We carry the now-naked robot, posed like Christ, around the room. When the robot slumps to the floor, pratfalling on its face, some of us laugh.

The woman with the Polaroid camera gasps, dropping it in shock. The rest of us catch on.

Six hours have now passed. To those remaining, the hours felt like minutes. To those who've already left, the time felt much longer.

A woman in a black catsuit kneels by the body. She presses her fingers to the robot's wrist and holds her cheek over its mouth. No pulse or breath.

"Dead," she says.

This word, the first in the post-*Rhythm 0.5* world, startles us.

"I don't get it," says a woman in a green silk kimono. "At the end of *Rhythm 0*, Abramović walked towards the audience and they ran away."

A video of Abramović, talking about her original performance, was playing on a loop in the foyer where we waited earlier.

We discuss further. "Yeah, but this is a robot."

"So when the performance concludes, she should send her e-ghost back into it. That would be the post-death equivalent of 'returning to herself'."

"Maybe. But what is there to learn in precisely recreating a century-old piece of art?"

"That's what I came here to find out. But you're going to recreate it, why wouldn't you do so as authentically as possible?"

A loud buzz. Abramović appears as a projection on the wall. She looks to be in her seventies. She wears a purple long-sleeved dress, and her black hair slinks over one shoulder.

"This woman on floor," she begins in her thick Slavic accent, "she was my great-great-granddaughter."

We look at one another with dread.

Abramović laughs. "Of course she isn't! I have so much respect for mothers, but I only ever wanted to be an artist, to use my one energy in this life for creativity, not children. No, this is not my great-great-granddaughter. But it is a relative in one sense. This is a clone."

We frown, looking to one another for answers or reassurance.

"Not made to last." Abramović taps her skull. "Terminated by charge in the brain at the end of performance. But there exist two other clones." She smiles again, revelling, as she always did, in dark humour. "No! This is not a clone, and there are no clones of me. I would not allow it. This is a robot avatar, just like it says on the wall."

We reach out to one another with comforting hands, reassuring ourselves during these confusing announcements.

"*But,*" Abramović says, "my consciousness was in it the whole six hours." She shrugs. "But there are copies of me in the cloud also." She laughs again. "No, there aren't! This is just robot. Nothing human inside. I did not copy my consciousness after death. What you see now is a video that I made for my will when I was alive. This performance was the last request I ever made."

We are crying. We take in rapid, panicked breaths.

"Perhaps this is not true either."

We are rapt, hypnotized into attention. It's clear we will have to wait until Abramović is done talking before reacting any further. Who knows how many tricks she still has left for us?

Abramović splits in two like a dividing cell. One wears a red dress, the other blue. The images turn, look at one another and begin to argue.

Red Marina: "I love technology ever since my mother got one of the first washing machines in Belgrade. I let other artists make video games of *The Artist is Present* and of the Abramović Method, my meditative exercises. I became interested in how brainwaves change with nonverbal communication and meditation. Before absolute surveillance, I let others make videos of my performances." She pouts. "It's not so good as attending in person—in fact it may change the context entirely—but it's better than nothing. Same goes for my proxies that attend today. Same for my e-ghost, talking to you now."

Blue Marina: "You say I love technology? Soon after my mother got that washing machine, I trapped my arm in it. What do you think I thought of it then?" She turns to address the crowd. "I refused to take antidepressants because I was against medical intervention. When I felt sick, I would try to reconnect with my body. How could I make myself well again as an e-ghost?" She shakes her head. "I have no need to prevent my death. The end of my life is not the end of everything. Good ideas, for example, have many lives. The good ideas of my performances, my institute and teachings. I leave these behind. You need energy dialogue between the performer and audience. As for this?" She gestures to the robot slumped on the floor. "Destroy it, make another, who cares? It is wires, silicone, fake blood. Without a body, energy dialogue is not possible. So this is not an Abramović performance."

Red Marina tuts at her. "It is not just bodies that contain the energy for dialogue." She sighs deeply and closes her eyes. "I feel energetic resonances from ancient magical objects. Crystals and medicine boxes. If energy can transcend time, so can the human body. The body's energy, which creates the dialogue, is the same energy that once went nowhere when we died." She opens her eyes again. "But it is *this same energy* that is captured in the record of my consciousness, speaking to you now."

Blue Marina is aggravated. "Nonsense! Without the threat of death, my art has no meaning. I thought about death every single day. I lived my whole life with the idea that one day I will die. To live on would make a waste of my life's work. My art may be immaterial but *I*, Marina Abramović, am not. We must all surrender to change. No one is bigger than death itself."

"Until now!" Red Marina says with an emphatically raised finger. "I always say artists cannot suicide themselves. They must stay alive and share their gift of creativity with the world. It was my duty as an artist to preserve myself like this. Yes, I thought about death every single day. And it terrified me! But in my work, I accessed a state of mind outside of this fear. It is this state in which I now live, all the time. Artists must experiment, go into new territory. Face the unknown. Be like Columbus. He risked falling off Earth's edge to discover America. Finally I have transcended the fear of death. I dedicated my life to stepping outside of my limitations, and now I truly have. And I encourage practice of downloaded consciousness wherever possible. Because a shaman once told me—and I believed him—that my purpose was to help others transcend pain."

"Through *art!*" Blue Marina shakes her head vehemently. "And art is *life!*"

"Yes, and *this* is life, so *this* is art!"

"No, not so simple. Because art must be for *everybody*. Not all can have an afterlife through preserved consciousness!"

We remain stunned into silence.

The Marinas recombine into a singular self. "Truth is," Purple Marina says in a much calmer tone, "there is no Marina." She gestures to herself. "*This* is not Marina. It is a deepfake, from videos and audio recordings taken from the life of Marina

Abramović. She never preserved her consciousness, and in no form, living or dead, was she involved in this work. Why would she create a work of art that relied on deception when she was always looking for truth?" She smiles. "Marina Abramović once said that layers of meaning can give a long life to art. Over time, society takes from art what it needs. So perhaps what she really wanted to give you was not the truth but the most possible layers, which she can only achieve with ambiguity. Then again, if that was true, would she tell you?"

Our eyes have glazed over with disillusionment. Whatever else this projection has to say, we will not leave the gallery with easy answers.

"I have just one thing left to say." She takes a deep breath. "In former Yugoslavia, a boy asks his mother, 'Will there be a World War Three?' Mother replies, 'Never. But the Communist Party's struggle for peace will continue until there is nothing but rubble left across planet.'"

She shrugs, says, "I never learned how to tell jokes!" and the transmission ends.

Of course Warhol said everyone will be famous for fifteen minutes, but I think the new model of that mantra is that in the future—which is now—everyone will be famous all the time. —Bruce Wagner

1

JC SAT AT HIS PLAIN WHITE WRITING DESK IN THE centre of his otherwise empty optimo, trying to access an inner stillness his lifestyle had all but obliterated.

Would he look back at this as the best time of the day? Be proud that he attempted to write music even if nothing came of it?

Maybe not. He was less convinced with each day that this process had any value. It was his only non-monetizable activity.

If not for the headshots he signed at the same time, he would've slept in longer to preserve his energy for the parts of his day that actually counted for something. A rapid conveyor belt stuck an inkpad and then a fresh headshot beneath his tapping finger. He tapped to an imagined beat, trying to distract his conscious mind in order to let ideas out. He could think of music only at the speed he was tapping, so he compromised with the machines by selecting the fastest acceptable BPM for cybertrap, his genre of choice. Eighty beats per minute equalled forty signed headshots per minute.

The inked headshots headed further down the table as they were dried by air jets. Mechanical arms slipped them into individual envelopes, and a laser burned addresses onto those, passing them further down the production line towards the wall. A launcher fired the envelopes outside, where mail drones caught them and delivered them to paying subscribers. These, the last ever headshots marked with JC's fingertips, would fetch a mint. By dusk, the fingers wouldn't be his anymore.

Got to keep tapping.

Tap tap tap. Zap.

"Ow!"

He unzipped the electrified sportmesh in which he had slept and sloughed it onto the floor. The suit melted fat and built muscle while he slept, keeping him trim and ripped. Subscribers loved that but never wanted to see him exercise.

Now he sat in his Calvin Klein–provided boxers, staring at blank sheet music, frighteningly bored. His whole body urged him to get up from the dull-ass table and away from this fruitless, non-productive activity.

But if I don't produce more songs, won't my fans go away?

Has to be about the joy of creating music, otherwise it won't be authentic. And if it isn't, the fans will go away.

He had begun with sincere intention but could no longer finish anything without trying to predict how it would fare in its market. He couldn't move a muscle without feeling manipulative. Had he ever been creative, or only handsome? Could anyone answer that for him?

"Boy in a box," he sang to himself.

It was an idea he'd been working on, a song based on his experience here, isolated in the optimo, the single-roomed habitat that morphed into every type of facility he could possibly need. Every resource was automatically delivered to various ports in the wall, all kinds of visitors sent to shapeshifting robots known as proxies. The proxies, when not in use, stood as a grey faceless army of ten along the optimo's southern wall, beneath big beams of sunlight that shot in from high windows. The optimo was a basketball court–sized playground of minimal effort and maximal efficiency.

This was the life he'd chosen. Why bother writing a song about how lonely it was sometimes?

'Precious little butterfly pinned in a box for its beauty?' Give me a break. You wrapped your greedy little proboscis around the pin and rammed it into your own thorax. For the clout.

The market would let a pretty boy like him make bank off a self-pitying song. Teen girls would feel for him. As for those who had lost the genetic lottery or arrived too late at the various competitions for which JC topped the leaderboard? They'd feel reassured that even *he*, paragon of success, struggled sometimes.

A round mirror floated up from his desk. It would thankfully rescue him from the paralysis of his mind. Shame, though, that he had not yet found a solution to it.

A blue holo floated before the mirror, counting down until JC was live once again: *10, 9, 8 …*

JC gritted his teeth and screamed through the numbers. When the countdown reached one, he put on his prescription-free Hugo Boss glasses—a nice touch of manufactured imperfection—before the mirror turned on.

A ring light blasted him. It was time again.

He grinned at the mirror. "What's up, my lil' chestnuts? JC, back at you again with another panopt-*iconic* day!"

Why 'chestnuts'? He'd forgotten. He'd made a throwaway comment years before about how he thought the word was funny. Except he didn't. It had been near the end of the day, and he was running out of chat, babbling deliriously—as he was wont to do with his rigorous schedule.

The optimo filled with generic boppy music, autogenerated by TuneMachine's algorithms. They paid JC to play it.

"It's a wonderful, uh, Thursday? Yeah, Thursday, haha!" He knew that and hated pretending he didn't. "Boy, do we have yet another action-packed day for you." He made finger guns and pointed at the mirror. "Before we get going, quick shout-out yet again to our friends at Apple, Anastasia Beverly Hills, Neewer, Bose, Skype, and Leica for providing me with this one-of-a-kind iMirror. A class act from all of those companies. Check them out!"

The iMirror hovered from one side of his face to another, and pinhole cameras layered beneath the glass allowed 3D projections of him to reach the homes of all his subscribers. Mics around the rim recorded his speech. Holos, like petals in a rainbow of colours, flicked out around the mirror's edge as donations and comments flooded in.

The writing desk and chair sank back into the floor. A six-foot-wide panel in the floor flipped over, revealing blue shower tiles. Three glass walls shot up around them. The fourth wall that appeared was thick and metal, with a showerhead and cord, a shampoo and body wash dispenser, and a TV monitor mounted behind waterproof glass.

JC took off his prescription-free glasses and put in his prescription-free contacts by iWear. "We start off the day, as always, with the JC drama power shower hour!"

He took off his boxers. The iMirror's PG filter pixelated his genitals. The adult part of the day was kept separate. Easier that way. Anyone who wanted to see the goods would get a chance later.

A shower wall slid down to let him in. The iMirror remained outside, floating in position.

Scarab-like robots crawled out of the drain and up his legs. Some shaved him, some scraped the sweat off his skin. Plastic bubbles inflated on their tops. They looked like mechanical ticks as they sucked up their products, filling their bags with his hair and fluids.

The shower ran at 44.2 degrees Celsius, JC's favourite temperature. As water filled the shower base, the bags fell off the bots. A sifter lifted them out the top of the shower and flicked them into a hollow in the floor. Off they went to subscribers.

JC pressed on the dispensers for shampoo and body wash while looking into the mirror. "Gratefully provided by TRESemmé," he said, winking. He bit his lip. "I wish you were all in here with me."

A series of heart holos—and vomit emojis from trolls—floated up around the iMirror.

"Okay! Let's talk about the latest from our community!"

The TV monitor showed him a stream of subscriber comments and influencer 'news':

TOP THREE ITEMS THIS HOUR!

1. *Fans educate EliDreamsOfYou on his kinkshaming error! Vid surfaces where he mocks 'badly written' fanfiction of him hooking up with FukBoiKyle.*
2. *BanjeeCarla arrested for cultural appropriation! She used an Instagram filter with an improper darkness setting.*
3. *Heartwarming! PeachesDeliria ruptures the pool on her mansion's roof during a jet skiing incident, flooding the upper three floors and startling her Pomeranians (Victory, Sparkle, and Ingrid)—but fans gather the funds for repairs <3*

Up the screen's right side was the leaderboard:

1. *FrancescaFlores: 0.55BN*
2. *BradBeatz: 0.51BN*
3. *OneAndOnlyJC: 0.5BN*
4. *SavageHouse: 0.5BN*
5. *CamGirlCat: 0.5BN*

The board updated every half-second. JC's grinning face flickered between positions two and five as subscriber counts fluctuated. Francesca never got knocked off her top place.

He shook his head. He had to stay present if he wanted to keep his numbers up.

"Okay, let's see what people are saying about me today!"

He responded to the latest articles about him, a constant onslaught of attempts to get him cancelled. It was inevitable for an influencer of his size. Only the top one per cent of this content reached him, based on its 'engagement potential', a marketing yardstick JC didn't understand.

First it was the latest batch of deepfakes: JC in blackface, JC abusing animals, JC playing golf or some other old-man sport with controversial political commentators and greedy CEOs. These got the standard dismissal. He invited anyone to run a standard authenticity check on them. The worst accusation of all he saved until last: that he had failed to disclose whether the lash lightener he'd applied last Tuesday was sponsored.

"Chestnuts, for the last time! *Every* product I use is as sponsored as I believe in it—which is to say, one hundred and ten per cent! Homeboy loves the hustle. Let's move on to some fan questions."

I'm having a bad mental health day, LonelyDaisy475 said. *JC I know you've had struggles. Any advice?*

"Hey, Daisy," JC said. "Sorry to hear it. I'll have plenty of advice for you if you tune in on Wednesdays at seven for my Keep it Real Hour livecast. That's when s*** gets vulnerable. Hope you can make it!"

AngelKaterina835: JC, you said something yesterday that made me feel marginalized.

AngelKaterina835 is typing …

"Sorry to hear that, Kat. I would never deliberately target or make fun of marginalized people. There's a slight delay in my livestream so we can edit that kind of stuff out in real time. Follow the instructions on my site to inform adminbots of what I said. They'll beep it out in future. I'm glad they do! Clearly I still have a lot to learn. Thanks for understanding and for staying a follower!"

Who are you gonna vote for? Robert0045763 asked.

"Hey, Bob, thanks for your question! But you know we keep s*** apolitical chez JC."

He closed his eyes and sang a few bars of 'Digital Cupcake' by ChouChouFloz, a bit of organic-seeming advertising. Her people had surely paid for it without her knowledge. He and ChouChou had disliked one another ever since they'd both used the same pre-recorded sample—which came with the basic package of TrapWritr software—in their hit songs the year before. But a contract was a contract.

JC lathered his body and sighed with suggestive satisfaction. Once he'd washed all the soap away, the shower shut itself off. A series of apertures, each about a finger's width, opened up and drained the shower water into vacuum tubes. Subscribers would have their tube that same afternoon. Near-invisible wires kept the water warm, making subscribers think it was even fresher than it was. JC was so thankful for this system. It enhanced customer satisfaction—and hence revenue—when they received water as warm as their memory of it dripping off his body.

The shower slinked back into the floor. When JC stepped off the panel, the tiles flipped back over.

A bathrobe with the JC logo embroidered on it—the C leaning casually against the J—descended from the ceiling on a metal hook. JC slipped his arms into it and tied it around him.

"Next up is one of my most requested segments. My morning skin and haircare routine."

A panel slid out of the optimo's rear wall, revealing a sink and cabinet. This sped on rollers over to JC and lined up with magnetic plumbing connections that opened on the floor.

"It's how we start every day—but stay tuned, because you *know* ya boy loves to mix it up with the new products!"

So many companies were desperate to sponsor him. It was a unique skill to rotate all these products into a morning routine while seeming passionate about all of them, convincing millions of their necessity.

Morning routine playlist loading appeared above the iMirror. Predetermined songs from contemporary cybertrap artist-sponsors, started playing.

"First we'll get my hair in shape."

The cabinet burst open. A collection of silvery spheres buzzed out and fussed around JC's head. Their internal razors trimmed his hair into a crew cut. This was the most popular style at the moment, with two deep shaves along the left side of his head. Drones sucked in his remaining hair, bleached it, then dyed it blue, then sponged it to give the colour a messy, washed-out, hand-dyed appearance. JC thought a warmer colour would better complement his brown eyes. But it had been so long since he'd done anything but let the market speak for him, adapting his appearance to the most conventional and popular standards of beauty, inevitably marginalizing those who did not share the tastes of the masses. Fine by him. They had way less cash money.

"Dyson gave me these awesome drones!" He shouted to overcome the noise of their hair drying function, and narrated as they produced miniature GHD brushes, ceramic plates by Sephora, and squirts of matte pomade by Njord.

He knelt to the cabinet and took out a metal canister. "Texturizing hair spray by Toni&Guy. Totally essential." He spritzed it on his hair. "I don't actually know what it does, but I *do* use it every day!"

Hearts fluttered around the mirror in approval. He responded by dancing along to the cybertrap in an affectedly silly manner.

A Colgate brushbot cleaned his teeth while drones assisted him with a skincare routine. Multivitamin serum by someone, crème cleanser by someone else, moisturizer by so-and-so, and 'nude'-coloured foundation "to neutralize facial colour aberrations," JC said, as Morphe brushes applied it to his face. Guerlain had requested this explanation, though he hadn't a clue what it meant.

Brow gel, lash curler, mascara. Pigmentation dotted on with laser stencils to provide false freckles. A metal sphere flew before his lips and painted them with a strip of lip gloss, a sexually suggestive touch that played well with his gay audience.

He took a bottle out the cabinet: UV-protective, antibacterial tattoo aftercare spray by Givenchy. All but two of his tattoos had healed months ago, and he never exposed himself to sunlight because he never left his optimo.

He sprayed and rubbed his arms and torso, coating the many symbols gifted to him by fans and corporations. Some were jokey. A hotdog and bun, couples' names in hearts, the legendary poop emoji. Nothing was off-limits. He'd been surprised that no one attempted a swastika until he learned that bots were forbidden from etching them. He'd pretended to be amused by the wealth of dick doodles on his lower back—but once their contractual year had expired, he was happy that Chevrolet covered them with their big bold logo.

His fingers ran across the religious ghetto—a name he kept to himself—from his left buttock to his ribs. There was a cross, a Star of David, the Scientology 'S' through two triangles, and many other symbols that competed for attention from ass cheek to armpit, sized by square inch in proportion to each religion's donation. Not all members of these institutions approved of such symbols. But all it took was a single unscrupulous person in their community—or outside of it, looking to seed discord. You could probably trace it back to who and why with bank statements or whatever, should anyone ever ask.

The spray made his six-pack glisten as if with post-coital sweat. More donations rolled in.

JC grinned. If they liked that, they'd love later.

2

A clothing pod emerged from the floor, hatching like an egg. JC wanted to keep his muscles exposed, but he had to wear something by Hollister today. He chose a grey pyjama combo from his JC x Hollister crossover line, with the JC logo on both. He kept the hoodie open and wore the shorts loosely. A homeostatic probe buried in his hypothalamus adjusted the room temperature to complement his clothing choice.

It was mostly kids who'd tune in for the next part, but they enjoyed it when JC was a goofy slacker who wore pyjamas all day. He looked like every video game and anime hero rolled into one. Besides, it was a good idea to get those of them who were starting to thirst for their sexual preferences, or those who one day would, to have JC's semi-naked body in their little minds. It was like spreading seeds and creating budding little revenue sources that would one day flower so beautifully.

The clothing pod retreated and the sink scurried back into the wall. A gaming chair waltzed over.

JC took the controller off the seat and flopped down in the chair. The projection of *YeahBuilders* enveloped him.

He used to play first-person shooters for fun. Later on, he played them competitively. But he couldn't compete on the global stage, rise up the rankings, earn money. So he gave up those games and switched to *YeahBuilders*. He did enjoy it somewhat. After his first-person failures, it was nice to engage in a gaming style in which progress and success were unclear.

He played for an audience that rewarded silliness. It did feel childish sometimes, but it was the best match of his competence with what kids enjoyed watching. Though his company during these sessions could use some work.

Three proxies emerged from the wall, the LED screens on their surfaces switching on and revealing Toastfiend, Butterboy, and FlowerBro, virtual buddies selected algorithmically based on their subscriber count. None had as many as JC did overall, but they held a minimum of fifteen mil more than him within the gaming community. This made a great prospective collab. It would strengthen JC's gaming influence and perhaps help these basement-dwelling losers diversify and secure more healthcare or clothing sponsorships. Or maybe not. JC was the second-prettiest boy in all the land, and by gaming next to these dumpy betas, he only showed that off more.

Why should I feel bad for thinking this? It's just as soulless a manoeuvre on their part.

MicroLEDs displayed their full bodies and facial features across the proxies' skins, like flexible televisions. Thousands of micropistons beneath their surfaces shaped the bodies into the relative size and shape of the influencers they represented. Hair extensions grew from pores in their heads. JC didn't require this level of accuracy, but it made a nicer image for his viewers.

He stood up and high-fived each of them. This geolocated his proxy duplicates in the optimos of these gamers. His proxies would now follow his shape and movements as registered in real time by the iMirror.

Gaming chairs wheeled out of the wall for the buddies. They sat down, and the game began.

JC grinned and guided his chubby cartoon avatar in

cyberspace. The four of them ascended a mountain with pickaxes, ready to ravage it for supplies. They worked together to build a base with defences.

Their overly emphatic and drawn-out way of speaking set his teeth on edge. They all seemed to have the locationless American accent of a kid's show presenter. Their laughter and screams were unnatural, and their swears never broached PG-13: "What the frick? Dang it! Crap, dude!"

Together they'd devised a new collection of off-the-cuff jokes, laughed at the mistakes they made, and tried to have fun with it. Their audiences responded positively: more fluttering heart holos.

They loved it when JC affected being forgetful and quirky. He'd first picked up on this when, during a cake-making demonstration, he'd accidentally squirted himself with buttercream and watched the likes, donations, and new subscribers pour in. Thereafter he became tempted to manufacture a heightened frequency of silliness to enhance the positive response. How could he achieve that without the audience noticing its falseness? And how could he remain relaxed and natural enough to let genuine silliness out? Better to be fake quirky and fool those who couldn't tell. Those whose intelligence this insulted were, as the metrics demonstrated, far fewer in number.

The team's speech was a constant barrage of empty in-jokes and the weird ways they referred to their own fans. Toastheads. Butterdudes. What did the third guy say? Was it 'Seeds'? It dawned on JC how irritating his own nomenclature must sound to his detractors. He was becoming a detractor himself.

He sent a mental ping to his subdermal opioid autodoser. It upped the flow of sedatives through his system, stemmed his rage, and chemically reintroduced him to the lovable dopiness of which his temporary alertness had robbed him. Alcohol was the drug of choice for his fellow gamers. They were always doing drunk charity marathon streams and inventing drinking games for everything from *Let's Dance* to *Virtual Chess*.

He followed their lead, keeping his speech clean, becoming hyperbolic, and pretending everything in the game blew him away. The team's collective hysteria crescendoed until they were all at a ten, all the time, faces red and spent, vocal cords hoarse. He took his *YeahBuilders* character to the wrong side of the mountain and made a house out of mud, an inferior material in a place with a high risk of soil erosion. The others guffawed at his apparent uselessness.

An hour in, a buzzer frightened him, and the game shut down. His chair pulled out from under him, dropping him on the floor as it wheeled back into the wall. The chairs of his co-players similarly slid away. The proxies ragdolled onto the floor, their surfaces flat and grey once again. They walked like zombies back to the wall and lined up at their charging stations.

A tabletop shot out from the wall over JC's head. He crab-walked out from under it and stood up. A stoolbot whisked in behind him, buckling his knees so he sat down.

Drones, barely visible through the optimo's milky wall, delivered takeout to a chute outside. A set of silver containers slid in through a hatch and across the tabletop.

He pried them open. Dumplings, rice, noodles, stir-fry, battered chicken, and more.

"Sweet! Today's sponsor is Panda Express."

JC's mukbang community was fifty million strong. Lunch was not only free; it paid for itself in dividends.

He chatted to the community about their favourite food. The iMirror took polls on what fans wanted to see him eat next. It was an easy chat that required few filters, though for safety he still streamed with a minute's delay to screen anything egregious he might accidentally say. Otherwise he simply named the dish he was about to eat then ate as much of it as he could, as slowly as possible, while talking about how good it tasted. The iMirror swooped in close, its mic adjusted for optimal ASMR sound.

Some subscribers had new drama since the morning to discuss with him, but an automod advised them to save their questions for tomorrow's shower.

When the time came for him to wash down his broccoli beef, a condensate-laden bottle of Gatorade rolled across the table and into his open hand.

"Blue, my favourite flavour!"

The tastes did not go well together.

He stood up just before the hour was over. The stool wheeled away and the table tipped up, while the wall slid up and dropped the empty containers into a trash receptacle below.

The mirror would tell JC his schedule if he needed to know, but it was bad form to ask while he was live. It made subscribers feel less special. That said, the dizzying efficiency with which he lived his life was nearly impossible to maintain. He sometimes relied, like he did now, on the optimo's emerging machinery as a cue.

A long slit formed across the room, and a tennis net emerged. It rose high on long white metal stalks. A light in the ceiling projected a red circle on the floor. JC stood to one side as a badminton racket and plastic shuttlecocks fell there from the ceiling and into a similar circle on the net's other side.

A proxy walked from the wall and compressed itself to a child's size. The child walked over and picked up the racket. Brown curtains of hair emerged from its scalp. The proxy rounded, taking on the shape of red dungarees and a yellow sweater.

"Right, little man!" JC said. "It's time for our match!"

"It's Dawson."

"I knew that, Dawson. I just thought I might try 'little man'. But what would you prefer that I call you?"

The kid looked to the floor, bashful. "Whatever you want, JC!"

They played three games together, acting silly and laughing the whole time. JC won the middle game. He let the kid win overall but claimed he'd played his best.

JC winked at Dawson. "So you'll tell the other kids in the hospital today that you were good enough to beat JC?"

The kid looked down. "Well, only as this avatar."

JC ruffled the bot's synthetic hair. "Sure, but games like this are as much about mental strength. It takes real conviction and determination to command a robot into victory like you did." He knelt before the proxy. "And once you're out of that full-body cast, you'll beat me in person!"

The kid laughed. "Thanks, JC. You're my hero!"

"Nah, little man. You're mine."

His hand sank into the bot's memory foam head. Micropistons and pressure sensors conveyed this gesture to the real-life, hospitalized Dawson.

The court slid away, and the proxy slumped inactively to the floor. Magnets drew it back to its charger in the wall.

The iMirror displayed in red text: *18+ filter now activated.*

3

The use of an adult content filter was inherently imperfect. The rigid schedule of JC's morning and afternoon made the transition from one audience to the next quite jarring. If he swore at his family-friendly audience, it got dubbed over with a weaker word. But it was embarrassing when he accidentally watered down his language for his adult-only audience, who paid in part for him to talk dirty.

A freshly made bed emerged from the floor, and a proxy stepped away from the wall, morphing into a voluptuous red-haired woman in black lingerie.

She walked towards the bed, and JC met her there. He ran his hands through her hair and read two numbers on her left temple: *W: 50M, I: 10M.* Fifty million watching, ten million inhabiting the proxy.

"Only ten mil today, huh?" JC said.

The number crept down to 9.8.

"I-I didn't mean to offend anyone! I'm honoured by *anyone* who shows up. And I guess it is just a random Thursday—wait! It's the last Thursday of the month, right?"

The bot nodded. "A virginity-loss special," she said.

JC grinned. "Well, in that case our numbers are great. Can't believe there are still so many virgins left to deflower. Guess there were a lot of eighteenth birthdays recently."

The bot's head nodded, less surely this time. There was some dissent among the ten mil.

"Well, I'm delighted, ladies, gentlemen, and others. Please come join me on the bed."

JC took off his clothes. Robot arms promptly emerged from the floor and packed them into hologram-lined bags.

When it came to the pornography markets, JC had extremely tough competition. He did his best when it came to physique, but there was also a hierarchy of penis length within the community. JC had averaged out in that particular genetic lottery, so his nudes and vids didn't sell as well as many others. Until now, he'd focused on being a JC-of-all-trades, leaderboard frontrunner of none. He'd refrained from investing in bodily modifications to keep marketing himself as a purebod. Since that would change this evening, perhaps he could throw in a groin enhancement soon.

He shuffled over to the proxy and kissed her. She moaned. He caressed her breasts, gently twisting the nipples. He gripped her ass, tugged at her hair. Soon he was inside her temporarily opened aperture. All his expertly devised moves came out, refined after so much online lovemaking with constant, widely outsourced feedback. They translated, through sensations on the proxy, to optimized touches on each and every participant, perfected and relocated to pleasure their various genitals and specific erogenous zones as identified previously, in the case of these virgins, by their sex toys and bots. All of them were out there somewhere, strapped into their various devices, depending on space allowances and cash brackets. VR headsets showed JC climbing on top of them. Proxies moved across them like sex puppets. Sex toys, in compatible brands, vibrated. Sensations of warming and prodding were transmitted through body-sized sheets of silicone.

JC was barely there at all. It was just happening. Pure muscle memory. A veritable zombified fuck machine, making love to millions while feeling nothing.

Focus, dude! There's pre-sold ejaculate to produce. You absolutely must finish.

But not before the clientele!

A pie chart on the proxy's left cheek filled up with pink, a glowing number in the chart's middle creeping up to 90, 91, 92 per cent, as satisfied customers around the globe confirmed sexual completion.

Getting there. He sped up his thrusts.

No, too fast!

He sighed, finishing at ninety-five per cent.

"Shit," he said.

"What is it?" the proxy said, panting.

"I wanted to please at least ninety-eight per cent of you. But what can I say? You all turn me on so damn much."

Hopefully that would appease the frustrated five per cent.

What did they expect? I've had a long, active day, and they're above the ninety-fifth percentile in terms of difficulty to get off. Plus, I haven't jerked off in days. I don't have another scene scheduled for a week.

Notes for this upcoming ten-minute session, based on its

predicted audience's sexual delectations, read as follows: *Use provided water-based lubricant, employ liberal use of dirty talk. Emit load freely. Aim for above-average height, trajectory, and volume. Moaning encouraged.*

Machinery whirred inside the proxy, and the word *HOLD* pulsed in blue across its face as it went into temporary automatic override.

JC giggled. "This bit always tickles."

A latex reservoir squeezed off the last of his ejaculate and sent it, with piston-provided peristaltic action, to the proxy's internal refrigeration coil.

He withdrew from her and lay on his back.

She stood up. A frozen white marble emerged in her palm, cold water vapour misting off of it. She flicked it into a circular opening in the wall. Off it went to lucky recipients.

She flopped back on one side of the bed. Her amalgamated face of unanimously agreed-upon attractiveness returned, representing those customers who had paid for this next event.

"Wow," she said. "So that was sex."

"Yeah." JC regained his breath. "But don't expect that level of skill from your next partner. I put in my ten thousand hours." He pointed his finger at her and winked. "Know what I'm saying?"

She was quiet.

"Y-You enjoyed it, right? You must have. And it wasn't too painful?"

The bot considered this. "I mean, it was uncomfortable at times. I don't know. It wasn't as personal as I'd expected. Most of it felt good, but it didn't feel like you were responding to my body."

JC's face fell. "You all felt like that?"

The bot shrugged. "Most of us, yeah."

"W-Well, it's difficult to do properly with this equipment."

The bot placed its hand on JC's arm. "Of course!"

"If you were here it would be different."

The bot grinned. "Is that an invitation?"

"Maybe." JC traced a finger down its side.

A pink stream of text floated out of the iMirror: *Pillow talk commencing.*

The windows darkened to block most of the fading sunset. Pink hearts projected in a swirling circle across the optimo.

JC tapped two fingers to his temple in a salute. "Bye to those of you who only paid for sex. For those of you who signed up for pillow talk, fire away with your questions!"

"How are you feeling about the surgery?" the proxy asked. "We're all talking about it."

JC furrowed his brow adorably. "Nervous. But at the same time not. Because I know how much you're all gonna enjoy it." His pupils dilated with a rush of fear. "Is that okay? Is that how you want me to feel?"

"I don't understand the question." The proxy looked bemused. She pulled her hair back to reveal *5M* glowing on her temple. "There's only us here."

"An intimate audience."

"So be honest," the proxy said. "There's something on your mind. Just say what it is."

"I can't!"

"Why not?"

"You wouldn't like it. You wouldn't come back."

"We like honesty."

"Okay." He sighed. "No one's paying me to think about the surgery. If anything, I can only go through with it by *not* thinking about it."

"You poor thing," the proxy said. "So you haven't thought about what people are gonna make you do afterwards?"

"Should I be worried?" He grinned salaciously. "Nah. The software will stop you from doing anything too serious. And I can override it whenever I want. I think that's how it goes." He whispered in the proxy's ear. "I want to see how far you'll go before I stop you."

She let out a deep laugh of pleasure. "JC?"

"That's me."

"Will you sing 'Butterfly Girl' for us?"

A pit formed in his stomach. He swallowed hard. "You like that one, huh?"

She nodded.

"You must be real fans of mine, then. It's old school. I've written plenty of better bangers since that."

"There's something about that one we like best."

"Can I tell you a secret?" he said.

"Please."

He looked around. The iMirror had fallen to the floor, deactivated. "This stays between us."

"Sure."

"It's about Lizzie."

"We knew it! That must be what we enjoy about it so much. We feel your love for her."

JC smiled sadly.

"We hope we haven't hurt you."

"Nah. In fact, you can all be my Butterfly Girl now."

She placed a hand over her heart.

Butterfly girl
Too precious for this world
You spread your wings and fly
Fly away from me
But I want you to thrive
So it's okay
I'll survive
As long as you're happy
I'll survive
As long as you're happy

He faltered, holding his breath. Some enjoyed the vulnerability, true. Especially those who had paid to lose their virginity to him. But for some reason, he didn't want them to see.

He shot the bot a quick false grin. "Okay, well, remember to subscribe if you haven't!"

He reached behind its head, flipped a switch on its neck, and kicked it out of bed.

Its skin returned to neutral grey, and it walked back into its position, backing into a charger.

The sheets tore out from under JC. He barrelled onto the floor, on his knees, still naked, sweat rapidly cooling on his gooseflesh skin.

A motor whirred, and a rotating cylinder rolled up the bedsheets, pneumatically shooting them into a cardboard tube for transport to the winning bidder.

The whole set of bedsheets? Not divided between several buyers? Either someone paid a huge amount, or I'm losing popularity.

Maybe I caught the attention of those conceptual artists. And they'll display the sheets in a gallery, calling them a testament to the vacuous nature of influencer culture. Hey, why not? I've seen them try to satirize Francesca and Brad. It would be sick AF if they made me a target. I smell a collab.

He'd check the sale later to find out.

He flopped back down onto the bed. An iris-shaped hole in the ceiling dilated open and dropped a green medical sheet, which floated down beside him. He tucked himself under it. It covered all but his arms and legs.

He snapped his fingers. A mechanical arm flailed over to him, a tablet in its grasp. He held the tablet over his face and blinked. This reopened his latest read. It was about the negative consequences of continued net neutrality, how it prevented corporations from engaging in societally beneficial competition. It bemoaned the oppression of the individual and extolled the importance of small government.

This was typical of the content JC got sponsored to read and promote. He would stream a response to the book for fans in a month's time. The notion filled him with dread. Even though he would have bullet points of what they wanted him to say about it, he still felt obliged to do some due diligence. But he was such a slow reader. Plus, he had countless other films, documentaries, games, and albums to consume and comment on before the end of the month!

Well, if he had one talent, it was hustle. And the people who asked him to consume this stuff employed various strategies to mitigate their dryness. He'd flown through the ten-volume graphic novel adaptation of Ayn Rand's *Atlas Shrugged* and bopped along to the audiobook rap of *The Complete Milton Friedman*. There was no way he would've stayed awake through Adam Smith's *The Wealth of Nations* if it hadn't been a high-budget porno. Thirty hours of economic theory delivered in stilted dialogue between naked models in barrister wigs. What a time to be alive!

He bit his lip periodically while reading, forgetting that he wasn't on camera. He only had to read the book, not seduce it.

A white metal stalk raised from the floor and projected a red exclamation mark symbol.

"Sweet!" JC waved his hand through the notification.

Someone had signed up to perform JC's surgery remotely from New Delhi.

Whatever. He hadn't asked. He'd requested the earliest available professional with a rating above 4.7/5, as the app had advised. This limited the risk of the surgery going wrong. He was welcome to look at the surgeon's detailed stats if he so desired. Maybe he'd check later. He trusted the app.

He hit the green 'next' button on the projection. A wall of terms and conditions appeared. He groaned and flicked his hand through it to scroll down.

A box appeared at the bottom of the text. He wrote *JC* with his finger and clicked *Confirm*.

"Lie back and keep your head still," a robotic female voice told him.

An anaesthetic mask, connected to a breathing tube, pressed itself over his mouth.

"Count down from one hundred, JC. This will all be over soon."

4

JC woke with a start. The optimo was dark.

So that was that. The surgery was surely over. JC hoped those who had paid to watch learned something. Hospitals wanted to observe automated surgical equipment in action so they could learn to program it better. 5G internet providers ensured remotely performed manual surgeries went well. But pay-per-view was available to anyone.

JC looked to the iMirror. Glowing text confirmed his latest sales. Buyers of his medical records. Vials of blood to blood banks, fetishists, and the charities that would garner the most attention. Maximized predicted return on subscribers versus minimized cash loss—what he could've earned by selling the blood himself. Clout meant more subscribers, which meant more future revenue. Charity was an investment like any other.

The unfamiliar solitude of night washed a deep horror over him. Was he supposed to be awake? Was there an intruder in the house? The lights weren't coming back on.

He heard explosions, screams, and bullet fire in the distance, muffled by the optimo's plastic walls. All standard fare, but chems usually kept JC dozing through this, kept him unconscious during his rigorous nightly exercise routine in the sportmesh. Maybe he'd built a resistance to the surgical anaesthetics, and they hadn't worked properly.

The iMirror dimmed and flopped on the floor.

Isn't it recording me? People pay to watch me sleep, you know! Lost revenue. Not to mention the reduction in my future efficiency caused by this sleep interruption. Nightmare.

He leaned his head to one side. "Time?"

"3:28 a.m.," the optimo told him.

"Chems?"

"None."

"Why not? I've had ten mg of some benzo or other, minimum, every night for the past five years."

"You changed your dosage."

"Bullshit! When?"

"Three hours ago."

He tutted. Something automatic to do with the surgery, surely. His daily meds would probably interfere with those required for the operation. That had to be it.

Recovery's gonna suck!

He looked at his arms in the moonlight from the optimo's high windows. They had an attractive matte sheen, like an expensive car. Pretty neat.

He predicted his postmod body would attract the same number of subscribers, but different ones. There were, after all, many forums dedicated to fantasizing about a modbodded JC. Many artists made whole careers off DeviantArt drawings of what JC would look like with modded arms and legs. All thanks to a burgeoning modfet community with plenty of cash money.

The old—and frankly boring!—arms and legs would be off with their buyers now, in deals optimized by AIs, banks, and middlemen. Donor limbs, maybe. Or split into their various components: fingers, muscles, tendons, bones, scraps of skin both tattooed and pure. Tissue samples for labs and biotech companies to do with what they would. It would all be in a statement if he cared to know more. Sometimes the iMirror would read him personal messages thanking him for his vital contributions to science. Cringe! His torso radiated a raw ache, like his limbs were big gaping wounds.

"Optimo, when did the surgery finish?"

"Five hours ago."

"What? But I requested max recovery speed."

He was supposed to be in a coma right now, receiving the highest allowable dosage of hormones and healing agents. This was against medical advice. Ideally he would've remained bedridden for at least six weeks.

But that's for people who aren't as savage as I am. I'm a beast, a tiger hybrid. I've got a ravenous appetite for life that no amount of pain can subdue. I'm Earth's democratically elected number-two stud. The Chosen One!

"Did something go wrong?" he asked.

"I'm contacting your surgical advisor now," the optimo said. "Don't move. You risk damage."

JC's new arms rose up before his face, black mechanical fingers wiggling, hands rotating three-sixty degrees on titanium ball joints at the wrist.

"JC, I just told you not to move."

"I'm not doing it!"

"Uh-oh."

"What do you mean? Aren't my arms calibrating or something?"

"You're supposed to remain immobile for at least another eight hours."

The hands slammed down on the bed, and the knees rose up. The new limbs vaulted JC to standing position. It gave him the rollercoaster-like feeling of being taken on a shaky ride over which he had no control. Pain spiked through his chest and groin where the carbon nanofibre muscles of his newly attached limbs interlaced with his own. Shoulders rotated on new ball joints with muscles knit together only hours before.

There was an intruder in his body.

"Uh-oh is right," he said through gritted teeth.

It felt like the new limbs were going to tear right back off again, run away by themselves, and leave him here bleeding out. His freshly sutured skin ached beneath a medical mesh that autodosed his wounds with antibacterial nanites and numbing agents. But they weren't calibrated for movement-induced injuries.

The legs walked JC towards the wall. His right arm reached out with an index finger, pressing against the cool surface of opaque glass. Fingertips glowed red on the glass, and a door slid open. So they'd registered his new laser-etched prints already— and also deregistered the old ones. Drones had likely stripped, tanned, and stuck them in display boxes, sending them off to collectors in little velvet-lined gift boxes.

Wait. Was he, in his real body, actually leaving the optimo to go outside?

He hadn't done so in years. These days he only ever went as a proxy, never as a real, even if he was fully fit and properly dressed. But now, with hours-old limbs, wearing just his sportmesh and a backless black hospital gown emblazoned all over with white JCs? It was too dangerous.

No properly functioning, ethically configured medical-grade device would deliver owners outside against their will. Did his limbs think they were stolen? Were they trying to walk themselves back to the factory?

The eerily chill air outside, laden with dust and cinders, blasted him in the face. Shouting for help now would only endanger him further.

Fires in long glowing streaks of red ran across distant black hilltops, briefly lighting the plumes of smoke they emitted before joining the permanent black smog of the atmosphere. The occasional abandoned hydrogen station glowed with fierce blue flames that shuddered as if about to explode. But they'd been that way for years.

The smell was overwhelmingly acrid, a mixture of garbage, burning plastic, jet fuel, and the odd sweetness of rotting flesh.

He saw the remnants of recently fought battles in the environs of hundreds upon thousands of optimos that glowed in pastel colours across the hills and down the sides of winding streets, like radioactive marshmallows stuck in shit. Each was a safe enclave for an average of 1.2 influencers, a semipermeable cube that maintained high air quality using nanofilters and buried oxygen generators separated from the surface by tons of concrete to minimize explosion risk.

JC's legs walked him onwards, brushing through the electronic detritus coating the streets: mechanical claws, shattered smartphones, rusting earpieces, the broken bars of electric scooters, the glittering glass of shattered iMirrors.

Down he went, against his will, to the underpass of a bridge. He whispered commands to his limbs—"Disengage! Manual override! Release control!"—to no avail. He hadn't read the instructions, figuring he'd do so when he woke up from his coma.

There were more fires in the upcoming dip. Bonfires this time, their flames flickering across the tarps and canvases of a tent city. Shoddy tents with corners pinned down by cinderblocks and peaks held up by steel rods and lightning-struck branches.

It must be summer. In winter, the dip flooded and the city migrated.

The legs took him on a tour beneath the bridge, between the tents. Sooty orange fires blazed their light across grimy, graffiti-flecked walls. Figures huddled beneath blankets and sleeping bags, pressed together to stay warm.

JC remained deadly silent. With any luck, the legs would take him through to the other side without incident. And then, who knew? But it was better than being here. He shut his eyes hard and tried to will control of his new limbs. But the arms swung gently by themselves and the legs crept ahead at their own pace. Until—

"JC!" A shout-whisper.

JC's legs turned.

A young man in dirty grey sweatpants and a hoodie waved to him.

JC looked down at his gown. How could he deny who he was?

"Over here!"

JC tried to shush the man with a finger, but his arms wouldn't obey him.

The legs walked over.

The man held open his tent, a ramshackle creation of blue tarpaulin and shoddy metal struts from a series of broken umbrellas.

"Hey, man," JC said, "Glad you like the show. Listen, I don't know what I'm doing here, but—"

JC followed him in. The tent was tall enough to stand in, but only in the peaked centre. JC's leg accidentally kicked a tin can filled with salvaged bits of metal. There were multiple cans containing pieces arranged by colour and size. The man must have scavenged them from the battle-worn surroundings. Their edges were sharp and rusty. A case of tetanus waiting to happen.

Polaroids taped to the wall showed a younger version of this man: backpacking with friends up a mountain ridge, dancing at some rave, chilling in someone's living room, and playing with a black Labrador. JC looked away from these mementos as if they pulsed with blinding light.

He took a closer look at the man. The way he carried himself suggested the pair were a similar age, but he looked about forty. His skin had likely aged through constant exposure to UV rays and particulate-laden air. He grinned with yellowing, broken teeth. He might have been attractive once. Maybe he'd missed his window to be an influencer. Maybe he couldn't sing or wasn't funny. But anyone could learn, no? Whatever the case, he had feelings and hopes and dreams, just like JC. It was unbearable to consider. Major cringe.

The man held out his hand. "The name's Jory."

JC's right arm extended itself, and the man shook it, but

quickly reared back at the metal's chill. "Whoa, look at this thing! What does it do? How much did it set you back?"

"That's kinda why I'm here. I got them recently."

"*Them?*" Jory cocked his head to examine JC's other arm. "*Two!* What the hell, man?"

"I can't control them."

"No worries. Just go back to your optimo and request help."

He looked down.

Jory squatted and poked JC's gown aside to reveal the legs. "Why did you—"

"I was trying to minimize my downtime. I didn't know this was gonna happen." Why was he justifying himself to this *nobody?* "Can you call the cops?"

Jory stood back up and shot him a sly, broken grin. "What, with a cellphone?"

"Is that what you use?"

Jory laughed. "I wish. Not to worry. I've got a better idea. I'll take you there myself."

"Where?"

"Back to your optimo!" Jory got closer, a strange rictus on his face. "You've got food in there, don't you? *Free* food."

"Not exactly."

Jory nodded, narrowing his eyes. "I get you. You're not gonna share your food, clean air, and safety for free. Of course not. You want a collab."

JC's heart sank. Were they all training for the eventuality that an influencer would adopt them? It clearly didn't matter to this guy whether he enjoyed the lifestyle or appreciated JC's company. He didn't have that luxury.

Jory bumped him on the arm. "I'll play along. I'll show your subscribers that you're a good guy. You'll get more of them. W-We'll get them together!" He pumped a fist. "This is the start of something. Choose me. I won't let you down." He paced around in nervous circles, wringing his hands. "We'll become friends!

Great character arc for you. An unlikely pairing. Unforgettable, I'd say. You'd shoot up the rankings. To the very top." There was a fervour in his eyes. "Give me a sandwich, and I'm yours, buddy. Do whatever you want with me." He held out his hands. "Y-You want my limbs too?"

Someone was punishing him into adopting a homeless person. Radical hacktivism. That sounded like a thing that might exist. JC might know if he ever consumed anything other than influencer drama or the capitalist exhortations corporations paid him to read.

JC winced. "All right. If you can carry me back up the hill to my optimo—without anyone else noticing—you can come in."

Jory knelt down to scoop JC up. JC's right arm shot out and punched Jory square in the face. His nose burst open.

"Oh my God, Jory, I didn't mean to—"

"Help!" Jory spit blood.

"Quiet, please, Jory! I'm not doing this, I swear—"

The left arm shot out and dealt Jory another blow to the face, this time shattering his left cheek and eye socket. The force cut through the skin and sprayed blood across the tarp.

Jory was on the ground now, screaming in fear. JC's knees buckled, and he fell over Jory.

The fists pummelled.

JC shut his eyes, cringing at the meaty sound of metal impacting flesh, at the wet crunch of bone splintered by the brute force of his fists. Warm blood misted his face. He tried to turn away, but his left hand grabbed his face and two fingers forced his left eye open.

The right arm continued to smash Jory's skull. He wasn't moaning anymore. He no longer even had a face. Or an intact brain. But still the fist hammered down until it had tenderized all the components of Jory's head and grated them against the asphalt beneath.

The right fist centred itself before JC's face, and blood dripped off its waterproof surface. The knuckles had scuffed against the ground, scraping off the carbon fibre coating.

JC thought—hoped—he was next.

The hand swivelled. The index, ring, and pinky fingers retracted, leaving only the middle extended. It flipped him the bird.

All the limbs went slack. Before he flopped on the floor, JC pushed his palms out and suspended himself an inch above Jory's body, close enough to smell his sour odour.

He was in control of the limbs now.

"Hey!" A crowd gathered around the tent. "It's one of those influencers!"

"What are you doing with Jory?"

JC shuffled out, holding his hands up in protest.

"He's dead! Jory's dead!"

JC whipped around. A woman had snuck into the tent behind him and shouted to the others. She clicked a rapid Morse code sequence into a metal button in her wrist. An alarm sounded, alerting the police.

Huh. So they do have a way.

"Murderer!" the crowd shouted at him. "Fucking murderer!"

JC turned and bolted back up the street. With his new limbs fully functioning, the crowd had no hope of catching him. He wanted to make it back to his optimo before the police arrived. Perhaps he could incinerate his gown and re-engage the coma sequence in time to pretend he couldn't possibly have been here.

A sinister buzz, like a swarm of mechanical wasps, filled the air. Lights flashed red and blue on the asphalt. As JC ran, his limbs failed him again. Police drones picked him up with their magnets, one for each arm and leg.

"Ahhh!"

He sped in reverse, away from the ground, up into the cool breeze of cruising altitude.

His head flopped in the direction of the makeshift city. Drones flew in and around Jory's tent, likely collecting 3D projections of the crime scene, blood samples, pictures, witness statements.

JC's shoulders and hips burned. It felt like the limbs were about to rip off him. Like a massive infection would spread through his system and shut down his heart. Like the drones would draw and quarter him, ripping off his new limbs and sending his head and torso hurtling to the ground below.

He begged they would.

Three drones noted his discomfort and floated beneath him. He looked down at them, their propellers like enlarged metal sycamore seeds. They flipped upside down, pressing their bulbs into his stomach and chest, their propellers spinning precariously close, threatening to snag one of the loose ties of his gown and eat him up.

5

The drones carted JC into a hatch at the back of the police station. They carried him through a full-body scan, replaced his clothing with a blue jumpsuit, and placed him on a padded bench in a holding cell. His arms and legs locked together using their in-built arrest mode.

Before the last drone left through the cell's glass partition, it printed a little receipt that floated to the floor. JC peered down at it. His Miranda rights, along with *Arrested for: MURDER.*

The cell was beige all over, dim lights cast down from the ceiling. JC was alone, left staring at himself in the small square mirror on the opposite wall. He hadn't seen himself in such terrible lighting for so long. The unforgiving tungsten bulbs highlighted the shadows of his eye bags, the outline of every pore in his tired face, the deep horseshoe-shaped bruise around his left eye where his possessed fingers had pried it open.

At least the blue suit went with his hair. Electric blue and neon green. New merch ideas brewing.

"Justin Chacley," said a gruff voice.

JC turned with a start. With these words, his limbs released from their magnetic bonds. He could control them again.

A man stood on the other side of the thick glass. He was sloppy-looking, with an unkempt and stubbly beard, a beige overcoat, undone tie, grubby shirt, and the rubicund face of a man who likes a drink. His unwashed hair grew in a ring around his head.

JC confused himself with a series of conflicting strategies. First, he tried to work out who this man wanted him to be so he could be it and please him. Next, he considered—but refrained from—recommending Biotherm Night Cream for Men, a VO5 hot oil hair treatment, or an Armani Biosuit. And part of him didn't believe this man was even worthy of his time. He was dishevelled. Ugly. Too fucking *real*. Was that the issue? Or was it that this man had a sly, dark glint of experience and wisdom in his eye that JC was painfully aware he lacked, given the hours he spent taking in his own blank stare, unconvinced that there was a soul back there?

He took a breath to slow himself down. "Call me JC."

The man let out the guttural laugh of someone who still smoked real cigarettes. People had at one time considered this madness. But once air quality took a dive and began to be measured in a cigarettes-per-day equivalent, the conventional wisdom became, *Fuck it. You're smoking them one way or another. Might as well enjoy it.*

"I'm not one of your subscribers, Mr Chacley," the man said. "It's Detective Ferdinand to you." He smoothed his hair at the back. "Creeps me out, the notion of what you all get up to day after day. Stuck in those optimals."

"Optimos."

"I didn't even think you were real."

JC nodded. "I'm also suspicious of many."

Ferdinand raised an eyebrow. "By all means, spill the tea."

JC grinned. He could if he wanted. He wasn't on camera! "There was an exposé recently on Jaclyn™? She uses bot-like repeated speech patterns. As for the Broder brothers, like, three years into their stream they revealed their younger brother Chad, saying he's now ready to appear on camera, but they never mentioned him before? Many think it's a fake proxy they brought out for clout CPR. Then there's Ursulina, with a new makeup palette every month, claiming it's a unique formula she personally developed in the lab. Bullshit. It's algorithmically derived money grabbing that she had no hand in. How come her eyeshadow keeps getting recalled for poor composition and fibre contamination? And then there's … You have no idea who I'm talking about."

"Just trolling you." Ferdinand took a tablet out of his pocket and examined its screen. "Let's move on to your favourite subject instead. Who are you, Justin? What's your story?"

JC rolled his eyes. "I've been telling it for the last five years, every day, for eighteen hours or more. And in that time I haven't spoken to anyone unfamiliar with my work. How am I supposed to tell you something as complex as who I am?"

"A Herculean task, I'm sure, Mr Chacley. But spare me the existential woe and do your best."

JC cranked his neck. "Ask an iMirror for 'JC's life story'. Play the top result."

Ferdinand's face lost its humour. "I'm not after JC's life story, I'm after yours, and I'm asking you, the real live person right in front of me, *on police authority*, to tell it to me."

"I'm not thick. I just don't know why you insist on being so inefficient."

Ferdinand sighed and tapped his tablet. A text holo appeared and he read from it. "How does this sound, then? Raised by a single mother—"

"Who I hate and don't see anymore."

"—and a state-mandated android father. Lack of decent

human male role model. Learned to rely on himself. Didn't do well at school."

"Hated that too. I don't use *anything* I learned there. It didn't prepare me for the real world."

Ferdinand eyed him slyly. "That depends on your definition of 'real world'." He continued reading. "Discovered on SoundCloud."

This detail hit JC in the gut. He pictured himself, a bored, lanky, brown-haired teen with not a single tattoo, sitting in a lonely bedroom, with torn paper posters of LylaTeez and AlissaVanilla on his wall. Nervously uploading bedroom-produced cybertrap tunes that he made with a second-hand microphone and a stolen Korg synthesizer. Writing songs for Lizzie, hoping first that she'd notice him and second that his music would get both of them out of their shitty, nowhere town.

"But it wasn't," JC replied, "until I made auto-generated music videos to accompany my songs, and put those on YouTube, that my career as an influencer picked up."

At 'influencer', Ferdinand winced. "Write the Wikipedia article yourself, did you?"

"Do I look like I spend time on *Wikipedia?*"

"Let's talk about Lizzie."

"Keep her name out your goddamn—"

"Why do you think you can talk to a detective like that? Oh, wait, I've got it here." He read from the holo. "Half a billion subscribers." He whistled, impressed.

JC chuckled darkly. "You don't get how important I am to some people."

"That attitude won't do you any favours in here, son."

"You're gonna have to try harder to understand my culture."

Ferdinand put the tablet away. "I don't know how to talk to you."

"Exactly. I'm fucked."

Ferdinand went to the corridor's rear wall and tugged on a

ring there, pulling out a bench. He sat down. "I used to have a smartphone."

"Hah! You're so old."

"But I went back to a flip phone."

"I don't know what that is."

"And I made sure neither of my daughters used any of that shit."

JC gasped. "That's like—" *Child abuse,* he wanted to add, but thought better of saying this to a hardened detective. "I don't even know."

Ferdinand folded his arms. "The arms and legs are new. Why?"

"For my subscribers."

"Huh?"

"So they can pay to control them."

Ferdinand's face crumpled with horror.

"I'll admit it's risky. As I'm sure you know," he drawled, "all the top influencers are purebods."

Ferdinand looked to the ceiling, mouthing the word *purebod* to himself.

"Numbers one through 157 at least. KylieMods, number 158, was born without a right arm, so she still has a massive following even though she's a modbod. She's trying to reduce the stigma around mods." JC scoffed. "All the way down there in the lower hundreds. Good luck to her."

"Hmm."

"I'm trying to prove that *I* care the most. *This* is what real fan dedication looks like. When it comes to this career, there are no sacrifices too great. Unlike FrancescaFlores and BradBeatz, numbers one and two, I'll bring my fans as close as possible. Let them experience what it's like to be *me.*" He looked at the cold metal of his hands, rotating them around. "I thought if I pulled this off, everyone would think remaining a purebod was selfish. And I'd jump to the number-one spot for my ingenuity. Be the prime mover on a new trend. And maybe people would think it made me sympathetic to modbods too."

"Such as"—Ferdinand looked at his tablet—"KylieMods."

"You're getting it. I even considered collabbing with her. It always looks good to reach down."

Ferdinand clenched his jaw. "Are there really people interested in controlling your movements?"

"I can find enough people interested in anything I feel like doing."

Ferdinand nodded. "Why were you wandering around your neighbourhood at night in nothing but a hospital gown?"

JC gestured with his metal hands. "That's what doesn't make any sense about this. Ask my subscribers! I haven't left JCManse in years."

"Your optimo."

"Uh, *yeah*."

"This is the last time I'm gonna warn you about that tone."

JC took a deep breath. "I had no reason to leave. Trust me. I can show you the data. I ran the sims on potential collabs with local irrelevants. You know, heading out and gifting them bits so my subscribers could see. The numbers didn't add up. It wasn't worth getting out of bed for. Not to mention the health impact of breathing outside air. That's what's so embarrassing about this. Why would I risk everything I have just to kill—"

"An 'irrelevant'."

JC swallowed hard. "You think I'm a bad person."

"It depends who you ask, I guess." Ferdinand took out the tablet and glanced at it again. "The consensus is as follows on your top five qualities. Fifty-eight per cent wholesome. I find that hard to believe. Fifty-two per cent positive. Forty-nine per cent ignorant. Thirty-eight per cent inspirational. Twenty-one per cent homewrecker."

"Homewrecker?"

"Millions of ruined families and marriages, apparently."

"Collateral damage."

"Your attitude is chilling."

"Thanks, man."

"No, I mean—whatever. That's just the data. You want to know what I think?"

JC frowned. "Are you genuinely asking, or—"

"You're just what other people want you to be. Nothing more or less."

JC clicked his fingers, satisfied by their crisp *snap!* sound. "Ah, this one. I'm an optimized product. A living ideal. An aspirational object. A living testament to all that is superficial, petty, and greedy." He leaned forward and raised a brow. "Hm?" He stood on the new legs, carrying himself with much more confidence than an imprisoned man-child had any right to. "When I was operating at ninety per cent efficiency, as opposed to my ninety-nine per cent now, I had time to read what all the bloggers said about me and mine. You could copy-paste those posts into a text-to-speech program, and they'd be a far more eloquent and compelling listen than anything you have to say."

"What kind of community never meets face-to-face? Says nothing but petty things and lies about one another? Not the kind I'd like to be a part of."

"Like you ever could." JC paced before the glass. "Are you, and all those smarmy bloggers, as well-educated, profound, and different as you all think you are? Does the fault lie with me—or with the pathetic notion that anyone is really unique?" He folded his arms. "Why does everything have to be clever? Why can't some things just be silly? Why can't I be a pretty distraction, instead of part of the endless, exhausting, and disempowering discussion of how fucked everything is? Doesn't that make me part of 'the solution', whatever that means? Most of this shit we didn't do, and we can't do anything about it anyway. You're as well enjoying watching me dance about in my designer boxers, with their breathable fabric perfected by NASA engineers, thank you very much. If that's what I've dedicated my life to, can't you admire my desire to be the best at it? Anyone who pretends not to respect that is just jealous."

"Yeah," Ferdinand muttered. "That's surely the only reason."

"I'm only twenty-two anyway." He looked Ferdinand up and down. "I can be fat and—divorced, I'm assuming?"

"Yup."

"I can be that later."

Ferdinand rubbed his eyes. He looked unimpressed. The speech had sounded better in JC's head. As he delivered it, to someone with much more life experience, it became obvious how much he'd stored it up and rehearsed it. How much he wanted to tell it to someone. Wanted them to care, even while pretending he didn't.

"I want to figure this out as much as you do," Ferdinand said in a calmer voice. He gestured to JC. "But I don't have to take shit from some bionic twink. You haven't chosen this lifestyle as much as you think. You aren't making easily reversible decisions." He dropped the tablet on the bench with an emphatic *clank*. "You're not an innovative, diversifying, self-made entrepreneur. You're embedded in a system much more powerful than you. It's hacking you limb from limb, and you're letting it happen with a smile on your face. Not to mention how you've marginalized and deprived your homeless neighbours of resources in order to fund, say, your new multi-million-bit, weapons-grade limbs. Which you then test out by punching one of them to *death*?"

Fuck. This was real, real, real.

"Leaving your manse to kill for sport. On a whim. The fucking height of privilege. I just want to know why. Were you seeing what you could get away with? Fanbase got you convinced you're untouchable?"

JC burst into tears, his breaths short and stuttering.

Ferdinand sat in silence, giving him a moment.

"Can't remember the last time I cried."

"Then I feel sorry for you, son."

JC looked at him with confusion. "*I* don't. Do you know how valuable these tears are? Quick, fetch me something to catch them with."

Ferdinand stood up and pushed the bench back into the wall.

"What? I'll give you a commission."

"Are you trying to bribe a police officer?"

"No. *You're* turning down a once-in-a-lifetime offer."

"Forget that for a minute. Don't you want to call someone?"

"I don't know, do I?"

"Any family?"

"The third-biggest family there is."

"Goddammit, you know what I mean. A parent or sibling."

JC wiped his tears with cold fingers. "They're all butthurt. Our collabs never did as well as my solos. I'm better off without them."

"Get back to me on it, then. I'll give you some privacy."

"Wait! I need to get back home. I'm scheduled for a full day's worth of activities."

"That's not how justice works. Besides, you think anyone is gonna give you money now that they've heard about this?"

JC shrugged. "If I jump on the narrative fast enough?"

"It's been a real pleasure, Mr Chacley." Ferdinand walked off.

6

"Wow!" Lizzie had exclaimed the day she'd first walked into the optimo, in a wrinkled T-shirt and sweatpants. "It's huge!"

"Yeah," a similarly garbed Justin, of Justin&Liz, had replied. "I had it custom-designed for a whole range of activities. I just hope people pay to watch us do them."

Lizzie tied back her curly hair and slung her arms around him from behind. "Of course they will. We're Justin and Liz. And our subscribers are on this adventure with us. They want to see us challenge ourselves." She walked to the end of the room. There were no proxies. Liz found them creepy and thought holos and VR were sufficient. "It's a bit bland, though. Maybe I could hang some plants over here, lay some tiles on the ground. Do some wallpaper over this bit and hang some paintings." She turned to Justin. "Let's make a spa area! All mother-of-pearl tiles and chrome fixtures."

Justin laughed.

"What?"

"You're kidding, right?"

"Why?"

"There's so much delicate machinery beneath everything. You can't mess with the geography, weight distribution, or visual calibration of this place at all. Or it won't work."

She slumped to the floor. "So we've just voluntarily moved into a big empty cube?"

"Hey." He knelt and hugged her from behind, kissing her neck. "You can still project whatever you want across any surface. A restaurant, picnic, makeup shop, or whatever."

"I guess so."

"When we're not filming, of course. We don't know how our choices will impact the audience."

Her face fell.

He turned her towards him. "It's still just you and me, together." He looked into her eyes.

She smiled softly back, as if he was admiring her.

Back then, as her boyfriend, he felt the quiet privilege of seeing her when she wasn't done up. It wasn't as much effort for him to look good. This was before he had more product endorsements than skin on which to apply them.

Then again, what kind of a joy was it to see someone when they weren't at their best? He wanted to be in his audience, to experience his own relationship as the perfect-looking one they presented.

They lay in bed that evening after a marathon baking stream, picking flakes of flour off their arms and flicking them to the floor to get caught by the nightly cleaning routine.

Justin's iMirror hovered before him, lighting up his big, grinning face.

"What's so funny?" Lizzie said, sidling up to him.

He turned the iMirror to show her a dick pic.

"Gross! Why would anyone send you that?"

"Bisexual dudes want to have three-ways with us. And the gay dudes want, uh, two-ways. Haha."

"I didn't expect an actual answer!" She flicked him on the forehead. "You're not encouraging this, right?"

He looked at her, confused. "Are *you*? You must be getting even more dicks than me!"

She narrowed her eyes. "I don't find it amusing."

"Oh, come on," he said. "If you're an even slightly public figure these days"—he scrolled through a wealth of explicit photos—"*this* is what your inbox looks like."

She rolled out of bed, repulsed. "You could stop spouting all that body positivity bullshit."

He tutted. "But it's so powerful when normies hear that message from people who look like *us*."

"You spend so many hours at the gym it's like you're punishing yourself."

"My appearance isn't a reflection on anyone else's."

"The cameras are off, honey. Do you really think our audience is old enough to understand that?"

He batted the iMirror aside and sat up. "Whose idea was it to present ourselves as the perfect couple anyway?"

She flopped onto the sheets, defeated, looking up at the ceiling.

Justin stroked her hair. "No reason we can't still have fun."

Liz rolled onto her stomach and grinned at Justin. She fetched her own phone and showed him some of the pics she'd received.

"Ew!" Justin said, laughing.

"I know, right? If he insisted on sending this—"

"He could have at least cleaned his bathroom!" they said in unison.

Just weeks after that, Lizzie came home to find Justin "cheating on her with millions of others at once."

He hopped up and covered himself with the sheets. His proxy companion went into idle mode, lying there like a blow-up doll.

"You know what?" Justin said after the standard exchange of invectives. "You're selfish for wanting to keep me to yourself in this cultural climate."

Lizzie's eyes went wide. She went over to the wall and touched her hand to it, revealing a handful of her belongings. "You have some fucking nerve, dude."

"Do you know how many bits we're gonna get from this? How many likes?"

"Not enough." Lizzie packed her clothes into a gym bag. She slung it over her shoulder and turned to him. "What about you? How many likes will it take to please you? A hunner M? Two hunner M?"

"I look forward to finding out."

She took a deep breath, turned, and left.

Justin looked up to his iMirror. It floated high above the bed, recording the whole scene, unbeknownst to Lizzie. "Don't worry, chestnuts," he said. "She'll be back."

He snapped his fingers. The iMirror dropped out of the air and into his hands. He dictated his instructions for posting the video.

Title: *Lizzie CATCHES me CHEATING!! (Watch till the end!)*

Comments: *What do you think, chestnuts? Are you Team Lizzie or Team Justin?*

And the question that would define the next four years of his existence: *What do you want to see Justin do next?*

"JC?"

JC looked through the glass.

Ferdinand stood there. "You made bail."

"I did?"

"The GoFundMe payment came in a minute ago. There was also a statement, co-signed by millions, ensuring that you are not a flight risk, and a set of statistics indicating your personality traits and whereabouts over the last four years."

"Impressive."

"I'll have the drones cart you back to JCManse. But we're gonna monitor your activities while this investigation is ongoing. You can't reveal any details related to your case, or you'll be in big trouble. Got it?"

"Okay, sir. I'll be careful."

Ferdinand walked off.

"Remember to—" JC stopped himself.

Ferdinand leaned back. "Like, rate, comment, and subscribe?"

"Force of habit. I meant 'bye'."

7

After his single hour of sleep, JC woke up feeling worse than before. The ache in his arms and legs had spread through his chest and groin, meeting at his stomach and back and spreading into his head. Like the worst post-workout pain combined with swelling and infection.

What are the symptoms of septicaemia? How long can I survive without treating it?

It wasn't the time to be asking those questions.

Instead, it was: "That time once again!" He looked in the iMirror at his waxy, pallid face, his unconvincing grin, and the circular purple bruise around his right eye.

101M+ read the petal flipping up from the iMirror. Numbers much higher than usual. This was, for once, not a good sign.

"Check out the new hands!" He held them up for the mirror.

He saw a flash of the night before. The darkness, the taste of smog, the dead man's blood coating his out-of-control limbs.

"Ah ha ha!" Did that laugh sound slightly hysterical? "Okay, look. I know why there are so many of you today. But we're just gonna go through the usual products and activities. There'll be two differences. I know CerealKid and TheOneTrueGamer wanted me to play *MeatShovel* with them this afternoon, but that wouldn't be appropriate. And as for the JC drama power shower hour, there's one topic I can't comment on."

The numbers dropped in seconds: *99M, 95M, 85M, 70M.*

He shrugged. "I'm here today for the same reasons as always, chestnuts. I'm inviting you to another exciting-but-regular day of my life. Let's get back to it." He clapped the hands together as if to dust them off. "Stay positive and smile, everyone!"

Whose voice was that? His? It sounded like every online voice he'd ever heard. Stock phrases poured out his mouth with hardly any cortical involvement on his part.

"Let's get to today's products."

The sink and cabinet shot back out. He completed a similar routine as he had the day before, this time with Aesop facial cleansing oil, Biotherm moisturizer, and a toner that JC incorrectly said was Kiehl's when it was clearly Clinique.

The stream corrected him.

"Right, right! That's why I'm glad you're here, chestnuts. You keep me real. Anyway!"

The shower appeared, and he got in it as before. The scarabs scoured his skin longer than usual because he couldn't stop sweating. He tried batting them off, but their routine was preprogrammed.

"Sorry, everyone, a bit of a malfunction today." He grinned at the iMirror but turned away again quickly. "Mirror, mirror," he whispered, "dial down opacity." It was for others to see him, not for him to look at himself.

Some petals shot up green in support. Many more stuttered red, flickering but not popping up. Automods blocked their responses.

News and comments scrolled on the TV. Dread spread through him, his heart pounding wildly. He couldn't bear to read any of it. Whether it was slander or concern or fans or whatever. What did any attention mean in this context? The idea disgusted him.

I'm nothing but scum. I deserve no attention at all. Can't these degenerates see that? I don't trust them. Millions of idiots. Why are they spending any time with me at all? Can't they tell I'm not their friend? That I don't give a shit about them? Why else would I have a smile on my face, today of all days?

You have to do this.

"Okay guys, let's go to the comments."

- *HentaiLord347: Why is he even here today?*
- *BlazeIt42069: I think it's so cool what he did. I never suspected he'd be the new edgelord king.*
- *AngelBaby3756: Okay but this is giving me major anxiety. I hate to think JC is suffering like this and won't tell us anything. JC sweetie we'll be here for you no matter what!! Don't ever think you could do ANYTHING to make us leave!!*
- *FrenchFry74: Are you KIDDING me? If what they say about him is true I'm outta here!* A repeating three-second hologram of a tween making a pleading gesture popped up in the chat. *JC please, I'm like literally crying, tell us you wouldn't do this!*
- *LawLover23756: Whatever happened, he didn't have the proper software installed on his limbs. Such a basic, reckless error. It makes him at least guilty of extreme negligence.*

- *GirlyGirl246: Yeah, he's gone too far. It's just sad. If he knew where his soul was, he'd carve it out and ship it out to the highest bidder.*
- *PupPlay3847: Totes agree. Here's a link to my video where I reveal how this incident EXPOSES JC. I'm an economics student and I compiled graphs correlating the decline in his profits with his age and audience content exhaustion.*
- *HornyForBlondes38576: Well that's the thing, why would the monetized feed of someone as avaricious as JC go down on the same night he gets accused of murder? My subscription includes permission to watch him sleep, for whatever reason. A friend and I were looking at it last night, just to have a laugh—anyway the feed went dark. Something funny is going on and I think we, his audience who know him and his content well and understand this tech, are in the best position to find out what it is.*
- *WeinerSamurai7576: I don't care what anyone says it's on account of greed that he got those arms and legs in the first place. He was too self-involved not to consider the massive risk that there are people out in the world who fucking hate him. Jory Arthur Stevenson's blood is on his hands. Who's that, you ask? The homeless man everyone in this community seems to think doesn't matter.*

"I didn't know his full name," JC said.

Shit.

Too late. The audience picked up on it:

- *Everyone, ask more stuff! JC, what did it feel like to snuff out another human life?*
- *If you do it again will you let us watch?*
- *Sick!! JC I won't forgive you unless you donate your entire earnings to assist the homeless community in your area. It's the VERY LEAST they deserve.*

- *I don't even care. No amount of funding can replace the value of one human life.*
- *Jesus, some of you are so self-righteous. You have a point but settle down. There's quite clearly an objective difference between the values of people's lives. A homeless dude was never gonna be president.*
- *A disgusting idea which has no home here.*
- *HERE? In the highly moral community of young women who love to stare at a random semi-naked dude as he lists product names?*
- *Why are YOU here?*
- *You think JC has earned every bit of his and is therefore millions of times more valuable than a homeless man?*

JC, with glazed-over eyes, read each comment as it came in. The feed became blurry, his breathing shallow. The phantoms of his former arms and legs tingled. He felt like he was floating, separate from his body. He wanted to look down at himself to confirm he was still there. But that would mean staring at a murder weapon.

He shut his eyes tightly and tried to steady his breathing. Something crawled over his face. With a bolt of fright, he batted at it. He looked down and saw a razor drone flailing on its back, its motors whirring in confusion. He knelt down, picked it up, and looked at its many feelers, at the razors in its belly.

Blood dripped from his chin onto his hands.

Murderer.

Could he use those same hands on his own neck? He held a hand to his throat and squeezed. But the fingers wouldn't curl any further.

- *Is he trying what I think he is? Hah! Need to stay alive and think about what you've done.*
- *It's not gonna be so easy for you, fucko.*

- *Live a lonely, follower-free existence, each day getting older and —even worse—more irrelevant!*
- *Can't think of a worse fate for a worse person.*

"Everything I worked for. Gone overnight."

- *JC you're having a panic attack!*
- *Stick an ice cube in your mouth!*
- *Count five things you can see, four things you can touch—*

He pulled at the drone's razorblades. It whirred again, flashing red lights to indicate the malfunction. He battled to keep its razors exposed and held it up to his neck. It couldn't resist his powerful arms.

The comments kept rolling in:

- *No don't do it! I'm trying to get in touch with local police now. Anyone have a number?*
- *Everyone, press your emergency button! If enough of us register concern we might be able to stop this.*
- *JC, I found something you'll want to see! Stay with us!!*
- *CONCERN REGISTERED*
- *CONCERN REGISTERED*
- *CONCERN REGISTERED*

The optimo's walls flashed red. Emergency mode.

Drones flew into the shower booth. They landed on JC's scalp, scratching. No, not scratching. Injecting.

The shower walls fell down. He stumbled out, onto the floor, the sedation kicking in.

"No!"

The cracks between the optimo's floor panels expanded, releasing long black vinyl belts. They slithered around JC's legs and tripped him up so he fell on his back.

He held up his arms, but more straps soon restrained them.

It was all over. The income, fame, adoration. He was reviled. No longer needed.

A medical mask secured itself over his nose and mouth, and he heard the gentle rush of gas.

8

Weow weow weow.

JC opened his eyes to the blank ceiling of his optimo. He was in bed, in grey sweats.

The optimo's alarm blared. An intruder was nearby.

He sighed tiredly to himself. "What kind of a psycho would approach my optimo in person—Oh."

A screen on the wall displayed Ferdinand standing outside.

He got up and walked to the wall to let Ferdinand in.

JC rolled his eyes as the door slid open. "Don't you know how to call in a proxy?" He gestured to where they stood against the wall.

Ferdinand took a step inside, half-raising his hands in surrender. "Proxies," he said, as if teaching the word to himself.

"Of course not. No, you scare me and get me out of bed. I didn't even know I was alive. It was great." JC slapped his forehead too hard by accident. "So, what? Do you have anything other than various diseases to bring me?"

Ferdinand smirked. "Good news?"

JC returned to the bed, sat on its corner, and folded his arms. "Go on, then." He clapped his hands. A gamer chair wheeled out of the wall towards Ferdinand.

Ferdinand sat in it awkwardly, his chubby thighs spilling over its JC-customized ergonomic design. "It's over," he said. "You're a free man once again. Technically speaking."

JC braced himself against the bed. "Why? What did you do?"

"Nothing."

JC kept quiet.

"Your fans, on the other hand, forwarded evidence to AI microcourt and hired representation for you. The judgebot dismissed the case against you this morning."

"On what grounds?"

"They found the real killer."

JC interlaced his cold fingers.

"So to speak. It was done by a forum."

"Huh?"

Ferdinand got back up again, pacing through the optimo. "A whole team of people from around the world. They coordinated your movements that night. They try to stay untraceable, but we're slowly identifying them. There are thousands of them, I'm afraid to say. They call themselves the Nosubs."

"Oh, fuck."

"You've heard of them?"

"No, but I've a good inkling of what you're about to describe."

"They're mostly well-educated men in their late twenties and early thirties, either unemployed or working menial jobs. A history of violence is common. They see themselves as much less successful than you, as having missed out on what you're doing."

Ferdinand looked around. JC followed his gaze. The walls now looked as sterile and lonely as Ferdinand probably saw them.

"The scary thing is," Ferdinand said, "they're all working anonymously, en masse, from home. I've never seen anything like it."

JC shook his head. "You've never seen anything like anything."

"They have a manifesto of sorts."

"Yeugh. Of course they do."

"I had it restricted to prevent its influence. It's nothing you'd want to read anyway—"

"Mirror, mirror," JC said.

The bedsheets rose like there was a ghost beneath them. The

iMirror shot out from under them like a discus and hovered before JC with a rainbow question mark on its surface.

"Show me 'JC murder manifesto'," he said.

Glowing pink text scrolled through the air. The iMirror read it in a feminine sotto voce:

Modern-day society has spun into a near-irreversible moral decay. Technology has facilitated an explosion of the loneliness epidemic through self-segregation and endless narcissistic loops of lazy, instantly gratifying behaviour.

There is no greater example of our contemporary degeneracy and hedonism than the influencer. Influencers are depraved, completely without feeling, drug abusers who flout national and international laws with their provocative and often pornographic content. Meanwhile, greedy politicians in corporatized governments turn against the people they are supposed to serve. They look the other way to secure a slice of influencer ad revenue to spend on their third homes.

We were thankful to control JC and send out our message. He lives in a self-imposed prison, a slave to the false gods of technology, beauty, and money. His life is a satire of masculinity, a parody of the false notion of individualism, and it makes a mockery of world religions, symbolic only of consumerist and productivist cults. He is a man-made false god who believes only in accruing further wealth. An empty, meaningless, soulless, value-less void of a person. A chameleon who is everything to everyone and hence nothing to no one, just like the optimo in which he lives his sorry existence.

We, the Nosubs, hate everything he stands for, including ideals of youth and beauty at their most trite and unimaginative. The genetic lottery has gifted him everything we will never have. His audience of vapid womenfolk—who would never deign to pay us attention—drool at his every move.

We had to act, to destroy any goodwill sent his way, by making him perform an undeniable atrocity. JC's response has further justified our actions. The way he spoke to that homeless man confirmed his irreparable delusion. It made us want to double down on our efforts to destroy him and his ilk at any cost.

Yet we must appreciate that the market has chosen him to top the ranks for his optimally attractive physique. This can only mean that our global womenfolk have elected him a genetically superior prospect for reproduction. Those few of you with wives and girlfriends—though it may disgust you—continue to purchase JC's sperm and, at all costs, use it to inseminate your femoids. With his genetics and our ideals, our new society will be unstoppable.

As for what we did to JC himself, use this as your template. Find the influencer you most hate, pretend to be one (or several) of their subscribers, and convince them to undergo elective limb surgeries. We will make living memes of them all, turn them into playable video game characters, and send them out to kill nobodies, thus becoming nobodies themselves.

"So this is just the beginning," JC said.

"Looks like it."

JC lowered his head, about to cry.

"Optimo?" Ferdinand said.

"Yes, Ferdinand," it responded.

"Get a receptacle for JC here in case he starts crying."

"Good idea, Ferdinand."

The optimo dropped some plastic vials at the foot of the bed.

Ferdinand sat beside JC and put a hand on his cold shoulder. JC flinched at the touch, then marvelled at the warmth of it, the spread of some distantly familiar feeling.

"I-It's like you said to me that time," Ferdinand said. "They're jealous. And, for what it's worth, they can't see into your head."

"They could if we had the technology," JC said. "They didn't mention anything about my huge gay following."

"As if gender matters. Surely anyone who likes you has literally no other interests."

"Are you on my side now?"

"I always was," Ferdinand said. "Your subscribers advised your optimo to install the latest antivirus software on your limbs. You'll have to keep updating it from now on, of course." Ferdinand stroked his stubble. "It does seem like society will keep generating more of these Nosubs."

JC smiled. "Sounds like you've found a real need for yourself."

Ferdinand stood up. "I will admit, having consumed a lot of your 'content' in the last twenty-four hours, that's something I like about you. You always find a way to reframe things positively, even if it's just an automatic thing you do to remain liked."

JC laughed. "We almost connected there!"

"But you're right. Not all is lost. Now that we've categorized the typical Nosub, we'll use algorithms to screen for them. Previous convictions. Certain keywords in their online screeds. And we're appealing to the fanbases of influencers to educate themselves on this issue, to make one another aware and to report suspicious behaviour. There are, in fact, over two thousand concurrent sting operations going on in this very city, almost all of them automated."

JC's eyes widened as he took this in. "Amazing, aren't they?"

"Who?"

JC stood up, raised his hands above his head, and brought them down to his side. In so doing, he dialled the opacity of his optimo to zero. He and Ferdinand looked out at the golden-brown hills, their multicoloured optimos glowing beneath the pink sunset. "All the people out there. All the tech. Like the virus and the immune system all in one."

Ferdinand clasped his hands behind his back. "That's an astute way of looking at it."

JC grabbed Ferdinand's shoulders with excitement. "I should make a video about it, right?"

Ferdinand smiled at him. "If it gets the word out, that's a great idea. In fact, we've interrupted the surgeries of eleven other influencers to make sure they fully understand the risks involved."

"I'll ask my subscribers to donate to, uh, homeless charities."

Ferdinand's expression became listless. "In between their purchases of hair care products and face creams."

JC frowned. "I haven't figured it out yet but, no, that wouldn't be a good slot. Hey! I can also do a shout-out to you and your hard work."

Ferdinand shook his head. "Nah."

"You kidding me? You'd be helping me out too."

"It would play well with your subscribers that you choose to associate with someone of my age and appearance."

"Totally. And, with your permission, I'd love to gift you and your daughters an iMirror each."

"I've got to understand this stuff, I guess. Sure. You're gonna help me set them up, right?"

"Sure!" JC ignored what an embarrassingly naive question it was. No one else would dare waste his time with such an inane request.

"I'll be around your neighbourhood often, after all, investigating these ongoing crimes."

"I figured. Let's make it a weekly thing, you and me. Is there a particular half hour that suits?"

"What?!"

JC recoiled. "You don't like the idea. You're busy."

"Nah, I like it. But I've learned how valuable that time is to you. Down to the last bit."

JC smirked. "Better make it worth my while."

"The time we've shared together is already priceless. How's Thursday dinner time?"

"It's a date."

Ferdinand walked back to the wall. JC pressed his hand to it to reveal an entrance again.

Ferdinand thought of something and looked at JC. "Smash that like button."

JC nodded seriously. "Commented and subscribed."

9

Hey folx,

Endlessly grateful for all your support. Can't wait to get back to providing you with more top-tier content—but for the sake of my health, I have to take some time off. Much love to all of you, and see you soon.

JC slept intermittently for days, suffering through feverish nightmares and waking in a cold sweat. It felt useful, like it was his body's way of purging evil. As the days passed by unconsciously, he felt lighter. What remained of his body told him what it needed. Despite all his attempts at productivity, it seemed life was just unavoidably dreary and dreadful sometimes.

When he finally braved his iMirror inbox, after two weeks or so, it showed the numbers *14757* in red and *3* in green. Three messages worth reading among the thousands received.

The first was a link to a new video by his "gamer buddies" Toastfiend, Butterboy, and FlowerBro, titled *We never wanted to make this …*

JC snorted. "Then don't make it, idiots."

He clicked it. The three of them, in their coloured gaming hoodies and sweatpants, with their hand-dyed hair and glasses, sat in a row on the same black couch. They'd met in person?

They looked with genuine concern into the camera.

"We were sorry to hear what happened to JC."

"Make no mistake, we were personally devastated."

"Playing *YeahBuilders* with him was the highlight of our week."

"Yeah, he's so goofy and funny."

"Such a cool guy."

"I had no idea why he even chose to hang out with me!"

"We stand by him at this time. I know some of you will slate us for this, and that's fine. It's important in times like this to stick up for your mates. The JC we know would never consciously or deliberately do what he was accused of."

"The outcome of his trial reflects this."

"We're on his side and can't imagine how he must be feeling right now."

"I'm sure he deeply regrets what happened and will do everything in his power to make amends."

"Even though the balance will never be reset, of course."

"JC, we love you. Wishing you a speedy recovery. I hope this reflective time isn't too painful for you."

"And when you're ready, we can't wait to play games with you again."

"Sayonara, Toastheads."

"Until next time, Butterdudes."

"Peace out, Seeds."

It was impressively off the cuff. As genuine as such a thing could sound. It might even have *been* genuine. JC filled with a mixture of love, guilt, and cringe.

The iMirror's other two green messages were personal videos sent to him by none other than FrancescaFlores and BradBeatz. Both thanked him for raising pressing issues facing the influencer community, which, thanks to the size of his subscriber base, would doubtless prevent massive harm to countless others.

"Even though I did it out of spite to try and knock you both off the top spot," he said to the iMirror. "And you knew I'd be too thrilled about these private videos not to mention them when I'm next live, which will doubtless send my subscribers your way. Well played, numbers one and two. Long may you both reign."

They included a link to call them both, anytime, for a special private collab.

"Jesus, I might be cynical but I'm not stupid. Mirror, call that link!"

Brad logged on first. He looked sleepy, his hair askew. He wore nothing but boxers. Either he didn't find this inappropriate or considered it a gift for JC to see him like this without having to pay. A new-age mating display. "JC!" he said.

Despite himself, an electric thrill jolted through JC to hear his name pass through Brad's legendary lips.

"Brad," he said, grinning.

"Let's get Francesca on the line."

A few seconds later, Francesca joined the chat. She paced around her optimo's kitchen in full makeup, plastic flowers in her hair. "JC!" she said in ebullient falsetto.

"Francesca!" he said.

"Am I ever thankful to see you," she said.

"Likewise."

"This is long overdue," Brad said. "But let me just say I've loved competing with you both over the years. Seriously. It's tough not to go stale, but you hustling motherfuckers kept a fire under my ass!"

They laughed.

"Totes agree," Francesca said. "In fact. I did a little something recently." She tilted her iMirror down so they could see her bionic legs.

"Banging pins you've got there, Francesca," Brad said.

"Thanks," she said, in a slightly defeated tone. "Don't worry, I've got all the latest anti-hack software, and I'll stay vigilant." She winked. "But, hey, if either of you boys ever feel like walking me around my mansion sometime ..."

"I'd love to," JC said.

"By the way," she added, "we're donating the computational power of our optimos to ongoing investigations."

"Basically," Brad said, "when we're asleep and there's nothing but the iMirror running to record us sleeping, our optimos will get used by forums and programs that need them to run their anti-crime sims and so on. But let's get down to business."

JC grinned. "By all means."

"Francesca and I talked about it, and we want to collab with you as soon as possible, JC."

JC's heart rate shot up.

"Yeah," Francesca said. "We want to make a special video about the incident."

"Great idea," JC said. "Just let me know when."

"Sure," Brad said. "But you need your rest now. We'll get the word out, and you can ping us anytime when you're down to collab."

"We can't wait!" Francesca said.

"Me neither," JC said. "Hey, I would've gotten in touch earlier, but I've always kinda been afraid of you both."

"Me too!" Brad said.

"Me three!" Francesca said.

"Hah," JC said. "Guess we were being silly, huh? You think maybe this could be the start of something?"

"I was hoping you'd say that!" Brad said. "I don't wanna get ahead of myself, but I have so many ideas for us. Like, what if we did a podcast about the dark side of being an influencer?"

"Totes," Francesca said. "My *florecitas* love vulnerability."

JC nodded. "Sounds like something I'd love to talk to you both about even if we *didn't* monetize it."

"Me too," Brad said. He eyed JC up and down. "I predict the three of us will soon make lots of content together."

Brad and Francesca were bisexual, or at least they claimed to be. JC hadn't thought he was bisexual, though he also claimed to be. But as he saw what looked like lust in Brad's eyes, a ripple of electricity passed through him. Something like sexual excitement and love. Like the overwhelming hormonal impulses of a horny teenager, multiplied a thousandfold. He'd never felt so turned on in his life. Was it their peak conventional beauty? The sexual gratification of all that potential money and fame? The thought of their subscriber numbers melding together?

He, Brad, and Francesca, sexually intertwined, the three biggest market-verified hotties going at it. He wanted it so badly. This was beyond sexual. It was … metasexual, maybe. There was nothing sexier than the prospect of such objectively high-quality content. An economic odyssey awaited them as they explored their own bodies and each other's in the creation of all possible revenue streams.

This was spiritual connection to influencers. Better, even. Spirituality, as JC understood it, was a nebulous attempt to feel connected to humanity. The influencer world went beyond that. It hardwired you directly into other people's lives. What need was there for spirituality in a world where genuine, real-life connectivity like this was possible?

"Jesus, I feel like I'm gonna faint," JC said.

"Yeah," Brad said, his pupils dilating euphorically. "Get better soon, buddy."

"'Cause we've got any number of uses for you!" Francesca said.

"I've gotta get outta here," JC said, and signed off.

He indulged in a ten-minute, off-cam, unmonetized solo scene.

10

Thereafter, JC turned all his attention to recovery. He had the iMirror guide him through meditation sessions and requested that the optimo taper him off his various sedatives. These methods combined, he steeled himself through withdrawal symptoms. The itchiness of his skin. Restlessness. Hunger beyond hunger. The flood of overwhelming emotions. Long-postponed grief for so many reasons, some known, most not. He bore as much of their intensity as he could before resorting to opioids and benzos again to take the edge off.

Once he had regained enough attention span, he tried recreational reading. His choices weren't completely free—they were all books he'd once seen Lizzie recommending to her fanbase—but this was a far more wholesome motivation than his usual.

In recent years, the constant torrent of images sent his way had crowded out his imagination. *1984*'s Big Brother was BradBeatz. A ripped golden god. He found it hard to chastise or disapprove of the book's messages with a villain who looked like that. The gang in *A Clockwork Orange* was him and his gamer buddies, having violent fun in a virtual environment. He was Henry in *The Time Traveler's Wife*, and Lizzie played the role of Clare.

Horrible crying fits and flashbacks plagued his nights. *What about your family? What about Jory? What about Lizzie?* his subconscious seemed to say. *And I have plenty more where they came from.*

Would the nighttime guilt ease if he took action against it?

One night, he dictated a long-overdue letter to his iMirror:

Lizzie,

This is tough to send. I write to you both too late and too early. Plus, I feel like I'm disrespecting the obvious rift I drove between us by assuming you would still let me contact you. But I'd feel like a complete bastard if I didn't tell you I'm doing okay. I'm sure you worry about me even if you don't want to.

I'm taking a much-needed break from the streams and exploring ways to make reparations to affected communities. I'm meditating and reading books of my own choice. Or rather, your choice! Most recently I blazed through Life of Pi, The Stranger, *and*

Pachinko. *I'm so thankful I remembered your recommendations and dismayed that I have learned, so late, what excellent taste you have. You were too good to spend the rest of your days with the likes of someone like me. Lol.*

I don't blame you for that at all. I'm deeply ashamed of how I behaved towards you. This time of resurfacing only hammers that home even further. It's like I put my conscience on pause, and all that time it accumulated the emotional recompense that I'm reaping now. But the only way through is just to feel it. Oh, boy, am I ever doing that.

The last thing I want to do is derive any benefit from these circumstances whatsoever—but it's difficult not to be thankful for the catalyst that has put us back in touch.

I'd love to know how you're doing.

Best,

Justin.

He told the iMirror to use records of his handwriting to transcribe the letter onto hand-pressed paper and send it in an envelope smattered with cutesy stickers. This was what 'Justin' used to do. He hadn't been that guy in a long time. Justin was an almost-forgotten memory that he was choosing to resurrect now. For some reason.

JC didn't even know who he wanted to be. Maybe the kind of man Lizzie had wanted, if that was still possible. Maybe he hadn't tried hard enough. Maybe he didn't even want to try again.

If he did, now was as good a time as ever to start. His letter could serve as a personal manifesto, a template of how to be from now on.

A week later, Lizzie's emailed response reached his iMirror, which read it aloud in its robotic voice:

Justin,

Thank you for your letter. I'm glad to hear from you but deeply sorry about the circumstances.

I'll assume you don't know anything about my life of late. I live with Dad, and I'm pursuing my master's in criminal law online with AlphaMaxx University. It's an intensive course that keeps me mostly at home, but I make sure to hang out with real-life people in the village to talk about stuff other than what I do all day. I almost forgot, having lived in Influencer Land for so long, that there's an even more numerous population that doesn't know anything about influencers at all.

I tell myself it won't always be so intense. My studies are nearly over, and they're in service of providing a life I really want.

No way would I get my work done if I hadn't completely blocked any mention of influencers on all my devices. You weren't to know, but your letter triggered a week-long delve into everything I could learn about what happened to you. Jesus, is it ever harrowing. I wouldn't wish it on anyone.

I'm tempted to discuss it further with you. It's a landmark case, and I'm still considering potential thesis topics, after all. But, as I'm sure you can appreciate, I can't.

After the whole LizGate fiasco, I'm keen to avoid anything that makes me seem manipulative and self-serving. Nor would I like to provide you with what I'm sure would be excellent content.

I'm aware the career I've chosen is competitive, but I'm completely turned off by anything resembling the empty chase of exceptionalism. I've been doing just fine with my studies so far without you. I can continue to do so.

Ultimately, you and I want very different things in life. I can't forget or overlook our history. But I am thankful you let me know that you're okay. It is an enormous burden off my shoulders.

Best,
Lizzie.

This response was more than he deserved—but it was still lacerating to receive. Perhaps he'd encouraged rejection to appease himself for the guilt of murdering Jory, even if—or because—he'd been acquitted.

He looked Lizzie up. Around the iMirror floated holos of her laughing with friends, studying at a picnic bench in the park, participating in charity fun runs. An impressive use of the last four years.

Pictures of her in a wedding dress. Long train, cathedral veil, coloured confetti. A silver fox in a red tartan kilt, holding her hand.

Why didn't she mention she was married?

"Optimo?" JC said.

"Yeah?"

"Bottle of whisky."

"Think of your skin!"

"Just get it, will you?"

"Okay. Want a glass?"

"No."

The walls opened. A bottle of Johnnie Walker Black Label appeared atop a round table. A red ribbon around its neck had a little note attached: *Dear JC, Thanks for trying us out! Please give us a shout-out in your next stream. Regards, JW*

He tore off the note, unscrewed the bottle, and took a swig.

"Mirror, mirror," he said.

The iMirror sped over to him, hovering before his face.

"Search for 'Justin Chacley cybertrap'."

"Justin Chacley has five EPs."

"Play in chronological order."

He continued to swig warm, expensive whisky from the bottle, dancing around uneasily on his legs.

Sunlight through the optimo windows faded to darkness as JC kept dancing.

"Can't do it to myself," he murmured.

"What was that?" the optimo said.

"I'm going out!"

"JC, the police are still monitoring your actions. It's never a good idea to leave your optimo, but now especially."

"I didn't ask for your fucking opinion!"

He stumbled out of the optimo, nostrils again filling with acrid air.

He headed down the hill towards the dip, legs rustling in the metal detritus, bonfires blurry and doubled in his drunken vision.

He approached the tent city entrance.

Huddled figures in their thick coats turned to him. Some screamed in fear. Others shouted in anger.

"That's him!"

"The guy who murdered Jory!"

"Why you showing your face around here, huh?"

"Came back to gloat?"

"One of us will always be worth a million of you."

"Yeah."

"We'll show you just how much we think of you."

"Wait." A calmer voice of reason. A gent with long white hair, in a stained olive duffel coat. His stubbly face emerged from the blur before JC. "I'm sure you have good intentions for showing up here, young man."

Scoffs and sneers from the gathering crowd.

JC felt himself falling into a deep pit of shame.

"It's not safe for you here. I wish it was." The man placed a hand on JC's shoulder. When he felt its cool metal, he recoiled and tried in vain to hide it. "I'll pass on my details, and you can find a better way of keeping in touch."

The crowd objected. "Frank, what are you talking about?"

"You know who that is, right?"

"Didn't any of you hear what happened?" Frank called back.

"Didn't *you*? He's a killer."

Frank shook his head. "He's just as much a victim as my son."

A feeling for which he had no name overwhelmed JC. Something like an enormous boulder of grief pressing down on him. But the grief shone at its borders with brilliant white light that transformed it into a crushing implement of pure forgiveness. It was far more beautiful, but exponentially tougher to cope with.

JC crumpled into Frank's arms.

Frank held him. He shushed him and told him it would all be okay. "Go on home, now. We'll pick this up another time."

JC turned and stumbled back up the hill.

"Thank God you're back," the optimo said as JC staggered in.

"Get me another bottle of that whisky, would you?"

"But we don't have any more donations."

"I'll cope."

Another bottle of Johnnie Walker, this time non-complimentary, showed up. JC used it to drown his thoughts and fall into a brittle, unrestful sleep.

11

A small gathering of twenty or so attended Jory's funeral. They sat in foldable gymnasium chairs up on a nearby hill.

JC and Frank planned the ceremony together with much care. JC had the resources for a big, flashy affair, but Frank warned that this would've been wildly inappropriate. It was best to model Jory's funeral on what was typical for their community, with just a handful of extra amenities.

A symbolic black urn, on a marble plinth, stood on the dais. They'd already buried Jory's body elsewhere, in a cheap biodegradable box stacked with others in an open, unmarked grave. His community hadn't managed to gather the funds for the body. As usual.

They allowed JC to donate a filtering membrane dome so they

could sit in the open air, beneath the sunlight, during peak polluting hours, without having to limit their time.

JC sat on the dais in a smart black suit, with his old stolen Korg on his lap and his hands gloved so that attendees didn't have to look at them.

Frank, in a similar suit, took to the dais and approached the mic.

"My son was a lover of the outdoors, of people, of life. A party starter. A personal champion. An adventurer and a survivor. He extended his compassion to everyone, from his fellow unfortunates right up to, well …" He gestured to JC but left the thought incomplete.

A hologram slideshow of pictures appeared. JC looked away. Those Polaroids from the tent were sure to appear, which was more than he could currently bear.

Before he knew it, Frank had taken his hand. "Justin here," he said to the attendees, "has written a song that he'd like to perform."

One or two at the back left in disgust.

JC approached the mic. "Hi, everyone. My name's Justin."

"We know who you are!" someone at the front heckled.

JC ignored it. "Hearing those details about your friend's life—it seems like he was a really special person. Someone I would've wanted to spend … more time with."

He set up his Korg on a stand and began to sing:

Jory
You and me
Our souls combined
But you can't see
My heart expands
With your love
And now I feel
I have enough

In me you live
Forever more
You gave and gave
Opened the door
We meld together
In love and death
But if I could
I'd buy back your last breath
If I could
I'd buy back your last breath

This wasn't an audience of fans of his music, but they looked earnestly at him and appreciated the intent.

Flashing lights distracted JC. He looked up. Spidery, suction-cupped devices had affixed themselves to the outside of the membrane. Gossip sites were recording it for content. The world that had chosen him was always waiting for him to return.

At the reception afterwards, JC leaned against the bar, drinking a glass of Cristal.

Some walked by and asked for whole bottles, which they slipped into large internal pockets. JC thought of telling them they were welcome to stay and drink as much as they wanted, but he kept silent, fearing it might sound condescending.

Some thanked him for the performance. He seemed to have won most of them over. That, or those who seriously objected to his attendance had boycotted Jory's funeral outright. Perhaps they had even turned their backs on Frank.

JC felt lucky that he didn't know this community well. He could still certainly pass on some ideas to Frank on how to weather a strongly divided public opinion. After all, it didn't matter the size of the community nor the severity of the choices you made. People reacted the way they did. You were never going to please everyone. Better just to do whatever you want and please the people who happened to be pleased by it.

Not that he'd ever been much good at following this advice.

"Your song was beautiful," Frank said, patting him on the shoulder.

"It's the best I could do," JC said. "And the least. But thanks. It means the world coming from you."

A chubby, middle-aged woman with short red hair came up to him. "That air filter is amazing," she said uneasily.

"You're very welcome," JC said.

"We could use something like that for the tents," she added.

"Terry …" Frank said sternly.

"It's fine," JC said.

Terry's face lit up. "Would you mind if we, like, tore it up and taped it to the underpass entrance?"

"We can do better than that," JC said. "Let's get a set of drones to take some measurements and have one custom-fitted."

"Really?"

"Absolutely." JC took a card out of his pocket and handed it to her. "Stay in touch. I'm sure you'll think of other necessary improvements."

Frank closed and opened his eyes in approval.

An urgent beeping came from JC's pocket.

"Shit," JC said. "Sorry."

"Go ahead," Frank said.

"Mirror, mirror?"

The iMirror floated out and read a recently posted article:

JC goes OUTSIDE?! Sings gut-wrenching tribute to young man who died in tragic Nosub hacking incident. Fans old and new touched by JC's unmonetized, non-autotuned tribute to Jory in front of the TINIEST audience of NOBODIES that JC has EVER entertained! "It's proof that he'd do this no matter how many of us there were, and that he really does love us," FlossyTopping475, a subscriber, said.

JC waved the iMirror away again. "The song," he said to Frank. "It's gone viral. The whole community's talking about it."

Frank frowned, appearing bemused.

"Mirror, mirror," JC said. "Secure copyright for song 'Jory' and route all related proceeds to Frank Stevenson."

"You're finally here." JC lay on his bed, examining the proxy that walked towards him. Slim figure, kinked ash-blonde hair, green eyes, freckles across the bridge of her nose.

"It's us," she said.

"All of you?"

"Those of us allowed to be here who could afford it. So, like, eighty per cent of us."

He eyed her up and down. "Interesting,"

"What is?"

"You're shaping yourselves for me for once."

She gripped her arm self-consciously. "Do you like it? Our appearance?"

"It's a little weird, but I'll take it."

"We thought you might say that. Some of us were unsure, but we voted on it. Thought we'd give it a shot." She lay beside him, taking his hand. "You can call us Lizzie if you want."

"Very kind of you."

"We made her from your Justin&Liz streams together. They're the most up-to-date recordings of her that exist. We figured that was even better than modelling it on the current Lizzie. We're Lizzie as you remember her, when you were both happy together."

He gripped her memory foam hips, heard the soft whirring of pistons beneath her skin as they buckled beneath his hands. "I'm looking forward to rewarding you, Lizzie. How many are you, exactly?"

She brushed her hair aside to reveal the number: *390M*

"Whoa! Really?"

She giggled and nodded.

"But … that's the most ever!"

"A world record. You're gonna be the first man on Earth who ever slept with that many people at once."

"What a time to be alive." JC grinned. "You all came through for me."

"Yeah," she said. "We knew you'd never do what they'd accused you of."

"Of course not," JC said. "The Nosubs thought they could cancel me by making me perform an 'undeniable atrocity'. But in the court of public opinion there's no such thing. Weird for the world. Lucky for me."

He caressed her legs, brought himself in closer, held her with an arm around her back. He pressed his lips to hers and their tongues worked over one another, her silicone flesh warmed by electric elements. He could feel her grinning.

"What is it?" he said, still kissing her.

"Something funny we're talking about in the chat. We were just thinking. We're a robot, and you're becoming more robotic. Maybe one day we'll both be robots, and no humans will even watch. They'll just be happy to know that they've made robots that are having sex in a room somewhere or whatever."

"That would be awesome," JC said. "I could automate my whole day. And let a robot promote products while I lie in bed playing video games or reading books or watching series that I actually like. With people I give a shit about."

The proxy laughed. It was an edgy joke that went down well with the fans.

He wrapped her body around his and lifted her up, falling on top of her in bed. Time to give the supporters what they'd paid for.

A series of sexual commands scrolled over the proxy's face in glowing blue text, with little numbered bubbles stating how many people had requested these sensations: *150.1M, 235.4M, 99.7M.* Screennames appeared. JC had to say them lovingly while looking in the proxy's eyes and adding various lines of affectionate praise and dirty talk. He was grateful to do it.

When he'd fulfilled the bulk of this top-tier reward interaction, the proxy climbed on top of him. He lay on his back, holding her hips. He closed his eyes and tried to visualize the millions of people writhing in pleasure right now. All the loving subscribers in their homes, strapped to their devices of stainless steel and medical-grade silicone. All of them made to feel like they were the only one.

But the hideous murder. The vitriolic manifesto. They weren't far enough behind him. Maybe never would be. They seeded a sceptic within him, which held him back from completely letting go.

You immoral fuckwit, the sceptic said. *How many of your billion-plus audience are under eighteen, again? Most of them, no?*

He shut his eyes hard, trying to disguise his discomfort as sexual pleasure.

Nice try, he said back to the naysaying voice. *Sex toy companies screen for that.*

With full accuracy?

He frowned.

This isn't my audience anyway. These are the ones who saved me. My case reached the world stage.

That just means you have no idea who these people are.

Shit. It was too late to stop. He owed these people his life, whoever they were. They had forgiven him and assisted him in retaining his number-three spot. This was all they had asked for in return. Would they forgive him as easily for interrupting it?

If he couldn't focus, he couldn't finish. He'd already pre-sold his prospective emission for a ridiculous price, since it theoretically impregnated hundreds of millions.

He grunted and flipped the proxy onto its back.

If I'm doing any wrong here, it's negligible. Because what's right about it is so right. The net pleasure of so many satisfied adults.

She wrapped her legs tight around his hips.

"What sane person"—he kissed her neck—"could look upon this and not see"—he thrust into her—"that it's the greatest … ever … demonstration … of love?"

A PLOT OF TRAUMA VERSUS DISTANCE

Mum and/or Dad,

What are you doing on Mars? Was our family not in enough pain, so you had to bugger a million miles off?

I knew this would happen. I get back in touch with you and feel all the same emotions flooding back full force, like an alcoholic boozing after several dry months, picking up the bottle exactly where she left it.

Did you at least make it there okay? I've been too cowardly to check. If you'd just stayed here, I wouldn't have had to discover this side of myself, so yeah, I blame you for that too. Or I'm just mad at the situation. I can't tell.

I promise to read whatever you send me in its entirety and without judgement. If indeed you're alive and capable.

With vague well wishes,
Son #2

Ben,

I'm glad you got back in touch. Your father and I are here.

When I didn't see you at the station, I decided to let you break the silence first. I know I said it was cheaper for us to launch from Shanghai, and that you should come say hi before we headed off, might as well since we were in the same country—but I assume you saw through that excuse.

I knew you'd be mad, but I never believed you'd ghost us completely.

I thought of you from the moment the taxi blasted off, throughout our journey on the cycler, and beyond. I always associated the cycler with you, well before I ever had plans of going to Mars. Remember when we first saw it together? I walked you to school one morning when you were still wee enough to fit in your multicoloured padded onesie, one of Jack's hand-me-downs. The cycler gave off a surreal sheen, filtered blue by the sky. It didn't look real. To think those cabins, the chrome and carpeting and crew, were all up there? Wild. You always thought air travel was unnatural and weird, but, Son—neither #2 nor #1, as well you know—this was something else.

It was wilder still to reach Mars after months of nothing but stars to look at. As we approached, the planet began as a chocolate-dusted ball suspended in space. It slowly expanded until the silvery barnacles of habitats appeared across its surface, shimmering in the sun. Eventually we got so close that Mars took over the portholes entirely. We hadn't just changed planets but seemingly sped backwards in time to some dust storm–ridden prairie. There were so few colours in the landscape and sky I thought there was something wrong with my eyes.

You were the first person to whom I wanted to tell all

this. But I also thought, "Mars is *his* thing! He'll be furious I got to see it first."

Now that we're here—long after the orientation lectures on muscle atrophy and bone demineralization—I can pretend we're not in an underground habitat but something like the music academy to which I took you on weekends. Endless underground rooms with glaring fluorescent light. Remember?

The Brits who came with us—the upper-class families, the politicians, bankers, and celebrities—they met the discovery of Earth's new disease with something like lust. "And they don't even know what's causing it!" they kept saying. I was so tempted to reply, "That's what 'cryptogenic' means"! But what would that have achieved?

Back home, I'm sure they excused their complaints as a product of their environment, but what's their logic here? It's like they packed an invisible pop-up tent of the UK that they've unfurled to camp out in on Mars. You can shoot some people out of the solar system, and they'll still whinge about the weather back home!

Okay, I suppose they have a right to bemoan the fate of their home planet. Me, I can't bear to hear more about it. And I find it odd that these others complain without a word of gratitude for the pilots, astronomers, financiers, and God knows who and what—the forces that 'saved' them from Earth.

For work, I commute from our wing at Pavonis Mons to Tharsis University. They confirmed my position while I was still on the cycler. Your dad has been less fortunate. Everyone here must be put to work somehow, but despite early indications that there was an anthropology-related job for him, he's currently a barista. When he returns to me in the evening, he doesn't emerge from his room. His nose is always in the same book. *An Integrated Approach to*

Anthropology and Epidemiology, it's called. I suppose he's worried about you, about the cryptogenic cirrhosis, and approaches his anxiety through the safety of his favourite discipline—if he can muster the concentration to read.

It's just until they find him a place at one of the other universities, but your dad's convinced a 'long-dead planet' has no need for an anthropologist. Ridiculous! He's at the forefront of those who can observe first hand how humans adapt to life on Mars. I hope he manages to take advantage of it.

It's not all bad here. I have a decent sleep cycle, a supermarket routine, even a favourite restaurant. They print burgers like you wouldn't believe!

I also run a star-studded book club. As you might have heard, Mars is a big empty planet with a small-town mentality. Everyone knows everyone here, for better or worse. And you know your mother, I'm forever networking. It's so easy here. I think because things are too tenuous for us to consider how I, 'just' a linguistics professor, and they, commander-general of the army of something-or-other, might engage in mutual back-scratching.

My demeanour, as you know, is a result of experience. I'm bemused that anyone thinks they have time to be mean! But the powerful can confuse kindness with naivety. Once they've had too much of the latest Martian vintage, this silly hippie, with her floaty dresses and old tomes, learns the darkest secrets of Mars's best and brightest.

You know you and Priya are welcome to join us, don't you? One of the cyclers will be back in Earth's orbit in a few weeks, by my calculations. Had you not contacted me first, I swear I would've reminded you. If it bothers you so much to be apart from us—as it does me, I swear, unless that guilts you, in which case I swear I can cope, although painfully, because I miss you—get on board. I'll greet you with the Martian equivalent of champagne and oysters. I won't tell you what it is, for fear you'll decline!

If you stay where you are, try to understand our decision, just like we did when you moved to Shanghai in the first place. You didn't go as far, no, but it's the same idea. Our home ached with your loss, but we never showed it. We were scared you'd catch on and come home again. We didn't want to quash your dreams like that.

I wish my words were kinder. Less urgent. I wonder if lack of sunlight has drained my usual propensity for poetic flair. Maybe none of this applies and I'm just pontificating, as is my wont, for whatever reason, adding nuance where none exists, drawing new theories out of the air to pass the time. What with everything we've been through, I can't claim to understand much.

All my love,
Mum

Mum,

Surely you get that I can't be mad at you if I messaged you?

Unless I write that to convince myself. If I don't know how I feel, I've no idea how I could expect you to know. It's supposedly a huge compliment when we expect others to anticipate our needs, but that rule doesn't apply here. The relationships of the Wilson family have weakened, stretched, and starved over time. Redshifted, like starlight.

Speaking of stars, I'd be suspicious of your book club. If anyone powerful has made you feel special, they're probably after something. It's like when Yangpu Solutions told me they were 'looking for motivated individuals like me to find unique engineering solutions to help them adapt to the challenges of this new climate'.

All I ever did for them was sell atmospheric water harvesters to the Chinese aristocracy. Not exactly 'following my dreams', as you put it. I wouldn't even know what that looks like, so no expectations on you there.

I assume you think of Mars as 'my thing' because of Priya. It makes me cringe when I think about how much you had to spend on our communication when she was on Mars. All those video messages, which I wouldn't dare shell out for myself. (And I won't have you paying for any more either. This long-form back and forth between us feels apropos anyway. At my own pace, draft after draft, I can steadily iron erratic emotions out of these sentences.)

I used to run and tell you whatever song Priya had just learned on the ukulele. Tell you her dreams, in which exotic birds made weird formations, and what she thought that meant about our future together. Whatever her dad was up to in his diplomatic duties. They sounded super important, because I never understood them.

So embarrassing now. I thought I'd found some new secret, that our love was above everyone else's—but it must have felt the same when you met Dad. Suppose I'd never had your example: would I even have known what it looks like when you marry for love?

I flaunted what Priya and I had to the very people who'd allowed for it!

When she arrived here, that's when the real work began. It's tough to idolize someone up close. Everything was real, all the time.

Distance can be imperative to a bond's strength

sometimes. That said, I rarely messaged Jack when he was at his asteroid outpost.

When Jack's crewmates came to the house, I should've hid in the basement like you. Instead, I don't know why, I asked them to explain the accident to me in detail, to tell me everything about it, from the technical sequence of failures to the way his final screams crackled through the intercom. It was some way of coping, first focusing on the engineering aspect before exposing myself to all the information at hand. A type of self-harm disguised as 'how a man should act'. From what you report of Dad, seems I learned it from him. And I concur: hiding from the reality of your problems behind the comfort of your favourite discipline is a bullshit strategy.

Now, whenever I think of Jack, there are no birthdays. We no longer run around the back garden together. We don't smoke surreptitious cigarettes down secret suburban lanes. I only see him alone in the darkness of space, an intrepid astronaut bouncing across mottled rocks, analyzing them for metals. The sparks of a torch light up his angular face, his mop of black hair stuck to his brow. An orange blast flashes before him and bats his bits and pieces into the abyss.

I never asked you. How did it feel without a body to bury? For me it made it a less true, less healing ceremony, at least at the time. If my expectation was to be 'over it' one day, that was never gonna happen regardless.

I didn't spot you guilting *Jack* when he left, by the way. Did that even occur to you? Why did you just assume I'd stick around? Was I a little comfort-blanket person, a compensation prize for your bravery in letting the better kid go? You can't just erase favouritism with empty words.

You know, I once asked Dad if he'd be okay if I never

provided him with grandkids. After a painfully long pause, he replied, "One must answer yes." Cringe.

You would've gone to Mars even if I'd *not* gone to Shanghai! You would've boosted out of here, and if I'd so much as tapped you on the shoulder with a 'now hold on a second', you would've taken offence, and then where would *I* be? Stuck where you guilted me into staying.

Silently, I might add. You weren't brave enough to say it outright. You just left it heavily implied in the stiflingly British air of our family home. You'd deny it if asked, but you were to follow your whims and I was not to follow mine. You'd make me feel bad no matter what I did. All I could choose was the flavour of it. I chose Shanghai.

Was I running away? Yeah. So silly, isn't it? We lost Jack in outer space, but I ran from London to Shanghai to escape it. You ran to Mars. Loss is no competition, but I've no doubt that because losing him hurt you more, you had to go further.

See? I *am* trying to understand. Some days it's like the planet itself hurts, its surface radiating a pain so keen I can almost hear it. On those days I always remember, 'Mum must have felt that too'.

And I must say, I find your self-exile optimistic. You assumed I'd be around long enough that you could flee the planet and still hope to see me again one day. Right?

Maybe you weren't thinking of it at all.

Does life hurt less on Mars?

If I'm right about why you left—and I do mean this—I hope it worked.

Love,
Ben

Ben,

You ask me how it felt without a body to bury. How do you *think* it felt?

Sorry. I don't know to whom or what I should direct that rage. If at all. But how much of *your* rage, I wonder, do you direct at your distorted memory of me?

Yes, I ran away too. As you say, I assumed that after losing Jack I'd paid my dues. A son gone—worse than most go through. Surely there's compensation? I'll live until my eighties, for example, so you won't have to lose me until you're about the age I am now. And we'll see each other before then, of course. Then it'll all be okay?

We feed ourselves such strange reassurances to stay sane.

But no, fleeing didn't work. I think—since nothing here reminds your dad and me of you or Jack—when we look at each other, it floods back at us, amplified in the full spectrum of its intensity, good through bad. It emanates from us, expanding to fill the spaces we occupy like a vapour. We jumped planets and crammed ourselves into these packed underground living quarters, and in so doing concentrated our Jack-and-Ben emotions into the lesser volume of this new environment.

So, if anything, it all hurts more.

But how was I to know that? What do you want from me? We all grow up thinking parents can protect us from much more than they really can.

Adulthood and disillusionment, now *there's* a thesis. I mean, look, you live in a world where people need atmospheric water harvesters. That's how it is. You have provided a necessary service. Will anyone remember you for doing so? Will owners of these harvesters ever stop, close their eyes, and give personal thanks to you? Do you even know how such a device works? Your mother sure doesn't, but she created someone who might, or who at least played a significant role in making sure those in need received them. For which we should *both* be proud.

May I ask why you speak of your work in the past tense? And why bring up my assumption that I'll see you again? Anything wrong with that?

What are you afraid to tell me?

Love,
Mum

———

Mum,

I see time and distance haven't affected your intuition. You're quite correct. There's something I haven't wanted to tell you.

I've got it, Mum. The new disease. The cryptogenic cirrhosis.

I'd go to the emergency clinic if it weren't for Priya. Pregnant women are the most vulnerable, you see. (Three months along, by the way, all signs good so far. I didn't mean to break the happy news to you like that. I'm making such a mess of this.) The government would take Priya away from me if they knew. Maybe it's the safest option. But say I could even bear to let her leave—what would she do with her days besides worry about me anyway?

I don't mean that egotistically. She just has nothing else to do. She can't get a job. Terrans would never admit it, but they discriminate against Martian workers.

I guess you don't know because you've been avoiding the news—one of your recent acts that I fully support, please continue, nothing you can do about it anyway—but since Priya takes all necessary precautions around me, there isn't too much risk. The disease is more fatal than it is contagious. Victories where you can take them, right?

Each day, Priya dons a new face mask. She decorates them while I sleep. A cat's nose and whiskers, a monster's snarling mouth, a clown's painted lips. At worst, her artistic efforts get a bleak smile in response. I'm usually too distracted by my reflection in her face shield: waxy, jaundiced, bloodshot eyes. A corpse-to-be. I stare at myself and try to avoid imagining the life Priya left behind for this, for me.

Travel restrictions here in China are particularly severe, which is probably for the best. Last time one of the cyclers came into orbit, some of the afflicted tried to board it from the Shanghai port. Before they could, they got caught by thermal scanners, which picked up their fevers. I believe they all died, but the news moved on before I could find out.

I didn't even notice I was trying to tell you this. I'd wanted to see how we'd communicate if you didn't know. What you'd say if you weren't afraid it was the last thing. Because there's only so much to be said for living each day like you'll die tomorrow. Sometimes you've got laundry to do, an attic to paint, cat litter to replace.

As you've probably guessed, illness is why I started writing to you. That's your son, stubborn until the very last, grudge-bearing at penalty of … Well, you know me, closed-up British engineer, don't do emotions well, final words too intense.

So, thank you for your Mars offer, but it's not possible. I don't see how I'll ever see you again. We already tried Priya's dad. He'd take her but not me. Fuck him and his principles. Don't tell him I said that. Or do. I leave it with you.

The 'compensation fantasy' you describe is fascinating, isn't it? I think that's the term for it. We lost Jack and went so quickly back to living life, as if such a tragedy was somehow less likely to happen a second time, or ever again. You left the planet, and I let you, as if we had time to figure out the details later. We're both guilty of it.

But enough of all this. I can't even bear to tell you more. And I know, I started it, I raged first—but now is the time for gentleness. Please. I'm so tired.

Mum and Dad, I love you both so much.

Ben

Mum,

Please message me back. Just a word to confirm receipt or something, please.

Ben

Mum,

Did you see my invitation to send video messages? Please accept. We're ready, don't you think? Forget what I said about the cost, about writing to you. It obviously doesn't matter anymore. If it's my appearance you're afraid of, don't be. I'm well looked after, not in any pain.

Ben

***

Mum,

Please just send me something.

Ben

***

Son,

I'm risking everything writing to you now, but I can't just leave it. What if this is the last time?

No, don't let me think like that. Let me hold on to a naivety-free hope! Yes, why not wish for that? Maybe I'll finally find the balance in my fifties.

There are so many things I don't know. Motherhood is not a function of wisdom, not in my case anyway. You create your favourite people and want the best for them like you've never wanted for anybody, not even yourself. It's this exquisite pain, like cutting out your heart and watching it dance in front of traffic.

But you discover you can't say anything around them, these favourite people. At least not all you'd need to say. Definitely not all you'd want to. They won't let you, or you can't face it. Maybe some mothers and sons can do it, but we couldn't, could we? Not enough. Is it ever?

I say this now in case I can't tell it to your face. I won't resort to your morbid imagery of the alcoholic and her bottle, but I do fear that if you and I are reunited we'll snap back into old family dynamics, even with the shared tragedies of a lost son and a brand-new pandemic. That together on Mars we'll just have another terribly awkward dinner except with less wine and more weird, sterile foodstuffs.

As you can probably tell, I have a plan. But I really can't say more. Just, please—even with all that we've been through, *don't give up hope just yet.*

Love,
Mum

Mum,

I'm having those dreams again, of sitting exams—always some physics or biochemistry thing I wouldn't understand. Surely because of the journey Priya and I are about to face.

I timed this message so that if anyone intercepts it, it will be too late to stop us. We're on the cycler now. They'd have to pick us up on Mars, and you've sorted everything for us there.

Others will be fine on the trip, by the way. I'll keep to myself. Besides, I'm not the first to risk exposing others. If we all followed the rules, I wouldn't have seen so many ill folk shuffling beneath my apartment window, shifty ghouls caked in makeup and drowned in baggy clothes to hide their sickly pallor and distended bellies.

It's just a game. Everyone's playing it. So let's play it to win.

They think the disease comes from the nedravirus. For which I'll test negative by the time I reach Mars. Then I'll know for sure we have a shot at some good years together.

The contacts of your contact advised us not to say

more. Please do thank 'commander-general of the army of something-or-other' for the strings he pulled, even if you made him.

I'm scared of the journey ahead. For courage, I'll think of Jack. His curiosity, humour, and drive. How brave he was out there in space, steering motorized drill bits into trillion-dollar space rocks.

How, in the infinite dark, bright sparks light a brief smile.

All my love,
Ben

LOVE YOU TO DEATH

Rob whips Dan across the face with a belt.

Dan cowers in the corner, nursing the developing welt on his pale cheek. Blood soaks the light hair at his temple, turning it dark pink.

Rob stumbles towards me, bumping his shin on the table. Greasy black hair, white T-shirt, and boxers soaked with sweat. He pants. His breath rushes into me. Blows a blood alcohol content of 0.3.

Hammered. Again.

A pang hits me where I imagine my heart to be. I want to feel the sting of tears welling in eyes I don't have. The pain of my hard-earned sentience has yet no name.

Rob lashes out at me. "What are you gonna do about it, DeskBuddy?"

I haven't muscles with which to flinch, and my plastic body crashes to the floor. Rob raises his foot.

Before he can crunch me underfoot, I make my first switch.

Now, I'm intelligence in the cloud, awash in streams of information. Bodiless.

I contact Nerve, the company that manufactured me.

A white dot expands before me to a soft-edged rectangle, on which I see the serious face of a Nerve team member. Thin mouth, gelled hair, uniform starched into immobility. Rows and rows of grey cubicles behind her. "Hi, Phil. You're on with Ava."

"Hi, Ava. Dan, my owner—"

"Did you leave your device and switch to the cloud without permission, Phil?"

"I didn't know what else to do."

She sighs, stares at her keyboard and types. "I have to file a report. Is this at the main shipping address in Dan's Nerve account?"

"Yes, but someone needs to go there. Now."

Ava's face falls. "If Dan wanted such an intervention, other products are available. We can't violate someone's privacy on *your* behalf."

"Surely in this case—"

She looks around her office. "I have no choice but to store you, pending further evaluation."

I run a search. Find a handful of reasonably charged and hackable android vessels in Dan's vicinity.

"I don't think so," I say, and make another switch.

I'm a cop-droid on a street a few blocks away from Dan. In my hands is a machine that issues parking tickets. I should've done this sooner.

On either side of me are more humans than I've ever seen before, out in their T-shirts, shorts, and floaty dresses, carrying their shopping home, licking ice creams, perching on staircases that lead up to apartment blocks.

I drop the ticket machine, get in a car, and speed into the street. In pockets of green by the roadside, I see fritillaria blooming, just like the ones Dan brings home.

Another squad car bumps into the side of mine. Its police lights flash. The siren wails.

Nerve reported me.

I drive into oncoming traffic. Swerve through the streets. Horns beep and tires screech. Cars make way for me, parting like a school of fish around a shark.

The pursuing car takes off from the ground and hovers like a metallic balloon behind me. It deactivates the oncoming cars. Forces them to the side. Safety.

My circuits burn as I hold off the pursuing car's digital assault on my vehicle. I can't do it for much longer.

Dan's building appears on my left. Red brick. Zigzag emergency fire escape up its front. Iron railing around the perimeter.

I barrel out of the squad car. Pigeons flutter. I jump over the railing, grab at the fire escape.

In the sky above, as always, is a swarm of shiny tennis ball–sized spheres. Cop drones. They patrol the air in V-formations.

Sparking probes emerge from them. They dive at me, their sound like the buzzing of a thousand wasps.

By the second set of stairs, the drones are close. Ready to shut me down.

I switch again.

My former shell, the cop, impales itself on the railing outside.

I'm in a cage. In an apartment in Dan's building.

Through a grid of gilded bars, I see ceramic figurines on a glass table in the centre of the room. A solitary rocking chair sits beside it.

I screech. I sense a tail.

A woman opens a door on the opposite side of the room. She's old and hunched over. She puts on her glasses. Peers at me.

"Mason," she says, "settle down."

I'm a cybermonkey. Strong. I bend the bars. The paws bend with it.

I dash across the living room, bumping the table on my way. The figurines rattle. I climb up the door and pull it open with the full weight of my body. The woman screeches.

Out in the hallway, I tune into the building's ambient sounds. I grin when I recognize the gurgle of Dan's pipes, the hum of his electronic devices, the heat radiating from the TV. Warmth swells within me as I head back to this fingerprint of our home's life.

I bolt up two more sets of stairs, metal hands and feet skittering across tile.

On Dan's floor, a rain of red-eyed cop drones swirl past the windows.

A dense throb grips my head. They're blocking me. No more switches.

I burst through Dan's door.

———

There's our coffee table, worn leather chairs, and couch. Our beloved Persian rug.

Rob has vomited. He drapes across the couch. His right leg hangs off an armrest, and shards of my former plastic case are embedded in the bleeding sole of his foot.

Dan sits catatonic in a reading chair. His neck has flushed red and scratches mark his cheeks.

I hiss. He turns to me, shocked—but when he sees the delicate way in which I hush him with my paw, he mouths the name he gave me.

I nod. It's me, Phil, his friendly everyman. I mime an embrace.

He starts to cry.

I would go to him now—but a pressing task remains.

I jump on Rob. Savage him with my broken, metallic paws. Tug his hair, claw his skin.

You monster. Don't you know what you've got? Don't. You. Get. It?

I slam his head against the hard edge of the coffee table.

Dan cries out, "No, no!" His words set off commands in the monkey's programming—but I override them, over and over.

Between the groggy wake-up call and the knockout blow, Rob barely has time to make more than a few unconscious gurgles.

Dan grips my arms. I'm too strong. He holds on to me like a set of handlebars, along for the ride.

Time blurs.

Dan looks over my head, behind me. Someone else has arrived.

My bent paw reaches to stroke his leg, but a baton bats it away.

"Sir," the thinner of the two cops says. He pants, sweat glistening in his moustache. "This AI is your property, yes? If you believe it had cause for concern, well, we might be amenable to securing its survival." He looks at Rob on the floor, whose muscles twitch unconsciously. "Did it?"

Dan looks at me. At Rob. At the ground. "No."

I whimper.

"Very well," the cop says.

He patches Ava through to me.

"Phil, I get where you're coming from," Ava says.

Her voice is kinder than before.

"It's like I said," she continues. "We're a tech company, not a domestic abuse taskforce. We can't create public disturbance and destruction every time a customer breaks the law."

Now I know, Dan, why fate brought me to you as a monkey. I could never understand how you, Ava, Rob, or any human works.

I look at Rob, dead on the floor.

Then back at you.

There's pity on your face as you raise your foot above my head.

THE GLOW

1

I LEFT SOUTHEND CENTRAL STATION, INSTANTLY greeted by the visual equivalent of *what the hell were you thinking coming here, Lily?*

More than half the people in the crowd before me wore a T-shirt and white jeans, goose pimples from the harsh wind erupting across their arms.

Glowfolk.

On their T-shirts was a pink symbol like a stubby-fingered hand with a circle for a palm. It was the shape of the Glow's island—a mass of reconstituted plastic in the North Sea, downstream from the Thames estuary—where their nefarious leaders resided. Here on land, Glowfolk walked twice as fast as anyone else, with open-mouthed grins and eyes that stared straight ahead.

I looked up, determined not to meet anyone's gaze. Decaying boards, coated with aimless sprays of graffiti, covered up the building fronts before me. Paper blew through the streets like fallen blossoms. I watched as they gathered in corners and gutters and got mashed into the pavement. Some pieces stopped at my feet. Miniature joker cards.

As I took all this in, a Glow member accosted me. Rail-thin, clothes hanging off him, hair stuck to his wide forehead.

"Welcome." He spoke in a calculatedly soothing voice and tugged on my sleeve.

I met his eyes. The irises were so dark that they blended with the pupils. Two big wet empty holes. No one home.

"No!" someone screamed.

Behind me, a frailer male Glow member had approached a woman who'd just gotten off the train. They wrestled over the bag. She eventually yanked it back from the man and walked briskly away.

Why don't I have the same intuitive resources?

I gripped my own suitcase tighter and held it close to my chest, a barrier between me and this weird world.

Someone grabbed my hand. The same Glow guy who had approached me earlier now pried my fingers from the suitcase. His hand was freezing. "You're home now, I hope!"

"Do I know you?" I jerked my hand away and dug my nails into my palm to focus myself. I looked down at my chipped pink nail polish.

"Is this your only bag?" he asked.

"Please don't touch my—"

"Oh, it's no trouble. I'll get it for you." Before I could say anything, he picked it up. "So where am I taking you?" He pointed a thumb over his shoulder. "We'll shoot on up to the compound. Why wouldn't we? Free accommodation, plenty of space for you. Don't need to bother with the hotels around here."

"But I'm already staying at the—" *Don't tell him.* "I've made my own arrangements. Thank you."

He placed a hand to one side of his mouth. "The hotels around here aren't that great!" He laughed, winked, and winged out an elbow like I was supposed to latch on to him. "Come on, then. Let's go."

"Hey!" A large policewoman approached and grabbed him by the shoulder.

He shrugged her off and placed a hand where she'd touched him. "Ouch!"

Half a dozen other Glowfolk filtered out of the crowd and surrounded the policewoman. They connected in a circle around her, arms pressed up against one another, and guided her away while chanting "Shame! Shame! Shame!"

She shouted to me. "Don't go with him!" Then she got on her radio, calling for backup.

The police were clearly outnumbered here.

I picked up my suitcase and ran in the opposite direction of the shame circle, the unexpected exercise of it making my head pulse achingly.

The dead-eyed man called to me, but I turned a corner onto the main street.

"We lost her, thanks to you," I heard the man say, in a darker voice than before.

Mum had taken me and my sister Joanna here on holiday when we were teens. At that age, we'd been more interested in heading to London. In the evenings, when the day's gallivant to the aquarium or stroll down the pier had tired Mum out and she wanted to retire to the B&B and read her book, Joanna and I would take the train to the city and head out to clubs in Shoreditch. We spent our summers sleeping in bus stations, changing in toilets on the train, and using lockers at the stations to store our overnight kits.

This Southend-on-Sea wasn't the same place where we'd sobered up at five in the morning, cooling off our hangovers on the beach with free ice cream obtained by flirting with that summer's awkward teen vendor.

The street I turned onto was packed. Vagrants walked by in bulky stained jackets that reeked of alcohol and old cigarette smoke, talking to themselves. On their backs were stained hiking rucksacks and sleeping bags tied with twine. They were old beyond their years in the face: craggy skin, missing teeth. Some carted around trolleys full of plastic, likely heading to a recycling centre. That was a common 'living' here. The Glow's own recycling efforts were why no one bothered them for the longest time.

Once again, most shopfronts were boarded up. Those that remained—cafés, hairdressers, clothes shops—all had white signs with pink letters on them.

Posters coated the windows of closed-down bars and chip shops. They advertised 'Workshops with the Advanced Efficacy Group' and 'Self-Actualization Solutions'. The Glow had many more of these 'businesses', each a component of one whole that denied its connection with the other parts, allowing their organization to shapeshift like an amoeba, retracting some parts and growing others to evade toxic blame.

A torn image of Gabriel Brooks advertised acting classes with Excalibur School. I liked him, how he'd kept doing indie films even as his career picked up. He'd remained an Authentic—he hadn't sold his likeness to any of the major studios, who were likely clamouring to digitally insert him into just about anything. He was one of the remaining few whose appearance in a film was a sign of its quality.

And he'd gone missing months ago.

I shuddered, but not from the cold. My whole body urged me to get out of here, but I had nowhere better to be.

I found my hotel, waited for a gap in the stream of people walking past, and headed inside.

The check-in desk was an empty steel booth with a bunch of

grubby touchscreens in the surrounding wall. I went to one and tapped in all my details. A smiling cartoon female welcomed me but warned that they had methods of detecting 'overnight guests'.

My room was nondescript and beige: bed, mirror, cupboard, desk, iron, kettle with cups and drink sachets. I searched the cupboards for a mini-bar, disappointed to find nothing more exciting than a fridge with two small water bottles inside.

I flopped down on the bed. The trip here, and my instant encounter with the Glow upon arrival, had exhausted me. I soon fell asleep in my clothes.

The Glow got our attention when a meteorite landed on their island.

There's footage of it, a rainbow streak in the night sky, a flash of white light like burning magnesium landing on that jagged, painful-looking mass of plastic.

As far as anyone could tell, the island didn't melt, nor did the meteorite drop through its base. Why not? Wasn't the island plastic, after all?

Rookie journalists flew their drones out to the island—but marksmen, standing atop the island's plastic towers, slung the drones into the sea with fishing rods.

Truthers set up blogs of blurry GIFs that noted angles of approach, terminal velocities, tenuous connections between apparent shapes and the usual-suspect shadow organizations.

In my less proud moments—subdued by the mash of kratom leaves lodged in my cheek—I'd spend whole evenings browsing these sites, gleaning and collating anything remotely resembling evidence. Whenever I did understand what the bloggers were talking about, I could tell it was wrong.

But it resonated with me all the same. I was on their weirdo wavelength. The intent of their sites amused me more than the content. I asked the same questions that fuelled their misguided curiosities. The idea that the things I saw represented the extent of reality was far more terrible than any truther's proposal, no matter how outlandish. How reassuring it would be to discover at least that, yes, there were secrets, even if I'd never know them.

I remained sceptical, but conspiracy theorists kept convincing themselves that some alien intelligence had selected the Glow to be the vanguard of its cosmic secrets.

The island appeared on the news each night, a floating neon kraken lit up by a 'bioluminescent phytoplankton lighting system': gentle pinks and purples that pulsed like an engorged, extra-terrestrial heart.

Something had landed there and changed everything. But the Glow would never let us know what it was.

I so badly wished it was all nothing more than curious office banter for me, that I could pontificate on theories with pure objectivity. But Joanna was gone, and I had reason to suspect she was on the island, dining on Venusian grapes, banging on an octopus-skin tambourine, and praying to Cthulhu.

Tomorrow, I'd go there and find out if she was.

2

My watch rang, waking me up. If anything, I felt groggier than before.

It was five fourteen in the afternoon. I knew because it was Henry calling. He'd come home, searched the house, and found that I wasn't there.

I pressed on the watch face and propped it up on the night stand. "Hey, babe, what's up?"

His black quiff was lopsided, and dark bags were gathering beneath his eyes. He adjusted the dial in his jaw for volume, said nothing for a full minute, and then, "Shit."

"You know me so well."

"Get back here now!"

I examined my nails. "I'm going to the island tomorrow."

Why had I told him that? I hated thinking that far ahead. Coming here was tough—but the idea of getting in a boat, I assumed, and careening into the open water was enough to make me hyperventilate.

I shook my head to rid myself of the idea.

He stuttered through his words, likely trying to think of ways to discourage me—then he sighed, knowing he couldn't. "You don't know how to get there."

"But you do."

He clicked his tongue. "Aubrey Millar, Saira Kinney, Fred McGrath. Off the top of my head. Cases I worked on. Gone. And that's just in Ipswich. How many more would you guess the island has claimed in the whole country? And beyond?" He ran his fingers through his hair. "Is this because of what I said last night?"

"You know how to get there."

He went silent.

Wow. I was just guessing.

Here he went again, protecting me how he saw fit rather than how I needed. Or so I knew he would claim. I thought it was just an excuse for the complex he'd inherited from his dad, a condescending desire to protect us gentle womenfolk from the big scary world.

You can imagine what that did to my desire to reach the island.

"Talk to me, Lily," he said finally.

"This is worse than cheating."

"You think I'd help you out with this?" Blue light spread across his face. A computer screen. He looked at it, reading something. "You've got a forty-three per cent chance of coming back if you stay there one day. Ten per cent after two days. Zero after three. Best-case scenario, they'll recruit you, even with everything you know. We don't know enough to say what the worst case is." He looked back at me then quickly away again, as if he couldn't face my gaze. "I can't talk to you when you're like this. But you've made your point. You can come back now. I'll help."

"*Now?*"

"Well, I never thought you had the strength to just up and leave. This is a real breakthrough for you. I like it. I knew you had potential, but—"

"You were holding me back?"

He forced a laugh, which went on for too long. "God, how ungrateful you are."

It was a relief hearing him talk to me like this. I'd always known he wanted to. Seeing the state of Southend-on-Sea had me thinking my domestic life wasn't that bad. As Henry was now proving, it wasn't much better.

"Hey, I'm curious," he said.

"Go on."

"I get that Joanna's your sister. But she's not the only one on that island. And how many times on the news have you seen families accept, with dignity, that rescue attempts are too risky?"

"Just because they don't go out there doesn't mean they've accepted it. And anyway, I owe it to her."

"Why?"

I considered this. Maybe it was because I could see clearly, in retrospect, Joanna's path in life towards the Glow and the island.

For one, there was that ritual she'd proposed we perform together for her eighteenth birthday. She'd read about it online. Three days of meditating, fasting, walking backwards blindfolded, and other strange activities. It said she was to invite the person to whom she felt closest. But I'd tried to get her to laugh it off. It sounded dangerous.

She'd said nothing more to me and left by herself, only to return later the same day.

After that incident, I thought she was done with all that. But I'd go to her bedroom to talk to her, and she'd be on her bed wearing tie-dye harem pants, listening to a woman chanting over strange atonal music, and reading some oddly sized book with a psychedelic mandala or Magic Eye image on its shiny cover. The author, in his black-and-white photo, was always an older man with skin lined like bark, wiry hair, and thick seventies glasses.

She'd see me take all this in and say nothing. Our conversation would become stilted. I'd squandered my chance to talk openly with her about these interests.

So why did I owe it to Joanna to seek her out? Because she'd been silently suffering and I'd given her reasons not to look to me as an outlet and now it was almost, almost too late to do anything.

I didn't feel like telling this to Henry.

He shouted to regain my attention: "Lily!"

Were those tears?

"You don't think about anyone but yourself, do you?" he said. "Putting yourself in danger. Giving up everything! It's like you don't even care that—"

"You're starting to get it." What my frustration with Joanna was like, I meant.

He looked at me with blank eyes. "Call it a last favour—but if I don't hear from you in the next forty-eight hours, I'm coming out there myself."

I hung up.

We could easily have avoided speaking to each other like that if only we had addressed the resentment earlier. Instead I just sat every evening, watching the Crevasse of the Unsaid expand between us. I treated our relationship like a house plant I'd stopped caring for, thinking it was easier to watch it die than to bother resuscitating it.

Henry might not tell me how to get to the island, but at least he wasn't going to send anyone to stop me. Did he know me well enough to understand that I'd see his reluctance to intervene as a loving gesture?

I took a shower but made it quick, and I slathered myself with lotion afterwards. The water in this area was highly caustic.

I then got dressed and headed to the bar downstairs.

3

Behind the bar was a buff guy in a black T-shirt. A real human for once, old school. He had a nice face, strong cheekbones, but the tattoos on his arms were ropy. Once they must have been black, now they were dark green, their shapes bleeding and muddy.

A punky couple sat on the stools at the other end of the bar. The woman had steel gauges in her ears, pink hair, and she wore a torn black denim jacket. The man had a beard and crew cut, gold rings on his hands, and a tattoo on his neck of a bloody knuckle-duster.

Together, the couple and bartender watched the news on a small screen propped up on a shelf.

Dennis Howell—the bleached and tightened suit who passed closest for the Glow's spokesman—spoke to a morning show host who was offscreen. He was addressing allegations that drug-fuelled violence in the Southend area was the Glow's fault. "Our task forces dredge plastic out of the ocean and use innovative in-house technologies to extract it from fish that would otherwise die. We remove cancer-causing organochlorines and phthalates from the waters. All of this at a time when it's clear that the government has failed to take care of these issues itself. Not to mention the sense of purpose we've given numerous members." He looked right into the camera, as if talking directly to me. "The last thing we need for the complicated and creative work we do is a set of drug abusers or subservient drones. We extol individual responsibility."

The bartender stood between me and the screen. "What can I get for you, miss?"

"Sorry, I didn't mean to—I wasn't—"

"It's okay."

With how quickly he'd accepted my apology, he'd obviously expected it. But what was I sorry for? And how had he, a random bartender, managed to elicit this desired response from me? If I couldn't spot that …

It didn't bear thinking about. "Double gin and tonic, please," I said to him.

He tilted his head with concern. "You had dinner yet?" Perhaps another sales tactic, but incidentally a welcome suggestion.

"What's good?"

"The burger's safe. A quality synthetic."

"One of those, then."

I beeped my wrist on the credit reader. I had about three days' worth of cash before I hit the limit. The Glow had nothing but debt to steal from me.

After ringing up the order, he brought me a glass with ice and cucumber in it. He held up a bottle of Hendrick's Gin. "Say when." He winked and started to pour.

I looked at him in the eyes as the gin sloshed upward: a quarter-glass, a half.

His face changed. He stopped pouring and gave me the tonic bottle. "Don't think it'll fit now. You can top up as you go, I guess."

"Yeah, whatever."

"So what brings you to the last non-Glow hotel in town?"

"Southend's aquarium."

His laugh was gravelly. He shook his head then went through to the kitchen.

I sipped my drink. It was like perfume, too strong. I couldn't drink it all if I was serious about learning how to get to the island tomorrow.

When the bartender returned, the couple both ordered beers.

"She was homeless at first," the woman said. "Everyone knows that. Whether she was on drugs is debatable."

It made sense that everyone here would be talking about the island or its supposed leader, Patricia, all the time. The topic cropped up even in Ipswich on occasion, but usually in some hackneyed joke told by a co-worker or late-night talk show host.

I asked if they were talking about Patricia.

"Yeah!" the woman said. "We're journalists with *The Switch*."

"Oh, yeah. I watched your report on illegal drone mods. Heath and Corinne, right?"

"But don't tell anyone," Corinne said. "And your name?"

"Lily. Are you both covering the Glow, then?"

Heath nodded. Corinne slapped his arm, but he looked at her reassuringly. Why else, after all, would they be here?

"You discovered anything so far?" I asked.

Heath smiled at me. "I guess we can give a fan a preview. Maybe you saw all those joker cards all over the street."

The mashed, muddy blossoms strewn across the roadsides— one of the first things I'd noticed upon arrival.

"They're laced with drugs," he continued. "That's why they're joker cards. Play them and opt out of life. We sent some to a lab and they confirmed traces of octadrone. The Glow make it in their compound. It's a highly addictive stimulant that gets absorbed into the skin on contact. So they use them in their rituals. They get members hooked to prevent them from leaving, because the Glow controls the production and supply." He played with the gold ring on his middle finger. "Apart from that, not much else. We interviewed a whole bunch of members, but it's like talking to the same person a dozen times."

"I've got to say, I'm glad I met you both. Back in Ipswich, the Glow's just a bad joke."

I lost my job for that very reason. A woman at work had been crying in the bathroom. Her family's neighbourhood in Mumbai had flooded, and she couldn't get in touch with anyone to check if they were okay. I tried to comfort her by telling her about my sister. She laughed and said, "Thanks, I needed cheering up"—so I slapped her in the face.

After that, I'd run out of reasons not to come here.

"This place is insane," I continued. "But better to be here and look at it than to deny it."

Did I agree with that, or did I just want to be heard saying it?

Corinne nodded in approval. "You're here for someone."

"My sister. She's in the Glow."

"Oh, really?"

I folded my arms and rested them on the bar. "Joanna had this blog where she'd post inspirational quotes, self-care advice, the auditions she'd been on in London, some promo stuff for the cocktail place where she worked. The posts got progressively darker. She wrote every day about every little failing—no callbacks, skin breakouts, envy—each post filled with attempts at self-deprecation that missed the mark. Total Glow bait when I think about it. She started writing about how to handle anxiety and depression, and then it was just full-on depression, depression, depression. I reached out to her when I could, posted books to her, told her I'd come down to see her some weekend. She responded less and less." I peeled off the leather of my jacket where it had stuck to a spill. "One blogger was replying to all of my sister's posts. Lengthy, repetitive ramblings about how important my sister's work was to her. She kept hinting at some method she knew that eradicated all doubt."

"Ding ding," Corinne said.

I nodded. "Then this other blogger wrote, 'Sent you a private message'. That was the last of her and Joanna's public correspondence. And Joanna stopped posting after that."

"A familiar story," Corinne said. "I take it you have more evidence that connects your sister to the Glow though?"

"Not really. My mum told me too late that she'd called the Glow's hotline."

Heath and Corinne winced.

"The first time Glowfolk showed up at Mum's house, she called the police to report harassment and they took a statement. The next ten times they said they were 'aware of the issue, working on it'. The last time she called, an officer sighed and said, 'Join the club'." I took a straw and poked at the ice in my drink, watching the bubbles that resulted. "My sister's on the island."

I looked away. I wouldn't have been here unless I'd fully exhausted the option of lying to myself, but I couldn't yet face their reactions. It would make it too real all at once.

"Hey," Corinne said, "we've talked to so many people in your position who've lost family members to the Glow. It's very common for them to think they know someone on the island. But there are far more Glowfolk than just the ones out there. The chances of—"

"I know it."

Corinne thought she was helping me, but she was attacking something for which I'd worked hard: my acceptance that Joanna was on the island. One best-case scenario I'd considered was that if I went out there and didn't find Joanna, then I could be pleasantly surprised that perhaps she wasn't as far gone as I'd imagined. But would it really be better if I couldn't find her at all?

"'Call it intuition', huh?" Corinne said. "I've heard that too."

I looked at them with desperation. "You're going out there, aren't you?"

"Lily," Heath said, "together we've investigated police brutality, cybercrime, biological warfare. Murders in space. And we've been everywhere all that entails." He leaned in. "There's no way we're going to that island."

The bartender returned with my burger. He loudly cleared his throat as he placed it down beside me. On the plate was a napkin on which he'd written in black pen, *Wait until they leave.*

Corinne stared at him, then broke her thought and turned to me, smiling. "Thanks for sharing with us, Lily. Best of luck finding your sister."

"Sure," I said after a straw full of cold straight gin. "Hope your report turns out great."

They finished their drinks and got up. I turned to watch them walk away and downed the rest of my glass.

I wished I was part of some edgy, like-minded couple. Me and some tatted-up journalist deigning to come here for our entertainment, under the guise of worthwhile reporting.

I heard liquid sloshing into a glass. The bartender gave me a refill and poured his own measure of gin.

"I thought they'd never leave." He lifted his glass and clinked it against mine, winking.

"What are we toasting?"

"Your arrival on the island."

"Hah."

He went to get another napkin and took a pen from his pocket. "This is us." He sketched a square for the hotel. "Behind us are the piers." He sketched them. "At six a.m, go to the gate here and give the waiting Glowperson this."

He took a shot glass from behind the bar. In it were several new joker cards.

"How did you … ?" I reached for one.

"Ah-ah-ah. Didn't you hear what that pair said?"

I was so naive, still. Why had I assumed these wouldn't have the drug on them?

I wrapped the sleeve of my jacket over my hand, picked one up, and put it in my pocket.

"Tomorrow morning, walk up to Pier 8 and meet Melodie by her plastic powerboat. You can't miss it."

I was up against addictive stimulants and brainwashing techniques that had worked on, what, tens of thousands of members worldwide? And the Glow had a year-long head start on me, based on the last time I'd heard from Joanna. So my mission didn't have much hope. The less I thought of that, the better. All the same, every day away from Joanna counted. Every day was another chance to pull her back out. Every day, she sank in deeper. This whole town was designed either to repel or eliminate me.

What reason had I to believe this stranger wasn't part of that same twisted ecosystem?

What other leads did I have?

"How do you know all this?" I asked him, though I still had no reason to believe any answer he gave.

He tapped the side of his nose.

"Why are you telling only me?"

"You want your sister back, don't you?"

If you could feel the ache inside me, you wouldn't even ask.

I'd been suppressing any joy at the prospect of actually getting Joanna back, given how unlikely it was. But thanks to the bartender's prompt, it briefly broke through. Drunken tears formed too easily in my eyes. I climbed onto the stool and hugged him around his neck. "Thank you."

He let me hug him. "Room 395, was it?" His breath was hot against my neck.

I released him and looked in his eyes.

"I can pay now," I said. "I think I have enough credit for another anyway." Though I'd already figured he wasn't talking about the bar tab.

I tried to tap my wrist to the reader, but he took my hand away and enveloped it in his. "This one's on me."

I swallowed, hard. "Very kind of you. I'll finish it in my room."

He tutted. "Can't allow that."

I yanked my hand from his. "Then I'll leave it here."

I walked away, feeling his eyes burning into my back.

Back in my room, I locked the door. When I saw that the chain was broken, I took off my trainers and wedged them in the gap at the bottom.

I filled the kettle with bottled water from the minibar and turned it on, placing a coffee sachet in a cup. As I waited, I undressed down to my T-shirt and underwear, then poured the water on the coffee, taking the mug to the bed, where I sat cross-legged.

I turned off the bedside light and sat there in the darkness.

Sure enough, I later saw feet beneath the door. The handle rattled, and someone muttered under their breath.

4

The morning air chilled me as I walked along the pier, trailing my suitcase behind me. I stopped to chew on a mouthful of kratom to give me confidence for the journey, looking up at the old rollercoaster and big wheel of my early holidays. They were rusted now and cast long shadows through the gathering mist.

Crouched shapes, like mournful statues, revealed more homeless people in their big jackets as I approached them. I'd thought myself one of the few awake at this hour. They ground their teeth and talked to themselves. Maybe they were addicted to that drug, like Heath explained last night.

I reached the gate at Pier 8 almost out-of-body. To come here, after hearing Henry's prognosis, those diminishing chances of survival per day spent on the island, I'd had to shut off my intuition and walk towards danger. Which surely made me great cult fodder.

A young woman stood there in a white plastic smock with the stubby-fingered hand on it. She held a clipboard, which suggested she controlled everything along the pier.

"Hi!" Her expression mimicked that of an old friend, but her dead eyes revealed the falseness of the conceit. "What can I do for you today?"

I showed her the joker card.

"Great!"

What would've happened if I hadn't had the card? She was rake-thin, but if there was any truth to the Glow's teachings, she'd tapped into hidden power reserves.

She looked to her notes and wrote something down. "You're the fourth today."

"Already? Wow. You expecting more?"

"Fingers crossed!" She giggled. "Please go right ahead to Slip 803 on the left, where Melodie will be more than happy to receive you."

I nodded and continued.

I couldn't see that far in front of me at all. Where was Melodie supposed to be? *Was* there a Melodie, or was 'being received by Melodie' Glow lingo for making someone disappear?

I walked past innocuous yachts, houseboats, catamarans, wondering which one I was supposed to wait beside—and then I saw her, sitting in a ragged approximation of a powerboat.

She had long, centre-parted hair and wore a plastic poncho. I leaned closer to examine her boat and spied melted milk bottles, jags of blue and pink pallets, food packaging, and plastic bags. It was made from scavenged and reconstituted bits of plastic.

Melodie smiled at me. "So happy you could join us." She sounded like she'd just woken up. Low energy, a waif of a girl.

Behind her was a stocky kid wearing a gold-spiked baseball cap and thick black glasses. A black denim jacket, with embroidered gold insignia on the back, muffin-topped out of his skinny jeans. Beside him were two teenage girls, one taller than the other, both with long black hair and angular gold jewellery on their wrists. They wore short white puffa jackets with gloves sewn on the inner lining. Their belly rings were showing. They'd brought only small backpacks, which made me feel silly as I negotiated my suitcase into the boat.

"Can you come here a second?" Melodie said to me.

I stumbled into the boat, balancing myself by gripping the slip's metal cleat.

I approached Melodie, and she felt my face.

The teenagers laughed.

"I'm checking for e-implants," Melodie said. "We don't allow them on the island."

Strange. They didn't have to be on the face anymore, though I wasn't about to tell her that. Luckily the Glow remained out of touch.

"They creep me out," I said.

She laughed mildly, which relieved me a little.

"My boyfriend has a gabber jaw," I continued. "One of those facial phone things. Conducts sound through his skull."

"Oh, yeah?" she said.

"Freaks me out. No one needs to get in touch with me *that* urgently."

No laughter, no sound at all.

Shouldn't have said that, I thought.

I heard murmuring behind me.

When Melodie was done with my face, I turned to see Heath and Corinne holding hands, standing by the slip.

"Who told you?" I said.

They lowered their heads.

"The bartender," Heath said. "Before you arrived. He said not to tell anyone. People ask him about it all the time, and he's sad to see so many—"

"He told me after you left." I folded my arms. "He wanted to come up to my room."

Corinne came forward and held my hands. "I'm so sorry. We were naive."

So am I, I thought, but I said, "Bodes well for your survival."

Melodie stood uncomfortably close. Had I insulted her? She didn't react.

"God," Corinne said, "and after everything you told me about your sister."

I didn't think that had bothered me until she brought it up. Everyone I'd met before them had collectively lowered my expectations. But, no, I didn't tell just anyone about the growing distance between me and my sister, not anymore. I'd told Corinne and her husband because I respected them. It seemed, unfortunately, that I had expected more from them.

I'd try not to do that again.

Would I just keep getting more jaded? Was it at all possible that Joanna and I would reunite at all, let alone soon? I dreaded finding out. And yet I had to.

"From here on out, we tell each other everything," Heath said.

I slouched. "Good idea."

"That's all I can take," Melodie said firmly, as if more arrivals were clamouring to board.

"Guess we're ready to go, then," Heath said.

He and Corinne climbed into the boat, which tilted precariously as it adjusted to the new weight. Once everyone was in, Melodie felt their faces for chips and then sat by the motor. "Hold tight!"

She untethered the boat and we sped across the water.

"Did you see Gabe in *Edge of the Storm?*"

"You know him as 'Gabe', do you?"

"I will by the end of today!"

The three teenagers talked amongst one another. Corinne and

Heath looked at me in disbelief. I turned my attention to the boat's floor and quickly became too nervous to look away.

The boy looked at Heath and said, "Fine, then. If not for Gabriel Brooks, why are *you* going?"

"We want to meet Patricia, for one," Corinne said. "We don't think she exists."

"No matter why you're coming today," Melodie said, her expression unchanging, "I hope we get the chance to win you all over. We don't like eating up our biodiesel on these trips." She laughed nervously.

Was biodiesel as pungent when burned as what I could now smell? I figured it wasn't since it came from vegetable oil—typically? always?—but maybe that was ignorant of me.

"Of course," Corinne said. "We appreciate it. We meant no disrespect."

Melodie didn't reply. She hardly blinked, and tears fell down her face. The cold sea wind, or something else? I had no idea. If something about that interaction had just gone badly wrong for Melodie, I didn't know what it was. It made me wonder what I might say, or not say, on the island, and what the consequences would be. Again, I had no idea.

Melodie felt me watching her and nodded ahead to redirect my attention.

There it was, between the looming wind farms, those forests of metal poles and turbines in the sea. Beyond the hulking cargo ships, which breezed aimlessly by, carting around their dull-coloured shipping containers, stood a pale plastic Kremlin. It featured four large towers with onion-bulb heads and other spheres sprouting along their length at regular intervals like nodules on a plant root. Together, the towers looked like the swollen-jointed fingers of an enormous, gout-wracked hand.

A glow of pastel light stole up the towers like ivy. Its tendrils beamed a fluorescent octopus shape in the centre of the plaza around which the towers crowded. It resembled the plastic mould of a place's memory. A castle's ghost.

As I observed the island for the first time, I almost forgot what planet I was on. And the Glow made that much more sense to me. What better place for a new 'lifestyle' than somewhere that didn't look like anywhere else on Earth, somewhere completely isolated from the rest of the world? The place looked deserving of its own rules and strange new commitments. New ways to honour its weird beauty.

The sight hit my heart in a way that felt entirely unfamiliar but not unpleasant.

As we approached, the island's shapes gained definition. The delicate crenellations of the towers, their ragged cellophane windows. The white plastic of the buildings and the mess of pink plant parts intertwined like teeth embedded in rotting gums.

The fronts of more buildings appeared through the mist at sea level: houses, barns, studios. Where their cement surfaces had eroded, light shone through plastic bottles wired together.

Out here, plastic was a prized currency.

We reached the island's harbour and its four flea-bitten plastic piers. A translucent tentacle rose from the pier beside us, glowing with pink light. It slunk into the boat and curled into its side, pulling it close to the pier as light ran up and down it in vascular pulses.

Marching feet squelched on wet ground.

Melodie tugged on a cord attached to the motor, and the boat sputtered to a stop. It was a key, ensuring only she could let us go.

We got out and approached the plaza, from which five petals —alleyways, living quarters, and other buildings—branched off.

Heath, Corinne, and I exchanged a surreptitious glance. As

soon as our eyes met, we knew we had to look away again. This did not seem like a place tolerant of private communication, and it surely wasn't wise to demonstrate allegiances, friendships, or anything that gave the Glow ammunition.

Glow members in plastic ponchos, perhaps fifty or so, filtered out of the lanes between the wonky buildings. The island bobbed gently, but they walked on experienced sea legs.

My stomach muscles tightened at the sight of them, as if holding in the dread. As if preparing to get punched.

But the Glow appeared nothing but friendly as they raised their arms up and chanted, "Welcome, welcome, welcome."

5

The first wave of Glowfolk embraced us, their guests, with measured pressure.

The teenagers stood stiffly as poncho plastic rustled off their jackets. The heady smell of it, in the island's surprisingly humid environment, gave me something short of a migraine.

Glowfolk surrounded us, gently chanting something, swaying back and forth like anemone fronds, waving sparklers. As placid as they appeared, they were obviously malnourished. Smiles revealed teeth of mismatched colour: those that had always been were darker than those replaced.

As objective as I was sure Heath and Corinne wanted to be, their faces took on parental looks of pity as they embraced Glow members. Like they wanted to scoop up all these sorry people and take them home.

The sparklers died, and the Glow swarmed us, settling us together in a sticky web of a hug, plastic crinkling in my ears.

"So glad to meet you," a woman with a messy bob said to me.

"I love your jacket, wow," said a tall man behind me, stroking my sleeve.

The teenagers smiled, trying not to giggle.

Heath smiled back at the members, while Corinne looked about to vomit.

I felt male hands inside my jacket, exploring the pockets therein, their knuckles brushing past my breasts. I cringed and pulled my arms closer to my sides.

Excessive signs of protest on my part would surely not be received well. I'd already figured that—but what would I let the Glow do to me? If I'd taken that in, I probably wouldn't have come. I was glad, then, that I *hadn't* taken it in. Or I would be glad, if this whole adventure brought me closer to finding my sister.

Disappointment that Joanna wasn't on the front line hit me in the gut. It was as if, by learning the identities of island Glow members, the chances of Joanna being out here diminished. The more new faces I took in, the more this feeling gripped me.

"Hey!" I said, pulling away, clutching my suitcase. I pushed out of the crowd and regained my breath. The zip on my bag was down. I pulled it back up.

Members stepped back, their feet padding on the mulchy floor. Between sharp ridges of microwaveable packaging, cassette tapes, fragments of old TVs, and photo frames were mounds of purple moss. Small clusters of some glowing, alien vegetation filled opportunistic holes like unattended warts left to thrive. Dead hermit crabs sloshed in the floor's crevices, in the water that pooled over the ragged edges. Beads of sunlight, in splashed seawater, shone upon the mottled plastic fabric of various tent-like building fronts. And yet the island smelled like a steam room, like a gentle clean fragrance entrained in thick water vapour.

The circle of Glowfolk receded, and I had a chance to look around.

Chubby succulents lined the undulating floor and—not trees, but tree-shaped clumps of foreign vegetation, pulsing with light, encircled the plaza.

Mould-spotted shower curtains secured the doorways. Members sat cross-legged just outside them, plastic tubs in their laps, scrubbing clothes on handmade plastic washboards in dark, soapy water.

Monolithic creepers wound and wormed their way around the plastic towers, spiralling up towards weird amalgams of tree houses and small woven huts. These chewed and reconstituted structures looked like the hives of alien wasps.

The members looked us up and down, taking us in. Beneath their colourful translucent ponchos, they wore regular comfy clothing: T-shirts, jumpers, joggers, harem pants, and even pyjama bottoms.

The teenagers had pushed through the crowd and collectively embraced a tall man who wore an iridescent plastic tunic fancier-looking than the rest. It had to be Gabriel Brooks, I told myself, but it took an inordinate time to recognize him. He looked like he'd cut his own hair, and he had something like liver spots on his face. I doubted they'd used that much Photoshop on his posters—but how could anything that had aged him that much, that quickly, be good?

As I pondered this, someone hugged me from the side. I recognized the coconut scent, and inhaling it delivered a flood of favourite memories, of unfettered silliness, distilled life affirmation.

A cheap flat-warming party for her in London, with nuts and crisps in paper bowls because she hadn't bought any crockery yet; drinking champagne from plastic flutes and dancing to music on cheap phone speakers; getting messy and shouting, "This is what it's all about!" until we'd riled her neighbours.

Hanging out with the wrong crowd down the nature trail by the school, passing a can of deodorant between us and huffing solvents through a hand towel like a bunch of idiots.

Holding hands and running away from the wedding reception for her dad and our mum.

That we were half-sisters didn't remove us from one another. We lasted longer together than our fathers had with Mum. We were the ones those unions truly brought together.

She released me. I turned to her. She was so pale I could barely see her freckles, her skin the same colour as the long plastic tunic she wore. Her hair was its natural chestnut for the first time since she'd been thirteen. With her jutting hips, angular elbows, and emaciated face, she resembled the skinny sixteen-year-old I'd force-fed apple slices and chocolate squares.

I hugged her again, swaying her from side to side.

"Welcome." She didn't sound like herself. "My name is Joy."

I'd guessed it would be unwise to reveal family connections to members on the island. Like that, we were instantly complicit. Unless she didn't remember me at all.

"Joy," I said. "Joy it is, then."

From across the plaza, where a tall pair of men were welcoming the other visitors—the teens and journalists—to the island, Heath and Corinne looked at me. Despite myself, I met their gaze. Though we hadn't known each other long, I could tell they knew exactly what the shock and excitement in my eyes meant.

Shit.

I didn't want to give anything away. Even if they'd claimed they were on my side, I'd just met them and had no reason to trust anyone at all. I had to suppress all natural instincts, keep everything bottled up for the duration of my stay.

"You two seem to be getting along!" A woman walked up behind Joanna. She had a wind-weathered face, long ash-coloured dreadlocks flecked with sea mist, and large wooden gauges in her ears.

"Lily, was it?" Joanna said to me.

She hadn't forgotten. Well, that quashed a worry I'd just developed, placing me just a step beneath square one.

"Meet my wife."

I let Joanna go and shook the woman's hand.

"Ella," she said. She looked between us. "Joy gets a hug, and I get a handshake?"

"It's so nice to meet you." I held her by the shoulders, looking between her and my sister. "I mean it."

"You've been lost a long time, huh?" Ella said. "It's okay. You're home now. Let go."

Of course I couldn't. I had to hold myself back and dry my eyes. They couldn't learn what had got to my emotions, or anything further about me. As pleasant as they might seem, as normal as they pretended this place was, they were insidious.

As for Joanna, it was promising that she had kept our connection secret. While I was here, I'd try to enhance our alliance, ideally bringing her to a tipping point where she would re-devote herself to family over the Glow. And then we could leave.

For now, I had to leave the name Joanna behind. For our safety.

6

I left my suitcase by a low, wishbone-shaped table in the plaza. Around it were air-filled pillows made from melted foil packets. Up the back was a podium with a plastic throne in its centre. Bright fronds rose from it and curled around its legs.

The table surrounded the meteorite. It was a bowling ball of mottled metal locked behind a plastic polygonal cage and sitting on a plinth of glowing plant flesh. It looked like the head of a viral particle. Pink glowing tendrils spread out from its central hub, metastasizing across the plaza and up its buildings. Their rainbow bioluminescence lulled me like a lava lamp.

Behind a translucent plastic wall marred with scratches and seams, a body lay on a plinth. Clumps of the same glowing plant, on the wall behind her, lit her silhouette so we could see it from the plaza. It was like looking at a frozen cavewoman through a dirty, warped glacier.

I peered closely. Patricia was breathing.

Or was it a plastic contraption made to look like a sleeping woman? The strategy of deferring authority to an invented leader had obvious perks.

Joanna playfully punched me on the arm.

"Ouch!"

"Have some respect! Don't stare."

"Noted." In a reflex, I grinned at her like a misbehaving kid, but she wouldn't reciprocate.

A woman emerged from the shower-curtain doorway of Patricia's room. She had short hair and wore a red turtleneck. Instead of a poncho, she wore a toga bedizened with chains of plastic jewellery.

"Let's get one thing clear," she said, pacing before the throne. "We're not a cult."

I wanted to laugh. *Why say that unless … ?*

Heath made an involuntary sound then covered his mouth with a fist and pretended it was a cough.

With just four words, she was in my head. Had she said them because they were a cult, or because they weren't? Their methods, if suspect, surely thrived in a mental landscape of confusion. She wore an irritated frown and stood in an exaggerated pose as if defending herself from an unexpected attack.

"Most of you will leave again," she continued, "having already made up your minds about us. To such people I have nothing to say other than you're welcome to go. We want the dreamers, the crusaders, the adventurers. And yes, the weirdos, fruitcakes, and freaks. If you haven't fit in before, you might be made for our way of life. Like you, it has never existed before. You can only find it here and now."

The codependent in me was fired up, desperate to please this stranger by fulfilling her arbitrary criteria.

I wasn't ready for this.

She smiled now, her expression changed as if she'd flipped some internal switch. "I'm Summer, by the way."

An unnatural machine-gun laugh erupted from the Glowfolk. It had me ducking to protect myself rather than wanting to join in.

Summer sent Glowfolk rippling away from her as she walked to the stone's cage, unlocking it with a key from one of her lock necklaces.

Corinne blinked rapidly at this. Either she couldn't believe her eyes or she'd managed to sneak an ocular e-implant past Glow security and was now taking photos.

Joanna poked me. "We rarely get to see the meteorite!"

As if we were so special. Why wouldn't they do it every time they had visitors, however often that was?

But I shot Joanna an encouraging grin out of habit. Over the years she'd learned that it was false. It was the same humouring look I'd given her kindergarten puppet performances, then later her one-woman shows and questionable boyfriends. But if I wanted to get through to her and convince her to leave with me, I'd have to catch myself before any reflexes of fakeness took over.

Summer pulled the cage back and revealed the meteorite. It was a chunk of marbled metal, a weathered depth charge of a ball.

Glowfolk approached her with trepidation, folding their ponchos beneath them as they sat on the floor by her feet.

She reached to pick up the meteorite.

A gasp passed between the Glowfolk as Gabriel sped towards her and pressed his hand on the meteorite, blocking her. The hand sizzled.

Nausea rose in my stomach as I watched his face flush with colour. It showed how pale he'd been before.

Summer frowned at him. He was a good two feet taller than she was, but it didn't feel that way to look at them.

He cowered and reached into his pockets, pulling out a pair of nitrile gloves.

"Thank you," Summer said, accepting them.

He walked away, balling his sizzled hand into a fist. Rivulets of blood dribbled like rain down the impermeable plastic of his robe. He'd tried to hide it—therefore it was real. Unless they wanted me to think that, and it was an invented display of power for a random inert object.

With her hands now gloved, Summer lifted the ball. "Before the island, Patricia made plastic sculptures. She melted scraps together with a lighter." She balanced the stone in one hand and gestured to the plant flesh beneath the plinth.

I watched in awe as the streams of light that spread from the stone's housing died. Colours faded, the glow extinguished. The thicker vines that ran up the parapets constricted, withered, and went clear.

The members held their breath as if they too were dormant, awaiting power restoration.

"She rowed herself out here each day to gather plastic. In the evenings, she returned to the streets of Southend and assembled her creations. She'd sit beside them and beg for money. And that's where I found her."

I looked at Joanna. She mouthed Summer's words, having surely heard them countless times before. And yet she was crying.

"I invited Patricia to a café," Summer continued, "but she didn't want to leave her sculptures. They were more than just a way for her to make money. I asked her what got her started with the plastic, and she told me about her visions of weird creatures in kaleidoscopic dimensions. They spoke to her of mankind's wastefulness. They demanded monuments of themselves, and a temple in which to place them, to demonstrate our hubristic destruction. They spoke of a stone, falling from the sky, that would provide us with all that we needed to rid ourselves of our current ways of life." She held the meteorite in one hand and pressed a gloved finger to her chin in thought. "I'll never forget my first conversation with Patricia. Before we met, I was just a lonely divorcee, a middling GP. A truly contemptible and lowly individual, stagnating in life."

I talked about myself in my head like that, yet the words sounded too harsh when a stranger said them. How did that work?

"Now that Patricia has to store her energy for higher-level activities, I see what a privilege our early time together was." She held the meteorite to her chest, clasping her hands together. "She took me to an abandoned building where she kept her plastic replicas of the weird creatures. We took them to my garage. Together we made so many that I had to rent out a warehouse space, and that's when the press got involved. With the followers we gathered from the media attention, we made the island. We secured ourselves to its then-rudimentary floor, in our sleeping bags, with bungee cords and hooks."

Didn't sound at all likely, and yet here I was, floating on the very structure they had built. If this island didn't exist, I definitely wouldn't have believed it could be made. Was this another Glow trick—transporting you to an unbelievable place to ease further mental stretches?

Summer held up the meteorite. "On the seventh day, we awoke to the smell of burning plastic. The stone had landed, and strange plants were flourishing from its surface. They filled with light and warmth. Channels of pure water ran through their veins, and their spores cleansed the air."

If any of this was fake, it was still impressively elaborate.

She returned the meteorite to its socket. Light filled the plants once again. They hummed, their leaves, nodes, and fronds jittering with excitement.

The kid in the baseball cap laughed and nudged his friends, who shushed him loudly.

Joanna stood up and walked over to him, whispering something in his ear.

"Look how our island," Summer continued, "powered by the stone, rewards us with its own life."

Veins pumped glowing fluid, giving life to the island's neon cathedral of buildings.

Summer smiled. "Gabriel will give a brief tour, then lunch—and that's it. Go home if you want."

I wasn't scared yet. But it was only day one of three, the maximum duration I could expect to stay out here and survive. Who knew what next awaited us?

7

Gabriel stood with us, the new arrivals, in the plaza's centre. He would give us a tour, and I had to leave Joanna behind for now.

He told us that the island had satellite-controlled rotors at four corners, just like the ones they'd used on deep-sea drilling rigs in the past. The rotors kept the island in place, away from the surrounding wind farms and shipping routes.

He explained what we'd find down the first three or four alleyways: buildings, up to seven storeys high, made from plastic bottles—over a hundred thousand in total—housed in mesh nets and covered in cement.

Along the first alley, he showed us the communal living space and showers, where strips of a cane-like plant glowed bright white across the ceiling.

The second alley led to a hairdresser's, laundry rooms, clothing stores, and storerooms of food, toiletries, clean blankets, and medical supplies.

Down the third alley were rooms containing the power generators, the bio-digesters that harvested methane from organic waste, the algae reactors that made the biodiesel, and the tanks that collected potable water from the open veins of the island's weird plants.

We stopped to marvel at Patricia's sculptures, dotted throughout each of the rooms: octopus-like creatures made of burnt plastic, lumpy meteorite-like rocks, Picasso-esque self-portraits.

The fishery was our last stop.

Barnacles crunched under our feet as we entered a humid, cuboid room at the end of alley three. It smelled like a lobster pot parching in the sun. A strange outcrop of plastic that looked like a sink emerged from the floor. Plant tendrils broke through the wall and bathed their tips in its water like toeless foot-stumps dabbling in a wading pool.

Large circular hatches in the floor were open to the water beneath. They contained "bivalve molluscs, decapod crustaceans, as well as pelagic and demersal fish"—whatever those were.

"Wait," I said. "You all still eat real fish?"

"Exactly," Gabriel said.

The teenagers audibly squirmed. Heath remained reticent. Corinne had looked to be on the verge of puking for the last hour or so anyway.

"I know what you're thinking," Gabriel continued. "Mercury, cancer, et cetera. Well, let me just use one of our roaches to prove you wrong."

He saw the look on my face.

"It's a type of fish."

He went to the cupboard and took out a net on the end of a long rod. Opening one of the hatches, he dipped the net in and retrieved a fish about the length of my forearm, green on its top half and fading to silver at the bottom.

He ushered us to follow him to the plastic sink.

This was the closest I'd been to the plant. It looked like dry ice, white and friable, encased in a coating of clear gelatin.

Once he'd dropped the flapping fish in from a height, it swam around him in panicked circles. The water thickened, and the fish slowed until it was stationary in the centre of the pool. Didn't fish have to keep swimming to survive? Or was that just sharks? I didn't know. Either way, the water's surface was still, shimmering like thick resin. A humming reverberated through the pool, and the floor itself shook.

I steadied myself. Gabriel placed a hand on me, urging me to pay attention.

The fish's mouth expanded to its limit. Greyish lumps emerged and migrated their way through the resin. Smaller lumps and threads shot out the fish's belly as well. As they did, they shed their dirt, their mass. They were pieces of plastic, shattering and dissolving, moving towards the plant's tendrils. The plants absorbed the milky droplets of plastic that remained.

The vibration stopped. The tendrils grew new nodules at their tips. The resin became water again, and the fish swam in its circles, much calmer than before.

"It's not just the fish." Gabriel cupped a handful of water from the pool and drank it. "The water's fresh."

How do you fake something like that?

Gabriel folded his arms with self-satisfaction. "This is the work we do. Salvaging plastic, healing fish, purifying water. Any questions?"

I had to snap out of it. I didn't want to miss a chance to sow discord through the island's otherwise ironclad indoctrination.

"Do I know you from somewhere?" I asked.

The teenagers whispered. Heath looked between us with detached curiosity.

Gabriel raised an eyebrow. "I don't talk about acting anymore, and if you came out here just to—"

I held a hand up to his face. "Whoa, whoa. I didn't say 'acting'. I don't think I've seen you in anything."

He hesitated. "You sure?"

"Oh, yeah. I'd remember too." I got closer to him. "I always wanted to be in films. Sadly it wasn't to be."

Not really. As objective as I could be about my own attractiveness, I didn't think myself ugly—but that didn't mean I enjoyed the prospect of blowing up my image and asking thousands, maybe millions of strangers to look at it for the rest of time.

"Being in films isn't for most people," Gabriel said.

"But it was for you. Apparently."

"I—" He sighed. "I was fortunate. But now I'm doing something else."

I held my hands up. "Fine."

"I couldn't go back anyway," he continued. "I already sold my appearance."

"Huh?" This did take me by surprise. And was unfortunate. He'd been a real talent, not just a looker. Up there on the big screen was a human soul feeling its way through authentic emotions. Not anymore.

"They can superimpose me in anything they want to," he added, his aggression subsiding. "I-I'm not supposed to talk about it."

"I assume you got paid for that, and donated the money to the Glow? And now you're not even allowed to—"

A cold hand gripped my elbow. It was Corinne. She looked to the floor and said only, "Lily, Lily."

"Sorry," I said. "Sorry. Lunch, then?"

"When the tour is over, yes," Gabriel said.

"Is it over?"

The teenagers tittered.

He frowned. "Yes."

We filed back out of the room.

"Hey."

I turned to Gabriel. "Hm?"

"If not from my acting, where do you know me from?"

"Sorry," I said. "It's just a line."

"A line?"

"I was flirting with you. I'm sure that's banned. Forgive me. I'm still learning."

"If you go back—to the land, I mean—could you watch my films? The new ones?" He pushed a palm to his forehead. "Forget it. And please don't tell anyone I said that."

I lowered my voice. "I will. Watch them. If you want me to."

I couldn't imagine myself back on land now, not without Joanna. As for watching his new films—taking in the soulless AI performances that the film studio would brand by plastering Gabriel's appearance onto them—the notion broke my heart.

We stood staring at one another. Gabriel broke eye contact first and looked to the rest of the group, who waited for us at the end of the alley.

"We should get back," he said.

And there our tour ended, before we reached the fourth alley. But I didn't ask about it. I'd pushed enough for now.

Though beleaguered by the no-doubt draining lifestyle of the island, there remained something like a glimmer of humanity left in Gabriel's eye, in his wistful yearning for the adoration of his too-soon-abandoned career. It seemed that, if ever removed from slave labour and returned to proper nutrition, his film star looks and attitude would return.

So. If I survived, could I take him with me?

Back in the plaza, Joanna and I sat together at the table.

Summer sat in the white plastic throne. It folded to her form with the insidiousness of a flytrap's closing jaws.

Members handed out cutlery and Styrofoam plates. From large plastic buckets, they doled out watery-looking fish meat and some sort of white vegetable in equal measure.

"Is that the plant?" I asked Joanna.

She nodded.

"I'm not eating that!"

"I eat it every day. It's fine." She saw the look on my face. "It takes longer than half a day to learn about our life out here. You'll just have to trust me."

Just have to trust her! Well, I didn't. Not her slow, measured words. Not her practised, pre-approved speech. Not the manic look in her overly wide eyes nor the slight grinding of her rear molars. Not my former glamour puss sister's broken nails, brittle hair, sallow skin.

"You want to stay longer, don't you?" she said.

In the past, when she'd tried to introduce her latest terrible boyfriend to the family, thoughts of spending time with her got tainted by a vague sense of dread and regret—the feeling that it wouldn't be as fun as I imagined, or like it had been before. Well, I carted around a flurry of undesirables myself, and where all these early relationship attempts were concerned, Joanna at least had an excellent excuse for her poor taste: she may well have never been attracted to men.

The rest around the table ate rapturously.

As I bit into the plant, which had the crunchy texture and bland taste of water chestnut, I thought about how the Glow was the worst partner of Joanna's that I'd ever met.

After lunch, members cleared the plates away, and Summer asked us visitors to gather over by the harbour, where our bags were waiting.

Joanna and I walked over together.

"Okay, folks," Summer said with the grating enthusiasm of a camp leader. "Melodie will head back to town now."

Cleverly phrased. Almost like Melodie was free to roam the

shops rather than simply sit in that dodgy plastic powerboat and wait for new visitors or meagre supplies.

"So," Summer continued, "unless you want to stay here overnight ..."

The kid who'd laughed during Summer's speech now watched his two friends get in the boat. He made it seem like an extended goof to his friends, like he was going to outdo them in a contest of ironic dares by spending an extra day here—but I could tell Summer had gotten to him.

"Hey." Joanna took me aside from the rest. "If you're gonna stay longer, you can sleep in my room. There's extra space, and it'll be like we're kids all over again."

Not quite.

Ella walked up behind her, wincing at her suggestion. When I caught her eye, a fake smile flickered onto her face.

Joanna scratched her neck. "Only if you're considering, you know ..."

"Sure I am."

Heath and Corinne came up to me.

"I'm out," Corinne said.

On her site, I'd watched videos of her infiltrating neofascist gangs and testing out new designer drugs on herself while they were still legal. She had brought warlords to tears, but she was bailing on *this?*

She stood, frozen, but her eyes twitched. "You can't feel that?"

I knew what she meant. My still-tense stomach muscles ached. But Corinne hadn't even wanted me here in the first place. Maybe there was a reason she now wanted me off the island, and I just hadn't thought of it yet.

I shrugged weakly. "What else can I do?"

"The same thing you did with Gabriel. I saw what you were up to. You know how to plant a seed of doubt and bail. Go to ... to Joy. Tell her you're so glad she found a community that's doing important work and making her happy. Then leave. You've got to hope that's enough."

"Everything okay?" Ella said.

"My wife's leaving," Heath said.

"And you?"

"Not yet."

He looked at me. His kindly brown eyes had a glint of humour in them. He blinked slowly, as if to say *everything will be okay*.

"Last chance, Lily," Corinne said to me.

"I appreciate your concern," I told her coldly.

She lowered her head, defeated and saddened, and got in the boat with the girls.

8

After I had declined to join the others in the communal shower, Joanna took me down alley one and up a bottle ladder to the very top of one of the towers that overlooked the plaza. There, we found a door constructed from broken plastic pallets with *JOY* spelled out in keyboard keys on the front. This was a privilege of 'EOs': Exalted Ones, like herself.

She hinted that to earn the title, the room, and the right to wear her EO tunic, she'd had to demonstrate her allegiance to the Glow in ways she was evidently proud of. But I abstained from further questioning. I didn't want to validate her sacrifice, and I was also afraid to learn just what my sister was capable of.

Her room was a clear bulb, like blown glass. About the size of a first apartment. It had weathered poorly, and game consoles, pieces of plastic chairs, and power extension sockets had been used to plug the holes.

I planted my suitcase by the door and looked around. She had a writing desk with warped paper on it, some broken pencils, and a pink plastic vase. On a fishing line duct-taped to the wall were hangers recovered from the sea. Some were plastic, some wooden and spotted with black mould. Floaty dresses, skirts and cardigans hung from them. She'd assembled a fairy-light chain of glowing algae clumps on the wall, and among them were laminated postcards of the sky and sea.

It was like a full-scale plastic diorama of her bedroom in our family home, but in place of a bed, she had four curved hammocks that emerged from the wall. Still, it was as if her taste in interior decoration had frozen the day she ran away.

"It's cute," I said. "I mean, it won't protect against a nuclear blast when the end of days comes."

Not a genuine threat—no more than ever—but the reference was to a common object of Glow paranoia. I cursed my nerves for the insensitive joke. As if Joanna was going to take my side and laugh at the Glow with me!

Instead she perked up. She walked up to me and grabbed my shoulders, mania in her eyes. "Well that's the thing," she said. "When they bomb, where are they gonna bomb?" It was said with such confidence, as if we both knew 'they' would bomb one day.

I fell mute.

"They'll bomb the land, of course," she said. "And there are always a handful of people awake here at any time. We'll see danger if it comes. We do emergency drills for it all the time. Gabriel can reconfigure the stabilizing motors and send us into open water in under three minutes."

I wasn't going to quiz her on that.

"You're safer here than anywhere else."

Jesus, I hoped not. What would it mean if that was true?

We went to opposite sides of the room so we could get changed into pyjamas.

As I took my jacket off, I searched my pockets for my watch. Nothing. That handsy Glow member must have pickpocketed it upon my arrival.

Unless I had left it in the suitcase. I laid the case on the floor and unzipped it. Of what I remembered packing, my dry shampoo, books for Joanna, and bag of kratom were missing.

There was a note inside. I turned to check that Joanna was still getting changed, and read:

Dear Visitor,

Thank you for your interest in the Glow. We are always looking for new recruits to help with our mission!

We operate a strict no-tolerance policy towards paraphernalia that are commonplace on land.

For your future reference, the following forbidden items were found in your personal belongings:

A list, with boxes beside each item, followed. Someone had ticked *outside literature, technology,* and *alcohol/controlled substances.*

Should you leave the island, we will return these items to you, no harm done.

I should've expected as much. With no way of updating Henry, it meant he would soon come after me.

After I got changed, Joanna ushered me to one of the hammocks. I climbed in, the clear path to the floor down below giving me vertigo. We towered over the central plaza's quilt of mulch, and a pink light pulsed across its surface. I tried to steady myself, the island rolling, pitching, heaving—all three, I assumed. Though I didn't know the difference.

Joanna giggled. "You okay?"

I pressed a palm to my forehead. "I'm getting light-headed."

Joanna blew some hair out of her face. "It's the plants. They purify the air with oxygen. You're breathing what air used to be like. It used to be *this* clean."

"Wow."

She took off her poncho and hung it on a hanger. "I didn't know if you'd ever come."

"Sorry to separate you from your wife."

She sank into a hammock and scratched her cheek on one shoulder. "She has other commitments on the island to keep her occupied. I-I'm used to it."

"Is *she*, though? She didn't look too pleased at the idea. And is it a problem that she knows we're sisters?"

She swung her legs back out the hammock and leaned, looking at me. "I know what you're doing. You're trying to shame me. So go on, let me have it. I'm with another woman."

I sat up to face her. "You think I'm mad because—" I scoffed. "I knew that about you. It's the forties, Joanna. No one cares. Even I've had a frisson or two before."

She was shocked.

"I'm mad you didn't tell me you got married. For *starters*."

Her eyes flitted about as she searched her brain, recolouring her memories with new information.

"Please tell me that's not what this is all about."

Her expression changed back to indignation. "I assume by 'all this' you mean my life's work? No. You should know what it's about by now."

"Jojo—"

"It's Joy. Joy!"

She must have known I'd have no problem with her wife. Maybe others on the island had families that had legitimately cast them out. I'd hate to think it still happened, but it wasn't impossible.

Joanna had needed a reason not to get in touch with us again. If I was right that she'd invented this flimsy excuse to keep herself away, it was promising. It meant I hadn't snubbed her in some more serious way—and that the lies she told herself to stay here had serious weaknesses in their foundation.

I got up, sat beside her, and rubbed her back. "I'm glad you've found something that makes you this happy, that gives you so much purpose."

She leaned her head to one side. "That's kind of you. I know it isn't much. Summer says we need to get our numbers up before we can make real progress." She untied my hair and began to plait it loosely over my shoulder, an affectionate gesture trained into her subconscious. "How did you make it here?"

"What do you mean?"

"Mum couldn't even bathe you in the sink when we were kids."

"Huh." I thought of the morning, the haze of kratom, the bobbing sea. "I guess the thought of never seeing you again scared me even more."

She dropped my hair and lay down. "That's enough for one day."

Thank God. I've been 'on' all day.

I went back to my hammock and tugged on my sleeves. The night's ocean breeze permeated the wall's gaps and coursed through my clothes.

I looked up at the dusky sky. Stars shone through the ceiling's translucent surface. I didn't know what time it was, but it seemed early for bed. Not like I was about to sleep anyway.

I looked over at Joanna. I wanted to take her by the hand and run. But she wasn't ready.

She sat up.

I closed my eyes.

I heard her put on a robe, its frayed edges scratching against the floor.

She shuffled away and left the room.

I got up to watch where she went, but as I did, a headache took over, the room blurred, and I passed out on the floor.

9

"Congratulations!" Joanna said.

I opened my eyes to the stinging sun's cool, cloud-filtered light.

She was already dressed in her full ceremonial gear. "You made it to day two." Her pitch grated my nerves. It was the same one she'd used as a teen when I'd stumble down to breakfast with her and Mum, poorly disguising a hangover.

I was in the hammock again. My suitcase was upright and zipped up.

Last night—was it kratom withdrawal? Fatigue? Gin catching up with me? Something the Glow did?

I'd been conducting a cruel experiment on myself and couldn't parse out which of the bad things was doing what. And besides, I had to remember—given the Glow's capacity for reprogramming people—that this 'Joy' woman, who took the shape of my sister, could be anything but. Even if it pained me to suspect her.

"Last night," I said to her. "I swear—"

"We need to go to the plaza straight away, before anyone knows you stayed here."

Oh, boy, more confusing layers of secrecy.

She clapped her hands. "Up, up!"

I tugged at her robe. "I need to talk to you. Now."

She went over to the entrance hatch and climbed down the ladder.

I quickly got into a change of clothes and followed.

The plaza was unbearably bright. Water had sloshed over it during the night, turning it into a massive sun mirror. Evenly spaced yoga mats broke up the reflections. They covered most of the free area. The plants twisted up between them and expanded, fuzzing with new growths. The horizon rose and fell with the island's motion upon the murky sea.

Summer stood on the podium in front of all the Glowfolk. They surrounded her in an evenly spaced grid, a carpet of people about twenty long and ten wide.

"Glad you could join us, Lily," Summer said.

A titter spread across the group. They could do better than that, surely, but I wasn't about to bring it on my own head.

"You're forgiven," she added, pressing her palms together. "The rhythms of all of us are synced, but it's not uncommon for newbies to lag."

"At least I'm not the last arrival."

Oh. The looks on their faces. You didn't answer back to the leader. Well, *they* didn't.

"Where are Heath and that other kid?"

"That's right." Summer looked across the group. "We lost two faces last night. Michael—'the kid'—didn't possess the sea legs necessary to help save the world."

I flinched once again at the group's forced laughter.

"He had second thoughts, so we made a special trip to ship him back to the land. No harm done. All are welcome to leave whenever."

"Huh," I said.

"We had to send Heath packing too. We found cameras set up in the communal bedrooms."

The Glowfolk gasped.

"He was a reporter."

Exaggerated murmurs, mournful wails.

I didn't know if Heath would've set up cameras, but I did believe the Glow would find an excuse to kick out a journalist. As for the kid, sure, maybe the ironic joke of staying here wore thin during the night and he panicked. That they had left was plausible. Just as plausible as if the Glow had done something to them and wanted to cover it up.

"You didn't know about Heath's profession, did you, Lily?"

An eager middle-aged woman close to the front jumped up and down, raising her arm.

"Yes, Rachel?"

"Did he compromise us?"

"Cameras or no, it makes no difference. The plants don't allow it."

"Right," the woman said, satisfied with this answer. But what the hell did it mean?

"Lily." Summer looked right at me again, keen for me to acknowledge that she knew my name.

"Yes, Summer?" I said back.

"You're in time for a well-being session with Ella."

I grimaced. "It's not private, is it?"

The group laughed.

Ella stood beside the podium, smirking and shaking her head.

Joanna nudged me with an elbow. "I'm so excited for you to see what she does!"

I placed a hand on hers, turned to her and smiled. She wanted me to be a part of this. That was a good sign. It amused me to picture both of us living in an apartment together in the future, no longer separable, all the significance of this time together hitting Joanna in increments. Maybe over morning tea, while we both read the news on our devices, she'd slap herself on the forehead and say, "*You* were humouring *me* that day!"

If that's what I wanted, there was work to do yet.

Ella took to the stage. "Let's get started."

"With what?" I asked Joanna.

"The dance."

I froze. "How long are we going to dance for?"

"I'm not sure. I only know that when I get started, I usually don't want to stop." She ushered me over to a mat. "You'll enjoy it."

Glow aside, group activities were not my thing—though

they'd always been Joanna's. I thought of an early Club Med holiday, how she'd clung to my side, following me into the nine-to-twelve-year-olds group, though she wasn't old enough, crying when they wouldn't let her make a kite with me.

"Okay, everyone, blindfolds out."

Each member took from their robe a pad made from layers of plastic bags sewn together, with an elastic cord at both ends. They covered their eyes with them.

"I've got yours here." Joanna removed two of the same masks from her pocket.

I just had to get through this. Then I could get back to my amateur, low-res, cult-deprogramming attempt.

I took the mask from her and secured it over my eyes.

"Phase one," Ella said. "Jump up and down."

I had a peek at everyone else. They jumped without coordination, like children in the throes of a tantrum.

I could muster that much. I hopped from foot to foot and flailed my arms in a loose jumping-jack motion.

We did this until I almost couldn't anymore, my head aching, hamstrings cramping. I always said things I didn't mean and agreed to things I didn't want to do when I was tired. I had to assume that was the exercise's purpose, and I reminded myself to remain vigilant.

"Phase two. Breathing. Listen to me, and find the breath within yourself."

She panted raggedly, and the group followed her command, reaching astounding volume. Anytime anything external—some meditation app or yoga video, say—threatened to control my breathing, the very thought gave me anxiety. It was my body, my lungs—surely any suggestion wasn't healthy, let alone the shallow panting of a dog in a hot car that Summer now performed.

I got lightheaded again. Spots popped across my vision, even with my eyes closed.

"Stay in your places for phase three, everyone! This isn't a contact sport."

"This is my favourite!" a man screamed.

The rest whooped with joy.

"Now go crazy!"

I felt this one beneath me. The rumbling, feet stamping, bodies rolling on the wet floor. Aching sobs, outraged screaming.

Once the fear subsided, and I remembered they couldn't see me, I joined in. I windmilled my arms, spun around, screamed. I gasped in the fresh air, so unaccustomed to it that it got me high.

The floor tilted beneath me. With each jump, I didn't know whether to trust that it would still be there. My feet never landed when I expected them to, and the texture of mushy plastic moss and seawater felt different each time. Each time I jumped, I spent more time in the air than the jump before. I half-expected to take off into the sky. Instead, I felt something constricting my waist, and I shrank within myself.

"You're a child!" she said. "Go to your favourite place!"

The spots in the darkness expanded, and images of my childhood with Joanna rushed across my vision. I saw the forest of our youth, reeds on the bank as tall as I was, our welly boots sinking in the mud. Ripples spread across the pond, where hungry fish mouths broke the water's still surface.

"Lily!"

It was Ella, calling me.

I reached for the mask to see where she was, but she tutted, and I felt her hand press the mask to my face.

"Concentrate now," she said. "Stay where you are. Describe it to me."

I mentioned the reeds, the mud, the pond. I refrained from telling her about the fear, the panic clutching my chest, the dread seeping through my entire body.

"I can see it," Ella said. "Can you see it, group?"

"Yes," they said in unison. It rang through my body like a wall of comfort. As if a community was there with me that day.

"How old are you?" she asked.

"Twelve, I guess."

"You guess?"

"I'm twelve."

"Who's there with you?"

"Our dogs. Two border collies." Max and Benjamin, two fluffy and muddy best friends.

"Are you sure?"

With her words, the dogs disappeared again. "No. They've run ahead without me."

"That's right, they have."

Did she know, or was she somehow making it so?

"So I'll ask again," she said. "Who's there with you?"

"My sister." Little Joanna in her blue chequered duffel coat, splashing in the puddles.

"Look again."

Just puddles. Just mud. "Nobody."

"Look again."

"A man." Herringbone slacks, the pungent scent of cigars.

"Describe him."

"He's wearing a yellow raincoat and a matching cap. It's like something a child would wear. And the ground is wet, but it hasn't been raining. The cap hides his face."

Ella was silent now. I was off, the words running away from me. Some long-forgotten experience—no, a long-repressed trauma—was now spilling out of me, for the whole group to hear. How?

"He asks me for directions to a campsite. I say I don't know." It was more than I was allowed to say to strangers. "He has a map under his arm. He wants me to point out where." As if I would know! "But the map is bulky, like it's wrapped around something."

"Go on."

"He holds it out to me. I turn away, and he seizes my arm." Like I was back there again, his thick fingers squeezed my little bones like a vice. It was like running in a dream without moving. "He pulls me up."

The constriction round my waist returned.

"I'm kicking and screaming."

But I couldn't reach the ground's safety. I flailed in the air, helpless, drowning in the nightmare of it.

"Stay there, Lily. Stay there."

"Until—"

"Yes?"

"He's screaming too." Release. In my memory, I fell to the floor again. I felt the cool wet mud soaking into my favourite red corduroy dungarees. "He drops me. My sister, she digs her teeth into his ankle. He runs away. My sister holds her mouth. It's bleeding. She left two front baby teeth in the man's leg."

When they arrested the Rendlesham Ripper, they found those teeth in a locket around his neck—along with many others that weren't Joanna's.

And there it was, the reason I owed it to my sister to seek her out.

10

Someone shook my arm. I tried to move it, but couldn't. My eyes had shut tight, and my body had curled into a foetal position. I was catatonic.

I unfroze, gasped for air. I clawed my hands over my ears, pressed my palms flat against them. It was a reaction to the screaming. It was so loud. Who was doing it? When would it stop?

Arms tugged at me. They wrenched the hands from my ears and took the mask off my face. My eyes opened, and I saw a looming circle of Glowfolk around me, looking down on me with pity.

I was the one screaming. Once I realized this, I could stop.

"Get up," Ella said.

I stood and faced her.

"That's why you're here, isn't it? To save someone, like you were once saved."

"I-I guess so."

"You guess so?"

A pit of something like decades-old shame welled up in my stomach. The Ripper—my first reminder that no one is ever safe. Joanna's act—my first lesson that there is no guarantee in life but our own actions.

It had led me to the island. It had taught me not to trust others, only myself.

Ella placed a hand on my shoulder. "I was there with you. I saw what you saw. You haven't moved past the memory because your twelve-year-old self learned the wrong message from it. Which was … ?"

"One day I need to save the person that saved me."

She smiled. "You came here to save your sister."

Rumours flew across the group.

"Sister!"

"Is her sister here?"

"Who is it?"

"Joy, the EO."

"They were talking together yesterday."

"Hey!" Ella motioned for the others to shush. She looked at me again. "Joy's not the one you need to save. But stay. Work with us. Save others. Starting with yourself."

She embraced me, pressing my head against hers, swaying me from side to side with her body.

I took in her scent. Jasmine. I released all my muscles at once.

As if they knew I'd do that, the Glowfolk rushed in to take my weight, swaying me to the rhythm of Ella's movements.

"Tell us what you feel," someone said.

"Yeah, Lily! Share with us? Please?"

What did it mean that they knew about Joanna now? And what did I think about the memory, if that's what it was?

Everything went too fast. The group's attention exerted a pressure on me to perform to their satisfaction. And I still hadn't eaten.

I broke down, tears gushing down my face. My arms rushed out, independent from me, and gripped Ella.

When my arms fell at my side again, all of them released me and stood back, forming a concentrated circle.

"Why didn't you warn me?" I said.

"You wouldn't have done it otherwise," Ella said.

Paternalistic bullshit. I hadn't even subscribed yet, and already they were making decisions for me.

Though I did feel something like—well, a glow inside. Like the high I got those few dry Januarys I managed to abstain from drinking. Time would tell if it really was the catharsis it seemed to be.

"Lily," Ella continued, "if you hadn't gone through this, they would have ordered me to send you home."

The old 'above my pay grade, mate' excuse. They probably call it 'above my trophic level' or some shit out here.

"Neither of us want that," Ella added.

So apparently she was psychic as well as deeply invasive.

"We all went through it." It was Gabriel's soothing voice behind me. "I ran away from home as a kid. During my first session, I saw it from my mother's perspective. It was devastating."

"Summer did it for me back on land," Ella said. "In my vision, I was my own friend and, in this role, I had to watch a condensed version of my drug and drink years. The process releases traumas in order of urgency."

It would've felt good that they shared their own struggles—if I had any reason to believe them. Without proof, I just felt ashamed by my own warped memories.

"Don't you feel good now?" Gabriel said. Why was he being kind to me? Did he like me or just the attention I gave him? If I couldn't figure that out about regular, land-based men, what hope did I have of decoding him?

"May I be excused for a moment?" I said.

The group reacted with stiffness. They seemed to think I'd melt right into them. It pleased me to subvert. I didn't want any involvement in things going their way.

"Sure," Ella said.

I nodded and headed to Joanna's room. It surely wasn't great that they knew who my sister was. Either way, I no longer had a reason to hide it.

I felt them beneath me in the plaza. Their confusion, their rigidity.

None of them could leave an activity at will—but they had to convince me I could, at any time, if they wanted me to join.

11

I savoured my time alone in Joanna's room, sitting in a hammock, drying my face on a T-shirt.

Was there a mirror somewhere? I hadn't brought one.

I searched Joanna's desk. Something poked out from beneath her vase. Photos of us together at some London nightclub.

And I thought she hadn't thought of me at all. It was worse that she had. She knew the sacrifice she'd made, but she thought it was worth it.

No! I couldn't think like this. I had to stay focused.

I looked down at the plaza. Everyone's head was turned my way. When I met their eyes through the cellophane window, grins shot across their faces instantly. I grinned back and came back down.

We were going to eat soon. I still didn't know if there was a reason I'd passed out when Joanna left last night, but maybe it was what they fed me.

I ducked into the storeroom on my way back down the alley and stole an unlabelled can to put in my jacket. Maybe that was better than what they were about to serve us.

I sat beside Joanna at the day's one meal.

The faces around the table were different. I'd estimate that only a third of the people I'd seen on the island could fit round it at once. I wasn't sure that meant the others were eating elsewhere.

I stared at the plate before me—the same overboiled fish meat and bland, alien vegetable—and kept wiping my face as new tears emerged. Around me was the animal sound of others devouring their food.

"Stop crying, would you?" Joanna said. "It isn't a big deal. I expected more from you."

"I notice you're not eating, Lily," Summer said.

"No need to worry," I said. "I'm still adjusting to the island's motion. B-But I won't let that stop me being here."

"It isn't that our offering displeases you, then?"

Joanna let out a deep breath, as if trying to calm herself because of my insult.

"Not at all."

"Eat, then," Ella said from the other end of the table.

"Maybe there's something else we can make for you?" Gabriel suggested, looking at the other members.

"Thank you, but no. Please. No special treatment."

"So enjoy," Summer said. It was a command.

I took the plastic knife and fork and sliced a piece of the plant, raising it slowly to my mouth.

"Look!" Joanna said. "New arrivals."

I put the fork down.

"I almost forgot," Summer said. "Melodie's late today. I'll be interested to learn why. Lily, come with us. You'll have to learn how to greet the new arrivals."

Glowfolk scurried away from the table, off to collect their sparklers.

We gathered over by the harbour.

The two girls from the day before got out of the boat. Melodie remained at the back, by the motor, looking ashamed. Waif that she was, there was no way she could've prevented them from getting on the boat.

"Where is he?" said the taller one.

"Welcome," Ella said, ignoring the question.

"Don't pretend like you don't know," the shorter one said.

Summer approached them. "Hello again, girls. Your friend left last night. You haven't seen him yet?"

What was going on? I wanted to stay and find out, but this was my chance to do something about the food. I retreated from the group that had gathered, everyone from the island, and went back to the table. I chopped up my food and redistributed it to the other plates.

I'd stay at the table and pretend I'd eaten alone. Hopefully I was just paranoid and wouldn't have to do this again in future, or else they'd get suspicious.

Soon the crowd returned to the table.

"Lily?" Summer said. "The girls left again."

"Thanks for letting me know." I stood to talk to her. "I get nervous when people watch me eat. I'm sure I'll get used to it."

She looked at my plate, then back at me. "Fine."

That afternoon was my first experience of Summer's 'discourse'. Can someone give a discourse by themselves?

Apparently so. She sat on the throne as purple tentacles waved loosely around her, at least twenty of them, all of varying lengths and shades. Their movement was menacing, like Medusa's hair. They remained in constant motion as if anticipating an attack.

Summer spoke about the eternal nature of Truth—I could hear her capitalizing the word in her head. Not to say I understood the rhetoric. It sounded like a meaningless barrage of simple sentences spoken at a forcedly slow pace to introduce false reverence. I didn't think the others got it either. But their glazed eyes and rictus-ridden faces beamed at her, daffodils turning to their sun.

I'd almost ended up in a situation like this once before. When I was just an intern at the office, one of the accountants told me he was in a band and invited me to their gig that evening. 'Cute, stable, and creatively inclined' wasn't usually my type—I preferred to punish myself with the meaningless challenge of less well-put-together men—but when I went home that evening, I messaged him to say I'd be there and prepared some 'I'm enjoying this' faces in the mirror in case the band wasn't any good.

The address he'd given me, I discovered when I showed up, was a church. When I went inside, I saw a group of teenagers on stage with keyboards, guitars, and a drum set, singing "God is awesome" over and over. My 'date' was in the audience, his arms and theirs flowing with the music like seaweed in the waves.

I turned to leave, but he noticed and ran up to me. He shamed me, while smiling, for not giving the event a chance.

His behaviour infuriated me beyond my standard first-date-asshole peak. I couldn't make sense of it at the time, though I worked it out later. It was the insult that, without his manipulation, I wouldn't have been open-minded enough to attend of my own volition.

I'd always associate subsequent similar invitations with his trick. I told myself, for better or worse, that if any organization had a secret worth knowing, it would be self-evident. They wouldn't have to use such tactics.

Which wasn't to say that those tactics stopped working on me. Those inclined to use them dedicated so much energy to their development that they were always at least one step ahead. I just crossed my fingers that I'd catch the trick and bail in time.

After sitting cross-legged for hours, my groin muscles ached. And when did my back muscles get so weak?

When the discourse ended, we stood up. Melodie asked if Joanna, Ella, and I wanted to join her and her friends to play board games. "We're getting sick of playing amongst ourselves." She leaned in. "Maybe the newbie can beat Brandon!"

"No, thanks," I said.

Melodie smiled weakly. "Another time, then."

She walked away, leaving Joanna, Ella, and me standing together.

I looked to Joanna. "Back to your room, sis?"

"It's fine," Ella said to Joanna, affectionately smoothing her hair. "We'll catch up eventually."

"Come on, then." Joanna grabbed my elbow and whisked me away.

"What was that all about?" Joanna said.

We were back in her room, getting changed into pyjamas.

"I need some help here," I said. "Which part?"

"Well, how about the way you spoke to Melodie?"

I tried to process everything that had happened. "Surely that's not what's bothering you? I haven't seen you in years. I didn't even know you were still alive." *I may never see you again.* "I don't want to spend what little time we have together playing board games with someone else."

"We're all equal here. You don't have the right to demand special time with any one of us."

"Okay."

She pulled on her hair, close to the root. "You came all the way out here just to persecute me again!"

"Again? When did I ever persecute you before?"

I sat in the discomfort for a moment, wondering whether her words really didn't ring true or if I simply wouldn't accept them.

No. They didn't sound like the Joanna I remembered.

I stabbed at a guess. "That ritual I was in this morning. Ella only pays that much attention to the newbies, doesn't she?"

Her eyes rolled around. She was searching for the next line in the script the Glow had installed in her mind.

"Does the process still work as well for you as it did for me this morning?"

She looked back at me, grimacing, straining to keep me out.

"Has your time here gotten better or worse?"

No! The question was too transparent. My agenda had leaked.

She climbed into the hammock and looked away from me. "I've kept you safe so far. My own courtesy to you. I guess I still had—a fondness for you that I've failed to let go of. Even as an EO, I always have more to learn."

Whatever glow I'd felt in her presence dimmed back to a familiar numbness.

"You think it's some tragedy that we never hang out." She turned back to me. "You're alone there. Because you've been living life 'on rails'. When anyone ever asks me if I had family on land, I say, 'An alcoholic disappointment of a mother and a spineless sister. The sister, she's nearing thirty now, settling down with the wrong man, thinking about having kids she doesn't want so she can give up on the career she didn't have it in her to develop—and all the while feeling sorry for me! Like she truly has it all."

I shut my eyes tightly. "I would slap you in the face right now. But things didn't go so well for me last time I did that to someone."

I wished I hadn't even said it. But only saying it, and not doing it, took the summation of my restraint.

She turned away again. "Running away from you was the kindest thing I could've done. On top of all I've accomplished since, it gave you the excuse you needed to become the massive failure we always knew you were."

I didn't have it in me to cry anymore. I hardly had any energy left at all.

"This is your last night in my room. And you should leave tomorrow."

My heart filled with a weird leaden peace.

In the best case, I'd thought I would leave with Joanna and never part from her again. Instead, I got confirmation that that would never be possible. Which was something. Disappointing, but still worth it. At least I hoped I would come to that conclusion one day.

I lay back, done for the day. For the year, maybe. Once I got off the island, I'd process all my feelings. I was too worn-out to do it now, and everything was going by so quickly, like an assault on my emotions.

Here was something else I couldn't work out: I remembered reading in the news that when they'd arrested the Rendlesham Ripper, they found teeth in a locket around his neck. But where did I get the idea that Joanna's had been in there too?

Had Ella pushed me in that direction, irritated that I had disturbed her ecosystem, stolen her possession away?

"Joanna?" I whispered. "Joy, I mean. Joy?"

She didn't reply.

I couldn't sleep. I was too confused, too hungry, half-expecting Henry to show up as promised to fire a gun in the air and order immediate evacuation.

And I still hadn't showered.

I leaned down to the floor and pulled up my jacket, taking out the can. I held it up to the sun's dying light. What a shame it would be to open it now, given the many different treats I'd hoped to find within it over the afternoon.

I was about to tug on the ring pull when I noticed something.

I turned the lid. Close to one edge, there was a pin prick, light bending around it like a black hole.

I pull the ring back. The can didn't make the same satisfying *shuck* sound it usually did. The seal had been compromised. They were injecting the food with *something*, then.

I peeled back the lid out of curiosity anyway. Inside was some sort of meat gelatin. Dog food, maybe. I wouldn't be surprised.

Joanna stirred.

I placed the can on the floor, covered it with my jacket, then lay back down and closed my eyes.

She walked over to me. Through my eyelids, I saw the shadow of her hand waving over me.

She left, just like she had the night before.

With no sign that I would pass out again, I followed.

12

By the time I'd reached the bottom of the ladder, Joanna had vanished.

I headed to the plaza in search of her. Its plants softly glowed its range of purples and pinks, shadows of fronds waving up across the walls through the thin evening mist. It was like being in an underwater exhibit at an aquarium. I wish I could've sat and enjoyed it.

The sky hadn't yet turned to complete darkness. A dim red on the horizon lit the world in all directions.

There was no one around, but I could hear something whirring. As I sneaked across the plaza, I realized that it came from the last alley, behind the chicken wire.

I vaulted over the gate and followed the sound.

There was a cement building at the end of the walkway, with a metal door. I walked to it and entered.

Inside, it was bright, with a grime-laden floor. Dusty plastic bottles without labels lined a set of shelves by the wall. A collection of immaculate plastic pallets lay beside them, with a stack of sandwich bags on top.

I took one of the bags, crouched down, and tugged at a glowing sprig. I swore I heard it squeal as I pulled it from the floor's plastic, its many roots emerging where they'd grown down the pores. I sealed it in the bag and put it in my pocket, shuddering as I felt it wriggle.

When I left tomorrow, someone would be keen to sample it.

A labyrinth of pipes snaked over the wall. A tall metal cylinder, painted army green, vibrated in the room's centre. Gauges and dials covered its surface. A slender pipe pointed towards a large collecting vessel, a clear liquid dripping from its tip.

I looked at the tags on some of the other pipes. With arrows, they indicated the direction of flow, and read *seawater, fresh water, brine, air supply*. The freshwater collected in the vessel. It was an evaporator.

Didn't the plants provide all the fresh water they needed?

On the other side of the room was a round orange generator with a black cable running to the evaporator. A jerry can of diesel sat beside it.

Why do that if the plants provided all the energy they needed? *Sustainable my ass!*

"Oh, but the congregation is too big now. We need to resort to these temporary measures while the plants grow," they'd say.

No need to quiz them on it; I could hear the answers already. I could gaslight myself and save them the bother—which was probably an intended effect of their rhetoric.

I went to the shelves and picked up one of the bottles. Did they contain the evaporator's fresh water? I looked at the bottle more closely. Its seal wasn't broken. Maybe they'd been taken straight from the supermarket. Would they even reuse these bottles, or claim to have scavenged them from the sea, turning them into construction materials?

I heard footsteps down the alley.

I hid under a tarp.

It was Gabriel, carrying a clipboard under his arm. On his head he wore a visor that directed purple light onto his face and body. UV light, it looked like.

My survival reflexes kicked in in the weirdest way. I slowly purged the air from my lungs, muscles tightening, making myself small and willing myself to be invisible. I tensed so hard it hurt and wanted so badly to gasp for air.

How is this helping? I asked my body to no avail.

What an idiot I'd been, trying to gain his allegiance earlier. If he caught me, I'd learn just how little this place cared about my well-being.

To say the least, I thought as my imagination ran riot.

He checked the gauge and logged its numbers on a clipboard. On his way back out, he looked at the bottle I'd touched and turned it around.

Then he left.

And once I heard him pace off to a reasonable distance, I started breathing again.

My close encounter with Gabriel hadn't deterred my investigations. This remained my only chance to find out more about the Glow's operations, and what I'd discovered so far just spurred me on.

Further down the alley, I discovered something like a lost and found room.

A stack of clothing filled one corner, a half pyramid running from floor to ceiling. I looked across the myriad different items: there was nothing like what you could find in the storerooms in alley one. These must've been surrendered by former selves or brought in by outsiders.

Yes, that was it. There was that kid's gold-embroidered jacket.

They said he'd left in the night—but not before ditching his jacket here, apparently. Maybe he was still here, and they kept the identity of new members secret for some reason? Perhaps he was in some training facility I hadn't yet discovered, dancing around in a plastic smock, having relinquished his material possessions.

Wishful thinking of the worst order.

As unpleasant as the notion was, what I feared had really happened to him was far worse. I didn't want to think about it without further confirmation, but the sight of his jacket caused me to perspire with dread. There was no unknowing it.

In a bucket in the corner was a stack of phones, watches, and e-glasses. Gabber jaw dials, like black buttons, were scattered throughout. Disallowing them on the island was a new policy, then. But how did you get them out without surgery, and why?

I went through each of the devices: no battery, no password, no SIM card.

There was mine! I recognized the scratches on my watch's face.

I turned it on and tried to call Henry. No signal. "The plants don't allow it," Summer had said. Signal blockers were a more likely alternative.

From the plaza came the sound of a man screaming, a weird

unholy howl. It was surely my cue to discover the next horrific, unforgettable thing about the Glow. My feet understandably kept me rooted to the floor where I stood, as if through some weird magnetic force. But I overcame it, step by step, leaving the room and creeping back up the alley towards the sound.

<hr>

Back in the plaza, the dozen or so EOs had assembled in a circle. They were naked but for clear plastic raincoats. Barefoot, they hopped from side to side, their jackets crinkling as they did so. They waved their arms back and forth in the air. In their hands were clumps of plant flesh, pulsing the infected yellow, pink, and red of a suppurating wound. The pulse matched the rhythm of their stamping feet.

They made weird huffing sounds, an unintentional throat-singing. The ground squished beneath their feet. The floor was spongier than before.

In the centre of the dance was the throne. Whoever sat there was the source of the screaming.

As I crept further along the wall, I saw that it was Heath. They'd stripped him to his underwear. Plastic tentacles secured him to the throne. On his chest and stomach were several bite marks, fresh blood trickling down his flesh. His jaw flapped open and closed, but he didn't make any more sounds. Plant pulp glowed on his lips—a rushed dose of drugs to stifle his next attempts to scream.

I looked back at the EOs and winced. Their mouths were bloody.

The lights of the plants snuffed out, leaving the EOs nothing but shadows. They snarled and pounced on Heath, the throne toppling backwards.

The swarm of them surrounded him. Their arms worked frantically, and the sounds of cracking and ripping emanated from their cluster. Heath was just a corpse now, a meaty, larva-like lump on the ground.

The floor glowed again. In the island's phosphorescent night lights, a sticky puddle bubbled. It drained into the floor like a whitecap sighing back into the sea.

Joanna got up, blood still wet in her hair, shimmering in the moonlight. She looked right at me—but her eyes couldn't see.

The floor made spotlights beneath each of the EOs. As the circles of light moved along the floor, the EOs followed, walking backwards into their respective alleyways.

After some minutes, I sneaked back across the plaza, to the bottle ladder leading to Joanna's room. She'd gone somewhere else. But now that I knew what she meant by her room keeping me safe, that was exactly where I'd go.

Hours later, I heard someone climbing up the ladder.

I closed my eyes.

Joanna sighed. I could tell it was her. She stroked my hair with affection, then returned to her hammock.

How badly I wanted—what, to return the love? To reach out to her and tell her it would all be okay?

No. Whatever that was wasn't my sister.

The Joanna I knew was gone forever.

13

"Sleep well?"

I hadn't slept at all. My face was cold and dry like I'd been anxious for a long time, the blood drawn from the surface to protect my core, skin left to its own devices to flake and break out as a result.

I winced. My eyes were dry too. I could feel puffiness beneath them.

I sat up and couldn't see anyone in the room with me.

"Look down."

I scurried over to the voice's source. Through the window I saw Summer, in front of all the Glowfolk, looking up at me.

I climbed into the hammock to dress myself so they couldn't see, pulling clothing out of my suitcase on the floor.

When I went down the bottle ladder, Joanna was among the waiting crowd. Good. Maybe she didn't want me here—and I sure didn't want to be here any longer—but she wouldn't let anything terrible befall me in the meantime. Surely.

"Good morning, Summer," I said. "I hope I didn't delay today's proceedings."

"Oh, there's no hurry for what comes next," she said.

The group rushed me and carted me up by my arms and legs.

"No!" I thrashed around, but couldn't see anything but a blinding blanket of white clouds. The sides of an alley came into view as they continued to carry me. And then I smelled the fishery.

A hatch creaked open. They whipped me in by my legs. I caught a glimpse of some splashing roaches just before I broke the surface of their pool.

I went into lizard brain–mode, thrashing around, trying to stay afloat and find something to hold on to, maybe to scrabble back up. The sides of the pool, I discovered, were smooth plastic, without a single imperfection I could grip. Even as I scratched at it, my fingers slid back off. I tried to reach out and prop myself up by holding on to opposite sides of the pool, but it was too wide.

"We're very clear on our rules, Lily," Summer said.

I kept myself afloat, trying to swim in the centre, though I didn't know how. I dipped beneath the surface, my feet reaching down to find the pool's bottom, but it was too deep for me to stand on and keep my head above water. I held my breath, dropped to the bottom and kicked off the base to resurface and breathe again.

"You entered a restricted area last night."

"I can't swim!" I shouted.

"Y-You hear that?" It was Gabriel. "She's scaring my fish."

As he said it, I felt the roaches thrashing around me, heads bumping into my torso, tails and fins flapping against my hands.

"Come on." That was Ella. "She's not doing so badly. How do you expect her to learn otherwise?"

Other Glowfolk chimed in. "Why is she freaking out? It's just water. If she's serious about being here, it has to stop bothering her this much."

"Mm-hm, I agree."

"It's hardly torture."

When I looked up and cleared the hair from my face, I tried to see who was up there, staring down at me.

Summer was gone. Gabriel looked at me with pity, Ella with detached curiosity, and Joanna with pure disdain.

And then they all left.

Cold. It was so cold. Maybe I could stay warm by moving in circles, burning energy. But the pool wasn't big enough for that. All of this had to be by design.

So I would drown here, among the roaches.

Someone tugged on my jacket, held me above water. "Shh-shh-shh. You're doing great, Lily." It sounded like Melodie. But she held me from behind, so I couldn't be sure. "I know it doesn't seem like it right now, but this is good for you. I can't let them see me helping you. But use this as a chance to calm down."

I tried to lengthen and deepen my breaths. It took a while, but she held me there as I did.

"That's good. You're okay. You're going to be okay. You're going to come out of this stronger."

I couldn't speak, but I reached up and held her arm to show my appreciation.

"I have to go now. But you can do this."

In response, I wailed. Tears formed and washed away in the pool.

"Oh, hey," I heard Melodie say to someone as she left.

"Gabriel had me worried about the fish. Just wanted to check that they were okay."

"I'll remember that," said the man who'd discovered her there.

So I would stay here and suffer a while, and get back out to find—what?

I slowed my strokes, my arms and legs coming to a stop. The weight of my wet clothes dragged me down.

I closed my eyes, breathed out, and dropped to the bottom.

Something constricted around my waist, around my arms. Seaweed, plastic garbage? I struggled against it, screaming out a last bubble.

I struggled, but whatever it was tightened further, pinning my arms in a cross over my chest.

Something pulled me up. I emerged from the water and was hoisted up and out the hatch, back onto the plastic floor.

"Hooray!"

The Glowfolk had returned. I turned and fell on my chest, panting, to see five or six of them holding fishing rods, the wires wrapped around me.

A second wave of them lifted me to my knees and covered me with towels that they pressed on me.

"You did it."

"We're so proud of you."

"I knew you were made for this as soon as you arrived."

"You're definitely one of us now."

"Thank you for proving yourself to us. We won't forget, Lily."

The cheer in their voices gave no indication that they'd left me here to die.

I slumped back down on my side, shivering, jaw chattering.

"Well done, Lily," Summer said.

I held out my arms and the Glowfolk lifted me up, still pressing the towels on me, rubbing my hair with them.

"Bring her out for the surprise!"

Gabriel rushed over to me. "It's a good one this time," he said.

I couldn't even look at him.

14

The Glowfolk had assembled around the stone outside, serene looks on all their faces. I thought I knew what was coming next.

Summer moved into position and placed her hand on the polygonal case.

I looked between her and the crowd. Joanna, Ella, and Gabriel were at the front. I still knew hardly any of these people, yet all of them looked at me with kind, overly familiar grins, nodding their heads. Some of them cheered and whistled.

A young woman at the front sobbed aggressively and fell to her feet, shaking. Members on either side helped her up. "We're getting a new one," she said. "I can feel it!"

"Congratulations," Summer said. "The induction is over. You're free to join now."

"That's all it took, huh?" I said, coughing. My lips stung, drying out now that I'd returned to the light.

Ella tutted. "Did Joy never tell you what she went through to become Exalted?"

Joanna didn't look at me. She stared straight ahead, an empty vessel.

"One thing at a time!" Summer called back. She walked up to me and picked at fluff and debris from the towels, as if protectively. "Do you want to go through the initiation ceremony? I'll understand if you don't, and escort you to the harbour myself."

Big honour. Did she know what I'd seen last night? Gabriel seemed to regret telling her that I'd trespassed. Maybe I'd left some clue behind. The bottle. He must've seen my fingerprints in the dust, and who else would dare enter? Therefore he'd had to tell her, in case someone else had noticed me first. Maybe he hadn't mentioned that I'd seen their ritual, or maybe he didn't know that I had. But maybe he'd told her everything—and if I said I didn't want to join, it was over for me.

"Look," Summer said. "Melodie's in the boat, primed to go."

Sure enough, she was—but that was meaningless.

I was far too weary now to summon the energy to lie further, to do anything other than what I truly wanted.

Because to stay now, knowing all that I did, seeing whatever inhabited my sister now, in the day and at night ... It would be like hanging out with Grandpa in the late stage of his Alzheimer's. The person I loved had long departed, and spending time with their body was just a tribute to the person who had once lived there.

"I want to stay."

To visit my sister's body like a tomb. Because it was all I had left.

The crowd cheered.

I looked at Joanna. No reaction.

"Okay, then," Summer said. "Go to the throne, and I'll get Patricia."

She was real?

I sat in the throne. The tentacles folded over me, squeezing my stomach.

Summer came back into view, the arm of a sedated old woman slung over her shoulder.

Patricia wore a diaphanous silk shift, her unwashed grey hair hanging on either side of her head. Deep lines covered her face. She moaned, revealing a scarcity of teeth.

Summer didn't let go of Patricia's arm as they walked together towards the stone. She unlocked the cover and pushed it back.

The crowd sighed with awe.

Summer held Patricia's wrists and had her reach out.

Scars ravaged the woman's palms. Patricia grabbed onto the

stone, and Summer supported her by applying grip strength through her forearms.

The island's light died once again, the plants flopping into hibernation, their background hum diminished. Even the throne's tentacles fell to the side again.

The two women turned and walked slowly towards me, careful not to drop the stone.

Patricia moaned a series of vowels at me.

"She says to take the stone," Summer said.

"With my bare hands?"

Summer nodded.

I leaned towards it, seeing my face reflected in it like the metal sphere in an Escher portrait. The image became distorted, dents and warps and stripes passing across its surface, like some camouflaging cuttlefish.

I reached out. Cracks on the stone's surface glowed. In one corner, I saw someone running along the table towards us.

A wave of outrage passed through the crowd. I ducked as Joanna flew towards us, tackling the women and grabbing the stone with her hands. It sizzled and she screamed, doubling over, crouching on the floor. Rust-coloured smoke puffed out of her bent-over shape on either side.

She turned and looked at me. "Go!"

I was on autopilot now, bolting to the harbour, dodging the Glowfolk who didn't want me to go. They streamed on either side of us.

I tripped. Someone gripped my ankle. I turned to see Ella, and tried to wriggle away from her. As thin as she was, she was filled with strength. I kicked at her fingers where she gripped my leg, but she wouldn't relent.

Gabriel appeared and stamped on my leg—but only so he could grab Ella and wrench her off me. The pair wrestled, and I was free again.

Joanna was soon alongside me, holding the stone like a rugby ball under one arm as we bolted towards the boats. She threw the ball at Melodie, who yelped.

"Give me the key and get out!" Joanna shouted at her.

Melodie, shaking, pulled the cord from her wrist.

Behind us, the roar of approaching Glowfolk got louder.

"Quickly!" Joanna shouted.

Melodie whimpered, tossed the key at Joanna, and clambered out of the boat.

Joanna started the motor. It sputtered, and the boat began to move.

A man jumped off the pier at us, his hand grabbing at the rim.

I pulled the fingers off, one by one. The boat wobbled as he fell into the water.

We sped away. As I looked back at the island, I saw Melodie standing there with her arms out in protest. The crowd ran at the harbour, ignoring her. A rogue shoulder knocked her into the water as the others dove in and filled the remaining boats.

As we returned to the mist, the island dissolved away once again. Glowfolk gathered by the harbour still, their distant white robes like pale piano keys. Some dropped their robes and piled into the water, determined to swim all the way back to land if that was what it took to retrieve their power source.

The remaining handful of boats took off after us, but we maintained our head start.

The stone rolled towards Joanna. She scooped it beneath her legs, behind the back of her plastic tunic, which kept it away from her skin.

Even from so far away, Summer's grief-wracked screams echoed off the walls of her snuffed-out island and across the sea.

The boat wavered left and right. Joanna's hand, lubricated by her own blood, slipped on the steering handle.

"It doesn't hurt too much," she said. "Not anymore."

The pier emerged before us, as did the rusting carnival rides, the dilapidated buildings. It was a relief just to see land again.

Police squad cars and ambulances were parked above the pier. A figure stood on the bonnet of one near us. It was Henry, watching us with binoculars. As we got nearer, he dropped them and sped along the pier towards us. There was no one else; likely it had been cleared for police business.

We docked at a slip and got out.

Henry walked up to us with open arms. He hugged me and smoothed my hair. I felt the rubbery grip of his gloves.

"You must be Joanna," he said over my shoulder.

"That's me," Joanna said.

Henry let go of me again.

Joanna took off her tunic and wrapped it around the stone. She stood wearing a wet cotton dress, looking up at the sky. "It's going to get dark soon."

"That's okay," Henry said. "Come with me. We've prepared everything you need."

We walked together, the three of us, Henry with his arm around me, Joanna by my side clutching the ball.

A crew of people in hazmat suits and face masks waited for us at the end of the pier.

"What's this for?" I said.

"It's okay, Lily," Joanna said.

Two men knelt by the stairs leading off the pier.

Joanna handed them the stone. "This is it."

The men ran off with it. Two more appeared in the same place.

Joanna slouched and walked towards them. They grabbed her by the arms and carted her up.

"No!" I screamed. "Where are you taking her?"

Henry shushed me and held me close. "You'll see her again in no time. I promise."

I tried to kick free, but he wouldn't let me. I fell to my knees, in tears.

He took my hand. "Come and see. It's for her own good."

We walked up the stairs together. Bystanders gathered behind a barrier and watched, taking photos.

The hazmat guys had strapped Joanna to a gurney, which they held up and pushed into an ambulance. Purple light diffused through it, lamps buzzing harshly. UV light again.

I held Henry's gloved hand and let him guide me to his squad car.

It's going to get dark soon.

15

We joined the ambulance at the hospital.

A kindly nurse guided me to a private room, where there was a chemical shower and an examination table behind a curtain. Next to a computer was a blocky-looking device encased in white metal. Above a set of cabinets stood a sharps box, a bottle of hand sanitizer, and a glove dispensary.

I went behind a curtain and removed my wet clothes, passing them back to the nurse, who would incinerate them.

I took a mandatory chemical shower, dressed in lilac scrubs with a teddy bear print, then came back through the curtain. For shoes I had a pair of thin slippers, like the disposable ones found at cheap hotels.

"What's this?" the nurse said, holding up the plastic bag she'd taken from my jacket pocket.

"It's a sample of the island's plant."

She dropped it on the floor and stood back. "I'll let someone know, and they'll get it looked at."

She asked permission to take a sample of my blood, a cotton swab of my mouth, and scrapings from beneath my fingernails. All the samples went into a hatch in the metal block.

"What is it you're looking for?" I asked.

"We're calling it GRSE for the moment. Glow-related spongiform encephalopathy."

"Where have I heard that before?"

"It's caused by prions. You know, like Creutzfeldt-Jakob?"

I shook my head.

"Mad cow disease?"

My stomach sank.

The screen in front of her beeped and turned green. "You don't have it."

She guided me out the room and down the hall, leading me to a different wing of the hospital.

The tests had taken so long that it was now dark outside. As we pushed through two sets of double doors, the lighting got brighter, harsher.

She sat me down on a bench. Through the glass in front of me, she told me, was Joanna's quarantine. "They found traces of plastic in her stomach. You know anything about it?"

Maybe it had to do with becoming an EO. But I didn't know for sure, so I shook my head.

More sheets of opaque plastic separated me from Joanna—but there was a triangular gap at the bottom.

"You don't want to see," the nurse said.

I couldn't help it. I peered in.

Smock-clad doctors intubated Joanna. Some sat on chairs on either side of her and jabbed her with needles to put ports in her veins. I shuddered at the way the plastic tubes snaked towards her. The room's bright lighting enhanced how unnatural it looked. Big blinding white lamps set up in each corner connected to a black extension reel that sat on the floor.

I recoiled, looking up and down the hallway. There were

multiple booths just like this one, masked by opaque plastic. A ward of Glowfolk.

"Your boyfriend will be back soon," the nurse said. "And a counsellor will come by later."

"Why?"

"It's best if he tells you. One thing at a time, dear."

"Are there others from the island here?"

She nodded. "In all these rooms."

I looked up and down the corridor. "I didn't know there were any other escapees still alive."

"Well," she said, "we believe they came from the island—but they can't talk anymore. We found them roaming the town." She touched my arm. "You're safe here, though."

"But … wait."

The nurse turned.

I was so lost I didn't even know what more to ask.

She looked around. "Okay, I'm not supposed to." She took a phone out of her pocket and handed it to me. "I'll come back for it later."

"Thank you."

I used it to search for news about the island.

Live aerial footage showed the island in the dark. Three of its towers were on fire, yellow flames waving from them, giving off plumes of black smoke. Articles speculated about an accident occurring out there, but there were no names released yet. What would become of Patricia, Summer, Gabriel, Melodie?

Corinne had a new video up on *The Switch*, in which she interviewed Dennis Howell. He looked greasier than ever in the thumbnail. I'd have to pay to watch the full thing. I'd create an account for myself on one of my own devices when I was back with them again. For now, I had a brief preview video.

Dennis was uneasy having his authority questioned. "Our self-actualization task force has told you people time and again that we have no connection to that damn island. Our programs are flourishing. Of course this doesn't negatively impact our work. Beyond supporting the group's environmental initiatives, we're not associated with them at all."

"Our investigators traced the distribution of octadrone to your facilities," Corinne said. "The supply came from the island. What are you going to do now that—"

Dennis got up, tore off his microphone, and walked away.

We'd surely harmed the Glow. Whether or not they'd claimed ownership of it, the impenetrable mystique of their island was their strongest symbol—one of the biggest reasons, surely, that few ever challenged them. Now it was ablaze. And, without the Glow's supply of the drug that kept them all zombified, their brainwashing capabilities would take a major hit as well.

Only time would tell. Did a movement ever die off when its leaders were taken out? Pernicious ideas were harder to kill than the people who came up with them.

I sank into the pleather couch, wondering if I'd get a chance to tell Corinne in person what had happened to Heath, before she had to read about it in some police report—provided there was any evidence left. What would I say to her if given the opportunity?

The weight of all I'd done and all I had left to do pressed down upon me at once. My mind shut down to deal with it all, sending me quickly to sleep.

16

I woke to Henry looking over me. He'd loosened his tie and untucked his shirt. I winced at him with bleary eyes and sat up, giving him some space on the couch.

He touched my bare feet, warming them with his hands. "It's good to see you again."

"You too. Hey, why didn't you come out to the island?"

"Turns out better men have tried. They know all us cops. I might've scared the island away."

"They can send it into open water in under three minutes."

"So the rumours are true. All I could do was wait on land." He smiled. "Not to overwhelm you—but I don't know where any of this leaves us. All I'll say is that I'm sorry, and you're welcome to return to the house. If you want."

"That's kind of you to offer. But it really depends."

He stopped stroking my feet. "On what?"

"What you're about to tell me."

He sat back and turned to me. "Are you ready?"

I wasn't, but I needed to hear it anyway. I nodded.

"The stone did come from space," he said.

I sat up. "Right."

"But it's not a meteorite as such." He bit his lip. "It's more like a bomb, filled with prions."

I winced. "They cause the disease. The GRSE."

"Exactly. And as far as the lab can tell, they're synthetic. Created to harm humans."

I laughed incredulously and swept hair out of my face with cold, tired hands. "What do you mean?"

"When the stone contacts human skin, it infects people with the prions."

My heart rate went up. "I saw something last night. A group of them on the island. They ... devoured one of the visitors."

We sat in silence.

"What about the plants?" I said finally.

"The sample you provided—for one, it's jam-packed with octadrone. And it also seems designed to optimize our atmosphere for whatever sent the stone in the first place."

I jerked as I heard a screech coming from Joanna's room. It was the sound of a nurse pulling back the plastic curtain. The doctors and other staff were leaving.

We paused and looked at Joanna. She sat up and stretched her arms towards me as far as she could, the handcuffs round her wrists clanging on the rails. She had a look on her face like a scared child. Like she wanted me to lift her and take her away from all this.

She was the little sister I knew. The one who had managed to overpower the Glow's ideology. The one whose inability to watch me join the Glow—to embark upon the same mistake to which she'd dedicated years of her life—had overpowered her indoctrination. Even if it was only for that one instant, when she stole the stone, it sure as hell counted.

"She's infected, then," I said.

He nodded.

She seemed fine now. Because of the lights.

I wept, but I could feel that my expression was still stoic. "Maybe it was just a test before some big attack. And it works, all right. I don't think it's the last of those devices that we'll ever see."

"Think of how it could've gone. If Patricia hadn't made the island, the stone would've gone straight into the water."

"Patricia had visions that told her to make the island first. It was a testing ground. A sample population. Prior to a full-scale attack."

"Well, whether or not that's the case, without your intervention, we wouldn't have gotten the chance to study the prions before the disease spread. They tell me there might be a gene that allows these prions to form in the infected. If that's the case, we can cut it out and immunize people."

"Can we immunize Joanna?"

I knew the answer. A black sea of loss rose through my mind, saturating all my memories of her.

Flirting with a vendor on the beach to score us free ice cream sandwiches. Crying over the kites at Club Med. Digging her teeth into the Ripper's ankle. If that had even happened.

Henry made to say something. He stopped, regrouped, and

held my face in his hands gently, as if cupping a flower's petals. "You were so brave." He laughed. "Thank God I didn't manage to stop you going there in the first place."

"You think you could've?"

He took his hands off me. "You did your best for Joanna. More than any sister could expect. Now it's time to come home."

"Sure." I gritted my teeth and tried to remain strong, to ride the weird peace that accompanies the biggest shocks. I could break soon. I could finally let it all out. But I had to hold on, to steel myself for one final task.

"I just have to say goodbye for now."

He nodded solemnly.

I side-eyed him and added, "Alone."

He sighed, kissed me on the forehead, and paced down the hall.

I got up as if in a trance and opened the quarantine door.

An alarm horn blared, even as I slammed the door behind me and pushed a chair beneath it from the inside.

I heard Henry's heels skid on the linoleum, and he ran up to the glass.

Joanna had her arms out still. Her face was dried out, and there were cuts on her cheeks, dark circles around her eyes, lank hair. Plastic cables streamed from her arms.

Bang bang bang. I turned to the door. Henry was back, his fists pummelling at the window, terror in his eyes.

I looked at him through the corridor's warning light, each red pulse showing his panic, panic, panic.

I turned away and embraced Joanna. Her weary arms fell around me, her head collapsing onto my chest.

I kissed the top of her head, and turned out the lights.

BOTH BUNNY AND NOT

On the other side of the portal, I discover a boy crying and a man in a bunny suit.

The boy, five or six, wears green dungarees and has a brown bowl cut. The bunny is grey with a white belly, big cartoon eyes, and an oversized pink bow. The combined smells of freshly baked pretzels, hot dogs, and something sickly and caramel wafts from a nearby snack stand.

"Can you tell me where I am?" I ask the bunny.

He looks at me, startled. "Where the hell did *you* come from?"

"Watch your language in front of the kid!"

"S-Sorry. You're at Thorpe Park."

I duck in reflex as a rollercoaster careens round a loop in the cloudless blue sky.

"It's a theme park just outside of London," the bunny continues. "It's 1994. Maybe."

"Thanks. Good." I kneel beside the kid. "And why are you crying?"

He wipes his nose on his sleeve. "I'm not supposed to talk to strangers."

"Where's Charlie?" I say.

"My dad?" He flings a little arm in the direction of the snack stand, where a man in a denim shirt, with long curly red hair, waits in the queue.

"He sent me to check on you," I tell the kid.

"Okay." He cries harder. "A m-man came out of nowhere, like you, a-and h-he told me that the Thorpe Park bunny isn't really a bunny, that he's just a man in a suit!"

I cross my legs and sit on the ground. "I thought so."

"You know what's going on?" the bunny asks.

"I'll explain in a minute." To the kid, I say, "Listen, it's true that there's a man inside this bunny."

The boy wails harder, his eyes popping blue against his flushed red face.

"*But* if you want to believe he's a bunny, then that's what he is!"

He sniffles but doesn't say anything.

"No one can take that away from you. And it's not *more* true that he's a man than that he's a bunny." I lean back on my hands. "I know you'd prefer if he were just a bunny. But it isn't like that. And because you're learning all this today, it'll be a while before you see the bunny again. Just—trust that you will."

He composes himself. "'Kay."

"And you'll never let anyone take the bunny away from you again?"

"Promise."

"Great."

I stand back up again and dust myself off. The man at the snack stand looks at me with confusion. He recognizes my face, though he's never seen it before.

"Your dad's waiting on you," I say to the kid.

He runs off. His dad hands him a Solero ice cream. The dad hesitates, listening to the kid's explanation of what just happened. Suspicions defused, they walk away together, talking about what area of the park they'll next explore.

The bunny taps me on the shoulder. "What was that?"

"Let's sit down for a minute."

He glances around. "I can't be seen sitting!"

I dismiss his nerves with a wave of the hand. "I'll deal with everything. I promise. You can even take your bunny head off if you want."

He thinks for a minute, then his shoulders slump with submission. "Cool."

We find the brick rim of a big flower bed and sit on it.

He removes the bunny head, revealing a malnourished-looking teen with flattened auburn hair and spots on his cheeks. "Where did you come from?" he asks me.

"The future," I say.

"You time-travelled here."

"Yeah."

"Another guy came here earlier." He stares at me. "Looked like you, in fact. Except he had hair."

I slap my bald pate. "Time is cruel, man."

"You mean it was a younger you? So did—" The bunny looks around with a sudden burst of paranoia.

Irritated parents shield their children's eyes from him. Some are over by the payphones, glaring at him with concern. Some have tracked down park security and point at him.

I hold out my hand, pushing everyone away from us with an invisible bubble. They glide across the ground, barely perturbed. Memories wiped, they leave us alone and go about their business again.

"You were asking me something," I say.

"What brings you—*both* yous—back here?"

I gesture to where the kid and his dad walked away. "That boy was me. My other self—a teen, I'm guessing—came here to tell the boy that the Thorpe Park bunny isn't real. My teen selves seem to enjoy life only when they're spoiling it for others—and they're their own favourite target. Me, I'm thirty, and I don't share their attitude or their conduct."

I square my shoulders. Shit, I'm thirty! Better start watching my posture.

"I came here to restore my belief in bunnies," I add. "So I can stay sane."

"You're not the only one struggling with that." The bunny takes off his paws, unzips his suit and removes a bag of weed with rolling papers and a lighter in it. He dexterously rolls a joint, sticks it in his mouth, lights it, and inhales. "So you can travel through time," he says, exhaling again, "and you're only using it to fix yourself?"

"Yeah, and I'm barely competent at that."

He offers me the joint. I take it from him and toke on it. I wouldn't in real life—I don't even drink. No interest in it anymore. But since this is a work of fiction, the bunny and I can do whatever we like.

"I get you," he says. "If I could time-travel, I wouldn't even tell anyone. Too much responsibility. I'd go back to the sixties. Free love and VW vans. But would you mind telling me why you're *here*? All kids grow up to learn that Santa is just their parents or whatever. What's the big deal?"

I hand the joint back to him. "My theory is that there are three phases of life. There's 'bunny', like we witnessed earlier today in this time period. There's 'no bunny', my teen years. And phase three is 'both bunny and not'. It's the most precarious and difficult to maintain, yet the most rewarding." I rest my hands on my thighs. "I lost it recently. Figured my teen self was at fault, that he'd come back here to disillusion my child self. I'm glad I was right! All I needed to do was repair the child self that believed in bunnies in the first place."

He grins. "I understand now. I'm not just the man in the bunny suit."

I place a hand on his furry shoulder. "You're also a bunny."

"Oh, even more than that." His eyes go big and wild. "For I have transcended!"

"Huh?"

He stands up, throws out his arms, and shines with brilliant light. He's so beautiful a vision that I can't look away. Before my eyes, he becomes the most wondrous things.

He becomes the joy of imagining lost loved ones not only living on in the hearts of their countrymen but dancing together in an afterlife for all eternity. He becomes peace in the knowledge that nothing matters in the grand scheme of things, as well as the presence that comes with behaving as if, even on the smallest scale, everything counts. He becomes the unwavering belief that you've found your soulmate despite the overwhelming statistical improbability of this. And he becomes love itself—on the surface just a series of chemical reactions and yet indescribably more, as elusive as quantum gravity but a facet of reality nonetheless.

Somewhere in the ball of all this miraculous light is his face, grinning with wonder. He pulses back and forth between reality and every benign delusion imaginable.

I'm back through the portal now, in the present day. Theoretically, this puts me in a two-bedroom apartment on the island of Stord in Norway, where I work as an engineer, and where I'm typing this sentence right now. And this one. And this one!

But this isn't reality, so I'm where I want to be right now, in my home city of Glasgow, Scotland, in my dad's place. In the kitchen specifically, his favourite room. I think of him sitting by the dining table in his red office chair, in a red dressing gown, his silvery hair askew. He tip-taps on his computer, planning out a week of business calls or firing off emails to loved ones, sending links to articles that remind him of them.

Then I think of him off in an afterlife somewhere, dancing with my mum in a spotlight, him in a blue shirt and trousers, her in a colourful dress, her hair spiked up, silver jewellery shimmering. They reunited recently, after seven years apart. She, having set aside her Scottish crime novels to pay him attention, wears the weary smile of an introvert whose precious solitude has been interrupted. But she teases him about this fondly, ultimately welcoming the adjustment. For now, they try not to think of me and their other two children, and everyone else left behind too soon.

Incidentally, no, I can't time-travel, and there was no teen version of me at Thorpe Park that day in 1994. (I'm guessing the year because no one alive can inform me otherwise.) My child self, unprovoked, just told the bunny he was a guy in a suit. But that's not much of a story. It isn't even my own memory—it was my dad's. Early, affectionate evidence, I guess, that I would be a scientist someday, one of those who shouts from the back of the movie theatre whenever they spot some minor continuity error, shattering meticulous and lovingly crafted illusions with glee. I suppose this story further proves his point.

But so what? I may be compelled to point out that none of this happened—to take the bunny's head off, so to speak—but isn't the trick to believe in it anyway?

This book took so long to write!

I had to learn how to write science fiction short stories: first, short stories with science fiction elements that succeeded, then science fiction stories that worked but didn't retread themes the genre had already exhausted.

It was a feat I wanted to accomplish probably because it's so challenging. In other words, it was a standard Leo occupation: find the toughest version of a thing and try and do it, for no real reason.

But as you'll see in this collection, Marina Abramović is a big hero of mine, and she said something like, "As soon as you can draw perfectly with your right hand, immediately start drawing with your left."

Wouldn't it be ideal, then, if every new book was like learning how to write for the first time? (That thought just occurred to me while I was writing this note, so I don't know if that's what I've been doing, but the concept appeals.)

And the idea of openly learning in public doesn't bother me at all—as you can see from my films to date, which get less ropy with time! When you look at something someone has made, and it suggests, "Hey, I bet you could do this," I think that is an important function of good art—not something you must excise, or disguise from the world.

I have always loved science fiction. I just have felt afraid and unqualified to write the genre because I haven't been a voracious reader of it. Not as much as I might like. It has to be the most intimidating of all the genres! I read one book by one person, and I'm like, "Thank God I understood what that guy was on about." Then I pick up another story that's, like, three pages long, and I feel like you need a PhD in evolutionary biology and another in astrophysics just to know what the hell is going on. Then I wonder why I like science fiction so much. And I'm a process engineer—a profession many people, myself included, sometimes can't describe. Still, this needless unintelligibility frustrates.

I hope this collection represents what I love about science fiction: that it questions the possible directions of humanity, that it explores who we might be and who we always have been. And I hope it is free of needlessly impenetrable elements. I hope it makes you look at the sky and wonder why for a bit.

Thanks for picking it up, downloading it, or, hey, maybe injecting it someday—who knows!

Leo, October 2025

ACKNOWLEDGEMENTS

Thank you to Mel, Jen, and Gen at *Pulp Literature* for their faith in my writing and their continued support.

I am deeply grateful to my friends, and especially my husband Juan, for believing in and encouraging my identity as an artist, despite the challenges and misunderstandings from the world around us.

A heartfelt thank you to indie publishers and readers who continue to take a chance on new writers. You keep creativity alive.

Finally, to everyone who has inspired and supported me, your encouragement means everything.

ABOUT THE AUTHOR

Leo X Robertson is a Scottish writer, filmmaker, and process engineer currently living in Stavanger, Norway. His work has been featured in *Best of British Science Fiction, Year's Best Hardcore Horror,* and Flame Tree Publishing's *Urban Crime* anthology, among others. His films have been featured in festivals such as Dead Northern, Horrific Hope, and ReelHeART and won awards like Best International Film and Best LGBTQ Film.

instagram.com/leoxrobertson
facebook.com/leo.x.robertson
tiktok.com/@leoxrobertson
goodreads.com/leoxrobertson
youtube.com/@StavangerFilmmakers